men

as

trees

walking

men

as

trees

walking

GEORGE
IMBRAGULIO

vantage
POINT

Vantage Point Books and the Vantage Point Books colophon are registered trademarks of Vantage Press, Inc.

FIRST EDITION: August 2011

Cover design by Michael Fusco.
Interior design by Neuwirth & Associates, Inc.

Published by Vantage Point Books
Vantage Press, Inc.
419 Park Avenue South
New York, NY 10016
www.vantagepointbooks.com

Manufactured in the United States of America
ISBN: 978-1-936467-04-4

Library of Congress Cataloging-in-Publication data are on file.

0 9 8 7 6 5 4 3 2 1

To all the Dulcies in the World

— o n e —

SHE RAN, SCREAMING, panic-stricken, with her umbrella in one hand and her wicker purse in the other, her arms straight out to keep her balance, knowing as she struggled one heavy foot ahead of the other on the shifting rockbed of the streetcar tracks that he was right behind her and would soon grab her. Bo Arthur Bilbo had pawed and harassed her for years, laughing and hollering like something wild so everybody would stop and watch to see if he was really going to do what he always said he was going to do.

Exhausted, she fell forward, trying with what energy she had left to cry for help but finding to her horror that nothing would come out. When she awoke, she was gasping for breath, sputtering meaningless sounds, wet with sweat and sore all over. The tears were real, she felt them sliding down her face and wiped them away with the sheet. She couldn't go back to sleep for several hours.

Dulcie Dykes wet the comb and ran it through her short blonde hair, then secured the recalcitrant strands over each ear with bobby pins. With her right thumb and forefinger she pulled down the hair on either side of her face and formed spit curls, then secured them with bobby pins that she would remove before taking the streetcar. She painted her lips, pressed them together on a piece of toilet paper, then highlighted her cheeks with rouge. She laughed. This part of her daily preparation for her nursemaid job in Laurel was always the most fun of all.

"Dulcie," her sister Annie Lois called from the kitchen, "you better shake a leg. It's near 'bout seven o'clock."

She gave another twist to the curl on the left side. "I'm comin'." Annie Lois was lifting bacon from the iron skillet onto three dishes. Wanda Faye, Annie Lois' five-year-old daughter, was crawling up into her chair at the table.

"Hey, Dulcie," Wanda Faye said as she slid into place.

"Hey, Pumpkin. Mornin', Annie Lois."

Annie Lois dropped some eggs into the skillet. "You must've had a nightmare last night. I heard you hollerin'."

She had almost forgotten. "Yeah. I dreamed that ol' Bo Arthur was chasin' me again."

"Has he been botherin' you lately?"

"Naw, thank goodness. I ain't seen 'im for 'bout a week now." She suddenly giggled. "Hey, y'all, how do I look on my birthday?"

"Is today really Dulcie's birthday, Mamma?" Wanda Faye asked, turning to her mother with a glass of orange juice halfway to her mouth.

Annie Lois turned around, holding the dripping spatula over the skillet with one hand and wiping the other hand on her apron. "Yes, it most certainly is. August the sixteenth, in the year of our Lord, nineteen hundred and twenty-three." She turned back to the eggs. "And just how old are you today, Dulcie?"

Dulcie giggled and pulled out her chair. "I don't know. How old am I, Annie Lois?"

Annie Lois finished filling the three plates and put them on the table. "How 'bout you tryin' to figure it out for yourself. You're one dozen and a half years old. Now how old does that make you?"

She laid her fork down, put her hands in her lap and counted. She knew a dozen was twelve and a half-dozen was six, yet she still could not figure out what the total was. She frowned and scratched the top of her head because Annie Lois always got upset if she didn't count correctly. "I cain't figure it out, Annie Lois," she said finally. "You tell me."

Annie Lois sighed and said calmly, "You're eighteen today, Honey."

Dulcie was so excited she had a hard time getting her breakfast down. She stopped between bites, holding her fork high over her plate. "You goan make me a birthday cake while I'm gone?"

"I've given it some thought. What kind you want? Devil's food?"

She giggled. "You bet! That's my fa-vo-rite."

Annie Lois had given her the mirror from one of her old purses and now, as Dulcie waited for the streetcar, she took it out of the handled and gaily painted wicker basket she used for a purse. She looked at herself. Except for the two collapsed curls, she thought she looked pretty. Her hair was not the curling kind to start with, and the weather was so humid nothing she could do was going to make them hold. She tried, nevertheless, by quickly sticking two fingers in her mouth, looking around, then dampening the curls and trying to make them stay put.

Mary Alice Shoemaker and Libby McElreath were walking to school, one on either of the streetcar tracks, trying to keep their balance. When Mary Alice saw Dulcie, she stopped, said something to Libby, then they both looked and giggled. They said something Dulcie couldn't understand, then ran as fast as they could down the street, their strapped books and long hair braids bouncing against their backs.

Most of the white children made fun of her. It was something she still had not gotten used to. She always tried to ignore the mean things others said or did, mainly because Annie Lois had told her to. Now she felt depressed. She opened her purse and fumbled for nothing in particular among the diverse things there.

"Is dat who I think it is?" A big, heavy negro woman was approaching the bench where Dulcie sat. She moved slowly and awkwardly, pulling rather than lifting each foot and stirring up the dust with each labored step.

Dulcie did not recognize her.

The woman shuffled a little closer and gave a low laugh that seemed to take a lot of effort. "Miss Dulcie, don' chu 'member me?"

Dulcie frowned and played with the purse handles. "You do look sorta familiar," she said, "but Lord have mercy, I don't know who in the world you are."

The woman put a hand on the back of the bench for white folks only and leaned her weight against it "'Member Kat'n Roscoe?" She waited, then laughed heartily as she saw the sudden change come over Dulcie's face. "Honey, dis is ol' Sophronie Grubbs."

Dulcie laughed, squirmed, and squeezed the purse against her stomach. "Why, my goodness gracious alive!" she cried. "Now I remember. Me'n Kat'n Roscoe used t'play while you was washin' our clothes."

"Dat's right, Miss Dulcie."

"Where's Kat'n Roscoe now?" she asked, pulling out the part of her skirt that got rumpled in her excitement.

"Why Kat, she be livin' wit me. Her'n her five kids. Roscoe, bless his soul, was kilt in de waw. 'Zackly one week to de day 'fo de 'mistice was signed."

Dulcie looked down at her hands and remembered:

Roscoe, then three years older than she was, glistening milk chocolate brown, lean and already tautly muscled in his arms and legs, stooped slightly forward to keep from hitting his head on the sills of the house, his clothes dropped in a heap in the thick dust around a brick pillar. Her initial shock had muted her tongue and flushed her pale fair face with a burning redness, but the shock soon turned to a kind of guilty pleasure that hovered tantalizingly over her conscience like faint wafts of incense over a sacred altar. After a few moments of mutual awkwardness, Roscoe reached out to take one of her hands. She pulled away. Then, suddenly, she stepped closer and clasped her hands together nervously. He put a hand on each of her shoulders and gently squeezed. She wanted to touch back but couldn't.

. . . She heard her mother's voice again and again, then saw the bent-over body, almost kneeling on the ground, one hand holding onto the house and the other supporting her weight, and the villainous face hanging sideways and shocked wild by what she was seeing. Roscoe bolted behind the brick pillar, but Dulcie was too slow. She reached down and grabbed her dress, dusty and inside-out, and tried frantically to cover herself. Her mother yelled at the top of her voice and ordered her to come out "right this minute!", made her stand naked in the harsh sunlight for everyone to see, then laid an inch-thick chinaberry limb time and time again across her back side until the blood ruptured forth from the scored flesh and dripped and clung like scarlet dew on the thick spring grass.

Dulcie had not heard. Sophronie asked again. "I says, Miss Dulcie, how Miss Annie Lois be doin'?"

"Oh, she's fine. She's got a little girl." Saying that seemed to amuse her. "I bet chu didn't know that, did ju?"

"No'm, I sho didn't. I knowed she was married. What huh husban' do?"

"Oh, he's dead." It sounded so matter-of-fact, the way she said it. "He got kilt in the war," she added, almost proudly, because she believed it was true what some of their friends had said when the news of his death had come early one morning, that Hershel had died a hero's death for his country. The truth of the matter, which Dulcie alone knew but would never admit, was that she was the only person who was happy when the news came. Before Hershel entered the army, she had become more and more resentful of him because of the likely-to-be-permanent wedge he had driven between her and Annie Lois.

"Annie Lois says she's goan start teachin' again as soon as Wanda Faye's old enough to go to school" She bounced the purse up and down against her knees. "I bet chu didn't know Annie Lois taught me how t'read'n write, did ju? . . . Well, not a whole lot." She bent over laughing. "She said I done pretty good to be so lazy."

"I see. And what kinda work you do, Miss Dulcie?"

"Annie Lois calls it nurse-maidin'. I take care of Miz Penny Welborn's little girl Melissa."

"You like doin' dat?"

"Ooooo, yeah! I just love it!"

"Dat don't s'prise me none. Fum what I 'members, you was always de happiest when you was 'roun' chirren." Sophronie laughed and coughed at the same time. "You 'member dat ol' rag doll I give you, Miss Dulcie?"

Dulcie saw the soot-covered cast-iron washpot in the backyard and the fat flame fingers her mother made her stand as close to as she could without catching on fire, then told her, after violently shaking her shoulders, "Get a good look at that! That's what hell looks like!"

"What chu evah do wit dat ol' doll, Miss Dulcie? You still got it?"

Her throat tightened and her eyes burned. She shook her head from side to side. "Mamma wouldn't let me keep it," she said hoarsely and rocked her purse back and forth in her lap.

"An' how come she do dat?"

Dulcie pulled on her dress and slid her feet around in the dust. " 'Cause it was black. She said I wuddn't s'posed t'have no nigger baby. She said niggers had nigger babies and white folks had white babies."

Sophronie seemed amused by that. "Dat's right," she said. "An' what she do wid it?"

Dulcie looked quickly up at the old woman's expectant face. She squinted her eyes almost shut. "Why, she burnt it up," she said. "She throwed it under the washpot one day and pure-dee set fire to it."

LONG BEFORE YOU saw it, you could hear the streetcar as it negotiated the grime-crusted tracks north of town, then rasped the sharp curve in front of Kelly's Drugstore onto Main Street, the three-block, tree-lined dirt road that bisected the business district proper. The end of the line was the Agricultural High School, eight blocks south, where it waited five minutes before returning to Laurel on the east side of town, one block over from Main Street. Where Dulcie was waiting was the most centrally located stop, opposite the back of the bank on one corner and the ice house on the other, under an enormous oak tree that reached out in a nearly perfect circle, shading the southeast corner of the L. C. Arnold yard and the full width of the street and streetcar tracks.

By now, a large crowd had collected, most on their way to jobs in Laurel, and Dulcie was feeling self-conscious. Most people, even those who knew her, ignored her or, if someone did speak to her, it always sounded insincere and condescending. She pretended to be interested in what was going on across the street at Free State Bank and Trust Company. Mrs. Maybelle Turner, secretary to the bank president, was unlocking the back door that led directly into his office. Any moment now, Mr. Hays Younger, the bank president, would emerge from the elegance of his corner mansion one block south, with his superior look of contempt, and proudly strut on up to the bank as the people watched.

Down at the other end of the block, a dray with oversize, steel-reinforced wheels and pulled by two dark brown horses, drew up to the platform at the ice house and was soon surrounded by five negro men summoned from the office by Mr. Elmo Poole, the owner. The business of loading the ice wagon every day was as routine to the people waiting for the streetcar as for the men doing the work, yet it never failed to absorb their attention. The fascination of seeing the hundred-pound blocks of ice suddenly and miraculously appear out of the chute and onto the platform, preceded, surrounded, and followed by thick clouds of frost vapor that quickly dissipated into the humid air, never seemed to lessen.

When the streetcar arrived, Sophronie and three other negroes stood to one side until all the white people boarded, then got on, paid their fares, and moved, with all eyes watching, to the back and sat down on the single, long seat reserved for them.

As Sophronie shuffled past, grunting and grabbing the backs of the seats on either side with her hands, Dulcie timidly put out her left hand and touched the old woman's warm, moist arm. She heard Sophronie give a little sigh but didn't know what it meant. As the streetcar jerked forward, she turned around self-consciously and smiled at Sophronie.

Clanging and straining, the streetcar slowed down as it climbed the hill at the Paulding Road intersection, where it came to a grinding halt. A young negro man got on, paid his fare and started to the bench at the back. Before he could get there, the streetcar lurched forward and he lost his balance. The folks at the front of the car laughed. The man grabbed the back of the seat where Dulcie was sitting and steadied himself without looking right or left. When he let go and continued to the rear, his hand touched Dulcie's shoulder. She turned her head and looked back without thinking. Sophronie, mopping her sweaty face with her handkerchief, propped her free hand on the seat and slid over to make room for him.

"Wha' chu doin' on dis hyere streetcar, Tyler?" she asked.

He sat down with some steadying help from another man. "I'm lookin' for work, Miz Sophronie."

"You reck'n you go'n' find it?"

"I don't know. I sho hopes so. I hear'd dey's hirin' at Eastman Gardner. Maybe I be lucky and git me a job dere."

Sophronie wiped her face again. "How's yo' mamma? I ain't seed dat sweet thang since 'fo de waw."

"She do right fair. Still workin' mighty hard. But she be use t'dat."

"She sho t'God oughta be. God knows dat sorry ol' daddy a yore'n never hep out none."

Dulcie listened and smiled, wishing she were sitting with them.

She could feel her mamma pulling her arm and dragging her away from a group of negro children she had slipped off to play with while they were shopping one day. And the burning hot hand across her face and the fierce look in her mother's eyes. The grip of her mother's hand around her arm was so painful she strained with her other little hand to loosen it. Her mother had only jerked harder and her ankle had turned over and she screamed.

Now she sat straight and proper in her seat, as Annie Lois had taught her to do, looking out the window but not seeing, both hands holding the purse in her lap. All at once, she felt so much like a little girl again that she'd momentarily forgotten today was her birthday. She wondered if she really wanted to be a little girl again. Whenever she remembered how it was, she always reached a point, a sky-high wall, that made her stop dead-still and wonder if she wanted to be on one side of it or the other.

The wall was understanding, the point at which she realized she was mentally retarded. The understanding had come slowly, imperceptibly, stealthily, with each insult, with each tongue-lashing, handgrip, arm-jerk, or the burning brand of her mother's big, calloused hand on her face, or the flesh-scoring thrashings with tree limbs.

She always felt guilty when she thought about her mamma and wouldn't dare for the world let anybody know how she felt, because you were supposed to love your mamma more than anybody else in the world except God. Her feelings were so strong and sinful she feared sometimes that people must know what she was thinking. This fear often caused her to pretend she was in a deep, dark hole in the ground, with a heavy stone slab on top of it, and nobody could ever find her or make her come out. She knew, though, that if God found her and lifted the stone, as Annie Lois had assured her He could do, He would yank her out of there so fast she wouldn't know what happened and would almost surely throw her under the soot-covered cast-iron washpot and set fire to her.

As the streetcar eased up under the tin-roofed station in Laurel, Selma Shoemaker grabbed her purse, leaned forward and looked up at the big clock on the front of Grand National Bank.

"That clock ain't right, is it, Buford?"

"No'm," Buford replied as he maneuvered the streetcar to a complete stop, then leaned over and swung the doors open. Looking around to the back of the car, he added, "It's been losin' time lately. One of the ladies that works at the bank said they're hopin' to get it fixed in a couple more days."

After Dulcie got off, she waited to one side until Sophronie, with the help of one of the negro men and both of her hands gripping the sides of the doorway, got off the streetcar.

"I sure am glad I got to see you again, Sophronie," she said, giggling and swinging her purse against her legs.

Sophronie, exhausted from the ordeal of getting off of the streetcar, lifted her eyes and wiped her forehead with her wet, wadded up handkerchief.

"Why don' chu come see me and Annie Lois sometime?" Dulcie said.

Sophronie shuffled to the curb and waited for a milk wagon to go by. "Yessum," she said distractedly, "maybe I do dat one a dese days." Once the wagon had passed, she raised one of her fat arms and hollered, "Hey, Tyler! Hold yore horses! I wanna ax you sumpn."

Dulcie took her time crossing the street so she could watch the two negroes. Sophronie was like one of the family, she thought as she stepped onto the curb and headed slowly in the direction of Magnolia Street. When she could no longer see them, she felt sad.

AT EIGHTEEN, DULCIE'S body had already outdistanced her brain by several years. Something went wrong during gestation, but it was not until several years later that there was any evidence of what the trouble was. Her mother, Dora Dykes, was the first to notice, then her older sister Annie Lois. Dulcie's father would have noticed, too, if he had stayed around long enough.

Her outward appearance belied the inner failings. In fact, she had been a very pretty child with bright blue eyes and a happy, flushed countenance. It was not until she reached the age of nine that there was any abnormal change in the way she looked. If she pinned her hair back, as she often did when preoccupied, one might detect something slightly disproportionate in the vicinity of the eyes, and in the eyes themselves sometimes, without apparent cause, a look of expectancy or surprise. Most people would never notice such subtle symptoms, would never suspect or know that Dulcie was not normal unless they became aware of her deviant behavior, slight at first, and her unusual way of talking.

She usually spoke in the higher register of her voice, exaggeratedly, excitedly, with little or no inflection. At other times, when she was nervous or tried to speak softly, her voice would crack, and the words would jump up and down across the break, back and forth like a yodeler's.

Dora Dykes was a mid-wife, and she knew, from having seen other mentally retarded children, that it was somewhere around the eyes that the affliction first evidenced itself. Her own suspicions notwithstanding, she was severely shocked when Dulcie's third grade teacher came by the house one evening to discuss the child's growing ineptitude. It was an even greater shock a few months later when Mr. Marcus Tatum, the new school superintendent, called Mrs. Dykes to his office and told her, in a fashion she thought highly undiplomatic and unsympathetic, that he was sure Dulcie was mentally retarded. Doctors at the Feeble-Minded Institute would later confirm the superintendent's crudely expressed convictions.

By the time Dora Dykes had walked the fifteen blocks from the school to her house, she had made up her mind. When she walked in the front door, she heard Annie Lois and Dulcie laughing in their room. She went to her bedroom, took off her hat and laid it on the dresser, then began unbuttoning her heavy coat.

"Annie Lois," she called as she finished getting the coat off and onto the bed. She struggled to get her dress over her head.

Annie Lois appeared with Dulcie close behind. "What is it, Mamma?"

Mrs. Dykes sat on the edge of the bed and started taking off her shoes and stockings. "Come in here and shut the door. Dulcie, you get back to your room."

Annie Lois gave Dulcie an affectionate touch on the head, closed the door and leaned against it. "What is it, Mamma?"

Mrs. Dykes got up from the bed, fingering some loose hair back into place, opened the closet door to hang up her clothes, then stopped abruptly, with one hand on the doorknob, and faced Annie Lois. "Annie Lois, we're goan have to put chure sister in the FMI."

Annie Lois squeezed the doorknob with both hands. "Oh no, Mamma!" she cried. "Why, Mamma, why?" She extended her arms out to her mother in a gesture of entreaty, then dropped them, covered her eyes and started crying.

"Why? Why, you ask?" Mrs. Dykes slammed the closet door, reached over and took the stockings from the chest of drawers, then turned, one hand holding the stockings on her hip, the other shaped like a big question mark with the three middle fingers thumping against the side of her head. "Because she's not right upstairs." She gave two more thumps and stretched her eyes wide. "That's why."

Annie Lois moved closer to her, shaking her hands up and down. "Please, Mamma. Please don't take her away. She's really not all that bad." She watched anxiously for some modified reaction from her mother, but there was none.

"Mamma, you cain't ever tell, she might get better after a while. Don't chu think so, Mamma?"

Her voice, though still firm, was now somewhat softer. "Annie Lois, don't chu know nothin'? Don't chu know feeble-minded children don't never get better? They get worse!" She opened a dresser drawer and stuck the wadded up stockings inside without realizing what she was doing. When Annie Lois ran over and tried to put her arms around her, she pushed her away. She took her robe from the hook on the closet door, pushed her arms through the sleeves and vigorously tied the sash. "Hand me my slippers."

"Mamma, please don't make Dulcie go down there. She's my little sister, Mamma, and I love 'er. Please, Mamma, *please*!"

As Dora slid her feet into the slippers, she straightened with a grunt, jerked some looseness out of the sash and retied it. She let out another gasp. "Did ju boil them potatoes like I tol' you to?"

"Yessum. And I washed the turnip greens, too."

As Dora put her hand on the doorknob, Annie Lois ran over and edged in front of her. "Mamma," she cried, "let me take care of Dulcie. If you don't put 'er in the FMI, I'll help 'er. I promise, Mamma. I'm already teachin' 'er how to read'n write'n count. And she's learnin', Mamma, she really is. *Please*, Mamma. I know I can do it. Won't chu please let me?"

Her mother hesitated for a moment, then, with her strong right arm, pushed Annie Lois out of her way.

OFTEN DURING THE past fifteen years, ever since Annie Lois was born, Dora Dykes had ample reason to doubt the high state of grace she used to enjoy in God's eyes. It was bad enough to lose two babies in three years, one at birth, the other several days after it was born. Why, then, had God not seen fit to let this last child die as well? It must be a curse. What else could it be?

During the night, she was better able to assess the situation. Certain matters which her high state of anxiety had distorted out of proportion seemed suddenly of relative unimportance. After getting on her sore knees and laying out all her concerns to God, she found, much to her surprise, that she was capable of carrying the extra burden He had laid on her. Next morning, she told Annie Lois she had given the matter some serious consideration and had decided, and here she pointed a thick, warped finger for emphasis, "for *your* sake," to let Dulcie stay at home.

Annie Lois was as good as her word and immediately made some elaborate though impractical plans for rectifying what she had come to think of as God's mistake. With a sudden, increased desire to be a teacher, and a zeal made more fervent for knowing her little sister would not be taken away from her, she began to teach Dulcie some of what she herself had already learned at school.

Almost every day after school she brought out her colored pencils and notebooks and, with exaggerated mannerisms inspired by her current favorite teacher, devoted two or three hours to teaching Dulcie how to read, write, and count. For a number of days, the adventure was mutually enjoyable, and Annie Lois was always happy to report her progress, more hoped for than attained, to her mother.

To expect a fifteen-year-old girl to maintain her initial enthusiasm for such an undertaking for any length of time, even if the results were commensurate with the time and effort expended, was highly unrealistic. Dora Dykes already knew this. Annie Lois, herself, was experiencing some new feelings and learning some things not taught at school.

She went to great lengths to keep her interest in Dulcie's education from dying utterly of frustration and futility and, at the same time, to convince her mother that she was still as enthusiastic as she was in the beginning. Without Annie Lois' former devoted persistence and the countless repetitions of the few things Dulcie was able with great difficulty to grasp, however, the child was destined to retain only so much, forgetting things or losing interest with resultant frustration and sometimes sudden withdrawals into herself, especially if Annie Lois lost her temper or showed in any way that she was disappointed in her.

So, in time, Dulcie learned enough to function in normal situations, which meant it was often necessary for her to rely on the honesty and good will of storekeepers and clerks and to avoid situations which might be too difficult for her to handle, even if and when good-natured others tried to help her. She told time by noting the positions of big and little hands and knew the denominations of coins and greenbacks, although she could do little more than say what they were. Annie Lois made sure, for instance, that she knew how many of what coins were required to ride the streetcar and to buy certain commonplace items at the local grocery store. She could read slowly and could spell a number of words if she took long enough and didn't get upset. From Annie Lois' example, she had learned how to cook simple things, particularly candy, and handle chores pertaining to cooking.

On February 4, 1916, Dora Dykes, after having delivered twin girls for Velma Caldwell shortly before midnight, walked back home, some two miles or more, in a steady, cold rain. Next day, with a fever of one hundred and four and aches and pains all over her body and in her head, she went to bed and never got up. Dr. Cranford had said it was pneumonia. She knew, as she lay dying, that it was exactly what she had willed herself to do two years ago upon learning the truth about Dulcie.

Dora Dykes' sister Lavinie, who lived at Ovett, agreed to come to Ellisville to live until Annie Lois finished high school. She made it clear from the day she arrived that the arrangement was temporary and, although she had never married, she had a life of her own to live. It didn't take very long before Annie Lois and Dulcie were more than pleased that Lavinie had put a limit on her stay.

One evening during Annie Lois' senior year, after supper was eaten and the dishes washed and put away, Annie Lois nudged Dulcie into their bedroom, where they took off their shoes and sat on the bed with pillows behind their backs.

"Dulcie, I've been thinkin'," Annie Lois said, using the middle finger of her left hand to push back and round off the cuticles of her right hand.

Dulcie rolled over on her side and laid her head on her bent arm. "What about? Sumpn good?"

Annie Lois drew her knees up and wrapped her arms around them. "Yeah, but chu might not think so."

"Well, are you go'n' tell me or not?"

Annie Lois pulled on Dulcie's ear, then threw her head back and laughed. "Well," she said, "I'm gonna get married!"

Dulcie raised up, covered her mouth and laughed. "You gonna do *what*?"

"You heard me. I said I'm goin' to get married!"

"Why that's the craziest thing I ever heard. You don't even have a sweetheart, so how you goan get married?"

Annie Lois sobered and looked straight ahead through the double window onto the side porch. "I'm not kiddin', Dulcie. I mean it with all my heart and soul."

Dulcie fidgeted with her hair, her face solemn now. "Annie

Lois, you ain't never said nothin' about havin' no sweetheart. You *are* lyin', ain't chu?"

"No, Dulcie, I'm not lyin'. You wanna know who he is?"

"Yeah!"

She hesitated before saying, "It's Guy Allen Musgrove, that's who." She pursed her lips confidently, then added, "That's who I'm goan marry."

"My Lord, Annie Lois, who in the world is *that*!"

She rested her chin on her knees and closed her eyes. "My sweetheart," she said finally, savoring the way it sounded. "I think he likes me. He's been writin' me notes almost every day."

"Did he tell you he likes you and wants to marry you?"

"Not exactly. But I think he does. In fact, I can tell from his notes that he does. He asked me if I'd go out with 'im."

"And what did you say?"

"I said I'd think about it. I didn't woant him to think I was just waitin' around for him to ask me."

"What's Aunt Lavinie gonna say about that? You know she ain't go'n' let chu."

"Maybe not," she said. "I'll ask her tomorrow."

Dulcie sat up on her knees and laid a hand lovingly on top of Annie Lois' head. "Annie Lois, why you woana marry anyway? What'll I do if you get married?"

She took both of Dulcie's hands, clasped them together, laid her face gently on them, then reached down and tickled her feet. "Why Silly, you know you goan live with me, no matter if I am married. Honey, we ain't never goan be separated. You can count on that."

Dulcie slid over so Annie Lois could put her arm around her.

"Dulcie, Honey," Annie Lois said, "girls my age just woana get married. That's the way God made us." She slid her feet onto the floor and sat on the edge of the bed, looking deeply into Dulcie's eyes. "You see, Honey, there comes a time in a girl's life when she just wants to be looked after and loved and be made a lot over . . . And to have babies."

Dulcie leaned over and played with her toes. "Annie Lois," she said, barely above a whisper, "tell me about havin' babies. You reck'n I'll have a baby one day?"

Annie Lois walked to the dresser and started brushing her hair. Dulcie slid down to the end of the bed to be near her. As Annie looked at herself in the mirror, she remembered how her mamma had explained the "curse" and the "mystery of life" to her in a way which raised more questions than she answered. What her mother had not told her or had confused in the telling, Annie Lois learned quickly from her friends who already knew. How could she explain it to Dulcie? Even though Dulcie would probably never marry and have children, she ought to know about such things.

Dulcie stayed awake past midnight, thinking about what Annie Lois had told her.

Next day, Annie Lois talked with Aunt Lavinie about Guy Allen's note. The old woman moved from the stove to the kitchen table, wiped her hands, removed her specs, blew her breath on them and wiped them with the end of the apron. "I don't see no harm in you seein' that boy if you woant to and if you think he's trustworthy and not just woantin' t'do ugly thangs with you," she said finally. Then she added, "You'n me both'll go out with 'im. How's that?"

On the following day, when Annie Lois tried to slip the note under her desk and over to Guy Allen, he seemed reluctant to take it. She had to poke it at him several times before he finally took it and stuck it in his shirt pocket. A little later, he pulled it out and read it behind a book, then crumpled it up and tossed it inside the desk. He never wrote her another note. Furthermore, he rarely if ever even looked at her after that and never spoke to her again.

A few weeks later, while Annie Lois was buying some thread and a sewing machine needle for Aunt Lavinie in Harper's City Mercantile, Hershel Harper, watching from the door of the storeroom while his mother waited on her, seemed to see her for the first time. He had never realized, he later told her, how pretty she was. He moved inconspicuously up to the front of the store and spoke to her.

Six months and many chaperoned walks and visits later, they were married. One month later, Aunt Lavinie went back to Overt with less enthusiasm than she had anticipated, and Annie Lois and Dulcie moved into the big Harper house on Main Street.

— t w o —

UP UNTIL ABOUT five years ago, Bo Arthur Bilbo had showed no signs of becoming the village bad boy. That's because he learned very early that he could get along much better if he kept certain things to himself. Over time, he became so successful that most folks in town thought of him as a fine-looking, well-behaved boy who was one day going to make some lucky girl a fine husband.

Bo Arthur was an only child, not because Brandon and Lily Ruth couldn't have any more, but because Lily Ruth didn't want any more. She didn't want any more because she was not at all satisfied with Brandon as a husband and lover. Consequently, she often sought the warmth and comfort of other men's beds and arms, even though she paid dearly for it in the way of beatings and threats of being killed whenever she would come home from one of her outings.

Lily Ruth worked as a waitress at Ben Rayburn's City Café and was able, for reasons most people already knew, to amass enough money to make up for what Brandon refused to give her. When Brandon was inducted and sent to France, she became more promiscuous than before with men, a few of whom were well known and highly respected city officials, frequently warming her bed rather than having her warm theirs.

Bo Arthur, whose room was two doors up the hall from where Lily Ruth entertained her visitors, could hear and, if he opened his door just slightly, could see them coming and going. One in particular. During the summer and at other times when Bo Arthur didn't have to go to school, Lily Ruth would sleep until around mid-morning, then make her way up to the kitchen, drop into a chair and make a weak effort to restore a little of the usual appearance of her hair by instinctively moving bobby pins from one place to another. The times when she was especially sleepy and drained, she would make a hand motion toward the cupboard and say, "You'll have t'eat some bread'n butter this mornin' Son. I don't feel like cookin'." At other times she would stay in bed until mid-afternoon, during which time Bo Arthur often sat on the back steps, leaning forward on his elbows, wondering what she and her men friends were doing. Later, when he knew what they were doing, he would close his eyes and try to visualize it. The anger and hatred consumed him and took over his life.

Sometimes he would sit on the back steps with the pocket knife Brandon had given him when he was six years old, whittling on a limb or any piece of wood he could find, pretending that what he was whittling was his mamma, and the longer he whittled, the more violent he became, making sharp, deep diagonal cuts across and back again to form pieces of different shapes and sizes, no longer pretending but by now actually believing they were pieces of her. On other occasions, when he tired of staying at home, he would wander off into the woods behind the house and shoot birds and squirrels with his slingshot or kill rabbits or turtles with a heavy limb or a brick. He always felt better afterwards.

Shortly after the news came of Brandon's death in France, Lily Ruth met an out-of-town salesman at City Café. The salesman extended his stay in Ellisville long enough for Lily Ruth to throw some things together and leave town with him. Because there was nobody else to take care of Bo Arthur, his seventy-eight-year-old paternal grandmother let him come to live with her. Folks one after another came to show their concern with love and gifts and proffers of being available at any time to help make things happy for him. He accepted it all with a winning smile and courtesy rarely seen in other boys his age.

Eula Bilbo lived about four miles from town, but within walking distance, just beyond Tula Rosa Church, a place secluded enough for Bo Arthur to put some slack in the vise he'd been keeping on his real feelings. It didn't take long for the process to begin. He had been in his new surroundings only three weeks or so when it happened. One of his responsibilities was to feed the chickens every day, a job he didn't like and complained about every time he did it. When Eula asked him one day why he had killed one of her best Rhode Island Red hens, he said she had tried to peck his hand while he was spreading the feed on the ground. "I figured I'd better put a stop to it before she got any meaner," he said nonchalantly.

Only a few days after that incident, Eula came across a smelly pile of dead animals Bo Arthur had evidently killed and burned down at the far southwest corner of her property. She was horrified. When she asked him why he'd done it, he said he had to, they were bothering him and he just got tired of it. Then he added, "Anyway, I like to watch 'em burn." What he did a little later left no doubt about that. One Monday morning, when Eula was washing clothes behind the house, she asked Bo Arthur to build the fire around the washpot. She had to remind him twice because he seemed preoccupied about something.

After he built the fire, he stood watching it, almost as though he saw something in the flames that fascinated him. Off a few feet to his left, Dodger, the dog, was playing with an injured bird that was trying to get away. As soon as Bo Arthur became aware of it, he hurried over, picked up the bird, then threw it in the fire. As he watched, he laughed and hollered like somebody gone mad.

By now, Eula's concern was keeping her awake at night. Something had to be done, but she didn't know what it was or how to do it. She decided finally that the best and only thing to do for the time-being was to watch him every moment he was around and give him fair warning that she would see that he was punished if he didn't change his ways.

Her resolve was put to the test a few days later, when she asked Bo Arthur to take Dodger the table scraps from lunch. She watched from the kitchen window. After feeding the dog, he walked slowly, head down, over to a pecan tree, pulled down and broke off a short limb, then slid into a sitting position, pulled out his knife and started whittling on the limb. From time to time he stopped and stared, as though transfixed, into the distance. As she watched, she wondered what he was thinking about. She felt so sorry for him sometimes, though her sorrow lately had been less intense than her fear.

Bo Arthur dropped the pecan limb, wrapped his arms around his bent knees, with the open knife still in his hand, and rested his chin on his arms. When Dodger came over and tried to engage him in play, Bo Arthur jumped up, caught him before he could run, and pulled him, yelping, over behind the privy.

"Bo Arthur," Eula hollered from the open window, "you take yore hands off'n that dog. I mean this minute!"

He paid no attention but, instead, pulled harder on the collar till Dodger started choking.

Eula stopped what she was doing and ran outside, picking up the first thing she could see, a piece of metal pipe propped against the side of the house. "Bo Arthur Bilbo!" she hollered as she puffed her way across the yard. "You leave that dog alone or I'm go 'n' bust yore brains out. Bo Arthur, I said for you t'let that dog go! I don't mean t'morrow, I mean now! This very minute!"

When Bo Arthur pulled the collar tighter around Dodger's neck, Dodger, normally gentle-natured, suddenly went into a rage, shook his head from side to side until it slipped out of the collar, growled ferociously and bit Bo Arthur's right hand until the blood gushed out. Just as Bo Arthur raised his leg to kick the dog off, Eula ran up behind him, ready to bring the metal pipe down on his back. He made no effort to stop her but turned around, instead, and looked solemnly into her eyes. She had never seen him look that way. All of a sudden she felt sorry for him, but when she dropped the pipe and started to put her arms around him, he moved away and started crying.

As she trudged back to the house she cried, too.

IT SUDDENLY OCCURRED to Eula, as she stood looking out the kitchen window, that she had rarely if ever seen Bo Arthur show a real interest in girls. There was ample opportunity for him to do so, since most of the neighbors who came to visit had daughters about his age. She made a serious effort to recall some of those visits. Yes, she remembered especially that he almost always looked happier, even transformed in some strange way by their presence. She remembered now how he and Lorice Parker used to play horseshoes out by the barn, Lorice evidently enjoying it as much as Bo Arthur did.

Eula's concern for Bo Arthur's feelings about girls would later prove justified. What would happen one week or so later would change the whole course of her life and of Bo Arthur's as well.

Lorice and her mother Myrtis came over on Sunday afternoon for a visit. After a few minutes, Lorice and Bo Arthur went outside and Eula and Myrtis stayed in the living room. At one point, when Eula went to the kitchen to make some coffee, she leaned over and looked out to see where Bo Arthur and Lorice were. They were sitting under the pecan tree, holding hands. Bo Arthur must have said something Lorice didn't like because she suddenly jumped up and started to leave when he grabbed both her arms and looked as though he didn't know whether to kiss or kill her. Lorice kicked and fought him furiously, then, breaking away, ran home as fast as she could.

Later that evening, Eula asked Bo Arthur why Lorice went home in such a hurry.

" 'Cause I told 'er to," he answered without looking at her.

"And why'd you tell 'er t'go home?"

With his hands deep in his pockets, he turned sharply away from her and seemed unsure about what to say.

Eula persisted. "I asked you, Bo Arthur, why did Lorice run home that'a way and I expect a answer. Since I'm the one who's takin' care a you, I have a right t'know a few thangs that go on 'roun' hyere."

All of a sudden, he kicked the leg of a chair and gave her a wild and fearsome look. "Listen, ol' woman, I sure as hell never asked you t'take care a me, an' just 'cause you decided you wanted to don't give you no reason t'be askin' so many questions. If I'd a wanted you t'know, I'd a done tol' you." He bolted out the door and slammed it behind him.

Myrtis Parker was outside doing her weekly wash when Eula got there next morning. "As soon as I git this hyere batch a whites in the pot, we'll go inside," she said, wiping her sweaty forehead with a sudsy right wrist.

"What's on yore mind, Eula?" she asked as she poured the two cups of coffee.

Eula kept her eyes on the coffee rather than on Myrtis. "I got a sneakin' feelin' you awready know," she said finally, looking directly into Myrtis's eyes.

"Bo Arthur an' Lorice?"

"Yeah, that's it exactly. I been worried sick about it. I tried t'git Bo Arthur t'tell me what happened, but he refused. Then he got mad and run out the door."

Myrtis tossed her head back knowingly with a low grunt. "That don't surprise me one bit," she said. "But if'n it'd been me, I'd a kicked 'im out right then'n there." She hesitated long enough, it seemed, to decide what to say next by taking a slow sip of coffee and holding the cup close to her mouth. "Eula," she said, "I'm goan be real honest with you. After Lorice told me what happened yestiddy, I'm convinced you got a real bad problem on yore hands."

"I'm aware a that, Myrtis, but I've got t'know what happened, though, no matter how much it hurts."

"Well, Lorice said evuhthang was just fine till Bo Arthur started foolin' aroun', tryin' t'touch 'er an' makin' vulgar suggestions. When she tol' 'im she dittn't like it and t'stop doin' it, he got real mad. Eula, she said sumpn real strange come over 'im, that all of a sudden his face changed and he looked like sumpn wild. She said she thought for a while there he was go'n hit 'er. Then she said before she knowed it, he put his hands down between her legs and she slapped 'im as hard as she could. He grabbed her with both a his hands and said he was go'n' git what he wanted if he had to knock her down and drag 'er to the barn t'do it. She jumped up and he grabbed 'er ag'in."

"I saw that part," Eula said, sitting forward in her chair with the coffee cup pushed aside.

"Well, he must a not knowed that Lorice's been playin' basketball practic'ly all her life and her arms are 'bout as strong as his'n, if not stronger. So she just flung her arms inside a his'n an' took off runnin' as fast as her legs'd take 'er. She said she even forgot I was still in the house with you." She touched Eula's arm gently and stood up. "I'll be right back. I gotta stir them clothes."

When she returned, she pushed the two empty cups away and folded her hands on the table. "Eula, I don't know if you know this or not, but Lorice said she ain't the onliest girl Bo Arthur's done that to. Lorice tol' me none a the other girls at school won't have nothin' t'do with 'im. That naturally makes him mad as the devil, and she said he uses the foulest, vulgarest language she ever hyeard in her life."

She could tell this bit of information had deeply hurt Eula. She placed both hands on Eula's and patted them gently. "Eula, what gits me is the way he makes folks think he's such a fine upstanding man when all the time he's got the very devil inside 'im."

"That's 'cause he ain't never had no upbringin'. You know that, Myrtis. He never really had a mamma. An' when Brandon got kilt, thangs just went from bad t'worse." She paused long enough to think ahead, then said, "God knows, Myrtis, I never wanted that boy t'come live with me, but they wuddn't nothin' else could be done. I wouldn't just let 'im go to the dogs an' maybe end up in jail." She gave a deep sigh and covered her face with her hands. "Dear God! I don't know what t'do. I simply do not know what t'do!"

"Have you ever give any thought t'puttin' 'im in Collinsville? The reformatory, I mean."

"Oh God, yes, yes, yes! But it near 'bout breaks my heart t'even think a that."

"Well, how else d'you plan t'deal with it? As I see it, you don't have a whole lot a choices."

"I know that. But d'you reckon Marcus Tatum could hep me somehow? I've give some thought to that the last few days. What d'you think a that?"

"Why, I ain't give it no thought, but now that chu mention it, it sounds like a pretty good idear."

"I hate t'impose on you, Myrtis," she said hesitantly, "but d'you reck'n you could take me into town one day soon? I could walk to the schoolhouse if I just had a way t'git t'town."

"Well, yes, I might in a couple a days. What about next Friday? I'll be goin' t'town t'git groceries."

"Friday'll be just fine. Maybe by then I'll have a better idear 'bout what I'm go'n' say."

WHEN BO ARTHUR left home that morning, he had no intention of going to school. When he reached Tula Rosa Methodist Church, he went around to the back and hid his books behind a pillar, then continued walking slowly toward town. He suddenly realized he was not feeling too good. There were some unsettling thoughts beating around in his head, from some of which he'd tried for a long time to keep his distance, and now they were pushing everything else out of their way. Ever since Lorice turned him down yesterday, he'd been trying to figure out why girls didn't like him. Was he doing something wrong, or was he trying not to let folks know what he really felt about girls, that whenever he went beyond a certain point, every one of them became his mamma?

He had never concerned himself enough about this problem. And it was a problem. He felt he had what girls wanted. He was good-looking, well-built, and had a smile which he'd learned long ago could get him almost anything he wanted, even girls up to a certain point. Each time he'd try to go deeper than that in his thinking, an alarm went off in his head and made him change course quickly. Sometimes at night, though, when his resistance was lower than usual, the ugly realization of why he was how he was would jump out of his head and refuse to go away. If he ever consciously let the thought take shape, it would leave him with equal portions of guilt and animosity. To admit even to himself that he actually hated women in general would almost always kindle the fiercest and most compelling fires of retribution.

When he realized he was still holding the lunch Granny had made for him, he decided he'd better eat it, otherwise folks would wonder why he wasn't in school. He stopped at the cemetery, found a shady spot, sat down and opened up the paper sack, grease-stained from the biscuit and egg sandwich. There were also an apple and three spice cookies, his favorite kind. When he finished eating, he wadded up the bag and shoved it down behind A. L. Townsend's (1878-1917) headstone, then wiped his hands on his overalls and walked on to town.

He spent most of the morning visiting with first one and then another of the store clerks or owners who knew and liked him and thought he was a fine young fellow. Every one of them asked him why he was not in school. He said he didn't feel good.

He always enjoyed visiting with Mr. Sam Barranco, who owned Sanitary Meat Market and Grocery Store on Front Street, even though he usually referred to him as Mr. Sam Dago. Mr. Sam spoke English pretty well but sometimes used words Bo Arthur didn't understand, words which he felt would be better said in Italian than in English. Bo Arthur enjoyed his visits for other reasons as well, for the fruit and candy Mr. Sam would give him and then laugh because it made Bo Arthur so happy. Mr. Sam's generosity notwithstanding, Bo Arthur couldn't resist the impulse to steal a couple of bananas off of one of the four bunches hanging out in front of the store.

With a banana in each of his front pockets, he walked around town for another hour or so. Heretofore, whenever he'd played hooky, he had felt wonderful, free and under nobody's control. Today things were different. Though he had managed to put some of his troubling thoughts out of his mind temporarily, others, like certain indigestible foods, continued to make their presence felt.

Around two o'clock, he decided to take a rest on the steps of the Confederate Monument. Nobody was around at the time, so he needn't be afraid he'd be seen in something other than his usual assumed mood. He propped his elbows on his knees, then cupped his face in his hands, his eyes looking at the ground and sometimes closed in deep thought.

MOST PEOPLE IN south Mississippi who knew Frank Haley Bankston would tell you, if asked, that he was the embodiment of everything a southern gentleman should be and something a lawyer almost never was. Protestants were sometimes heard to say he was the nearest thing to a saint they'd ever come across. The few Catholics in Ellisville and those on the Gulf Coast sometimes said he had already met all the requirements for canonization and, therefore, was already a saint. All the requirements but one; he was not a Catholic. He was a dyed-in-the-wool, fire-and-damnation Baptist.

At age fifty-two, he had earned an awesome reputation for his dazzling courtroom victories during his twenty-one years of practice. He had won so many cases that, when and if he ever lost one, his faithful followers were sure and quick to disseminate the information, true or false, that a post-trial investigation had proved that the jury had been tampered with. His prowess as a courtroom lawyer was due in large part to his knowledge of the Bible and his quick, forceful use of pertinent scripture when defending or prosecuting. Even in casual conversation he was given to frequent use of scriptural references at what seemed to be pre-calculated junctures of what he was saying. Folks meeting him for the first time were usually surprised, then dubious by what seemed to be pretentious show. Those who already knew and admired him found it to be extraordinarily edifying.

Frank's father, who died two years ago, had also been an outstanding attorney, a religious zealot, and a very rich man. He often told folks he had never been happier and more fulfilled than when his first son, Frank Haley, Jr., was born on November 3, 1871. You would have thought it was the Christ Child he was carrying in his arms as he strutted up and down the streets of Ellisville. His son was, as far as anyone could tell at the time, as perfect a baby as a baby could be. It was not until Frank Haley, Jr. tried to take his first steps that his father and mother were made aware that what at first was thought to be the perfect offspring of their illustrious family had been born with an impairment. His left leg was slightly shorter than the other.

At about fifteen minutes after two on that Monday, Frank Haley Bankston, who had just been going through some deed registrations in the Chancery Clerk's office, walked cautiously down the courthouse steps, seemingly lost in thought, and down the sidewalk. Before descending the steps to the sidewalk, he looked in the direction of the Confederate Memorial and stopped abruptly, looked around thoughtlessly, then walked over to where Bo Arthur was sitting, bent over, oblivious to everything else than his own problems. Frank Haley got closer, bent his head forward, peering, trying to make out who was sitting in such a position.

He reached over and tapped Bo Arthur's shoulder. "Bo Arthur, is sumpn wrong?"

Bo Arthur thought it was Granny, waking him up for breakfast. When he straightened and tried to make out who was talking to him, he was momentarily confused. He knew, yet he did not know who the man was. His instinctive first reaction was one of dislike. It took a few seconds to decide which of his guises to use and what to say. "Who're you?" he asked finally, rubbing his hands together.

Frank Haley laughed softly and shifted his briefcase to the other hand. "Why, Bo Arthur, you know me. I'm lawyer Frank Haley Bankston, a long-time friend a your family."

Bo Arthur was not impressed and felt his resentment growing at knowing it was a lawyer talking to him. He laced his fingers together and looked at his hands rather than at Frank Haley.

"Aren't you s'posed t'be in school, Son?"

Bo Arthur suddenly became viciously alive. "First of all, Mister, I don't know who you are, but I shore as hell ain't chure son! An' I'm go'n' tell you sumpn else. Why I'm not in school ain't none a yore business."

"You're right about one thing, Bo Arthur. You're not my son. But you are my brother."

"Since when, Mister?"

Frank Haley leaned closer and said softly, "Since Jesus came. You do know who Jesus is, don't chu?

Bo Arthur hesitated. "Yeah," he said with a shake of his head. "I know who he is."

"Well, then, tell me, Bo Arthur, are you saved?"

"From what?"

"From your sins. That's why Jesus came. Are you, Bo Arthur?"

His anger was mounting. "Look, Mister, I thought chu said you was a lawyer. Then how come you started preachin' all of a sudden?"

"I am a lawyer, but lawyers can be Christians, too. Didn't chu know that?"

"I ain't never heard a one. And anyway, I don't need to hear no sermon from you or nobody else. I feel just fine the way I am."

The last thing Frank Haley would do was to show facially what he was feeling. "Young fellow," he said slowly and firmly, putting his face closer to Bo Arthur's, "you are a mean and disrespectful boy. Now, as for it not bein' any a my business why you're not

in school, let me set chu straight about that. As chairman of the
school board, I can see to it that you are duly punished for playing
hooky. And another thing . . ."

If Bo Arthur had been perceiving the meaning of the words
instead of their sounds, he would have reacted in a way that might
have caused Frank Haley to wonder about his mental condition.
He closed his eyes in order to separate the sound from the speaker,
with lips tightly shut pout-like and his broad hands gripping his
knees as though on the verge of springing loose from the stone
steps and lunging forward at Frank Haley.

"I've heard from reliable sources that since you went to live
with your grandma you've been causin' her a lot a trouble. And
some a the students at school say you cain't get along with any
of the other students, especially the girls. I heard that most a the
girls won't have anything t'do with you. Is that true, Bo Arthur?"

Bo Arthur threw his head back and laughed. "Man, you don't
know what chure talkin' about. I can have any one of them girls
anytime I want 'em. I bet I know where you heard that. Them girls
that tol' you that are the ones I won't have nothin' t'do with."

"Then tell me sumpn, Bo Arthur. If you're such a lady's man,
how come you keep chasin' after that feeble-minded Dykes girl?"

Bo Arthur averted Frank Haley's eyes by pretending he was
cleaning his fingernails. He finally looked up and grinned. "Man,
don't chu know I do that just for the fun of it?"

"You're sure that's the real reason you do it?"

"Of course it is. What other reason would I have? You don't
really think I'd lay that crazy thing, do you?"

"Yes, Bo Arthur, I do."

"Then man, you must be crazy. You gotta be."

Frank Haley sat down on the step next to Bo Arthur. "No, Bo
Arthur, I'm not crazy. I've been dealin' with people like you for
most a my life. And d'you know why I really think you run after
Dulcie the way you do?"

Bo Arthur tried to look at him but couldn't. He was rapidly
losing his temper and didn't know how to respond.

For Frank Haley, it was like being in the courtroom, waiting
for the right moment to say something he'd already carefully

structured in his mind, something that would startle the jury and cinch his case. He leaned over as far as he could to see the full effect of what he was about to say. "Bo Arthur," he said, the way he would have said it in front of the jury, "it's not for fun, as you say, that you chase poor Dulcie Dykes the way you do. Young man, you chase her simply because you don't know how to deal with other girls. Because Dulcie is feeble-minded you feel like you can do with her what chu cain't do with other girls. Now, ain't that the truth?"

If Frank Haley were in the courtroom, there would now be an audible unison gasp from those in attendance, followed by an uproarious stirring and talking which the judge would allow for a moment or two before gaveling everybody back to order. The defendant, most likely, would be bent forward, head in hands, either crying or restraining to the best of his ability the shock, pain, and futility he was feeling.

What he didn't know was to what extent Bo Arthur, during the sixteen years of his life, had learned not only how to conceal his malicious side but, also, how to react when faced with the threat that somebody suspected it and seemed intent on proving it. His skill at doing this was such that he could transcend for the moment the inner turmoil of mind and body and still transmit a countenance of composure, even of inner peace, leaving little or no doubt in the minds of most people that he was being truthful. The last thing he wanted to do was to give Frank Haley even the slightest indication that the walls of his true self had been climbed over or were on the verge of being razed.

He remained seated because to stand up at that point would give Frank Haley the impression that he was scared and caught off-guard. Instead, he threw his head back, clapped his hands together and let out a yell that caused people across the street to turn and look. "Man," he said, laughing, "you've been a lawyer too long. I don't care how many crazy people you've saved or put in jail, you ain't gonna fool me. I know who I am an' you'n nobody else don't know and never will."

I rest my case, Frank Haley would have said at this point if he were in court. Every feature of his face conveyed assurance and self-satisfaction, and justifiably so. No matter how skilled in the art of self-defense Bo Arthur felt himself to be, Frank Haley knew from the outset that he was dealing with a novice. Bo Arthur, in spite of his proportionately developed skills, had not, until a few minutes ago, been challenged by someone of Frank Haley's mental and legal stature. For a few moments he said nothing, during which time he took a mental inventory of the several subtle features of face and voice that convinced him fully that Bo Arthur was lying. "It's possible, though highly unlikely," he said finally, "that I really don't know you. But don't be too sure nobody else does. God knows, young fellow, and He's the one who's ultimately goin' t'judge you, who you are and what you are, and where you're gonna end up." He stood and brushed the seat of his trousers. "I have t'go now. I've got better things t'do than waste any more time with you."

As he picked up his briefcase and turned to go down the steps, the elevator shoe on his left foot slipped and he almost fell. Bo Arthur made a quick, instinctive gesture to help him, but Frank Haley regained his balance.

"If I were you, Bo Arthur, I think I'd give some serious thought to mendin' my ways."

It was the first time Bo Arthur had noticed that Frank Haley was wearing an elevator shoe on his left foot. He closed his eyes, lowered his head and resumed the remembering that had begun the moment Frank Haley started talking. It was several years ago, an experience that had had such a strong and lasting effect that he could call it forth at any time. Though he had heard any number of night visitors to and from his mamma's bedroom, there was one that was different enough to cause him to get out of bed and run to the slightly open door and watch. The man said something to Lily Ruth which Bo Arthur couldn't understand, started down the hall past Bo Arthur's open door, lit a cigarette as he neared the dark area of the hall where the back door was, then disappeared, giving the slightly warped door an extra shove to close it. It wasn't the voice that got Bo Arthur's attention. It was, instead, the dotted rhythm, the relatively loud sound the left foot made as it hit the hollow, uncarpeted floor.

He played the scene over and over in his mind until all the pieces fit together and, as soon as they did, his mind exploded. He jumped the two steps to the ground, then watched as Frank Haley limped his way up the sidewalk across the street. "God damn the dirty, low down son-of-a-bitch!" he sputtered between his clinched teeth as he kicked the base of the memorial. "After whorin' aroun' with my mamma, he stood right there, preachin' t'me about bein' saved an' tellin' me how bad I was!" More than anything, he wanted to run over there, catch up with Frank Haley, and tell him point-blank that he had seen him leaving the house one night. Instead, he started walking as fast as he could, growling obscenities under his breath as he passed people on the street. He drove his hands deep into his pockets where the bananas had been. The odor was good and reminded him of Mr. Sam.

Mr. Sam was holding some freshly cut steaks on a piece of wrapping paper for a spruced-up lady's approval when Bo Arthur got there.

"Fine, Sam," she said. "Maybe you better give me two or three more."

From the top of the meat counter to the ceiling a screened partition separated the customers from the back part of the store, with a door on the right side which was always locked unless Mr. Sam had to come out to sell groceries when his wife, who usually took care of that part of the business, was cooking in the back of the store, washing clothes, or taking care of the two babies.

Bo Arthur walked quietly up to the counter and looked over to where Mr. Sam was cutting the steaks. The lady moved slightly away and looked as though she didn't like seeing him. He suddenly became fascinated as he watched Mr. Sam stop, then give the knife a quick backward and forward lick or two on the steel sharpener he was holding with his other hand, then start cutting the other steaks. Mr. Sam knew just how thick or thin to cut the meat and, as he brought the knife from back to front, the line was precise and even, and each steak was exactly the same size.

The knife claimed all of Bo Arthur's attention. As he watched, he could feel the knife in his own hand and could feel the resistance of the meat against the knife and the need to hold the other end of the leg in order to make the slices come off just right. In a matter of moments, he was somebody else and somewhere other than in Mr. Sam's meat market and grocery store.

"Allo, Boy," Mr. Sam said after the lady left with her steaks. He had never been sure of whether Bo was Bo or Boy, but it really didn't matter, he liked him anyway. " 'ow you feela? You no feela good?"

"Un unh," he said, looking directly into Mr. Sam's eyes.

"What's a matter? You no do good in a school a t'day?"

"No, Mr. Sam, I just don't feel good. I better be goin'."

Mr. Sam came through the door at the right of the counter. "You wait a minute'a, Boy." He went to the front of the store where the fruit had been neatly arranged by Mr. Sam's wife Rosa. He looked at first one and then another of the apples, then picked one out and, after polishing it against his apron, gave it to Bo Arthur. "Here. You eat'a questa apple'a. You feel'a better."

"Thanks, Mr. Sam."

Bo Arthur went outside and sat on the steps, took one or two bites of the apple, then lowered his head and closed his eyes. He was finding it hard to keep the ugly thoughts inside where they belonged. Little by little the trivial experience of seeing Mr. Sam cutting the meat assumed gigantic proportions. He could feel and hear his heart racing as though something which he couldn't control was about to happen. He suddenly jumped up, threw the apple on the ground, and started running up the street as fast as he could, yelling and waving his arms in the air, with no idea of where he was going.

— t h r e e —

HURD CRAWFORD WAS president of Grand National Bank of Laurel, where Penny Welborn was a teller. For some time now, Mr. Crawford had been calling Mrs. Welborn into his office to discuss, so it was thought, matters pertaining to her employment. His concern about her work, if that's what it was, was justified. Up until the time of her divorce, she had never done an honest day's work in her life. So it need not be a matter of her embezzling funds but, rather, of her not being competent enough to handle her responsibilities. Word soon got around, mostly among the other employees, that Penny was about to lose her job.

When, however, her visits to the president's office continued, now more often and for longer periods of time than before, and she continued, day after day, to occupy her teller's cubicle at the front of the bank, the other employees began to suspect that something unseemly was going on.

One Monday morning before the bank opened, Hurd Crawford called Penny to his office. She thought it was mighty early in the day for a "visit," but locked the door behind her anyway as she entered.

"How was your weekend?" she asked and moved closer to the desk.

He opened and closed some drawers, then pulled out some folders and laid them on the desk. "Not so good," he said without looking up.

This caused Penny to wonder. Sometimes he seemed preoccupied. It was, after all, the beginning of a new week and he usually had a lot on his mind.

"Is it Sylvia?" she asked finally, nervously fluffing the blonde hair over her ears.

He closed a folder and sat down. "No, not Sylvia. At least not yet." He took out a cigarette and lit it. "I've been doin' some serious thinkin', however."

Her heart jumped into her throat. She had feared the expression on his face, and now this. *Dear God*, she thought, *what will I do?*

". . . and I think we're gonna have t'do things a little different from now on. I have a feelin' the other girls are beginnin' to suspect somethin'."

She laced her fingers together behind her back and squeezed so hard they hurt. "Yeah. They are."

"We're gonna have t'cut out these office visits and find some other way." He opened a desk drawer and pulled out an ashtray in the shape of a dollar sign, then tapped his cigarette in it. Finally, he looked up at her. "You got any suggestions?"

Oh God! How thankful she was that he hadn't said it was over! "Not right offhand," she said and cleared her throat.

"What about chure place?"

Oh merciful Jesus, yes! Yes, yes, *anything*! The release of tension over her entire body was so immediate and complete, she felt a sudden silly impulse to laugh and cry at the same time. Then she remembered. "Melissa," she said, covering her mouth with her hand. "What about her?"

"What d'you mean? Don' chu have somebody takin' care of 'er while you work?"

"Yes, the only thing, though, is she lives in Ellisville and has to ride the streetcar."

"So? Don't the streetcar run 'til midnight?"

"Well, yes. But surely I couldn't ask her to stay that late."

"I'm not askin' you to. I'm only suggestin' the girl could stay over a couple'a hours, say, on Fridays, and go somewhere with Melissa when the time came."

The thought sent chills all over her and made her head and body feel light. It was always so exciting to hear him talk that way. Her heart began to thump itself into her ears. "Yeah," she said. "I'll think of sumpn'."

He flattened what was left of the cigarette in the ash tray, pulled out a sheet of paper and uncapped the fountain pen. "All right, then," he said, putting the pen to paper, then stopping and shaking it to make it write. "You take care of that end of it and let me know how it turns out." The smile on his face, when he looked up, was anything but convincing. "So, back to work," he said, "and make us a lot of money."

She laughed self-consciously and walked out feeling only slightly satisfied. She spent much of her free time Tuesday trying to decide how to get rid of Dulcie and Melissa every Friday afternoon. Her first thought was to send them to the park only a few blocks from where she lived, but realized it would soon be getting dark and cold before six o'clock. While she ate her Blue Plate Special at The Dinner Bell Cafe, a splendid idea occurred to her. Maybe her sister Voncille would let Dulcie and Melissa stay with her for a couple of hours every Friday. Voncille might agree if she was approached in the right manner, which might prove difficult since the two of them had never gotten on well together. Voncille had become even more difficult lately since she and her husband Maynard were having marital problems, and she had taken to drink.

She went to see Voncille on Wednesday after work and they settled the matter amicably. In fact, Voncille said Penny's visit was like a shot in the arm, a pair of good strong shoulders to cry on and someone with lots of experience in dealing with marital problems to listen to her. There was only one catch, however, Voncille told her as she uncorked another bottle of bourbon, she was going to be in Meridian this Friday but saw no reason why Dulcie and Melissa couldn't come over the following week. Penny assured her with an awkward kiss on the cheek that that would be fine. This Friday, Dulcie and Melissa could go to the park where Dulcie would probably have more fun than Melissa would.

As she walked down the steps and started home, she turned and waved good-bye to Voncille, then checked her watch. She didn't know what exactly was bothering her. She should have felt better now for having arranged things for her Friday afternoon trysts with Hurd, but she didn't. Somewhere in the cold depths of her dying conscience she felt a dark uneasiness. Was it guilt at last? Voncille had warned her that she was playing with fire, doing exactly what Faye Henderson, "that other woman," had done to her, and heading straight ahead and hell-bent for trouble. Voncille conceded, however, that Penny might as well have fun while it lasted.

As soon as she got home, she threw her purse on the dining room table. "Did y'all have a good time today?" she asked as she gave Melissa a big hug and kiss.

Dulcie laughed and her face turned red. "We sure did, dittn't we, Melissa?" She reached down and tightened one of Melissa's long curls around her finger. "Tell mother what all we did today." She laughed again.

Melissa said they had lots of fun cutting out paper dolls and Dulcie was real good at it. Dulcie snickered as she went into the kitchen to get her purse.

Penny looked at her watch. "Oh, by the way, Dulcie. Do you think you could stay a couple of hours longer day after tomorrow?"

"Yessum, I reck'n," Dulcie said. "How come? You gonna have t'work late or sumpn?"

Penny had hoped she wouldn't have to explain and didn't know why she should, yet she did. In her own way. "Some of the girls at the bank woana start playin' bridge every week."

Dulcie interrupted. "What's *that*?"

"Why, it's a card game, Dulcie. We thought we'd start a bridge club . . ." She stopped long enough to clear a path forward through her improvised performance. ". . . 'nd meet here every Friday after work."

"I see, yessum."

"You think you can do that, Dulcie?"

"Yessum, I reck'n so."

Penny smiled. Thank God! One less hurdle. "You an' Melissa can go to the park and play while we're playin' bridge. Now don't that sound like fun?"

Dulcie looked at Melissa and they both giggled as though they were bound together in a conspiracy. "Yes m'am," Dulcie said emphatically.

"Alright now, when you get home this evenin', you be sure an' tell Annie Lois you're gonna be two hours late gettin' home on

Friday, you hear?" She held up two fingers, "Two . . . hours . . . day after tomorrow."

"Yessum, Miz Welborn, I will."

THE WEATHER ON Friday was soggy and warm, the sky layered in dirty grey clouds that stretched beyond sight in edgeless, congealed shapes. Frequent, sudden gusts of wind which should have brought some degree of comfort brought, instead, only cloying humidity.

Penny Welborn came home early on Friday afternoon, clearly in a state of high anxiety, every nerve in her body sensing and responding to the anticipation of what was about to happen. After stooping over and kissing Melissa and saying hello to Dulcie, she hurried to her bedroom, kicked off her shoes and massaged the soles of her feet. What a damnable way to make a living, she thought. Yet she realized and often reminded herself that if it wasn't for the damnable job she would not be worked up into this wonderful frenzy. There were so many things to do before he came, but the item of top priority was to get rid of Dulcie and Melissa. She sat on the edge of the bed and pulled her stockings off.

"Dulcie!" she called.

Dulcie appeared, smiling. "Yessum?"

"You know where the park is, don't chu?" She started unbuttoning her blouse.

"Yessum. Me'n Annie Lois have been there lots of times."

Penny finished undressing, then reached inside the closet for her robe. "I'm gonna take a bath now, but I woant chu and Melissa to go on to the park. Now look." She took her watch from the dresser. "I don't woant chu to come back till six o'clock. Come here." She held the watch out for Dulcie to see. "When the big hand is right here and the little hand is right there," she said, pointing to the six and the twelve and watched Dulcie's face.

Dulcie clasped and unclasped her hands in a gesture of frustration, tilted her head sideways and widened her eyes. "Why, Miz Welborn, I know how t'tell time!"

"Well, I'm certainly glad to know that. But chu don't have a watch, do you?" *Oh dear, another problem! Do I dare let her take my watch? Good God, I know she'd lose it as sure as anything.* Then the frown relaxed into a smile. "I tell you what, Dulcie. You know that big ol' clock on the front of the bank? The bank where I work?"

"Yessum."

"Good! Then you can tell the time by that. It's plenty big, so you won't have any trouble seein' what time it is, will you?"

Dulcie laughed so hard she almost choked.

Penny watched for a moment, something bothering her. "Remember, Dulcie, six o'clock. Not one minute before! . . . You understand?"

"Yessum, Miz Welborn, I done tol' ju I understand." She reached out and took the watch. "We ain't comin' back till six o'clock. The big hand'll be right here, and the little hand'll be right there," she said proudly.

Penny took the watch and put it back on the dresser, then opened her purse. "Here," she said, holding her hand out to Dulcie. "I'm gonna give y'all two nickels to buy yourselves sumpn with."

"Oh, thank you, Miz Welborn," Dulcie said, taking the nickels and pulling her handkerchief from her purse. Her hands shaking from the excitement, she opened the handkerchief up, folded it over the two nickels, then pushed them to one end and tied a knot in the handkerchief, chuckling as she did so.

"All right, now, y'all have a real good time. And Dulcie, y'all be careful, you hear?"

Laughing, holding hands, they ran down the front steps, Melissa with her pink-ribboned braids bouncing out of rhythm with her fleet feet, and Dulcie, heavy-footed, with her long, full gingham skirt billowing up as far as her knees, showing the gathered legs of her bloomers.

THEY HAD SLID down the chute t'chute and Dulcie had snagged the end of her skirt, and they had whirled around on the flying jenny until they both were dizzy, and now they wanted something to eat. They went to the tin-roofed pavilion and bought some peanuts from a man operating a kerosene peanut parcher.

"Have you girls seen th' organ grinder and his little monkey yet?" he asked as he handed Dulcie the peanuts.

"What monkey?" Dulcie asked. "I ain't seen no organ grinder, have you, Melissa?"

"Un unh," Melissa answered. "Where is he?"

"Look." He pointed to a big oak tree just beyond the stone-rimmed pond. "See all them people? Over yonder. Why don't chu take the little girl over to see 'im? She'll get a kick out of his little monkey."

Dulcie snickered and threw a peanut in her mouth. "I bet I will, too," she said. She unknotted her handkerchief to pay for the peanuts, gave him a nickel, then waited a moment, wondering if he was going to give her any change. When he thanked her, she knew he wasn't.

As soon as she heard the organ-grinder, Melissa pulled her hand free of Dulcie's and ran as fast as she could toward the big oak tree. Dulcie stuck the bag of peanuts in her purse and ran, too. Some of the peanuts spilled onto the ground and she stopped and stooped over to pick them up one by one, talking to herself, afraid the organ-grinder would be gone before she got there.

"Melissa! Melissa, wait for me!" she hollered. "You better not run away." She grunted herself to a standing position and wiped her hands on her dress. With the bag of peanuts now in her hand, she ran down the hill, muttering her own childish excitement in repeated gasps and grunts. She was exhausted by the time she got there.

After watching and feeding the monkey all their peanuts, Dulcie wanted to sit down on one of the benches beside the pond. Melissa wanted to play with a little girl and boy she saw on the other side of the pond.

"Aw right," Dulcie consented, spreading her legs apart as far as they'd go and her shoulders resting against the back of the bench. "Now don't chu go runnin' off," she said as she replaced one of her bobby pins. "I'm goan sit right here and rest a while."

As she began to relax, the gnawing and growling in her stomach reminded her of how hungry she was. Usually she had eaten supper by this time of day. "I wonder what time it is," she said. She couldn't see the bank clock from where she was sitting, so maybe she ought to get Melissa and walk up town so she could see it.

She was so tired! She stood for a while, watching some ducks trying to catch pieces of bread a little boy was throwing into the water, then limped over to where the children were playing.

"What chall doin'?"

Melissa stopped and looked in her direction. "Playin' tag, woana play?"

She shouldn't. She was so tired. "Aw right, but just for a little while. Melissa, me'n you goan have t'go home pretty soon."

She should have known better than to play tag with three tireless children. Once she was tagged, she stayed tagged. Finally, falling against a tree with her head down and both hands over her heart, she gasped for breath and began to sweat. She turned suddenly when she heard a woman's voice.

"Alice Mae! David! Y'all come over here." The woman motioned them over with her purse.

"Mamma, we're playin' tag," David said.

The mother folded her arms. "I said *come here!*"

Alice Mae ran to her mother, holding her side and trying to talk between gasps.

"Who's that big ol' girl y'all are playin' with?" the mother asked.

Alice Mae swallowed hard. "That's Dulcie, Mamma. She takes care of Melissa, my new friend."

"The very idea! That girl is entirely too big to be playin' games with little kids. You go get David right this minute."

Dulcie watched as the woman pulled the two children over to one of the benches, bent down with her left arm around David and her right hand, holding her purse, on Mary Alice's shoulder. "Now you young'uns listen to me. I don't ever woana see y'all playin' with that girl again. She's not right upstairs."

"What does that mean, Mamma?" Alice Mae asked, looking in Dulcie's direction.

"What does it mean? It means she's feeble-minded and will never be like you'n David. What I'm wonderin' is why she's not in the FMI where she belongs."

Dulcie heard. She took Melissa's hand and gave it a gentle jerk. "Come on, Melissa. We better go see what time it is."

"Why'd their mamma make 'em stop playin', Dulcie?" She did

not feel like answering. Sometimes, if she had something good to look forward to, she could think about it and forget the hurt. Now, no matter how hard she tried, she couldn't think of anything good that was about to happen. Not even having the next two days off and being able to play with Wanda Faye and go shopping with Annie Lois made her feel any better. There wasn't ever going to be anything good to look forward to.

A negro woman with a bundle of dirty laundry on her head walked past them and across to Pine Street. As she shuffled along, her laceless, turned-over shoes flopped on and off the back of her feet, showing the slick, pale pink heels. From time to time she reached absent-mindedly down and pulled the back of her skirt loose when shoe and skirt came together at the same time. Dulcie watched with a near-desperate longing to let go of Melissa's hand and follow the old woman, no matter where she was going.

Melissa saw the clock first. "There it is, Dulcie! What time does it say?"

It took her a while to bring her thinking around to telling time. Frowning, she stood with her legs wide apart, her right hand tracing the dial of the big clock and her lips shaping the sounds of the numbers as she said them half-aloud. The frown suddenly turned to a look of shock.

"Oh, Melissa! It's done past six-thirty! Lord, Honey, we better go home right this minute or your mamma's go'n' tan my hide!"

Dulcie hurried through the gate, forgetting about the loose sidewalk slab, losing her balance and almost falling, stumbled up the steps to the front porch and pulled on the door. The screen was latched and the wooden front door was shut. What did it mean? She looked around for Melissa, who had stopped next door to play with Mr. Crumbley's collie, Missie, then trudged around to the back door. She pulled on it and almost fell backwards. It was also locked.

What in the world was going on, she wondered as she gasped for breath and chewed on her fingernails. She pulled once more on the door handle, then sat down on the steps and slapped her hands continually on her knees. And, to make matters worse, her stomach was making hunger sounds she could hear even above the clapping of her hands. What would she do if Miz Welborn fired her? Where on earth can she be?

She was so tired!

She stood, waiting for some reassuring sound or movement, then hobbled down the steps, turned from side to side, and finally started walking aimlessly around the other side of the house. Suddenly something got her attention. Sounds, whether of people or dogs or cats she couldn't tell. She stopped and looked over into the neighbor's yard where only a lazy cat lay sprawled over the top of an overturned washtub. She waited until she was sure that what she was hearing was coming from the open but shaded window of Miz Welborn's bedroom.

It wasn't the sound of people talking, but it was people, she now realized. And it wasn't the girls from the bank that Miz Welborn said were coming to play bridge. Then, suddenly, a man's voice that didn't say anything she could understand, a slow and deep voice she'd never heard before.

She covered her mouth with both hands for fear that what she suddenly realized would slip out and be heard. *I should have known! Annie Lois told me about it a long time ago. Before Wanda Faye was born, I heard it every night and even saw it one time through the keyhole of their door.*

She looked around to make sure nobody was watching and got as close to the house as she could. She almost fell forward as she tried to get herself into a sitting position, with her back against the house, forcing her unwilling knees to support her weight as she struggled to raise herself up enough so she could pull some of her full skirt up and behind her.

There was another sound inside, now, of feet hitting the floor.

"I better get out'a here," the man said.

"No. Not yet," Penny pleaded. "It's only five-thirty. They're not comin' back till six."

"I cain't afford to take any more chances, Penny. I've gotta get back to the bank somehow without bein' seen. . . . Where'd you put my britches?"

Miz Welborn's wrong. She means it's six-thirty. That's what the clock at the bank said. But no matter about that, if Miz Welborn knew she was anywhere near that side of the house, she'd give her hail Columbia and most likely fire her to boot. Crouched forward, supporting herself with her left hand against the side of the house, she made her way as quietly and quickly as she could to the front of the house, where she stopped just long enough to look for Melissa. Where was that young'un? She ran out to the sidewalk and up two houses to where Mr. Crumbley lived. She heard Melissa and Mr. Crumbley talking and laughing on the screened front porch. She stumbled up the steps.

"What's the matter, Dulcie?" Mr. Crumbley asked, folding his newspaper and laying it in his lap.

"Come on, Melissa. We gotta go back to the park."

Melissa ran behind Mr. Crumbley's chair. "No, no, no! I don't woana go back to the park and I ain't goin' to."

"Calm down, Dulcie," Mr. Crumbley said, motioning her to the other rocker. "What's the matter, Honey?"

She gave a big sigh, laced her fingers together and wrung her hands up and down. "Mr. Crumbley, what time is it?"

"I don't know right offhand. Must be 'roun' five-thirty or so."

"No, Mr. Crumbley! You mean six-thirty, don't chu?" She ran her nervous, wet hands up and down the front of her dress and shifted from one foot to the other.

He got up stiffly, hanging onto the wide arms of the rocker. "Well, there's one way of findin' out. I hardly think it's that late though, Dulcie."

When he returned and said it was a quarter to six, her fear increased and brought on the tears.

Mr. Crumbley took her arm and helped her sit down. "Tell me what's the matter, Dulcie."

She told him the orders Miz Welborn had given her.

"Well, now," he said consolingly, "There's no use you bein' all upset about that, young lady. You'n Melissa can just sit here and talk with me till it's time to go home."

THE STREETCAR STATION, located on the corner opposite Woolworth's, was lighted by two bare hundred-watt bulbs that hung on crusted cords from the rafters of the tin-roofed ceiling.

The moment the lights were turned on, every bug within flying distance aimed for them like metal to magnet, surrounded and collided with the dirty bulbs and left them only to make periodic assaults on whoever was waiting for the streetcar.

Two long wooden benches, separated by a framed screen partition, were for waiting, the one on the right marked white, the other colored. The one on the right had divided arm rests; the one on the left did not. The front of the station was open to the elements, the three other sides walled and plastered with posters and advertisements for local businesses. At a central spot on the back wall, framed by a red border, was a poorly printed streetcar schedule in need of touching up.

The wind at a quarter till seven still came in sporadic humid gusts, making the light bulbs swing in all directions and the bugs to dance around them like revelers paying homage to and drawing sustenance from an elusive deity. Dulcie sat with ankles crossed, her basket-purse resting on her legs, each hand holding one of the handles. It felt strange being out so late! It didn't matter, though. She was so preoccupied with what had just happened that the darkness seemed friendly.

Everything had worked out well, even though she was so afraid Miz Welborn would know she had heard her and whoever it was in the bedroom with her. She had been especially curious, when she and Melissa got home, to see how Miz Welborn looked and acted. She acted the same as always, Dulcie thought, though her hair was messed up on the back and some of the penciled-in eyebrows was missing.

The crunch of footsteps on gravel drew her attention. Turning her head, she peered into the darkness, in the direction of the sound. Gradually, the feeble bug-studded light rays revealed a negro man about twenty-five years old in dirty overalls ripped at the left knee, a cap pulled down on his head, and a dirty denim jacket thrown over one shoulder. She watched the shiny kneecap as it came and went through the tear as he walked over to the colored section and sat down. She watched but he did not see her watching. When he took off his cap and replaced it at a different angle that revealed a little more of his face, she recognized him.

"Hey, did you get chureself a job?" she asked.

He seemed surprised. After a while, he said softly, "Yessum," and turned his eyes away.

She wanted to keep talking but for the moment was forced to do battle with her conscience. It wasn't a matter of whether it was right or wrong to talk to a black man. When you're eighteen years old and have managed somehow to survive all the tongue-lashings, the face-slappings you felt long after they were made, and the agony of a flesh-scoring chinaberry limb whose criss-cross markings turned the green grass red and left a brand you would carry the rest of your life on your bottom, you knew. When, for every day of your eighteen years you have been made to live by rules that need not be written in a statute book so long as they were written at various crucial points on your body, you didn't question if it was right or wrong.

What she had heard and seen Annie Lois and Hershel doing was right. What Miz Welborn and that man had done was wrong. Yet they were both doing the same thing, something nobody else was supposed to see or know about. And if nobody saw or knew about it, why would it be wrong? It was wrong because God saw and heard! God saw and heard everything! And she knew He had said that what Miz Welborn and that man were doing was wrong. All she wanted to do, though, was to talk with the negro man. Was that wrong, too? Even if nobody saw or heard? Nobody else would see or hear now

"What's your name?" she asked.

She couldn't tell whether he had heard or just didn't want to answer. "I said, what's your name?"

Without turning, he answered softly, "Tyler." It sounded as though he hoped that would be the end of it.

"What's your last name?"

He got up and walked over to where the streetcar schedule was posted. "Canfield," he said as he got up. "Tyler Canfield."

"You know how to read?"

He laid the denim jacket across the back of the bench, took off his cap and scratched his head. Putting the cap back on, he answered quietly, "Yessum."

"Did ju go to school when you was little?"

He turned and walked outside, almost beyond the light. "No'm," he said finally. "My uncle, he learnt me," then pulled out the makings of a cigarette and rolled and licked it.

"You remember that woman you was talkin' to that day on the streetcar? You know, Sophronie?"

He lit the cigarette, took one draw on it, then took it out of his mouth, studied the end of it and blew on it. "Yessum, I knows her."

She giggled and began to play with the purse handles. "I know her too. She used to wash for my mamma. My mamma was Miz Dora Dykes. . . Did ju know Kat and Roscoe too?"

"Yessum."

She laughed again, little snickers. "Me'n Roscoe'n Kat used t'play together when we was little. We had the most fun!"

He blew a puff of smoke at the ground near his feet and looked down without answering.

Three white men walked up, then she heard the clang and saw the yellow headlight as the streetcar turned onto Mason Street.

— f o u r —

ANNIE LOIS TOOK Dulcie's heated-over supper from the oven and set it on the table. Dulcie sat with one hand under her chin, looking blank-eyed across the kitchen to nothing in particular.

"I bet chu're starvin', aren't chu?" Annie Lois said.

Dulcie looked down at her food. "Lord, yeah!"

Annie Lois pulled out a chair, sat down, and asked how she and Melissa had spent the day. Dulcie told her about going to the park, stopping now and then with her fork upended, looking distractedly at the plate of food she wasn't enjoying. She soaked a piece of cornbread in the turnip pot liquor, stuck it in her mouth and gulped it down, then leaned her elbow on the table again with her chin on her hand.

"Annie Lois, you reck'n I'm ever goan get married?" she asked, looking directly into her sister's eyes.

Annie Lois looked down suddenly and played with the salt shaker. Slowly she turned her eyes on Dulcie and smiled weakly. "You just might, Honey. How come you t'ask that?"

"I don't know. I just wonder if anybody's ever gonna like me because of the way I am. You know, Annie Lois." Her lips quivered.

Annie Lois put her hand on Dulcie's shoulder. "Yeah, Honey, I know. I surely do. But you never can tell. Maybe one of these days a nice understandin' boy'll come along and fall in love with you and wanna get married."

Dulcie ran her fingers around the rim of her glass. "Don't chu ever woana get married again?" she asked, turning to see the reaction.

Annie Lois shook the salt shaker from side to side, then took the top off to see if it needed refilling. "I don't know, Honey. Maybe one of these days."

"Don't chu never woana have another baby?"

She set the shaker down beside the pepper and lined them up. "Yeah, I really would like to." She reached over and pulled Dulcie's face around. "Would ju like for me to have another baby?"

"I don't know," she said, looking down at her hands and remembering what she had seen and heard in Miz Welborn's bedroom. In a soft, weak voice, without looking up, she said, "I'd like to have me a baby, too." What she saw in Annie Lois' eyes when she finally looked up scared her.

Annie Lois put a hand under her chin and made her look up. "Did somethin' go wrong today, Dulcie? Did Penny fuss at chu?"

"No, un unh,"

"Then what is it?"

She wanted to tell her, even though it hurt so much to do so. She played with her fork. "Well, me'n Melissa were playin' with this little boy and girl we met at the park . . ." Her eyes began to burn, so she stopped.

"And what happened?"

"Well, their mamma came over to where we were playin' and fussed at 'em and made 'em stop playin' with me. She told 'em I was too old to be playin' with little kids, that I oughta be put in the FMI." She quickly covered her face with her hands and cried until the tears ran down her arms and onto the floor.

Annie Lois leaned over, took both of Dulcie's hands and pulled them toward her. "Here," she said, spreading her legs apart and bracing her feet, "sit on my lap."

Later, while her bath water was running, Dulcie undressed and, before putting on her robe, stood at the dresser mirror and studied herself. With the inquisitive fingers of someone sightless, she traversed the reachable parts of her body, stopping from time to time to ponder and enjoy. She pulled her hair behind her ears, then pulled it back and down, crossed her arms and squeezed herself gently. Looking directly at her reflected mouth in the mirror, she whispered, "Tyler . . . Tyler Canfield." Saying his name thrilled her. It had to be wrong. She grabbed her robe and covered her face with it for fear somebody would know what she was thinking.

Later, she prolonged her bath, stretching out the length of the tub and letting the silky warm water caress, cover, and tantalize her. Yet, at the same time, she felt like a little girl again. She reached out for Wanda Faye's green rubber fish and propelled it around the edges of the tub, laughing at how funny it looked and how good it made her feel.

Saturday nights, without fail, were for studying the Sunday School lesson. On this particular Saturday, Dulcie, sitting on the floor, legs crossed, hands cupping her face, listened with more than her customary interest. Annie Lois yawned and gave a long stretch as she laid the book down, then leaned over and looked at Wanda Faye, asleep on the floor beside Dulcie.

"Time for bed, little lady," she said, gently stroking the long blonde hair.

While Annie Lois was putting Wanda Faye to bed, Dulcie took the book of Sunday School lessons from the table, lowered her head close to the book, looked for a while at the picture on the cover, then, licking her fingers over and over, flipped through the pages, stopping now and then to pore over certain words and pictures.

When Annie Lois came back, she stood for a while, watching Dulcie, who, sensing her presence, looked up suddenly and snickered. "Annie Lois, you read so good."

Annie Lois slumped back into the chair and tightened one of her toilet paper hair curlers. "*Well*, Honey, not good."

She had been absorbed in the book. When she realized Annie Lois had said something, she looked up suddenly. "Hunh? What did you say?"

"I said *well*, not good. Somebody does something *well*, not good."

"Oh, all right," she said and snickered again. "I'll say it again and get it right this time. Annie Lois, you read so *well*." She laughed so hard the book fell to the floor.

BEFORE GETTING INTO bed, she opened the closet door and looked for her old book sack. Just when she was beginning to think Annie Lois might have thrown it away when they moved, she felt it down in a far corner behind a lot of boxes and other things she had thrown there. Seeing it again after so long made her feel sad. She laid it on the bed, then crawled in under the covers, picked it up and laid it across her knees.

The original blue canvas was faded unevenly and white traces of mildew were etched over it in random patches. The bag had a main compartment for books and paper and two smaller, outside pockets for pencils, colors, and whatever else one wanted to put there. When she pulled up on the strap of the first small pocket to disengage the holding pin of the rusty buckle, the leather, already cracked around the stretched hole, broke all the way around and bits of it fell onto the bed. The pocket held a discolored box of crayons with its own flap missing. She emptied them onto the bed. Only one, the grey, was still in one piece. The others were of uneven lengths with all or most of the paper wrappings gone. The other pocket held three pencils with their lead worn down almost to the wood or broken off and the erasers slick and hard, used down to the tin sleeves.

As she opened the flap of the main compartment, a sour whiff of mildew dust blew up in her face. For a moment she looked at the four books and what was left of a coverless tablet before pulling them out and laying them beside her on the bed. All the book covers were splotched with mildew and the yellowed pages were marked with brown stains of all sizes and shapes.

Sticking out of the speller and the reader were several of her lesson assignments, sheets of lined and discolored tablet paper folded down the middle, smudged with oily fingerprints, wrinkled and dog-eared where they lapped over the edges of the books. She pulled them out. The first thing she saw on each one was her smeared name, printed shakily in large, irregular letters, and the grade, a D or an F, and only one with a C. She opened them up and looked at them in wonder until she began to feel upset. Not about the grades, necessarily, even though she was surprised and embarrassed all over again to see how badly she had done, but mostly because the book sack and everything in it reminded her of her affliction. She could not possibly know all the reasons why the book sack made her so sad. She could only feel it. It represented the brief part of her life, almost completely forgotten until now, when she did not feel or know she was different from the other children.

Her sadness would not last long. Something more compelling than the book sack consumed her attention, something only momentarily displaced by these ugly, tangible dregs that had lain dormant for so long. As a matter of fact, it was this special something which had prompted her in the first place to seek out these tortured relics of her aborted education. Now she put the books, pencils, tablet, and crayons back and dropped the book sack onto the floor. She rubbed her hands together to wipe off the mildew, then turned off the light and slid all the way under the covers.

But she did not sleep. She did not want or intend to sleep. Now that the light was out, she could think better. Just having the bedroom door shut wasn't good enough, because what she was thinking was so dark the light would have exposed it for the horrible thing it was, and she would have been too scared to think about it. She lay on her back with her legs extended, the covers pulled up with both hands over her head, as she used to do when she was little. It made everybody else seem far away and beyond knowing what she was thinking or doing. Now, even more than then, she feared her thoughts would be sensed by those around her, no matter how far away, unless she covered her mouth. Moreover, her thoughts now that she was eighteen were so much more wicked than they were when she was nine.

For several minutes she lay still and only now and then moved her tense fingers into a new position to hold the covers. Suddenly, she threw the covers off, swung her feet onto the floor, and turned on the light. She picked up the book sack and opened the pocket where the pencils were and pulled out the only one that still had enough lead to write. Next she pulled out the tablet, which was stuck now to something on the bottom of the sack, got back in bed and pulled the covers over her legs. With both pillows propped behind her back, she laid the tablet on her knees and licked the stubby pencil point several times. While lying under the covers, she had finally decided how to spell the word. As she bent forward, her hair fell over her eyes and blocked the already weak light. She made a distracted effort to tuck it behind her ears but that didn't help. No matter, she would get the job done. Holding the pencil as tightly as she could with her right hand, she stuck her tongue out the side of her mouth and began to shape some letters.

When she finished, she brushed her hair back once more and sat up, holding the tablet at arm's length and the pencil between her teeth. She was pleased with what she had written. It was the single word she had been thinking about all day:

TILER.

– f i v e –

PENNY'S SISTER VONCILLE was making candy when Dulcie and Melissa got there the following Friday afternoon.

"Now it's all right for y'all to play, but chu goan have t'do it outside. Understand? I got a splittin' headache and the last thing I need is a lot a stompin' and hollerin'. As soon as I finish this fudge, I want chall to take it outside and stay out there till I tell you it's time to go home."

Dulcie stood with her hands self-consciously behind her, taking everything in. It was all such a mess! The first thing she noticed was how different Voncille and Penny were. Voncille had on a thin, wrinkled and dirty smock, the sash of which she seemed to have trouble keeping tied. Her head kept falling forward and her whole body seemed ready to collapse onto the stove. She looked tired and unhappy.

On a little enamel-topped table next to the woodstove was a bottle of bourbon and a glass with bright red lipstick smudges around the top. The sink was full of dirty dishes and several dish rags and towels wadded up beside and inside it. The linoleum on the floor, in a pattern of big red roses against a green background, was worn through at the sink and stove where the light coming through the single back window picked up an assortment of spills and droppings that had been allowed to stay and set for a long time, and it had a lot of fairly uniform, parallel worn and cracked lines following the raised edges of the unevenly laid floor beneath it.

Voncille told Dulcie to sit down, then began asking her questions as she stirred and tested the fudge from time to time by dropping some of it into a glass of water. At first Dulcie was embarrassed and hoped the candy would soon be ready so she and Melissa could go outside, but gradually she began to enjoy having somebody interested enough in her to ask questions.

"How old are you, Dulcie?" Voncille asked as she opened the door to the stove and put in another piece of wood.

"Eighteen," she answered as she smoothed down the front of her dress.

"You got a beau?"

"What?"

"I said, have you got a beau?"

"I don't know what chu mean?"

"A sweetheart, for God's sake. That's what I mean. You got chu one?"

Her face reddened and burned. She looked over at Melissa and they both laughed. "No'm," she said, squirming.

"What chu waitin' on? Santa Claus to bring you one?"

"I don't know."

"What chu mean, you don't know? You sure as hell ain't got to be eighteen years old without havin' at least one hot crush on somebody."

"Aunt 'Cille, can I go watch the gold fish?" Melissa asked.

Voncille moved the pot of candy off to one side. "Sure, Honey," she answered, laying a limp hand on her forehead to suggest her headache was getting worse. "But don't chu go givin' 'em nothin' to eat. Last time you was here, you fed 'em so much they near 'bout died."

She buttered a dish and poured the fudge into it, then sat down with a sigh, looking around for the bourbon. "Tell me 'bout chure beaus, Dulcie."

"I ain't got none, Miz Martin. I done tol' ju."

"And how come that is, you reck'n?"

She suddenly wanted to cry. "I reck'n cause none of 'em like me."

"You sure 'bout that, or you just too timid?"

"I don't know. Both, I reck'n." Her face solemned and she lowered her eyes, wishing now that Voncille would change the subject. When she looked up, Voncille was staring at her. Her tangled yellow hair, the dark hollows under her eyes, and the right eyelid that seemed to want to close defiantly gave Dulcie an uneasy feeling that she was an evil woman. Annie Lois had often said that women who drank whiskey were wicked and would go to hell.

Voncille got up, brought the candy to the table, and started cutting it into squares. When she finished, she folded her hands under her chin and looked thoughtfully at Dulcie for a while. Dulcie knew, somehow, what she was thinking. She could see the change that came over the haggard face.

"I see," Voncille said finally. "Is that chure trouble, Dulcie?

Dulcie bit her lips to keep from crying.

Voncille reached over and lifted her chin. "Hey, now, 'Cille don't allow no cryin' in her house," she said hoarsely and attempted to laugh. "If anybody's go'n' cry in this house, it's goana be me." She waved a hand in front of Dulcie's face to get her attention. "Look here at me, Dulcie. . . . Now, that's better. Now you listen to 'Cille. You ain't dumb, Honey. I can see that for myself. And anyway, a girl don't have to be no genius to catch a beau." She seemed to strangle on the words, then broke into a coughing seizure that seemed to exhaust her even more. Finally, pounding both fists against her chest, she recovered, swallowed a time or two and then continued, her face red and splotched. "Good god-amighty!" she said and whistled, "I caught this damn cold four months ago, and it looks like I'm goan take it to the grave with me." She stood up long enough to take the bottle of bourbon from the table with one hand, holding it close to her body to keep from dropping it, then brought it to the table, poured herself some and gulped it down, holding the glass with both trembling hands as though afraid it would get away.

"You all right, Miz Martin?"

She blew out a few deep breaths and sprawled out in the chair, fingering her hair aimlessly as though she had only now realized what a mess it was. "Yeah, Honey, I'm all right . . . Now, where was I? Oh yeah, I was gettin' ready to tell you how to catch you a beau, wuddn't I?"

She giggled. "Yessum, I guess so."

"Well, Dulcie, if you woana catch a beau, the first thing—the *very* first thing is—you gotta have a beau to catch, now ain't that right?" She laughed at herself, then the coughing started again.

Dulcie's opinion of Voncille was changing, she felt a little more comfortable. So much so that she began wondering if she should pretend that Tyler was her boy friend, and if she could do it without letting her know he was black. The locked-in horrors of childhood numbed the muscles of her tongue and throat. She crossed her legs and picked absent-mindedly at a short loose thread in the hem of her skirt.

Voncille told her to hold out her hand, then laid a piece of fudge in it "Well," she said, looking around suddenly, "there's little Miss Melissa. Did ju get tired watchin' the goldfish? You didn't give 'em nothin' to eat, did ju?"

"No'm," Melissa said and looked at the fudge in Dulcie's hand.

Voncille gave her a piece, then got up, took a plate from the cupboard and put several pieces on it. "Now y'all go on outside. Aunt 'Cille's goan lay down a while."

"Melissa," Dulcie said with her mouth full of fudge, "you go on out chonder. I'll come out there d'reckly."

This seemed to surprise Voncille. She was pouring another drink but stopped abruptly, letting some of the bourbon spill onto the table. "Melissa," she said, running her fingers through the spilled bourbon, then licking them, "you go on outside like Dulcie said and play with Poker while me'n Dulcie do some more talkin'. She'll come out there as soon as we're finished."

"Who's Poker?" Dulcie asked.

"He's my lazy ol' dog. Him'n Melissa like each other." She held the glass with both hands and Dulcie noticed that every time she took a drink her hands shook so that the whiskey almost sloshed out of the glass. She noticed, also, that Voncille's right eye had almost closed completely.

Voncille watched as Dulcie, legs crossed again, played with her skirt. "You woana tell me sumpn, Dulcie," she said after a while, "or are you just go'n' sit there all day playin' with your goddamn dress?"

She straightened quickly and smoothed her skirt down. "The hem's comin' loose," she said.

"Well, of course it is, and if you don't leave it alone it's goan all come loose. Now, what did you woana tell me? Hurry up, now, cause I'm goan have to go lay down pretty soon."

Dulcie blushed. "Miz Martin, I ain't got no beau and I ain't never go'n' have one."

"How come you t'say that?"

" 'Cause nobody don't like me the way I am."

"You sure? How can you tell?"

"Just b'cause. White folks make fun a me. They always have, ever since I was a little ol' girl. Annie Lois said I ought not let it bother me, but I cain't hep it."

In spite of the effect the bourbon was having on her, Voncille seemed genuinely interested in and affected by what Dulcie was saying. At one point, she reached over and gently laid a hand on Dulcie's arm.

"I know, Honey, how much that must hurt. An' what about niggers? Do they make fun a you, too?"

The response was instant. "Oh, no! Niggers don't make fun a me, Miz Martin. They never have. When I was a little bitty girl, Sophronie, this nigger woman that used to wash our clothes, would bring her little boy'n girl with 'er and we'd play together and have the most fun!" Remembering caused her face to redden and brought a sparkle to her eyes.

"I gather from what you just said that you get along better with niggers than you do with white folks. Is that right?"

It was suddenly difficult for her to admit what she had privately felt for so long. "I reck'n so."

"Now, Dulcie, I hope you ain't tryin' t'tell me you'd like to have a nigger beau. You ain't, are you?"

"Oh, no m'am!" Voncille's question was like a heavy-fisted belt to the head that made the words pop out of her mouth before she could think. The quickness and vigor of the response seemed to convince Voncille, but what she didn't know was that the quickness and vigor were signs only of Dulcie's fear of having her secret found out.

"Well, I sure as hell am glad to know that." She stopped long enough to pour herself some more bourbon. "Now," she said as she cupped her hands around the glass, "let's get on with what we were talkin' about. Beaus, wuddn't it? I was gettin' ready to tell you how to catch you one. . . ."

Dulcie bit and held her lips together for a long time, wondering what she ought to say now. "Miz Martin, I do like somebody a lot," she said slowly, lowering her eyes.

"You do?"

"Yessum. Sorta . . ."

"What does that mean, Dulcie, 'sorta'?"

"Well, he ain't a beau or nothin' like that. Just somebody I like, that's all."

"Well, Dulcie, that ain't exactly the same as havin' a real beau, is it? Now tell me about this whoever it is you say you like a lot. Where does he live, Ellisville? And what kind a work does he do, and what does he look like? Is he good-lookin'?"

She couldn't possibly answer those questions without getting into a lot of trouble. She was not skilled at inventing stories as she went along, and she knew if she tried to she'd sooner or later let Voncille know she was talking about a black man. Not only that, but a black man who didn't even know her, let alone like her.

She was unable to conceal her frustration and she knew Voncille could tell by the way she was staring, waiting for her to answer. She'd better put an end to it. "Miz Martin," she said, squeezing her purse against her body as she stood and pushed away from the table. "I better go on out there'n play with Melissa, 'cause she's go'n' tell her mamma on me'n I'll get in trouble."

Voncille needed to hold on to the table as she got unsteadily to her feet. "Well, aw right, Miss Priss, if that's the way you feel, that's just fine with me. You go on out there and play and don't come back in 'till I call you. Now let me make sure, when does your streetcar leave?"

"Six-thirty."

"Aw right. Now don't chu and Melissa make a lot a noise 'cause my head feels like it's goan split right down the middle. You understand, Dulcie?"

"Yessum, we won't. I promise."

But Dulcie did not want to play. Playing suddenly seemed like such a silly waste of time. Instead, she sat down on the back steps, spread her skirt out over her feet and played distractedly with the broken thread which was now longer than before. Melissa called her several times to play, but she only nodded her head and looked off into the distance. Her thoughts were so muddled she wondered how she'd ever straighten them out She knew now, more than ever before, what a terrible thing it was that she wanted to do.

She leaned forward with her elbows on her knees, hands cupping her face, and all at once she wanted to cry her heart out. It wasn't altogether because of what Voncille had said, or at least she didn't think so. In fact, she thought she really liked Miz Martin. She was the only person she'd ever known besides Annie Lois who seemed interested enough in her to want to help her. The more she thought about that, the more obvious it became that all the white people she knew, or most of them, were rude and mean to her. Negroes, on the other hand, had always treated her nicely and she had always felt happiest around them. She thought about Roscoe and the day they were naked under the house. But now, all of a sudden, Roscoe was Tyler. She played out the fantasy as it might have been if her mamma hadn't found them. Before she knew it, she was crying.

She could never tell anybody what she was thinking and wishing, but the unshaped words cycloned around inside her head, just waiting to blow her whole world apart if they ever got loose. Yet the thought persisted, over and over again. I wish I was black! I wish I was a nigger!" She dropped her head onto her knees as some strong and ceaseless source inside her fed and replenished the deep dark well of her despair.

Melissa ran over. "What's the matter, Dulcie? Why you cryin'?"

Without looking up, she said, "Go 'way, Melissa, and leave me alone."

"Did you hurt chureself or sumpn? Did Aunt 'Cille hurt chure feelin's?"

She straightened slowly and wiped her eyes with the hem of her skirt, noting that about a foot of the hem was hanging loose. "I tol' ju to leave me alone! I don't feel good. Now go on and play by yourself."

"I'm tired playin' by myself," she screamed, slapping her hands against her legs. "An' anyway, you're s'posed to play with me. Mamma said so."

She pulled her knees up and wrapped her arms around them. "We ain't got much more time t' play nohow. We goan have t'go pretty soon." When she finally felt like it, she smoothed her skirt down over her knees and stood up. "What'd ju do with that fudge?"

Melissa ran to where she'd put the candy and brought it back to her. Dulcie put a piece in her mouth and took two more pieces for later.

Melissa seemed happy now. "Come on, Dulcie, let's play."

"What are we go'n' play?"

"Hopscotch."

THE SUN SETTING made a bush burning of the big magnolia tree in Voncille's back yard. While Melissa was taking her turn, Dulcie watched the tree with equal parts of fascination and concern. The air had chilled, too, and as she rubbed her bare arms and squeezed them against her body, her instinct translated what she was seeing and feeling into a certain time of day when she was usually at home. She turned suddenly, threw her blue glass marker on the ground, and started to the house.

"Wait, Dulcie!" Melissa cried. "It's your turn. Where you goin'?"

"I'm goan see what time it is. Miz Martin was supposed to call me and I bet chu a dollar she forgot."

She started calling as soon as she entered the back door. "Miz Martin! Miz Martin! Ain't it time to go home?"

Inside the kitchen, she looked for a clock but didn't see one, then ran from one unfamiliar room to another, stopping suddenly at Voncille's bedroom door. "Oh, my Lord! My Lord!" she muttered, covering her mouth.

Voncille lay on her back, arms and legs thrown out from her body, and her dull yellow hair ravaged and lying wildly across the pillow, over her face, and even into her open mouth. The empty bourbon bottle was all but hidden under the bed and the glass not far from it, broken into several pieces.

Dulcie looked around the room, but there was no clock anywhere. She ran back outside, grabbed Melissa's arm and pulled her along, running, and gasping for breath. "We're goin' home. Miz

Martin's in there dead drunk and she was s'posed t'tell me when it was time to go home. Now I bet I done missed my streetcar." The thought that she might have already missed seeing Tyler deepened her anxiety as she gasped her way to Penny's house.

She tried to tell Penny what had happened while she frantically collected her things.

"You don't have time, Dulcie," Penny said. "You better hurry. I expect you've done missed your streetcar."

Never in all her life had she run so fast or so long or had such a compelling reason for doing so. She had lost her bobby pins in one of her frustrated attempts to get and keep her gnarled, wet hair out of her eyes. The increased effort of every step tightened the vise around her chest another notch, making her gasp for breath, and strengthened her fear that she would never get there, let alone in time to catch the streetcar.

As she staggered on in a direction she wasn't even sure was the right one, she swung the little wicker purse so violently that it popped open once and she had to retrieve its contents, crying and talking to herself in her panic. She used her free arm for abrupt, spastic jabs outward to keep her balance and her free hand to hold her skirt up as she arduously negotiated what seemed like a thousand high curbs. Only the hope that Tyler, not necessarily the streetcar, would be there kept her from sitting down on one of those curbs and screaming her already exhausted lungs out.

When she looked up for an instant and saw Grand National Bank, she gasped a labored, dubious sigh of relief that allowed her the sinful luxury of thinking about who would be there. Only a few more strenuous steps! She stumbled as she turned the corner of the bank and would have fallen if the brick wall had not prevented it. She steadied herself and swept her hair from her eyes, then looked up to see if the streetcar was there. It was!

"Wait for me! Wait for me!" she hollered. She looked up again, holding her skirt up to her knees so she could step over the streetcar tracks, to see if he was there. In her excitement, she let her skirt fall as she waved her arm to let the driver know she was coming. Her right foot caught the loose hem of her dress and she fell face-down on the graveled track bed.

Two thick black hands gripping each of her wrists pulled her up. He watched as she wiped the dirt and grime from her hands and arms and the front of her dress, then he stooped down, picked up her purse and started putting back the things that had spilled out of it.

Buford, the streetcar driver, seeing what had happened, jumped down onto the track bed. "What chu doin' with that lady's purse, you black son-of-a-bitch!" With his left foot, he pushed Tyler backwards, grabbed the purse, then put his other foot on Tyler's hand and ground it into the gravel.

"I was just puttin' back what fell out'n it."

"Like hell you was!"

"No! No!" Dulcie screamed, wringing her hands and stomping her feet.

"Did this nigger attack you, Miss Dulcie?" Buford asked as he handed her the purse.

"No! *No, he did not!* I fell and he picked me up."

"You hurt, Miss Dulcie?"

"A little, I reck'n."

Buford took her arm. "Here, let me hep you."

It was then that Tyler saw something else that had fallen out of the purse. He picked it up and looked at it, then put it in his pocket.

After Buford took Dulcie to her seat, he came back, jumped down and, before Tyler could get on, pushed him back and, with both hands, nailed his shoulders against the streetcar. "If I ever hear of you layin' one a yore dirty black hands on that white lady or any other white lady again, I'm goan break every goddam bone in your stinkin' black body, split your wooly black head right down the middle and spill what little brains you got down the front a your shirt. You understand, nigger?"

"Yessuh."

"Now get cho' black ass on inside."

Dulcie was picking tiny pieces of gravel from her elbow as Tyler trudged by to the back of the streetcar. She looked at him but he turned his head. As he did so, he dropped something on the seat beside her. When she heard him sit down, she turned around, hoping she could thank him with her eyes for what he had done. He was holding his head down with his hands between his knees.

She saw the piece of paper he had dropped. She knew what it was. That quick, short thrill that sparked all the nerves in her body seemed suddenly to put her life back in focus. She held the paper tightly and close to her body to make sure nobody saw. There was that one beautiful word, and now he knew: TILER.

– s i x –

ON THAT SAME Friday afternoon, while Voncille was trying to tell Dulcie how to catch a beau, Joe David Armstrong and fourteen other young negro men, who had been picking cotton all day at Mr. Elihu Carter's place ten miles east of Ellisville, had just been brought to town and paid their wages.

After they got back to town every evening after ten or more hot hours in the fields, the first thing they did was to crowd around the drinking fountain on the courthouse lawn, happy, laughing and hollering and getting their fill of cool water. Now, after collecting their wages, they tried to outrun one another to see who could get to the fountain first.

The two-story courthouse was justifiably the pride of Jones County. It was a beautiful square building conceived along Georgian lines, with recessed porches and entrances on three sides with a balcony over each and supported by four stone columns running the height of the building. It occupied an entire block on the northeast corner of town, opposite the ice house. The street with the northbound streetcar tracks separated it from the business district proper. The lawn and sidewalks were kept immaculately clean. On either side of the sidewalk leading to the west entrance was a stone water fountain, each identical to the other except that the one on the left was designated in large carved letters, colored, and the one on the right, white.

Closer to the street, on the southwest corner of the lawn, was a Confederate Memorial, a stone figure of a Confederate soldier, his rifle at his side, looking sternly, proudly upward and away to the north. He stood atop a square pillared pedestal, open on all sides and surrounded by joining stone steps.

While Joe David waited his turn at the fountain, he took the money from the bib pocket of his overalls and tried to figure out how much he'd made.

Comer Jackson, the fellow just behind him, watched. "How much chu draw, Joe David?" he asked.

"Look like 'bout three dolluhs an' fifteen cents." He folded the money carefully, put it back in his pocket and snapped it shut.

"How much chu pick t'day?"

"Little ovuh three hunderd poun's."

"Ooooe! Hey, y'all, guess how many poun's a cotton Joe David pick today."

When he told them, the one ahead of him in line shook his head, took off his cap and laughed. "Dat doan't s'prise me none. Joe David, he be good at evuhthang he do."

Joe David was growing impatient. "Aw, come on, Robert Lee," he hollered to the fellow at the fountain. "Git choself 'way fum dere an' let somebody else have some."

"Robert Lee say he so thirsty he gwine drink dat thang dry," Comer said.

Somebody else laughed. "If'n he do, I reck'n de rest of us go'n' haft' git our's fum dat udder'n over yander."

That seemed to amuse everybody except Joe David.

"Joe David," Comer said, "don' chu woant some a dat good ol' cool, white folkses water?" He bent over laughing and slapped his knees.

"Look like I mought haf to less'n I woana die waitin' on Robert Lee."

"Go on," Comer said, shoving him out of line. "I double-dog dares you!"

"Yeah," one of the others added, "go on, den tell us how much bettuh hit tastes dan de colored folkses."

"Just make sure you don' let none a yo' black rub off on it," Comer said, giving him another shove.

At first Joe David balked, digging his heels into the grass. All the others now, even the one at the fountain, were watching to see what he would do.

"You ain't skeerd, is ya'?" Comer asked. "Joe David ain't skeert a nuttin'," somebody else said. "Is you, Joe David?"

Joe David looked around, then walked slowly over to the foun-tain, turning his head from side to side to make sure nobody was watching. When he reached the fountain, he put one hand on the lip of the basin and the other on the faucet handle, bent over, looked around once more, then turned the faucet.

Denny Weems, Speck Barber, and Lyle Dennis were sitting on the ledge at the base of the Confederate Monument, facing the ice house, waiting for Mr. Elmo Poole to get back from the bank with the bag of money he drew out every Friday evening to pay them and the others that worked at the ice house.

"How 'bout us goin' frog giggin' tonight, Speck?" Denny said. He didn't ask Lyle because he knew Lyle's wife Lois wouldn't let him go anyway.

"Don't b'lieve," Denny said and spat a thick dark stream of tobacco juice almost out to the sidewalk.

"Oh, come on, man, why not? You can't ask for no better weather. And just think how nice it'd be to wake up in the mornin' smellin' yore mamma's coffee, then git up an' eat cho belly full a fried frog legs and buttermilk biscuits."

Speck laughed. "Does sound temptin', but maybe some other time, Denny." He stretched his long legs out and grinned slyly as he tapped his boots together.

"Why you lucky son-of-a-gun," Denny said. "What low-down thang you got on yo' mind now?"

Speck laughed again and let out a yell that made the folks waiting for the streetcar turn and look. He lowered his voice in mock confidence and said, "It's like this, Denny. While you giggin' frogs, I'm goan be doin' some giggin' a my own, 'cept it ain't go'n' be the same kind you talkin' about."

Denny faked a swing at Speck's head, then poked his fist into his arm. "Why, you two-timin' son-of-a-gun! And what chu goan do when Willodean finds out?"

Speck was about to answer when Lyle stood up all of a sudden and motioned in the direction of the water fountains. "Hey, look over yonder, y'all! One a them niggers is drinkin' out a the white fountain!"

Denny's face went red and he took off across the lawn as fast as he could. "That goddamn black son-of-a-bitch!" he shouted as he took off. "Come on, y'all, let's kill that black bastard!"

As soon as they saw what was happening, the other negroes ran off in different directions. All except Comer, who, with the bill of his cap pulled far down and one hand holding it on, ran around the corner of the courthouse, then, with his mouth open, stopped long enough to see that Joe David was in for some real trouble. He pulled back out of sight, then took off as fast as he could across the street in the direction of the quarters.

Speck's long legs got him there first. Denny was right behind. Joe David, hearing, straightened suddenly, looked around and froze where he stood, his right hand still on the water faucet. Trapped like a new-born wild animal with all the instincts for surviving but not old enough yet to have mastered them, he looked like an extraneous extension of the fountain itself. He wanted and knew he should run but realized it was already too late.

As Speck grabbed the back straps of Joe David's overalls, he turned his head and spat another stream of tobacco juice onto the sidewalk dividing the two fountains, then pulled Joe David away, leaving enough room for Denny to wedge in with his back to the fountain. With his left hand on Joe David's shoulder, Denny shoved him back, then drove his right fist time and time again, first into his face, then his stomach, and finally several times to the chin, one quick blow after the other. Blood erupted from Joe David's nose and mouth, drenching Denny's hands and the front of his overalls.

By now, a large crowd had gathered on the sidewalk, laughing, shouting, cheering Denny on, even the women who covered their faces with their hands. Sheriff Lee Anderson walked up to where Lyle Dennis was standing and asked what was going on. Lyle told him.

As Joe David dropped to the ground, Denny kicked him several times in the groin. Joe David let out a scream and doubled up. Denny shook the blood from his hands, bent down and wiped them on the grass, then, with his foot, rolled Joe David over on his face. He stepped over him, took a step or two back, then drove the pointed toe of his right boot three times into the base of Joe David's skull.

Joe David's mouth sprang open and his body convulsed violently, then stiffened. The last weak breath of life struggled its way up from the collapsed lungs, through the dark, blood-clogged tunnel of his throat, out the battered double gates of his mouth, and finally disappeared somewhere among the stained and trampled blades of new-mown grass.

"Anybody know who this nigger is?" the sheriff asked.

"Yeah, I do." Elmo Poole was holding the bag of money. "He used t' work for me. His mamma lives down yonder in the quarters."

The sheriff started to walk away, then turned. "If anybody knows where she lives, go tell 'er she better come get this nigger off the courthouse lawn."

"OUCH, ANNIE LOIS!" Dulcie screamed and kicked as her sister dabbed iodine on the cuts and scratches.

"I know it hurts, Honey, but it kills the germs. I think Penny's sister must be a mighty unhappy woman to go and get drunk like that. Looks like you might have to find some place else to go on Fridays, or we might have to buy you a wristwatch so you can tell when it's time to come home."

Dulcie brightened suddenly. "A wristwatch? Oh, Annie Lois, please buy me one." She looked at her left wrist and rubbed it, smiling. "Boy howdy, that'd make me the happiest girl in Ellisville. Do you really mean you might buy me one, Annie Lois?"

"I said maybe. After you eat your supper we'll look through the Sears and Roebuck catalog and see if they've got one we can afford."

When Annie Lois finished, Dulcie went to her room, changed clothes, and came back to the kitchen. "What'd y'all have for supper?" she asked and sprawled out on a chair at the table.

"I made me and Wanda Faye some pancakes. I saved some batter for you. You want some?"

She said she did. Annie Lois stoked the fire, then took a stick around which she had wrapped a piece of rag, and greased the iron skillet. "We had us some excitement while you were gone," she said as she waited for the skillet to get hot.

"What kind of excitement?"

"Some black nigger thought he'd be smart and drink out of the white water fountain at the courthouse, and some white fellows beat 'im up."

"Why'd they do that?"

"Why'd they beat 'im up, you mean?"

"Yeah."

"I just tol' you, Dulcie. He was drinkin' out of the white water fountain. I was ironin' and heard all the commotion and ran out to see what was goin' on. I never saw so many people in all my life! Miz Winnie Rogers happened to come by while I was standin' out there and she said she'd heard a nigger'd been killed."

Dulcie covered her mouth with her hands. "You mean they killed 'im just because he was drinkin' *water?*"

"Not just drinkin' water, Dulcie," Annie Lois said with increased exasperation, *"but drinkin' water from the fountain for white people only!"*

Dulcie had often wondered, when she was a little girl, why the water fountains were like that. All of a sudden, she could think of lots of things negroes weren't supposed to do. But to think they'd be killed for doing them was more than she could understand. "How come?" she asked without thinking.

"How come *what?*" Annie Lois was pouring the batter into the skillet.

"How come it's like that, Annie Lois?"

"You mean how come niggers and white folks aren't supposed to drink out of the same fountain?"

She nodded.

"Dulcie, sometimes you can ask some of the silliest questions. You know very well niggers aren't like white people. God made them that way." She tapped the spatula against the skillet to underscore her words. "They're just not *normal.*"

"Like *me?*"

Annie Lois was taken aback. "Oh no, Honey. What I meant was that niggers . . . well, that's a different matter entirely."

"Is it, Annie Lois? White people don't woana have nothin' to do with me 'cause I ain't got much sense."

"No, no, Dulcie! You're wrong about that. I don't think that's the reason at all. I just think white people don't understand your situation. And let's face it, some white people are simply ignorant and mean."

Dulcie felt something was wrong with what Annie Lois was saying but didn't know exactly what it was.

Annie Lois lifted the pancakes onto the plate. "And don't forget, niggers are dirty and they stink!"

Dulcie propped her elbows on the table. "Some white folks stink, too," she said as though to herself. "Remember ol' Jesse Folks? She stunk. You said so yourself."

"I know. Some white folks do stink. You're right about that. But that's still not the same thing."

"Why not? And you used t' say when you was teachin' that some of the little white kids couldn't spell or write or do nothin'. Don't chu remember, Annie Lois?"

"Yes, Dulcie, I remember. But you still don't understand. Those kids didn't have the same opportunities other white kids had when they were growin' up. Get me the m'lasses out of the pantry, Dulcie, and reach in the ice box and get the butter."

She got up and distractedly did what Annie Lois had told her to do. Annie Lois laid thick pads of butter between and on top of the pancakes and set the dish in front of Dulcie. She pried the molasses can open and spooned some over the pancakes, then sat down.

For a while, Dulcie played with her fork, then started sticking it into the pancakes, watching them soak up the molasses. She suddenly didn't want to eat at all.

"Go on, eat chur pancakes before they get cold."

"I will after a while." She took a deep breath and slowly let it out. "Annie Lois, I just been thinkin'. If niggers and white people ain't supposed to be together, why do niggers cook for white people? And do their washin' and ironin' and cleanin' house. And niggers even haf to help white women have babies."

"That's simply because that's all they're good for."

"But they're still niggers."

"But clean ones, Dulcie. That's the difference."

"Ol' Della wasn't clean. You said that's why you fired 'er, remember? I remember hearin' you say lots a times, 'Della stinks just like marigolds in the summertime.' "

"Yes, I remember. Della was careless about her personal hygiene.

The only reason I hired her in the first place was because Miz Shoe-maker recommended her."

Dulcie cut absentmindedly into the pancakes without eating. She ran her fingers slowly around the edge of her plate. "I still don't understand why niggers cook for white people and touch what white people eat but they can't drink out of the same water fountain white folks drink out of."

"Dulcie, you're bein' completely unreasonable. I'm surprised at chu! I thought chu knew better. There's a law against them drinkin' out of the fountain for white people. How many times do I have to tell you?"

"Why ain't there a law against niggers cookin' for white people?"

"Dulcie, I'm tired tryin' to make you understand. Now are you gonna eat those pancakes or do you want me to throw 'em out?"

"I don't want 'em, Annie Lois. I really ain't hungry."

ALONE LATER IN her room, she remembered what she had seen and heard in Miz Welborn's bedroom. It seemed so long ago already. So much had happened in the meantime. By the time she had taken her bath and was ready for bed, she had consciously put that out of her mind. She also shoved aside what Annie Lois had told her about the killing at the courthouse.

As she got into bed, the muscles of her legs and shoulders ached and the burning returned ten-fold on her hands and especially on her knees. She wondered how she could keep the bedclothes from touching all the sore spots. When she turned over on her left side, it felt a little better.

Now that she was all alone, she could think of Tyler. She drew herself tightly into a fetal position and closed her eyes. She felt his hands on her wrists, the added pressure as he pulled her up. She could see now, better than at the time it was happening, the look on his face. Now, however, she misconstrued it because it made her feel good to do so. The look on his face had been one of honest concern for her injuries and her embarrassment, and, possibly at best, because he knew or suspected already that she was limited in some way, and of sympathy, the knowing look of one tethered animal for another.

The remembering caused a sudden, complete erotic thrill to titillate the surface of her skin, stimulating her heart to a pace of near-continuum, rendering her whole body warm and weightless. By now she was so stimulated that she couldn't lie comfortably in any position. She turned convulsively from side to side. Then, in a sudden frenzy that caused her to think she was suffocating, she threw the covers from her and sat up in bed, pushing the hair away from her eyes and rubbing them in an effort to calm down.

But the excitement continued. It intensified. It was like the time years ago when she stood naked in front of Roscoe, knowing she shouldn't but wanting more than anything in the world to put her hands on his brown body, and like this afternoon when she saw and heard Penny and Hurd Crawford on Penny's bed.

Inadvertently, she had succored the pilot light of her passion to such a volatile state that no amount of rationality, none of the cautions and fears, none of the cruel and terrifying laws could prevent her doing what she wanted to do.

She slid slowly and quietly out of bed, even though it was unlikely that Annie Lois would hear her otherwise, then turned the light on. What she wanted and was about to do was so serious, so perilous, that she instinctively called forth all of her defenses as she set about to do it. Barefooted, she opened her door, looked up the hall to make sure Annie Lois had gone to bed, tiptoed up to the vestibule, past Annie Lois' room, and found her way to the desk where Annie Lois kept all of her unanswered mail in a lacquered letter rack shaped and colored like a flower-decked rural mailbox.

Back in her room, she opened some of the personal letters and spread them out on the bed. Kneeling first by the bed, later sitting up under the covers, she struggled to read the letters. A recent one from Aunt Lavinie was especially helpful because Aunt Lavinie's handwriting was big and clear. She remembered most of it, anyway, because she had had such mean thoughts about her aunt while Annie Lois was reading it to her. Aunt Lavinie was complaining about her failing health and bemoaning the fact that she was having to depend more and more on "nigger help."

She got out of bed, opened the closet door, got her booksack, then crawled back under the covers. She took the tablet and the only pencil that had a point, laid the tablet across her legs, unfolded Aunt Lavinie's letter again and flattened it out against the tablet.

"Dear Annie Lois and Dulcie," she read, then looked fixedly across the room and waited until she was sure about how to start, then leaned over as far as she could and drove the pencil point into the tablet. Slowly, arduously she printed in big, shaky letters the first word, then the second. She straightened, pushed the hair from her eyes and read what she had written. *dear tiler*. Just reading it and knowing she had written it thrilled her and made her laugh. *Oh*, she thought, *the comma*! She bore the blunted pencil point into the paper and pulled heavily down and around to form the tail of the comma. As she did so, the point broke.

"Oh, my Lord!" she said aloud. What must she do? Annie Lois always kept her pencils sharpened to such a fine point that every time Dulcie used one she broke the point off and Annie Lois fussed at her, then took a razor blade from somewhere and neatly made another point. But she didn't know where Annie Lois kept the razor blade. She scratched her head again and bit her lips. Maybe a paring knife would do.

She went stealthily to the kitchen and got the knife, brought it back to her room and clumsily shaved away the end of the pencil until there was enough exposed lead to write with. She took the paring knife back and quietly laid it in the drawer.

It was past midnight before she had found enough words to add to the ones she already knew or could guess at. Her right hand hurt and her fingers sometimes stiffened and refused to bend until she rubbed them and coerced them with her other hand. The total strain of writing the note exhausted her. When she finally finished, she moved everything onto the floor except the note. She lay back, and as the rays of light enlivened the erratic markings on the tablet page, she read it time and time again and laughed to herself, priding herself on her stupendous success.

She lay back with the note against her breasts. How can I get it to him? I wonder what he'll think. What'll he do? A happy chill of ecstasy charged her heart and flesh as she thought about what would happen when he read it.

— s e v e n —

TWO DAYS LATER, on Sunday afternoon, after helping his mamma into the wagon, Tyler Canfield jumped up and in beside her, pulled the collar of his coat up around his neck and the bill of his cap farther down on his head and laid the long, thin oak limb slowly but firmly on the mule's right flank. Turning onto Paulding Road, they headed east on their way to visit Sophronie Grubbs.

Tyler had convinced his mamma that all the work she had to do would still be waiting when she got back. She thought it mighty strange that after all this time Tyler had decided she ought to see the old friend she used to see almost every day before the war.

During the night the weather had changed drastically, with continuous heavy rain followed by an abnormal drop in temperature. The deep-rutted road had crusted over and the water in the ditches on either side was frozen solid. Neither of them spoke. It was still, a quiet time of Sunday afternoon. The regularly spaced, hollow clop-clops of the horse's hooves and the synchronized, strained but unbroken rasping of the four steel-wrapped wheels against the crunchy road surface would have lulled Arrilla Canfield to sleep if she hadn't been so cold. She leaned as far forward as she could, with the army blanket that covered her head and shoulders pinned together under her chin. From time to time she quickly brought a hand out to pull the blanket farther down, then pulled the hand back and squeezed her arms close to her body.

The wind came in erratic, icy gusts, dispelling momentarily the sense of life suspended, sending old foliage fluttering soggily to the ground and causing the mule to turn its head and shut its eyes.

When, from time to time, Arrilla opened her eyes and looked around, she saw the early reminders of another dreadful winter, days and weeks on end of cold and misery, bare tree limbs rain-soaked and dark, glazed over with ice and a thousand pendants of unequal size and length, depending on their relative success in reaching the ground. Up ahead, off to the right, three ravenous buzzards were taking frantic jabs and tugs at the remains of a possum. A covey of blackbirds in a dense, elastic formation flew south and disappeared over toward Ellisville, and two hawks perched ominously on a high limb of a sweetgum tree.

She smelled it before she saw it, the hickory-scented, weak, grey smoke coming from Sophronie's tilting chimney being whipped shapeless and colorless by the wind.

Sophronie had fallen asleep while she and Kat were shelling pecans in front of the fireplace. When Tyler knocked on the door, she jumped, spilling the pecans from her lap onto the floor.

They all agreed it was a wonderful surprise. When Tyler asked Kat where her children were, she said they were playing out back on the iced-over ditch. A little later, Sophronie told Kat to heat up the coffee. "An' bring de rest a dat fruit cake what Miz Wallace give us."

"Come with me, Tyler," Kat said, taking the bowl of pecans with her to the kitchen.

He followed and watched as she stirred the fire in the stove. She was still a good-looking woman, he thought as he remembered how things used to be between them. It was a long time ago, but he could still feel it. Before he could think better of it, he went over and wrapped his arms around her slim waist.

She turned around, laughing, and pretended she was shocked. "What chu up to, Tyler? What kind a woman you think I is?"

She resisted as he tried to kiss her, pulled away and motioned toward the next room where Sophronie and Arrilla were visiting. "Dat ain't right, Tyler. Me'n you ain't right fo' each other no mo'."

"What chu talkin' 'bout, Kat? Me'n you done mighty good befo'."

She straightened her dress and started cutting the cake, then stopped suddenly and walked over to the ice-laced window. "Looky yonder," she said, pointing with the knife to where the four children were playing. "See dat un sittin' down?"

Tyler wiped a clear spot through the sweat on the window with the back of his hand. "Yeah, I see 'im."

She looked at him and seemed surprised that he didn't understand. "Well," she said finally, "dat's yore'n."

"You lyin', Kat. You ain't go'n lay dat on me, woman. Anyhow, how come you so sure it's mine? How you know who any a dey daddys is?"

She didn't answer.

He watched the kids for a while. Suddenly, he turned around and pointed to one of them. "Fo' instance, Kat, who be da daddy a dat littlest un? De one what be near 'bout white?"

He didn't know what to think when she suddenly burst out laughing. "Dat 'un, Tyler, be my bread an' butter."

"Wha' chu mean by dat?"

Laughing, she motioned him over closer, then stretched up on tiptoes to whisper in his ear. "He da onliest one I be sure of. You know how come?"

"Naw, how come?"

She managed to pick up three of the plates and motioned him to get the other one. As she started into the other room, she turned, "'Cause I works fo' 'is daddy!"

He stayed at the window for a while. Maybe it was true what Kat said about the one that was sitting down, that it was his. He thought back to the many times he and Kat had fooled around, in her bedroom if Sophronie was away, or lying naked between the rows of corn if she was at home. All of a sudden, it seemed funny. Any one of them could be his, come to think of it. Except that near 'bout white one. So Kat's white boss has been servicing her! And paying her extra for keeping house for his wife. Good for Kat! He knew, she knew, and just about everybody else knew she wasn't the first or the only one. He laughed to himself. And what if it was the other way around? What if the black one was on top and the white one on bottom? What if . . . He knew *what if*, and he sobered at the thought. You don't do dat, nigger, less'n you be tired a livin' and ain't partic'lar 'bout de way you dies.

When he joined the others, they were talking about Joe David Armstrong.

"Tyler, how come you never tol' me 'bout dat?" his mamma asked.

" 'Cause I didn't wan' chu worryin' 'bout it. I didn't know nothin' 'bout it myself, nohow, till late yestiddy. I happen to see Comer Jackson and he tol' me what happen."

"Well, 'xactly what *did* happen?" Sophronie asked.

When he told them, their faces solemned, iced over like the rain-soaked trees outside. Arrilla laid the forkful of cake back on the plate, lowered her head, and closed her eyes. Sophronie flattened the left-over crumbs in her plate with her fork but didn't put them in her mouth. Kat, standing near the fireplace, looked down into the cup of coffee, swishing it around for no good reason.

"Comer say th'others egged Joe David on. He knowed it was against de law. Dey all did. Dey know, now, dey never should a did it."

For a moment, no one said anything. After a while, Sophronie licked her fork and handed her plate to Kat to put on the mantel She slapped her legs playfully, then reached over and patted Arrillia's knee. "Come on, eat cho cake, Honey," she said.

"Mamma, I reck'n me'n you better be gittin' home," Tyler said. "It's go'n' be dark 'fo long."

"Well, if'n you says so, Son." Arrilla stirred slowly out of her chair. "But I sho hates t'leave dis good comp'ny. I've enjoyed myself so much. It's been so good t'see ol' friends ag'in."

Tyler took his jacket from the back of the chair and warmed the inside of it, then his cap. "Miz Sophronie," he said, "I been aimin' t'ax you sumpn. I met dis white girl d'other day at da streetcar station in Laurel, and she say you use t'work fo' her mamma. She say her name be Dykes."

Sophronie squinted her eyes shut for a moment. "Oh, yes, yes, yes!" she said. "Dat be Miz Dora Dykes, de meanes' white woman I do b'lieve what evuh walked da face a dis earth. I'll never forget as long as I live how she whipped little Dulcie when she found her and Roscoe under the house, boaf of 'em buck nekkid. Miss Dulcie was de youngest. She had a older sister name a Annie Lois. But po' little Miss Dulcie, she were a little off in da head."

"How you mean?" Tyler asked.

"Why, she be feeble-minded. Not real bad. Not bad 'nuff t'be put in da FMI." Then she laughed. "Oh, now I recollects. Why, I seed Miss Dulcie jes' a few days ago, waitin' fo' da streetcar up town. Tyler, you say you seen 'er in Laurel?"

"Yessum."

"Oh yeah, dat's right. Now I remember. She say she be takin' care of some little girl in Laurel. Po' little ol' thang, dat mean ol' mamma a hers was always beatin' on 'er for first one thang'n then another. I don't know how dat po' li'l girl evuh live dis long."

Tyler rolled a cigarette, bent over and put it to the fire to light it. He helped his mamma into her coat and blanket. The old women hugged and kissed each other. Arrilla pulled out her handkerchief and wiped her eyes.

Sophronie laid her hand gently on Arrilla's face and smiled. "Dis has been so pleasure'ble. I hopes y'all'll do it ag'in real soon."

On the way home, with his head pulled as far down into his collar as it would go, Tyler remembered what Sophronie said about Dulcie. He tried to see her and Roscoe under the house, imagined what she looked like, a naked little white girl. Inwardly, he laughed as he thought about what they were up to. In a way it was funny. In another way it was strange. *Is dat why she wrote my name? Could it be she's got some crazy ideas in her head, by writin' my name and carryin' it aroun' in her purse?*

Out of the corners of his eyes he looked at his mamma, who seemed to be sleeping. An ugly, guilty, scary feeling came over him and he stopped breathing for a while without knowing it. *I gotta make sure Mamma never know what I'm thinkin'. Godamighty! I gotta make sure nobody ever know.*

That night he had a lot to think about. He squirmed, tossed, and turned for over an hour, thinking about what Kat had said, "dat's yore'n." And he hadn't even known. It made him feel pretty good to know he had made a baby. It was good, too, remembering the way Kat felt when he put his arms around her waist, then slid them farther down until she stopped him. Lying on his back, he saw Kat and Mr. Seth Wallace together, black and white, making that near-'bout white baby he saw playing in the yard. *A white man can do that with a black woman, but a black man better never do that with a white woman.* Dulcie Dykes came to mind again, changing shapes back and forth with Kat. Aroused, he quickly rolled over on his stomach and buried his face in the pillow. *Put it out a yo' mind, nigger, an' go t'sleep.*

His brain, nonetheless, was giving the orders, not taking them. He slid farther down under the covers until his feet touched the icy spot where they hadn't been before. He rolled over on his side, drew his legs up behind him, and tugged at the sheet, blankets, and quilts to cover his head. Then, just when he thought he'd better get on up, put on his clothes, and build a fire, he remembered Coletta Johnson.

Why hadn't he thought of her before now? Was it because he hadn't seen her for so long, or was it because the last time he was with her, they had had a bad fight and she had given him a choice of leaving or having hamburger meat made out of his face with the long kitchen knife she seemed to pull right out of the thin air. But that was a long time ago. Things would be different now, better. He remembered how it had been, how pretty, how sweetly plump and soft she was, how pleasurable when they were on good terms.

By now he was so worked up he felt like getting out of bed, dressing, and walking out to Dacetown where she lived. That was just an idea. A crazy one. *If I don't git some steep, I'm goan feel like hell tomorrow. Yeah, git choself some sleep, den when you gits home from work t'morrow, go over yander'n see Coletta face t'face and hope maybe things'll just slide on down from dere.* Contented, he drew his knees up close to his chest, wedged his hands between them and squeezed hard. He was smiling inside and out.

THE SMILING, INSIDE at least, continued all the next day. It was as though his strength and endurance had at least doubled since last night and his excitement about seeing Coletta later made the long day creep and run at the same time. As soon as he got home that evening, he cleaned himself up and told his mamma he wouldn't be eating supper and he might be gone all night.

He had almost forgotten where Coletta lived. He stopped and looked around, blowing his fingers to warm them, trying to see in the cold dark which house was hers. He suddenly remembered, straightened, rubbed his hands together, then climbed the lop-sided steps to the front porch. His heart was beating so fast he could feel and hear it. He knocked four times, rhythmically, the way he used to do when they were on friendly terms, waited a while, then knocked again, louder. He heard footsteps. Heavy ones. He took off his cap and grinned at the prospect.

Almost before the door was opened, he smelled the fried pork chops. Holding the door open was a man about six feet tall and almost as wide as the door itself. He was wearing a pair of over-alls with one strap hanging loose over his long-handles. He didn't speak; he just held the door open and looked mean.

"I was lookin' for Coletta. Coletta Johnson," Tyler said, playing with his cap and feeling the cold wind whipping around and numbing his ears.

The man came outside and pulled the door shut behind him. "An' what chu woant wid 'er?"

"I just happen t'be in de neighborhood an' thought I'd drop by for a little visit. Us used t'be friends."

The man took one heavy step forward and crossed his arms. "What's yo name, nigger?"

"Tyler Canfield."

"Dat's what I thought it was." He reached over and tapped the three middle fingers of his left hand on Tyler's shoulder. "Well, Tyler, I'm go'n' tell you what chu do." He pointed north with his thumb. "You face dat-a-way an' take yo' black ass jest as fast'n as far in dat direction as it'll go. An' if'n I evuh sees you on dese premises ag'in, I'm go'n' put a forty-five bullet thugh yo head, an' if'n you got any brains in dere, I'm go'n' scramble 'em. Do you understand, nigger?"

HE HEADED NORTH with his head down and bent forward against the strong, crisp wind. He was not going to spend another rest-less night with his blood in high gear and his manly cravings unsatisfied. It would take him a while to get over his disappoint-ment. He couldn't help feeling there was something wrong with him, even though he could count on the fingers of one hand with two fingers left over how many times he'd been denied private access to any woman he wanted, whether the property legally belonged to somebody else or not. There were lots of women he could spend the night with, but none of them, for one reason or another, appealed to him in his present state of mind. They were either married to men he was scared of, not clean enough, or they liked to do things he didn't like to do, or they were just too hard to get along with, demanding that any pleasures of the kind he wanted were available only if he married them or lived common-law with them.

There was just enough moonlight for him to follow the edge of the frozen, red clay highway. About an hour later, feeling instinctively a sort of familiarity with the surroundings, he stopped and looked around. A few yards ahead, a road intersected the highway, running east and west. As he neared it, he remembered what was just over the railroad tracks. Before the war, when he and his mamma lived closer to town, he often used to go to Kissy's Café. Unless Kissy had gone or was put out of business by the law, he knew he could get a bottle of shinny there. The more he thought about it, the better he felt.

He started drinking as soon as he was outside in the cold again. By the time he got home around midnight, he was too numbed in body and spirit to remember where he had been or why. He fell down twice before he got inside and into bed. He didn't realize what had happened until he woke up next afternoon around three o'clock.

— e i g h t —

DULCIE THOUGHT FRIDAY would never come. When she and Melissa got to Voncille's house that afternoon, Voncille seemed a little more sober than she'd been the week before, though most of another bottle of bourbon was sitting on the side of the stove. As she sat down, she touched Dulcie's arm affectionately and smiled, then crossed both hands under her chin with a look of expectancy on her face. When she began asking Dulcie some of the same questions she'd asked last week, Dulcie couldn't understand. Time and time again she had to remind Voncille, "Why, Miz Martin, I done tol' ju that. Don't chu remember?" Voncille reminded Dulcie that she'd had a very bad headache last Friday.

As soon as they got there, Dulcie told Melissa to go outside because she had something to tell Miz Martin. Melissa jumped up and down a few times but finally left when Voncille reached over and gave her a shove. Even if Voncille had asked the same questions over and over, Dulcie wanted to visit with her and maybe learn some things she wanted and needed to know. Voncille, nevertheless, still had one thing on her mind.

"Well, Miss Dulcie," she said with a mischievous look in her eyes, "have you found you a beau since you was here last time?"

Dulcie blushed and squirmed in her chair. "No m'am, I sure ain't. And why d'you keep askin' me if I have?"

Voncille drew back as though offended. "Well, maybe we better talk about sumpn else more to your likin', though I sure as hell don't know what that'd be."

"I don't neither," Dulcie replied, not knowing how to say what she was really thinking. "I just like talkin' with you, Miz Martin," she said. "There ain't many people that'll talk with me like you do."

"Maybe that's because you're so timid and scared to talk. Have you ever thought about that?"

"Yessum, I sure have."

Voncille gently laid both of her hands on Dulcie's. Something seemed to prevent her own words from coming out. Finally, she cleared her throat. "Would it make you feel any better to know I feel the same way sometimes, Dulcie?"

"You do?"

"Yes, I do. You see, Cille has some problems of her own. Kinda very private ones I don't woana talk about right now. Know what I mean, Dulcie?"

"Yessum, I think so." She was surprised to know Voncille had some private problems, too. It made her feel good.

From outside, Melissa kicked the screen door and stomped her feet. "Dulcie, you come on out here and play with me or I'm goan tell Mamma on you. *Come on*!" She kicked the door again.

Voncille jumped up from the table. "You kick that screen door just one more time, little priss, and I'm goan put some big white blisters on your little pink ass."

Dulcie was relieved when she left Melissa with her mother. She took the front steps two at a time on leaving. She was on the verge of panic. As she hurried along, she fingered her hair and at one point took out her mirror to see if the spitcurls were still holding. They had stopped holding hours ago. She wet her fingers and tried to reconstruct them. She ran for a few minutes until she gave out of breath, then had to stop to rest.

Thank goodness, the streetcar hadn't come yet. She squinted her eyes and frowned, hoping she'd see Tyler. He wasn't there. Nobody was there. She sat for a while, then got up and walked out to the street, then back to the station. Why hadn't he come? She opened her purse and took out the note. She had read it and refolded it so many times it had begun to tear at the seams. She put it back, closed her purse, and kept hoping.

The streetcar came but Tyler never did.

Later, while she was eating supper, Annie Lois asked why she was so nervous.

"I nearly missed the streetcar again," she lied.

"Looks like we're goan have to order you that wristwatch after all."

After supper, Annie Lois got the Sears-Roebuck catalog, then she, Dulcie, and Wanda Faye sat on the couch, trying to find a watch Dulcie liked, one which didn't cost too much. "Go get my fountain pen," Annie Lois said, carrying the catalog to the kitchen table. "If we send this off in the mornin', you oughta have it in about a week or so."

The excitement of having her own wristwatch helped put the disappointment of not seeing Tyler out of her mind for a while. That night, though, she awoke several times, wondering why he hadn't come.

Next Friday, it rained continuously with frequent thunder and lightning. Mid-afternoon, winds of gale force blew intermittently, sending tree limbs to the ground and anything else too light to resist whirling through the air. Voncille told Dulcie and Melissa they would have to play in the living room and they'd better not make one bit of noise because she had another headache. She took the bottle of bourbon to her bedroom and lay down. The thunder and lightning made her nervous. She finally got up and shuffled aimlessly about the room, then went to the kitchen, bottle in hand, and started looking through the recipes she took from a shoe box in one of the cabinet drawers. As she pulled it out, she called Dulcie and Melissa. They came running, noisily.

"How'd y'all like for Cille to make some oatmeal cookies?" she asked, reaching inside a cabinet to get a bowl.

They showed their extreme delight by squealing and jumping up and down.

Voncille quickly put the bowl down. "*Stop that*," she yelled, grabbing Melissa's shoulders and shaking her until the big blue ribbon fell from her long blonde hair. "We'll have no more of that! Now, y'all get the hell outa here and if I hear one peep outa either one of you I'm goan crack this bowl on top of your heads. And that'll be the end of the oatmeal cookies. Go on, now. I'll call you when they're ready. Good Godamighty!"

Later, when it was time for Dulcie to leave, Voncille put some of the cookies in a bag and told her to divide them with Melissa and take the rest home.

"I guess I better let chu have an umbrella, Dulcie. Get that old blue one over yonder behind the door. It don't look so good but it'll keep the rain off. You just remember where you got it and bring it back next week, you hear?"

"Yessum, I will," Dulcie said, taking Melissa's hand and starting out the back door.

She was soaked by the time she reached the streetcar station, in spite of Voncille's umbrella. She knew she must look awful but there wasn't a thing she could do about it. She looked anxiously into the rainy dark to see if he would come. The streetcar was late. He never came.

Dulcie's wristwatch came the following week. Mrs. Hulon Walters from Ellisville was waiting for the streetcar when Dulcie got there the next Friday evening. Mrs. Walters was a long-winded, steady talker. Dulcie looked time after time at her watch, mouthing aloud as she reassured herself she was counting correctly. At one point she opened her purse and felt the note inside.

Tyler did not come. She wished Mrs. Walters was not there. She wanted so much to cry.

The cold days came but Tyler never did. Thanksgiving was just around the corner. One morning, about a week before, as Dulcie was waiting for the streetcar, Sophronie Grubbs appeared. She was wearing several coats, one on top of the other, and what looked like a towel wrapped around her head. She had on a man's high-topped shoes and her hands were deep inside frayed, knitted mittens.

Dulcie's first impulse was to get up and put her arms around her. Instead, she laughed and twitched excitedly. Then she pulled up her coat sleeve and showed Sophronie her new wristwatch.

"Ain't it the prettiest thing you ever saw?" she said and giggled.

Sophronie leaned over to look at it and said it was.

"Annie Lois said she guessed she'd better buy me a wristwatch or I was goan kill my fool self tryin' to get to the streetcar station on time every Friday night."

"You mean you's workin' nights now, Miss Dulcie?"

"Oh no. Well, on Friday I do. You see, that's b'cause Miz Welborn . . ." She stopped. Her face suddenly got hot. "Miz Welborn and some other ladies at the bank get together and play cards every Friday after work. Miz Welborn didn't woana bother with Melissa so she asked me to stay a couple a hours later on Fridays."

"I see."

Suddenly, Dulcie's face brightened and her eyes widened. "Oh yeah! D'you remember that man you was talkin' to that mornin' I first saw you waitin' for the streetcar? You know, the one that said he was lookin' for work."

Sophronie's brow furrowed. She pulled the towel farther down on her head and tightened the knot under her chin. "You mean Tyler Canfiel'?"

Dulcie burst out laughing. "Yeah, that's him! D'you know what he did?"

Sophronie shook her head. "I sho don't."

"Well, one Friday night I near 'bout missed the streetcar. You see, Melissa's aunt Voncille was s'posed t'tell me when it was time to go, but she forgot to. I mean I nearly ran my fool legs off tryin' t'catch the streetcar. And guess what? Just as I got to the streetcar station, I fell down. I mean flat on my face! And you know what he did? He picked me up! I didn't even know who in the world was heppin' me till later when he hepped me pick up all the stuff that fell outa my purse. Did you know he did that, Sophronie?"

"Why no'm, Miss Dulcie. I had no way a knowin' dat."

Her eyes were aglow. For a few moments she stared into space, playing absent-mindedly with the purse handles. "And you know what?"

"What, Miss Dulcie?"

"I didn't even thank 'im. I slap forgot to b'cause I was hurtin' so."

"Well, I wouldn't worry 'bout dat. He know how you felt."

She thought about that for a while. "I guess so. I kept hopin' I'd get a chance t'thank 'im the next time I saw 'im but I ain't seen 'im a single time since then."

Sophronie looked puzzled.

"I bet chall are good friends, ain't chu? You ever see 'im?"

"Well, yessum. As a matter a fack, Miss Dulcie, I seed 'im jest a couple a days ago. He say he done lost his job and was lookin' fo' sumpn t'do."

"You mean he got *fired*?"

"Hit look dat a way."

She suddenly felt light and empty all over. She shuffled her feet and lifted and lowered the purse repeatedly against her knees, not knowing how she could keep from crying right there in front of Sophronie.

"Miss Dulcie, you aw right?" Sophronie asked, leaning over and lightly touching Dulcie's shoulder.

She slowly straightened. "Yeah," she said hoarsely. "Say, d'you reck'n you go'n' be seein' 'im any time soon?" she asked, trying to appear calm.

Sophronie coughed into her tattered mittens and shifted her weight from one foot to the other. "Why, I don't know, Miss Dulcie. Not for sure. I lives a fur piece from where he live. How come you ask?"

Something told her to be careful. She heard the streetcar as it slowed down to a stop, but she didn't want to get on it. She wished she and Sophronie could talk all day long, and right now she'd like to run off by herself and cry her eyes out.

She sat still and dejected all the way to Laurel. She wished she could come back home on the very next streetcar and never have to go back and never have to take care of little ol' Melissa. Now, all of a sudden the fun was gone.

The day went slowly. She was irritable and made life difficult for Melissa. Melissa, equally skilled in that regard, missed no opportunity to use it on Dulcie. When and if Dulcie agreed to play with Melissa, she did so with a total lack of enthusiasm. At the end of the day, she had a severe headache.

As the streetcar that evening neared Paulding Road, someone who looked like Tyler was walking in the opposite direction. She quickly put her face to the cold window and felt her heart beating against her ribs. Was that Tyler? She wasn't sure, so, when he was no longer in sight, she sat tensely erect and started biting her fingernails. What she wanted most was to ask the streetcar driver to let her off so she could run back and see. Her despair deepened. She buried her face in her hands and tried to keep from crying.

After almost losing her footing as she got off of the streetcar, she stood for a few moments, not knowing what to do. She did not want to go home, no matter how hungry she was and no matter that Annie Lois had told her this morning that they were having fried chicken for supper. She turned from side to side, looking in all directions, then started slowly, reluctantly toward the house.

She finally stopped and looked back as the streetcar, one street over, was heading back to Laurel. She was so confused! She visualized the streetcar coming to a stop at Paulding Road, and maybe Tyler would get on. Paulding Road wasn't very far from town.

She looked at her watch, then in the direction of the house where Annie Lois and Wanda Faye would be waiting for her. Why couldn't she turn around and walk as far as she could toward Paulding Road? She could follow the streetcar tracks. It would be easy. The only thing was that she was so tired. As the reckless scheme took shape, her spirits lifted. Whatever concern she might have had for Annie Lois and fried chicken dissipated as she strengthened her resolve to go. If she walked fast, she could be there in a little while.

But she couldn't walk fast. She was too tired, and she never had been able to walk fast without getting out of breath or tripping over her feet. She had never had, however, so compelling a reason for doing what was ordinarily impossible to do. From time to time she looked at her watch. It was now five-fifteen and soon it would be getting dark. That thought maximized the urgency of what she was about to do as well as her determination to do it.

She had just crossed the railroad tracks and was trudging northward with more and more effort, near the school house. Something behind her suddenly drew her attention. It was footsteps. She turned to see somebody running in her direction with arms flailing the air like something about to fly. She panicked, turned around and around, not knowing what to do. There was no one else to be seen in the neighborhood, nobody to help her. She started to run toward the school house, the loose gravel on the street making it almost impossible to move.

Bo Arthur Bilbo cut across Mrs. Chauncey Beard's yard, jumped the fence on the other side and stood, panting, legs wide apart and arms still flailing the air, waiting for her.

— n i n e —

SHE WAS SO scared she didn't know what to do. She stopped dead still and looked all around. It seemed there were fences everywhere and not a single gate to be seen. She screamed as loud as she could but, like always when she got too excited, her voice broke, jumped an octave or so, and weakened at the same time.

Bo Arthur ran straight at her, laughing and rubbing his hands together in anticipation. She remembered Mrs. Chauncey Beard, a woman she sometimes used to talk to while waiting for the streetcar.

"Miz Beard!" she screamed as loud as she could. It was not loud enough. She didn't know Mrs. Beard had been confined over a year to a wheelchair and had for even longer been hard of hearing.

As Bo Arthur reached her, he grabbed her skirt. She swung her purse around and hit his head. That made him mad.

"Who you hittin', lame-brain?" he said, then drew back long enough to avoid being hit again. As she swung the purse at him, he grabbed it and threw it over into a ditch running in front of the school superintendent's house. She tried in vain to reach his face so she could scratch it, but he was too swift and cagey for that. He grabbed her hands, then shoved her backwards onto the ground.

SCHOOL SUPERINTENDENT Marcus Tatum, having come home fifteen minutes earlier, was in the process of changing his clothes in the front bedroom. The once-stylish dark grey serge suit, one of two suits he wore on alternate days, was clouded and splotched with chalk dust, especially on the right trouser leg where he usually wiped his hands after writing on the blackboard. The jacket sleeves at the wrists and elbows and the cuffs of the trousers were of a lighter color, not the result of chalk dust. The shirt was ordinarily a bright white because Elsie Tatum believed in boiling all her white clothes separately when she washed. The collar, now, was unbuttoned just enough to show the inside ring of discoloration which had accumulated wearing after wearing and which Elsie had tried unsuccessfully for months to remove. The necktie was pulled haphazardly off to one side.

Having changed, he took the suit to the dining room, where Elsie was darning socks in front of the fireplace, and laid it on the table. She knew what to do with it. She would shake and brush away the dust, then, with a damp cloth to prevent any shines, she would iron it so it could be worn day after tomorrow.

She looked up with a tired smile. "We need some stove wood, Dear," she said, adjusting the right bar of her glasses. "I'll start supper just as soon as I finish this pair of socks."

He was about to take an apple from the bowl of fruit Elsie always kept on the dining room table but stopped, slowly put the apple back and walked over to the front window. "Something's goin' on out there," he said, grabbing his army coat from a hook just inside the kitchen door.

Elsie laid the socks down and got up. "Where? What's happenin', Marcus?" she asked, moving in the direction he indicated by a nod of his head.

"Don't chu hear somebody hollerin'? I'm gonna see what's goin' on. I'll be right back."

He hurried out the back door, stopping just long enough to break a thick limb off of a chinaberry tree, then moved out to the street as fast as his not-too-agile legs would take him.

Bo Arthur apparently didn't hear him. He was frantically tearing at Dulcie's clothes with his right hand while holding her ankles down with his knees and pressing her head into the ground with his left hand.

Mr. Tatum, with an adeptness acquired over more than twenty years of administering punishment to unruly students, came down with the chinaberry limb as hard as he could on Bo Arthur's back, then, with the toe of his right shoe, pushed him head-first over onto the ground.

As soon as she felt she was free, Dulcie went into a convulsion, kicking her legs up and down and slapping her face, despite Mr. Tatum's attempt to console her. He lifted her up and felt the old pain in his back as he did so.

"Why, Dulcie, it's you! I didn't know it was you. Are you hurt? Are you alright?" He tried to straighten her clothes and brush some of the dirt and gravel off of her back, but she made it virtually impossible.

Elsie Tatum, in a heavy coat, with a scarf around her head, hurried to where they were. Bo Arthur, apparently injured, made a frantic attempt to get up.

"Mrs. Tatum," her husband said, "you come and look after Dulcie while I take care of that scoundrel. Here, use my handkerchief. She's in a state of shock."

He picked up the chinaberry limb and stood over Bo Arthur, watching him trying to get up. He knew he shouldn't do it but the impulse was too strong to resist. He brought the limb down again. Bo Arthur screamed and spread out lengthwise on the ground. Mr. Tatum reached down with his free hand and tried to help him up.

"What in the hell are you tryin' t'do t'me, old man? You tryin' t'kill me?" Bo Arthur pushed himself against the ground and gradually stood up, brushing himself off and making an abrupt effort to get away.

Mr. Tatum grabbed his coat collar and pulled him back. "Nothin' I could do to you, you sorry, no-good savage, would be enough. You have always been a disgrace to your grandma and a disgrace to this town. If it's the last thing I do, I'm goan see to it that you're put in the reform school."

Bo Arthur pulled away as hard as he could, freed himself, and took off down the street.

"I cain't believe what I'm seein'," Elsie Tatum said, trying to calm Dulcie. Then, softer and in her husband's direction, "Was that mean ol' boy really tryin' to do what I thought he was?"

"From what I've heard, he's been tryin' to do it for a long time. I think it's time to have him put away."

He faced Dulcie and smiled. As she slowly calmed down, she watched Mr. Tatum, frowning, trying to speak but not able to.

The tears started again, rolling down her pale cheeks and into the corners of her mouth.

"Don't chu know who I am, Dulcie?"

She continued to look, then slowly shook her head.

"I'm Mr. Tatum, the school superintendent. Mrs. Tatum and I are here to help you. Are you hurt anywhere? Do you woant to go inside so Mrs. Tatum can take care of you?"

She shook her head repeatedly, wondering how she could let him know she wanted to go home. "Annie Lois . . ." she finally managed to say weakly.

"You woant me to take you home?"

She nodded, wiping her face with both hands.

He looked at his wife. She nodded. "Alright, Dulcie, I'm goan take you home, but first, let's go inside where it's warm. I know you must be freezin' out here. Mrs. Tatum will clean you up while I crank the car."

Dulcie squinted her eyes and looked from side to side.

"Did you lose somethin', Dulcie?" Elsie asked. "Is that thing over yonder in the ditch yours?"

"Yessum," she quickly answered, her voice stronger.

As Elsie started toward the ditch to get the purse, Dulcie remembered the note.

"I'll do it!" Dulcie said. *"I'll do it, Miz Tatum!"* She didn't care how much it hurt. Miz Tatum must not see the note. Nobody but Tyler must ever see it!

Elsie Tatum seemed more than mildly shocked to see Dulcie get down on her knees, wincing as the pain shot through all her limbs.

"Oh, my goodness!" Dulcie cried, holding up the handle which had come loose from the purse. "The handle's broke. He broke it, Miz Tatum. And look." She picked the purse up and turned it over. "My purse is all bent."

"How did it get way over there, Honey?" Elsie asked, helping her to her feet.

She gave a deep sigh and grabbed her right knee. "I was hittin' 'im with it an' he grabbed it and chucked it over there in the ditch."

Elsie stooped down to help her put back into the purse the things that had fallen out of it.

"No!" Dulcie cried, putting herself between Mrs. Tatum and the scattered items in the ditch. *"Don't! I'll do it!"*

Mrs. Tatum was obviously shocked by what she was seeing. She smiled when Dulcie finally stood, holding the purse in one hand and the handle in the other. "Don't worry, Dear," she said. "I think we might be able to fix your purse. The most important thing, though, is that you seem to be all right."

It was the wickered repository of some of the most precious moments of her life. She pressed it tightly against her body.

"Here," Mrs. Tatum said, putting her arm around Dulcie's shoulder. "Let's go inside where it's warm. Mr. Tatum will take you home in a little while."

BY THE TIME she got home, Dulcie was feeling more of the pain she would continue to suffer during the next several days, pain which would intensify to the point of making it impossible for her to get out of bed. As the pain intensified, so did the terrorizing realization of what had actually happened and what could have happened otherwise.

After Mr. Tatum left, having told Annie Lois what had happened and having suggested they both make a formal complaint to the law about Bo Arthur, Annie Lois scolded Dulcie severely. Later, she helped her with her bath and put iodine on the scratches and bandages where the more severe injuries continued to bleed.

"You still haven't told me why you were way over yonder by the schoolhouse in the first place. You don't mean t'tell me Bo Arthur chased you *that* far."

Dulcie was still too scared to tell the truth. She kept repeating what she'd already said or she said nothing at all. This time, she pretended to be hurting so much she didn't hear what Annie Lois was saying.

She got almost no sleep that first night. No matter what position she got into, the burning and the soreness worsened. Annie Lois gave her aspirin with warm milk, neither of which did any good.

Despite the pain, what had happened kept pushing everything else temporarily to the back of her mind. Having Bo Arthur chasing, then holding her down against the cold ground was so much worse than it had been in the dream she'd had about him earlier. What would he have done if Mr. Tatum hadn't stopped him? She recalled what she had heard that day when Mrs. Welborn and that man were in Mrs. Welborn's bedroom. She thought about the times she watched Annie Lois and Hershel through the keyhole, and the day she stood naked in front of Roscoe Grubbs under the house. That had been the first time anyone besides Annie Lois and her mamma had seen her naked. Why was being naked something God punished people for? Being naked was how babies were made. She tried to imagine how it would have been if, instead of Bo Arthur, it had been Tyler. The guilt and the shame of thinking such a thing made her slide farther down under the cover, wondering what would happen if anybody ever found out how she felt.

At every point on her body the nerves that were not already working full-time to send pain to her mind suddenly responded with tingling alertness, causing quick erotic spasms that made her feel weightless. At the same time, if she stopped long enough to consider the possibility of what she was thinking, her mamma, a dark, remembered presence, hovered over and all around her bed, reminding her that the fires of hell, like the fire that consumed her rag doll, burned without ceasing, and, by comparison to what she was now suffering, was always ready to show her what real pain was.

When Annie Lois came to check on her early next morning, Dulcie said she didn't feel good.

"Are the cuts and bruises still hurtin'?"

"Yeah, they sure are. But it ain't just them. I feel bad all over." Annie Lois put her hand on Dulcie's forehead. "I believe you've got fever," she said. "Open your mouth. It sure looks like it. Your throat's mighty red. Let me get the thermometer."

Her fever was one hundred and two. Annie Lois pulled the covers up and around Dulcie's shoulders. "You won't be able to go to work today, Honey. You're goan have t'stay in bed. I'll call Penny and let 'er know you're sick."

She stood for a few moments, wondering if this meant Dulcie, like hundreds of others in Ellisville, was coming down with the flu.

"What would you like me to fix you for breakfast?" she asked.

"Nothin'. I don't woant *nothin'*, Annie Lois."

Annie Lois continued to take Dulcie's temperature during the day. By late afternoon it had reached one hundred and four. Dulcie now started coughing, long, strained coughs that only used up what little energy she had left. Annie Lois called Dr. Cranford and he came over two hours later, apologizing and explaining why he couldn't come sooner. "We need at least four more doctors in this town," he said as he stuck a thermometer in Dulcie's mouth and opened her gown to put the stethoscope to her chest. He checked her pulse, then stood back a few feet and put the stethoscope back in his bag.

Annie Lois waited apprehensively.

He asked Dulcie some questions but she didn't answer. It was as though she had not heard. He slowly put on his overcoat and hat. "Do you know I've lost three patients today? And no telling how many more I'll lose before morning."

"Who were they, Doctor Cranford? I knew Verda Holston had the flu. How's she doin'?"

"Verda's holdin' on by the hardest. Juanice Camp died first thing this mornin' and Isaac Bentley and the youngest Fairley child died a few hours ago."

"Did they all have the flu?" Annie Lois asked, unable to suppress her fear.

"Every one of 'em."

"Well, what must I do, Doctor Cranford?" she asked, trying to adjust to the shock.

"You might try puttin' some mustard plasters on her chest, give her a lot of hot liquids, and keep givin' her aspirin every few hours. We'll just have to wait until mornin' to know what to do next." He reached over and took Annie Lois' hands. "Try to keep calm, Annie Lois, and make sure you don't come down with it, too."

She wanted to ask something else but was afraid to.

"Do you understand everything, Annie Lois? If so, I'm goin' home and try to get a little sleep. Otherwise I won't be much good to anybody."

She watched him as he walked down the hall ahead of her. As

he opened the front door, she asked, "Do you think Dulcie's goan make it, Doctor Cranford?"

He turned slightly. "You know, Annie Lois, Dulcie's physical condition hasn't been normal from the time she was born. A person like her can't take too much sickness, especially nothin' as serious as the flu."

Her throat tightened and her eyes burned. "You mean . . . she might not recover? Is that what yure tryin' to tell me?"

"I'm sorry, Annie Lois." There was the slightest indication that he really meant it. "I hate to have to tell you this, but from the way she looks right now, I don't think she will."

— t e n —

WHEN THE LAST log burned itself out, crackled, and collapsed onto the fireplace floor, Annie Lois suddenly awoke. Wrapped around with a blanket, she had fallen asleep from exhaustion. She got up with difficulty and walked over to look at Dulcie. Dulcie was sleeping but, judging from the expression on her face, not peacefully. Her mouth was open and from deep down inside her chest came congestive sounds that meant all was not right. At least she's sleeping, Annie Lois thought. That can only help. She put some more wood in the fireplace and stirred the embers to get the fire going again, then pulled the blanket closer around her shoulders and sat down in the rocker.

The short, erratic sleep, instead of calming her, had only increased her distress. A barrage of ugly thoughts trampled one over the other, carrying her back and forth in time to the beginnings, to the remote happy times before she became aware of life's deceptions, before she learned that, no matter how often or how credulously you dreamed, dreams remained dreams and little or nothing more. It was like learning there's no Santa Claus. Her compromise with life had been long and bitter.

Now she faced up to the all-too-likely horror and loneliness of losing the little sister she had taught and nurtured and loved so much. The thought, heretofore suppressed enough to allow her to function, was suddenly so painful she wondered how she would ever be able to bear it. There was nothing in the future which could in any way offer hope. She was not prepared for what was about to happen. She pulled the blanket up around her face and prayed for God to help her.

Dr. Cranford came around seven-thirty next morning, examined Dulcie and took her temperature. He called Annie Lois, who had gone to the kitchen to start breakfast.

"When did ju last take her temperature?" he asked.

"I haven't taken it since last night around ten o'clock. Once she went to sleep I hated to wake her up."

He shook the thermometer and put it back in its case. "It's gone up," he said, getting into his coat. "If it gets any higher she very likely will become delirious. I think you should know that."

She leaned against the door and wanted to cry. "What can I do, Doctor Cranford?"

"To be perfectly honest, Annie Lois, I don't know. This thing's got all of us baffled. I know you're a very religious woman. I suggest you do some very serious praying. Lots of it."

"Doctor Cranford, I *am* prayin'. I always do. But isn't there anything you can do? Isn't there some kind of medicine that might help?"

"That's what I mean, Annie Lois. We simply don't have anything that'll do any good. We're having to do a lot of guessing." He walked over to the fireplace, holding his hat and obviously eager to go. "I see that Dulcie's breathing through her mouth and I can hear her lungs are congested. Do you have any camphor or mentholatum?"

"Yes, I've got some mentholatum."

"Then put some in some very hot water and let her inhale it. That might help, but, like I said, we're not sure about anything at this point. As I told ju last night, you must make sure Dulcie gets plenty of liquids. It's extremely important that she doesn't dehydrate."

"I understand," Annie Lois said weakly.

"Then I must be goin'. I'm sorry I cain't be more helpful. At times like this we have to rely fully on God's mercy. Remember that, Annie Lois."

She followed him to the front door. He started down the steps, then turned. "Annie Lois, do you think you goan be able to handle this? You mustn't let yourself get run down or you may very well come down with it. And there's Wanda Faye to consider."

She covered her mouth to keep from crying. "I know that, but I'm beginnin' to wonder if I can do everything by myself. I feel so helpless. Do you happen to know of anybody I could get to help me?"

"Not at the moment, but I'll give it some thought. If I think of somebody I'll let chu know. In the meantime, do the best you can and don't give up hope. I'll be back as early in the morning as I can."

She closed the door and leaned against it. The house had never seemed so big, so cold, and so lonely. There wasn't a single comforting hope or memory to be sensed anywhere.

She had just wakened Wanda Faye and had started to the kitchen when someone knocked at the front door.

"Good mornin', Miss Annie Lois. I didn't see your milk bottles out and was just wonderin' if maybe you forgot to put 'em out."

"Oh, for heaven's sake! I did forget, Mr. Crosby. If you've got time to wait, I'll just be a minute. Come in out of the cold."

"Thank you, m'am. I'm in no hurry. I done made all my other deliveries. I knew it weren't like you not to have your bottles out. I went ahead and brung you your three bottles as usual just to make sure. And if I recollect right, this is your butter day, too."

"That's right, it is. I don't know where my head is." She took the milk and the two molds of butter to the kitchen in two trips and returned shortly with the empty bottles. "I think I ought to tell you why I forgot so you won't think I've lost my mind. My sister Dulcie's come down with the flu and I'm beside myself with worry."

"You ain't got nobody t'hep ya?"

"Nossir, and I don't know how to get anybody. I wish I could get somebody if only for a few days. Maybe you know somebody I could hire."

"I got a lot a customers down with the flu, and several of 'em has had to hire colords to hep out. Folks like you, that is, what don't have no family or kin folks to come hep 'em. They tell me the colords is mighty good with sick folks. But for the life of me, right off hand I cain't think a nary a one, Miss Annie Lois."

She thanked him, and he had just put his hand on the doorknob when he suddenly stopped and turned around. "I just thought a sumpn," he said. "There's usually a bunch a colored men what stands aroun' outside Riley's Feed Store lookin' for work. I have a feelin', Miss Annie Lois, they might be able to put chu on to some good colored woman t'hep with Miss Dulcie."

"That sounds like a good idea," she said. "But on second thought, I cain't possibly leave Dulcie long enough to go uptown. D'you see what I mean?"

"I do see, Miss Annie Lois. Now I got another idea, but I don't know what chu'll think of it."

"What's that, Mr. Crosby. I need all the help I can get."

"Well, I was just thinkin', if you trust me to stay here while you go uptown, I'd be most happy to do so. Like I said, my deliverin's all done for the day, and I don't need to get home quite yet. I don't know what good I could do Miss Dulcie, but at least I could stay here just in case."

That was all it took to bring on the tears. "That's very kind of you, Mr. Crosby. I don't know how to thank you."

"You don't need to thank me. It's just a matter a one friend hepin' out another'n."

"Well, if it's not too much trouble, would ju mind waitin' a few more minutes while I get ready?"

"Not at all, Miss Annie Lois. I tell you what. You got any coffee left?"

She felt better. "Yes, I do. I was just gettin' ready to cook some breakfast when you knocked."

After pouring his coffee, she put the milk in the ice box and picked up the butter. "Oh, look at that!" she said, smiling. "That's the same little design that used to be on Mamma's butter mold. I remember it so well. When Mamma was too busy to churn and make butter herself, she let the old colored woman that worked for us do it." She quickly put the butter in the ice box and turned around. "Mr. Crosby, a wonderful thought just occurred to me."

The men stood around a fire burning in a washtub between the depot and Riley's Feed Store. From a distance, they seemed to be in good spirits, but, as Annie Lois approached, their mood seemed suddenly to change and a few of them stepped back a little out of respect for her. One of them took a cigarette from his mouth and snuffed it out on the ground.

"Good mornin'," she said. "I'm Mrs. Hershel Harper. I was wonderin' if any of y'all might know somebody who could help me take care of my sick sister. She's come down with the flu and

I'm not able to take care of her by myself." She looked from one to the other. "I really need help badly." They looked at one another without answering.

"I used to know a fine woman by the name of Sophronie Grubbs. She worked for my mother years ago, and my sister said she'd seen her a while back. Do any of you happen to know Sophronie?"

Several of them turned their eyes on the fellow who had snuffed out the cigarette, waiting, it seemed, for him to say something.

Annie Lois looked at him. "Do you know her?"

He nodded his head slowly but averted her eyes. "Yessum, I knows 'er."

"Do you know where she lives? And do you know if she's workin' for anybody now?"

"Yessum, I knows where she live. But Miss Sophronie be too old to be workin'. She stay pretty close t'home now she be slowed down."

"I know she's not able to work like she used to, but I was wonderin' if she could just stay at my house long enough to help me take care of my sister. She wouldn't need to do any hard work. I really would appreciate it if you could see 'er and ask 'er if she'd be willin' to do that."

She waited apprehensively. *Oh God, please help me!*

"Do yo' sister be de lady what goes t'Laurel t'take care a some little girl up yonder?" he asked.

"Yes, she's the one. Her name's Dulcie. Dulcie Dykes."

He toed the remains of the cigarette around in the dust, digging his hands into the pockets of the old army coat he was wearing.

After a while he looked up but still avoided Annie Lois' eyes. "She live out on Ol' Ellisville Road, but I could go home and git my wagon'n drive out chonder to see 'er. I could tell 'er you really needs 'er bad."

"Oh, how wonderful! And would ju please tell 'er I'll pay her well. Whatever she woants. An' you, too. Do you suppose by any chance she'd be able to come back with you? I realize that's askin' a lot."

"I don't know 'bout dat, m'am, but I can fine out an' let chu know."

"Thank you so much. Now, my house is the big white one with grey shutters directly across the street from Mr. Hays Younger's house. D'you know where he lives?"

"Yessum."

"Oh, I forgot to ask what your name is."

He hesitated. "Tyler Canfiel'."

MR. CROSBY SAID he could easily change his delivery schedule again next day if Annie Lois thought he could be of any help.

"That would be too much of an imposition, Mr. Crosby, but I certainly do thank you with all of my heart. I'm hopin' the old colored woman who used to work for us can come to help me. One of the men I talked to said he knew her and would go out and ask her if she could come."

"Miss Annie Lois, don't chu have no kinfolks a'tall what could hep out?"

"Nobody in travelin' distance. Aunt Lavinie, Mamma's sister, used to be a lot of help but she died three years ago."

"Now, ain't chu related somehow to the Harpers what used to run the mercantile store up town?"

"Yes, I am. Hershel, the oldest boy, was my husband. He was killed in the war. A short time afterwards, his mother moved to Johnson City, Tennessee, where her youngest boy Aaron lives. I also have some distant cousins and another aunt on Papa's side livin' on the coast, but I rarely ever see 'em."

"I'm right sorry to hear that, Miss Annie Lois. All the same, if I can be of any hep whatsoever, you can let me know when I bring your milk next time."

As soon as he left, she made a mental list of things she needed to do immediately. She told Wanda Faye she'd cook their breakfast as soon as she took care of Dulcie.

Dulcie was awake when she went to her room. Her face was red and her lips were chapped. With difficulty she squirmed herself into a sitting position.

"How do you feel, Honey?" Annie Lois asked, helping her to sit up.

"I hurt all over and my head's about t'kill me. I gotta go to the bathroom."

Later, as she helped Dulcie back into bed, she told her she was going to fix something good for her to eat. "I know you must be starvin'. And Doctor Cranford said you've gotta drink lots of water."

"Annie Lois, I don't woant *nothin'*."

"But Honey, you've got to. You'll never get well if you don't. I'll bring you a cup of coffee, then I woant chu t'eat somethin' solid. Then, after you eat, I'm goan give you a bath, rub some more Vick salve on your chest and give you a couple a more aspirins. That oughta make you feel a lot better."

She started to the kitchen, then remembered she hadn't taken Dulcie's temperature. It was one hundred and three, slightly better than it was the last time. This was encouraging, even though she realized it would go higher this afternoon.

She felt an all but imperceptible sense of optimism as she prepared breakfast. Mr. Crosby had been so understanding, kind, and helpful. And the thought that Sophronie might be able to take care of Dulcie brought a bit of order to her mental disarray. As she scrambled the eggs, she closed her eyes for a few seconds and prayed.

She knew deep down inside that there was no reason to feel optimistic, but she did, nevertheless. Perhaps her prayers were being answered. She was encouraged to the point of going out to the chicken coop, selecting the finest of her Rhode Island Red hens, and wringing its neck so she could make stewed chicken and dumplings, one of Dulcie's favorite dishes.

Making the soup added to her sense of encouragement. She began to remember how things used to be before the war, before she inherited the sudden woes of single motherhood and the added burdens of taking care of Wanda Faye and Dulcie. It all seemed so precious by comparison with things as they were now. She realized it was only natural that she should feel the disparity more painfully now than she usually did. She had learned early in life that the joys of the past are always made more joyful by the extreme miseries of the present.

Financially, Annie Lois was quite well off. When she was teaching, she managed to put aside each month a certain percentage of her salary, which, in turn, she put into a savings account at the bank. Aunt Lavinie had remembered her and Dulcie in her will and had left each of them a small amount of cash that would be found, she had specified, in a black wool stocking hidden beneath a loose floor board behind the kitchen stove. Upon Hershel's death, the mercantile store became hers, but when some difficulties between her and her mother-in-law became too stressful, she leased it to Mr. Marshall Unger, who was still operating it.

WHILE SHE WAS trying to get Dulcie to eat some of the chicken and dumplings, Penny Welborn called to ask about Dulcie and to let her know she and Melissa missed her. Melissa had been staying with Voncille since Dulcie became sick, but things were not going well. Did Annie Lois have any idea about when Dulcie would be able to come back to work?

"Miz Welborn, Dulcie is very sick," Annie Lois said. "And the doctor said she may not recover." Her throat tightened and she covered her mouth to keep from crying aloud.

"I'm so sorry, Miz Harper. I didn't realize it was that bad. We do miss her a lot. And please tell her we love 'er and we'll be prayin' for 'er." It was obvious that she was trying to conceal her own distress.

Annie Lois had not given more than a passing thought to Penny or how much she must be needing and missing Dulcie. She felt sorry for her.

In an instant, as a result of the phone call, she had lost her composure. The dark fears she had tried so hard to dismiss had now been verbalized, obliterating the feeble, assumed optimism of a few minutes ago and all foreseeable, retrievable hope as well. As she neared Dulcie's room, she heard gasping sounds and Dulcie's futile attempts to call her.

Wanda Faye, apparently having heard the sounds, was standing in the door of Dulcie's room as Annie Lois hurried inside and over to the side of the bed where Dulcie lay among the twisted bed clothes.

"Get out of here, Wanda Faye," she shouted as she tugged the covers loose, then threw them on the floor. Dulcie's face had gone colorless and her eyes rolled back in their sockets. The continuous gasps suddenly grew louder and came more quickly than before.

Annie Lois, straining and fighting back her fears, pulled Dulcie to a sitting position again. The gasps abruptly grew weaker and farther apart.

Somebody was knocking at the back door.

"See who that is, Wanda Faye."

Wanda Faye ran to the front door and back again. "It ain't nobody, Mamma."

"Try the back door. I know I heard somebody knockin'."

Dulcie's head suddenly fell forward. Annie Lois grabbed her and tried to hold her up.

Wanda Faye came to the door again. "It's a nigger man, Mamma."

She remembered. "It must be Sophronie!" she cried. *Oh, merciful God, please let it be!* Then, with more dread than joy, she asked, "Is anybody with 'im?"

"No m'am. He's by 'is self an' said he woants t'talk t'you."

Oh Jesus! Oh merciful Jesus! She pressed a hand to her heart. "Tell 'im t'come in here. . . No, Wanda Faye, not in here. . . Wait a minute. Just tell 'im t'come out to the hall where I can talk to 'im. *And hurry!*"

Dulcie's head fell back against the headboard.

"No! No!" Annie Lois cried, then bent down and listened for a heartbeat. Her own heart was beating so fast and loud she didn't know whose heart she was hearing. She sat on the edge of the bed and cuddled Dulcie in her arms. *Please, God, please help her!*

Tyler Canfield came slowly, awkwardly to the door, holding his wool stocking cap in his hands.

Annie Lois turned around, unable to conceal her anguish. "Sophronie couldn't come?"

"No'm. She say she got too much t'do t'day."

"Well, when *can* she come? Tomorrow?"

"She say she be able t'come t'morrow. An' she say ax you if n you woants 'er t'stay over."

For an instant, she allowed the hopeless possibility of Dulcie's recovery at Sophronie's hands to mock her despair. What an insane idea! By tomorrow it will all be over.

When Dulcie collapsed in her arms, Annie Lois turned her eyes pleadingly to Tyler. *There was no other choice, nobody else. She had to.*

"I've got to call the doctor right now. Would ju please stay with 'er while I call 'im?"

"Yessum."

She ran to the front hall and rang the operator. "Mrs. Watson, call Doctor. Cranford's house . . . quick, quick!"

She waited for what seemed an eternity before Mrs. Watson answered. "His number is busy."

She hung up and immediately called again. The line was still busy. Again. The line was busy.

"Miz. Watson, this is an emergency! Dulcie's dyin'. Please put me through to Dr. Cranford."

"Annie Lois, his line is still busy. You'll just have to wait like everybody else."

— e l e v e n —

WEAKLY, HER HAND shaking, she hung the receiver up and stood for a few moments in the cold hallway, wondering what to do. It was then that the full impact hit her head-on, knocking over every one of the props she had been using to bolster her spirit, and bringing her muddled, hope-motivated thoughts into focus. The most immediate and painful consequence was that she must now face up to what she had dreaded facing up to for so long. Since Hershel's death, she had been lonelier than she had wanted anyone to know. Now she would be lonelier still.

Upon entering Dulcie's room, she looked first in one direction and then another, seemingly unaware that this was where she was supposed to be. As her eyes finally came to rest on Tyler, she felt a new anguish. He moved to the doorway.

"The doctor cain't come," she said. "I don't know what else to do."

Without warning, in spite of all she could do to prevent it, her eyes filled to overflowing. The tears crept warmly downward between her fingers, over, under, and around the hands she pressed so tightly and ineffectually over her mouth. She hated herself for crying in Tyler's presence. How humiliating that he should be witness to a white woman's weakness and vulnerability! Surely he must be feeling some kind of satisfaction. Yet he had helped her when no one else could; he had been kind and yes, he represented the meager, only hope remaining that Sophronie's coming in the morning gave her.

"Thank you. . . . I'm sorry. I can't remember your name."

"Tyler, m'am. Tyler Canfield."

"I do appreciate what chu did. You may go now."

He started to leave. "Does you still woant me t'bring Miss Sophronie in da mornin'?"

Tomorrow seemed a year away. All she could think about was what would probably have already happened between now and then. She knew, nevertheless, that no matter what happened, she needed Sophronie for herself if not for Dulcie.

"Yes. I'm goana need 'er."

After Tyler left, she did all the things Dr. Cranford had told her to do and some of her own devising. When Wanda Faye came to the door and said she was hungry, Annie Lois told her she would have to wait, that she could not leave Dulcie.

While she was washing Dulcie's face with cold, wet towels, Dulcie squirmed and tried to pull her hands out from beneath the cover. She tried to open her eyes but their lids were stuck together.

"Dulcie, can you hear me, Honey? It's Annie Lois." She laid her hand on Dulcie's forehead, wondering as she did so, if the cold towels could have helped at all. As she reached over for the thermometer, someone knocked at the front door. She called Wanda Faye and told her to see who it was.

Seeing Dr. Cranford come through the door caused another outburst of tears and sobbing. He put an arm around her waist as he approached the bed.

"How is she?" he asked, trying to assess outwardly, it seemed, Dulcie's present condition. He opened his satchel and brought out his stethoscope.

"I thought she was dyin'," Annie Lois said. She wiped her eyes and tried to regain her composure. "I tried several times to get you but your line was always busy. I was at my wits' end. I didn't know what to do. It seems like a miracle that you came by just now as you did."

"I've just come from across the street. Hays Younger's wife Hannah has come down with it." He moved the stethoscope over Dulcie's chest. As he straightened, he added, "Hannah might pull through. She's a healthy woman. And she's got plenty of help, as you know."

Annie Lois was trying to interpret the expression on his face as he put the stethoscope back in the satchel.

He checked Dulcie's eyes, then put a thermometer in her mouth. She made an effort to help by slightly parting her lips.

"Have you noticed any significant change in her condition since I saw her yesterday?" He straightened, yawned and stretched his arms and shoulders back and forth while waiting to read the thermometer.

"It might be my imagination," Annie Lois said, "but just before you came, I felt her forehead and it seemed a little cooler than it's been. It was probably just the cold towels I used to wash her face."

He took the thermometer out, read it, and put it back in its metal case. He gave a quick look around the room as he snapped his satchel closed. "And how are you doin', Annie Lois?"

"I'm doin' the best I can. I haven't wanted to eat anything. I've been too worried." *Is he waiting for the right moment to tell me something bad?*

"That doesn't sound too good. I warned you, you know, about letting yourself get run down. If you don't take better care of yourself you might very well be the next one to get it." He took his prescription pad and wrote something on it.

She waited anxiously.

"I think Dulcie may be coming out of it," he said finally.

Her appearance visibly changed. She felt like laughing. "Oh, do you really mean that, Dr. Cranford?"

"Yes, there are some meager indications that her condition is improving. The congestion in her lungs is breaking up, and her fever has come down to one hundred and two. Those are good signs. That gives me cause for some guarded optimism."

"Oh, Dr. Cranford! You don't know how wonderful it is to hear you say that! And I forgot to tell you, Sophronie Grubbs, who used to work for my mother years ago, is comin' in the mornin' to help me."

"That's mighty fine, Annie Lois. I'm glad you're goana have some help. That'll give you a chance to look out for your own self now. Praise God!"

She asked about the prescription.

"It's something I believe will help get rid of the congestion, now that it's breaking up in her lungs. I'm gonna run by Miller's Drugs Store and have him deliver it to you. He should have it here in a little while." He put on his coat and hat. "I'll try to come by again tomorrow. It may be late."

She followed him to the door. As he walked onto the porch, he turned. "This afternoon at exactly eighteen minutes past two, I lost my thirty-fourth patient. These are mighty sad times, Annie Lois."

Later, she made a pallet at the foot of Dulcie's bed, one of a number of indications that she was feeling better. She had eaten a good supper and, after putting Wanda Faye to bed, had taken a bath with the door open, just in case, since the bathroom was some distance away from Dulcie's room. As she lay down, with the remains of the last burning log casting warped shadows on the ceiling, the edges of every thought were still laced with doubt that diluted and threatened to destroy her gradually returning optimism. But her body took over and she fell asleep suddenly and did not wake up until almost six hours later when she heard Dulcie calling.

"What is it?" she asked in a shocked, fear-altered voice as she got up and lit the lamp.

Dulcie was sitting up. She covered her eyes with her hands and frowned as the light fell on them. "I'm hungry, Annie Lois," she said. "I want sumpn to eat."

The knock on the door came while Annie Lois was making biscuits a little before six next morning. When she saw Sophronie standing there, she had a strong impulse to throw her arms around her and laugh and cry at the same time. She almost did. Last night's good sleep and the encouragement about Dulcie's possible recovery had restored her and, as she might have put it, brought her back to her senses.

Sophronie was exhausted by the time both of her feet made it to the top of the steps leading into the kitchen, and so afraid of falling that all she could do by way of acknowledging Annie Lois was a quick, nervous glance in her direction. Once secure, she allowed Annie Lois to help her inside where, still panting and muttering to herself, she took in every inch of the kitchen. The two of them stood looking at each other in awed silence, a long moment of remembering how each had looked years ago and all that had happened in the meantime.

At that moment, Annie Lois was reacting on two levels of consciousness. Outwardly, and to a great extent inwardly as well, she was so happy she became almost giddy, reaching out to touch the old woman, even taking her hand at one point and squeezing it. She was genuinely moved to do these things. At the same time, lurking in her subconsciousness like never-sleeping watch dogs, was the need for caution, for maintaining her proper demeanor as a white woman in the presence of a negro. This caused her a moment of misgiving. She let go of Sophronie's hand sooner than she had planned to and stepped back a little toward the stove.

Sophronie was talking, but Annie Lois was still remembering. Lightning-fast images from her childhood displaced thoughts of the present while her face with its fixed, pleasant expression shielded Sophronie from what was taking place behind it. Things were different then. She had played with Kat and Roscoe as Dulcie had done, but it was almost always in the guise of who and what she wanted to be later on. She spent hours some days behind an apple box she called her desk, pretending Dulcie, Roscoe, and Kat were her pupils. Sometimes she even came out of character and romped and screamed with them, even though she was older than they were and even though, often, she would later feel silly and would fuss at herself. She would then assume the demeanor of a young lady with better things to do than play in dirty dresses or even sit behind an apple box pretending she was a teacher.

What Annie Lois was thinking now was unsettling. When and why had her childhood feelings about negroes changed? As she watched and listened to Sophronie talking about the way things used to be, about Roscoe getting killed, having Kat and her kids living with her, and having seen and talked with Dulcie, and how often she'd thought about how she used to work for Mrs. Dykes, she tried consciously to find answers to some of the questions she was asking herself. What was there about Sophronie that made her feel this way? What had she ever said or done, what, if anything, was she saying or doing now which could truly be considered reprehensible? She could not answer at the moment; the answer lay somewhere in her head, undefined, amorphous, and, up to now, not needing and not wanting to be known. She suddenly slammed shut the door to that part of her brain. "Did you come prepared to stay, Sophronie?" she asked.

"Yassum. I brung me some thangs."

In her anxiety, Annie Lois had failed so far to work out all the details of having Sophronie stay in the house. There were, she suddenly realized, no alternatives; there would have to be adjustments, more compromises. That was the price she must pay for some much needed comfort, for helping Dulcie recover, and to stay well herself.

"There's a little room right next to Dulcie's where you can stay. I think you'll be comfortable, and it's so close to Dulcie's room you won't have to do so much walkin'. Here, let me show you."

"Why don't we wait till you finishes yo' breakfast, Miss Annie Lois. While you be doin' dat, I'll go'n tell Tyler t'bring my stuff in."

Tyler made two trips, bringing first an old suitcase, scratched and overstuffed and held together by a man's belt. Next, he came in holding a thin, lumpy single mattress rolled up and tied with a piece of rope.

Annie Lois, seeing this, stopped what she was doing, suddenly repulsed by the sight and the very thought of having the mattress in her house, yet the alternative of having Sophronie sleep in one of her beds was even less to her liking. Another compromise, she told herself. "Why did you bring that?" she asked, her voice belying what she really felt. She turned to Tyler. "Take it back. She's not goana need that."

Sophronie leaned over and grabbed Tyler's arm. "Jest a minute, Tyler. No'm, Miss Annie Lois. Dis hyere's my bed."

Later, as she saw the room for the first time, Sophronie knew she would have to change things around a little to accommodate the mattress. "Come 'ere, Tyler," she said. "See if'n you cain't put dat dresser over yander in da corner'n then I'll hab enough room t'git aroun' widout knockin' sumpn over."

In the next room, Dulcie was still sleeping, but she heard. Suddenly every muscle in her face seemed to constrict and her hands and legs flailed and kicked beneath the covers as she squirmed and tossed from side to side and, finally, while still asleep, tried to sit up and crawl out to the floor. Then, from the congested region of her lungs there came a rapid succession of strained, muffled, and indiscernible word fragments followed by violent sobbing and a torrent of tears which she tried with tight fists to wipe away. She was evidently trying to scream but was unable to. She rolled over suddenly and brought her arms and hands to the back of her head as though to protect herself.

The old bedsprings had long ago lost their resilience. There had been too many nights, and days too, of tortured sleep and sickness. Now, having lost their capacity to support her weight or comfort her in any other way, they could only signal their condition with erratic, raspy death rattles, as first one and then another of the rusty coils scraped together. When she threw herself over in a cowering, protective position, the front right leg of the iron bed left the floor, then came down with a force and sound that startled her partially awake.

She struggled herself loose from beneath the heavy covers and managed to sit up, but when she tried to call Annie Lois, nothing came out. Her voice was lodged inescapably in the taut confines of her still fevered throat. She looked apprehensively from wall to wall and from ceiling to floor, trying to recover from the horrible thing she had just dreamed.

Sophronie heard. "Tyler," she said, motioning him to the door with a jerk of her head, "you go on back to de wagon. I gotta see 'bout Miss Dulcie."

Dulcie's consciousness was still in transit. Besides the wetness of her tears on her face, the pillows, and the bed clothes, she could actually still feel at different places on her body some of the pain she had felt in the nightmare. Seeing Sophronie made the transition more difficult. How could she be here in this room, in this house, unless this room were really the room she used to sleep in when she was a little girl. *Sophronie was in my dream, so I must be dreaming, she concluded, because there she is.*

"Miss Dulcie, dis be ol' Sophronie. 'Member me?"

She pulled and squeezed the covers up and over her mouth and nose, just below her shock-filled-and-fixed eyes, and stared with mounting suspicion, pressing her body down as far as she could into the mattress.

Sophronie grabbed one of the posts at the foot of the bed and leaned her weight against it. "What's de matter, Honey?" she asked, placing her hand lightly where Dulcie's feet were. "Is you havin' trouble?"

"What're you doin' here?" It took almost all of her energy to speak the hoarse, weak words. She looked toward the door. "Where's Mamma?" she asked, tightening her fingers around the bed covers.

"Why, yo mamma, she ain't hyean, Miss Dulcie. Miss Annie Lois, she be eatin' her breakfuss in de kitchen. You wants me t'call 'er?"

This bit of information gave her a degree of satisfaction. It was good to know she was not dreaming any longer and, even though she wouldn't want anybody in the whole world to know it, she was glad her mamma was not in the house. She was having a difficult time, just the same, forgetting the nightmare. Even when she managed to speak audibly enough for Sophronie to hear, she kept faltering as she recalled disturbing bits of it.

"Does Annie Lois know you're here?" she asked finally.

Sophronie chuckled. "Yassum, she sho do. She axed me t'come take care a you. Dat's why I'm hyeanh."

"How'd you know I was sick?"

"A li'l ol' bird done tol' me." She reached down and patted Dulcie's feet.

"Oh, he did no such of a thang! How come you t'know I was sick. Tell me the truth."

Sophronie gave some serious thought to her answer. "Miss Annie Lois sunt word out t'my house and said she needed somebody t'take care a huh li'l sister."

Dulcie suddenly threw the covers back, smiling. "Did she really say that? She asked you t'come take care a *me?*"

Sophronie straightened the covers and pulled them back over Dulcie's shoulders. "Yassum, I done tol' you she did. An' I's gwine stay hyeanh till you's well ag'in." She put her hand on Dulcie's forehead to see if she were feverish, then straightened with effort and a few deep groans. "Does you be happy 'bout dat, Miss Dulcie?"

"Boy, *am* I!" she said, slapping her hands up and down on her legs. "Yes, yes, yes!" The laughter abruptly turned into a violent spasm of coughing.

Sophronie hurried to the kitchen as fast as she could. "Miss Annie Lois," she said breathlessly, "Miss Dulcie be coughin' up some a dat congestion she got in huh ches'. I needs a pan or sumpn real quick."

"Oh, good!" Annie Lois said. "That means the medicine Dr. Cranford prescribed is doing what it's supposed to. *That's wonderful!*"

— t w e l v e —

DULCIE RECOVERED FULLY from the flu but not from the nightmare. For weeks after she returned to her nurse-maiding job with Melissa, certain parts of the nightmare recurred like involuntary pain spasms, interrupting and overpowering whatever conscious thoughts she might be having. At night it was even worse. Sometimes, after being startled awake by it and having tried every possible position for going back to sleep, she would lie flat of her back, recalling it. The darkness gave her a sense of security as it always did when her thoughts were of things she would be ashamed and afraid for others to know about.

In the dream, she was walking somewhere she had never been before when someone grabbed her and threw her down, then straddled her. He was as real as anybody could be. She could see the glistening chocolate-brown skin just the way she had seen it once before. She felt the pain and screamed. All at once she could see again and the person on top of her was not Roscoe. The face kept changing. It might be Bo Arthur Bilbo or somebody else for an instant, then it changed again. Her mother appeared from somewhere and beat her with a limb for what seemed an eternity. But it wasn't really her mother; it was Mr. Tatum. He pulled the man off, wrapped his big hands around his neck and tried to choke him. Through the pain and the tears she was finally able to see who it was. It was Tyler.

As a result of Dulcie's sickness, things had changed considerably for Annie Lois. Sophronie, when not taking care of Dulcie, had made herself useful in a number of other ways. At first, Annie Lois protested and reminded her that her only responsibility was to Dulcie, there was no need for her to sweep and mop and help with the cooking. At the end of each day, Annie Lois felt less tired, more secure, and happier than she had been for a long time.

Sometimes she thought about visits she and Sophronie had had, especially when they had talked about the past. Each day the comfort and security increased and she found herself, upon waking each morning, feeling good and eager to be up and doing.

When Dulcie was finally able to sit up and her recovery seemed imminent, Annie Lois found herself thinking more and more about being once again on her own. She dreaded seeing Sophronie leave and told her so one day as they were shelling pecans in the kitchen.

"I suppose you'll be happy to get back home, won't chu, Sophronie?" she said.

Sophronie seemed more concerned about what she was doing than what Annie Lois had said. She reached over and got another handful of pecans and dropped them in her aproned lap. "Yassum, I reck'n so."

"How do Kat and the kids get along when you're not there?"

" 'Bout de same as when I is. You done see, Miss Annie Lois, I ain't what I use t'be. Dat mean Kat haf t'do most a de cookin' 'fo she go t'wuhk an' when she git back of a evenin'. She make de kids do de cleanin' and evuhthang else what needs doin'."

"And how old are her kids?"

"D'oldest un be fifteen next July. D'udders be twelve, six and fo'. Ruby Dee, d'oldes', ack jist lak a mamma to d'udders. Hits funny sometime t'see how she tike t'boss 'em 'roun'."

"Are they as well-behaved as Kat and Roscoe were when they were little? I bet if you had anything to do with it they are."

Sophronie chuckled. "I don' know 'bout dat. Chirren go'n' be chirren, no matter what. You know dat, Miss Annie Lois. But all'n all, dey be good young uns, thank de Lawd."

Annie Lois fell silent. She realized she had allowed herself to become too dependent on Sophronie and had, consequently, created another problem. Just how much did she need and want Sophronie to stay? That was what she needed to decide immediately, before all responsibility once again fell on her shoulders. To admit to herself just how dependent she had become was one thing; to admit it too soon or eagerly to Sophronie would be to condescend again, to give form and awareness to still another of her white woman's frailties. Yet, having already conceded on similar problems, she should and would find it a little easier to rationalize herself out of this one.

Her hands, which had slowed to near inactivity, now came alive again. She sat straight against the back of the chair, her face reformed in a look of repose. "Sophronie, didn't chu tell me Kat worked for Mrs. Luke Wallace?"

"Yassum. Mistuh Wallace, he de one what runs de hardware sto' on de cawnuh next to de drug sto'."

"I know. But it just occurred to me, how does she get back and forth every day?"

"Mistuh Wallace hab ol' Jess Bynum come git 'er an' bring 'er back and fo'th evuh day. Jess, he be de one what delivers for Mistuh Wallace."

This meant that what Annie Lois had been thinking and hoping was true. She laid her pan of pecans aside and put both of her hands on top of Sophronie's. "Sophronie, I've been woantin' to ask you somethin' and I wonder what you're goana think about it."

"What chu thinkin', Miss Annie Lois?"

She faltered. It was harder to do than she had expected. Before she knew what she was doing, she took Sophronie's hands and squeezed them. For a moment she was unable to speak. Then she looked up and smiled. "I woant chu to stay. I don't woant chu to go."

Sophronie laughed in short, hoarse episodes. "I figgered dat's what you was thinkin'. I been watchin' you lately an' I knowed sumpn was on yo' mine."

"You're too smart for me, Sophronie. Well, what do you think about that?"

"I awready thunk about it, Miss Annie Lois. I seed how run-down you was dat first day I come, an' I thought right den and dere you needed somebody t' hep out. As a matter of fack, I done see how much better you lookin' now dan when I first come."

"That's true. I feel so much better. I think you know how hard it's been on me since my husband died. Dulcie can be something of a problem, you know."

"Yassum, I sho' does. But Miss Dulcie be well now. You wouldn't need me 'cept in de daytime, would ju?"

"No, I wouldn't. I was wonderin', could you possibly come in every day with Kat? Do you think that would work out?"

"Hit might. I don't see why not."

ON THE FRIDAY after Dulcie resumed her nurse-maiding job, Sophronie made her way up town to see if she could find Tyler and ask him if he could take her home. She had told Annie Lois she would arrange things with Kat and the children and, unless something happened to prevent it, she would come back on Monday and continue coming as Annie Lois wanted her to do.

Tyler was not with the other fellows when she finally got there. "He be heppin' out at de ice house," one of them told her. "Mistuh Poole say one a de fellows what wuhks for 'im be sick t'day an' he had t'find somebody take his place."

"You reck'n you can find 'im an' tell 'im sumpn f'me?"

"Reck'n so, Miss Sophronie. What chu want me t'tell 'im?"

"You tell Tyler I needs t'git back home an' come git me an' my belongin's as soon as he be through."

Later that day, the same fellow came to tell Sophronie that Tyler said he wouldn't be able to take her home today because, by the time he got off from work, it would be too dark. He said he would be working only half a day on Saturday and would come and get her as soon as he could go home and hitch up the horse and wagon.

When Dulcie came home later, she was surprised and happy to find that Sophronie had not gone home yet. After eating supper, Sophronie washed the dishes, stopping from time to time to lean against the sink and rest.

"Sophronie," Annie Lois said, "leave those dishes alone and come sit down with us. You look tired. You've been on your feet all day long. Dulcie, you finish the dishes."

"I'bout finished, Miss Annie Lois. Den I sit down," she said, straightening and putting her hands back in the water.

"How come you didn't go home today, Sophronie?" Dulcie asked.

Before Sophronie could answer, Annie Lois said, "The man who was go 'n' take 'er home is workin' and won't be able to take 'er till tomorrow afternoon."

"Is that the same man that brought 'er?"

"Yes. The one, incidentally, who stayed with you that day when I thought you weren't goin' to get well."

"I don't remember that, Annie Lois?"

"Of course not. You were so sick you didn't know anything. I asked him if he'd stay with you while I called Dr. Cranford. He'd come to the house to tell me Sophronie wouldn't be able to come help out till next day."

"You mean . . ." Dulcie stopped before she said what she was thinking.

Annie Lois understood. "He was somebody Sophronie knows. His mamma and Sophronie are good friends."

This answered one of her questions, but she was still surprised that Annie Lois had let him in the house. In her bedroom!

Sophronie took her hands out of the water and listened, her head tilted slightly in the direction of the conversation. It was as though she knew what Dulcie was going to ask next.

Later that same afternoon, when Annie Lois and Wanda Faye started outside to pick up pecans, they saw people coming and going across the street at Mr. Hays Younger's house. Several cars were parked in front and around the side of the house. When Annie Lois saw Mr. and Mrs. Tatum walking back to their car, she crossed the street and asked what had happened.

Mrs. Tatum looked at her husband, then waited for him to speak. "Mrs. Younger died this morning."

"No!" Annie Lois cried, cupping her face with her hands. "I was sure she'd recover. Dr. Cranford said she would."

"She almost did," Mrs. Tatum said, "but she relapsed yesterday."

"I must go over there," Annie Lois said.

As soon as she changed her clothes, she went over and offered her condolences. She kept remembering what Dr. Cranford had said, pondering the irony that someone who seemed most likely to survive had died while Dulcie had lived. Next morning, she cooked a pot roast and Dulcie carried it over to the Younger house. Mrs. Younger would be buried Monday afternoon, Dulcie told Annie Lois later.

* * *

ON MONDAY MORNING, while Dulcie was waiting for the streetcar, she saw Tyler loading ice up the street at the ice house. She wanted to walk up there and say something to him, but the streetcar was already coming one block away. She got a seat on the left side so she could see him as the streetcar went by. Tyler looked up for an instant, then bent down to lift another block of ice onto the wagon. Dulcie started to tap on the window but suddenly realized how dangerous that would be. Instead, she squeezed the handles of her purse and pulled it up against her stomach, then lowered her eyes and thought about the nightmare and the brief, scary part Tyler had played in it.

Remembering was somewhat different now. Her previous feelings had been unencumbered, she had been able to enjoy, to thrill to the wildest of fantasies about him, even to the point of actually being involved with him in a sexual way. Now when she consciously stripped her mind of all restrictions in order to enjoy as before some of the fantasies she had enjoyed so much, she found the enjoyment to be much less. It was as though what had been vivid, tantalizing, and complete had been diluted, as, in fact, it had. Every time she willed herself into one of her fantasies, the guilt, which as yet she had not admitted to herself, put a restraint on the enjoyment. The restriction, which this as-yet-unadmitted guilt put on her enjoyment, did not, as one might expect, deter her in any way. There was something more powerful than guilt which would determine what she would feel and do now. It was something she knew less well than guilt. No matter how or to what extent Dulcie was limited mentally, she was otherwise whole, with the capacity to feel all those dark, private cravings of the body which, even before she had begun to ask questions, she had been warned to shun as things of the devil.

She spent most of the day thinking about Tyler and wondering how she could see him without getting into trouble. Melissa soon realized that Dulcie's mind was on something besides what it should be on, so countered with several tearful tantrums and finally a threat to tell her mother that Dulcie was not doing what she was being paid to do, and that she should be fired.

By the time she got to the streetcar station, Dulcie had decided on what she would do when she got home. She would get off when the streetcar stopped in town on its way to the high school, then she would have to pass by the ice house on her way home. It was not until she had waited almost an hour that two ladies told her they had heard the streetcar had had some trouble and no telling when it would arrive. By the time she got home more than two hours later and hurried down the street to the ice house, it was closed and nobody was in sight.

Annie Lois had become frantic and was standing at the front door when Dulcie came home, red-faced and irritable. When Annie Lois asked why she was so late getting home, Dulcie shouted, "Because the streetcar broke down, that's why!"

She resisted Annie Lois' attempts to comfort her, went directly to her room and slammed the door. Next morning, she got up almost an hour earlier than usual. From the moment her feet touched the floor, her every agitated thought was to get out of the house as soon as possible, so much so that on several occasions her body was too slow to execute what her mind told it to do. She became upset and would have cried except for the thought of what was yet to happen.

When she looked for her lipstick and couldn't find it, she stomped her feet and started moving things around and off the top of the dresser. In a fit of frustration, she emptied her purse onto the dresser and finally saw the lipstick down inside the little coin purse. With a swift gesture of her hand, she swept the other things back into the purse. She was not aware that something had fallen on the floor.

"Why are you up so early?" Annie Lois asked as Dulcie walked into the kitchen. "Did you think you'd overslept?"

"No, I just couldn't sleep no longer. I figured I might as well get on up."

She ate hurriedly with an obvious urgency and disinterest in her food. When she put on her coat and scarf and started out the door almost fifteen minutes earlier than usual, Annie Lois stopped her.

"Dulcie, what in heaven's name has gotten into you?" she asked. "Why all this rushin' around this mornin'?"

"Ain't nothin' the matter, Annie Lois," she answered irritably.

"You always fuss when I don't get up on time an' now, just 'cause I'm tryin' t'do better, you're still fussin'."

As Annie Lois watched her hurrying down the sidewalk and up the street to the streetcar stop, she knew something was wrong. Dulcie's anger was almost always directed to others, not to Annie Lois or Wanda Faye. Nor, as a matter of fact, to Sophronie, she realized now. Even after Dulcie had turned the corner out of sight, Annie Lois continued to stand at the front door, looking through the frosted glass at nothing in particular.

She remembered the day her mother came home and told her that Dulcie was mentally retarded. She had chosen not to think about what else her mother had said, that people who are that way usually get progressively worse as they get older. Nothing so far had given her any reason to worry about that. Now she wondered. Had there been a change too subtle for her to discern, or was it at this point in Dulcie's life where the real change would begin?

Or could this be the aftermath of Dulcie's critical bout with the flu? She had never heard of anyone's having survived the flu and later undergoing personality changes. She wondered if Penny Welborn might have scolded Dulcie for some reason, or if something else might have happened yesterday which Dulcie wished not to talk about.

Dulcie did not stop to wait for the streetcar but walked on up to the ice house. Two negro men, one on either side of the chute, were taking turns sliding the blocks of ice to the edge of the platform, then lifting them with their tongs onto the wagon. The one facing her was not Tyler. She looked cautiously around, then moved a little closer so she could see. She thrilled at the sight of him.

"Hey, Tyler," she said softly, cupping her hands around her mouth.

He turned around just long enough to see her, then back around to tong the next block of ice.

She moved a little closer. "Remember me? Dulcie. You hepped me that time at the streetcar station when I fell."

"Yessum."

"When'd you start workin' up here?"

"I be jes heppin' out, Miss Dulcie. Dis ain't my reg'lar job."

She looked around to see if anybody was looking at her, then walked a little closer to the platform. "I sure am glad to see you. It's been a long time. Did ju know I've been sick?" She laughed and swung the purse against her legs.

"Yessum, Miss Dulcie. I brung Miss Sophronie to yo house t'take care a you. You didn't know dat, did ju?"

"No, I sure didn't. How come I didn't know that?"

He lifted the block of ice with a grunt and walked back to the chute. "'Cause, I reck'n, you was too sick."

Mr. Elmo Poole came out from the office and looked at Dulcie. "How're you this mornin', Dulcie?" he asked.

She could tell he didn't really care how she was. He wanted her to stop talking with his hired help. "I'm on my way to Laurel," she said. "I'm go'n' miss the streetcar if I don't get on down there."

She had no sooner taken a seat on the streetcar than she began to make plans for later, when she would be coming home. She had tried so hard for so long to give Tyler the note, now she would simply have to do it. No matter what. She could, she told herself, if she thought long and hard enough about it and made sure nobody knew about it. She became so lost in her thoughts that she momentarily forgot where she was. She looked around and became oriented. No one was looking at her, so she slowly and quietly opened the purse and put her right hand inside. She tried to find it without looking, recognizing the feel of most of the things she touched, but the note was not one of them. She knew so well how it felt, its size and shape and the degree of pliability her many handlings and readings had given it. In a fit of panic, she looked inside the purse and scrambled frantically to find the note. It was not there.

— thirteen —

WHILE ANNIE LOIS was giving Wanda Faye an early bath so they could go to Laurel before lunch, Sophronie made up the beds and swept the floors. When she saw the piece of paper on the floor in Dulcie's room, her first thought was to sweep it onto the dustpan with everything else. That would have been easier than to put her large and stiffened body through the agony of stooping over to pick it up. She laid the broom against the bed, grabbed the bedpost with her left hand and strained and grunted, barely touching the piece of paper with her fingertips. It took three sweeps of her hand to pick it up. Straightening her body took as much or more effort than it took to bend over.

She gave herself time to recover, then slowly unfolded the paper and strained to see what was on it. She moved closer to the window and pulled the curtain back to see better. It took a while to make out some of the words. She sat down on the side of the bed, folding the note back up and wondering what to do. After a while, she stood, put the note in her apron pocket, and slowly, absent-mindedly pushed and pulled the broom across the darkly stained pine floor. She began to feel sick at her stomach.

Her concern deepened as the day wore on. After Annie Lois and Wanda Faye went to Laurel, unable to put the matter out of her mind by working, she sat at the kitchen table, remembering Dulcie standing naked behind the house as her mother riddled her flesh with a limb, and trying at the same time not to think about what terrible thing could yet happen unless she could find some way to stop it. Their schedules were such that they usually never saw each other. Then maybe she should talk with Tyler. But how could she when he worked until six o'clock every day?

She looked at the clock over the stove. If she left now and walked as fast as she could, she might be able to go to the ice house and back in time to cook lunch. She started to get her coat, then, looking out the window, considered what might happen if she did what she felt she had to do. And, anyway, how would that help matters? She realized that to do anything with her mind so muddled would almost surely be a mistake, yet the dreadful thought of what would happen if she did nothing kept pushing all other thoughts out of the way.

She tugged her arms into the sleeves of her coat, pulled the collar up and buttoned it, wrapped her shawl over her head and started cautiously, fearfully down the back steps, holding on to the bannister with both hands. She kept reminding herself that she must be extremely careful with her feet and just as careful with her tongue. Even if she died on her way to the ice house, it would be better than not to do anything.

She could see, even before she reached the ice house, that nobody was outside. She stopped for a moment and looked around to see if there was anyone she could ask about Tyler. Across the street, sitting on the sidewalk that ran in front of the Confederate Memorial, were several older black men.

"Has any y'all seed Tyler Canfiel' dis mornin'?" she called. "He s'pose t'be workin' at de ice house."

"Dey be deliverin' ice, Sophronie," one of them answered. "He be heppin' John Riley Carmichael wid deliverin' 'cause ol' Charley Sumrall be sick."

"When you reck'n dey be back? Sometime dis mawnin' ?"

"Not likely. Mos' days dey don't git back till late of a evenm'."

She wondered what to do now. "Would j'all do me a favor? If'n you sees 'im anytime b'fo' fo' 'clock, tell 'im I wants t'see 'im real bad. Would ju do dat fo' me?"

He said he would.

But he forgot to.

Later, while cooking lunch, she decided what to do. She went to Dulcie's room, pulled back the bedspread, laid the note on the pillow, then pulled and smoothed the bedspread back over the pillow. She stood for a while, looking down at the pillow and trying to feel what Dulcie might feel tonight when she got into bed. The plan had just suddenly occurred to her, and now that she thought about it, it seemed the best thing she could do under the existing circumstances.

As soon as Penny Welborn got home around three-thirty that afternoon, Melissa ran, crying and screaming, to meet her.

"Why Melissa, Darlin', what ever's the matter?" Penny asked, picking her up and kissing her.

"It's Dulcie, Mamma! I hate 'er and I don't never woana see'er ag'in!"

Dulcie, hands behind her back, was leaning against the porch rail, looking down at her feet.

Penny put Melissa down and started up the steps. "What's this all about, Dulcie?"

Dulcie was unable to defend herself. She had spent almost the entire day worrying about the note. She finally muttered, "I don't know."

Melissa furnished all the details, giving mean side glances at Dulcie as she did so.

Whenever Penny had scolded Dulcie before, she had made sure not to upset her because, first of all, she sympathized with her and, secondly and more importantly, though she would never admit it, because she needed Dulcie and never more than now. Melissa had complained several times last week about the way Dulcie was behaving and neglecting her. Dulcie promised to do better. Merciful God, Penny thought, things were bad enough while Dulcie was sick. She would have to decide quickly how to handle this present situation.

"Let's go inside," she said to Dulcie and Melissa. Once inside, she told Melissa to go to her room so she and Dulcie could talk. Melissa reluctantly obeyed.

"Shut the door, Melissa!" she added.

Dulcie found it easier to talk now that Melissa was out of the way. She apologized and said she still felt bad and thought she might even still have some fever. Penny listened as she thought about what she would cook for supper. Dulcie gathered up her things to leave. "I better hurry or I'm go'n' miss the streetcar."

"You will try to do better, won't chu, Dulcie? We both love you and don't want chu to leave. Melissa don't really mean what she said. She'll get over it, I promise you."

As Dulcie walked out the front door, she saw Melissa push the bedroom door shut.

Getting away from Melissa was a wonderful but brief relief. In fact, it seemed to intensify, by comparison, the unrelieved anxiety she had suffered all day. Every step she took on her frantic walk to the streetcar station only put her one step nearer the source of her trouble. The note had to be somewhere in her bedroom. She had reached that conclusion as soon as she opened her purse on the streetcar and found it missing. She remembered, also, that she had not opened her purse after leaving home until that very moment.

What if Annie Lois had found the note? How could she ever explain it? What terrible lie could she think of right this very moment, just in case that did happen, and she was all but sure that's what *would* happen. Convinced of that, she started imagining how different things would be if she had never written the note. No matter what she pretended, the horrible reality of what she had done made her wish she were dead. She thought about God. She wondered in what way He was going to punish her for her sins.

She saw the little black doll Sophronie had given her as it burned, and she heard and felt her mamma standing beside her and telling her that's what hell was like. Whenever she'd tried to pray before, she never felt anything. It was all she could do just to find something to say to God, and, when and if she did, she was so preoccupied with how it sounded that she was never able to feel the words had gone any farther than out of her mouth and into her own ears.

But she had been told often enough to consider, at least, asking God for help in times of trouble. As the streetcar clanged along the crunchy tracks near Paulding Road, she looked around to see if people were looking at her and, if so, if they seemed to know what she was thinking and feeling the need to talk with God about, then drew herself as close to the window as she could, closed her eyes, and said, "God, please hep me. *Please!*"

Later, she nearly fell several times as she hurried to the house.

She closed the front door as quietly as she could, then went directly to her room, closing the door behind her.

Annie Lois heard. "Is that chu, Dulcie?"

"Yeah, it's me." She started looking even before she took off her coat. She went to the dresser first, pulled out drawers and dumped everything onto the bed, then put it back clumsily, looked in the closet, even in the fireplace, where for an instant she thought she saw tiny scraps of charred white paper, and finally all over the floor, around the furniture and under the bed. Her heart was beating so fast she could hear it. She finally stopped and wrung her hands.

Annie Lois opened the door. "Dulcie, what in heaven's name is wrong with you? You look like you've seen a ghost."

Dulcie dropped onto the bed. "Oh, nothin'. Penny fussed at me again." She had not expected to say that at all. It just came out. Then, in an attempt to be more convincing, she added, "She said she was goan fire me."

"Fire you? What for?"

"Because Melissa told 'er I wuddn't doin' what she was payin' me t'do. She woants me t'do a lot a silly things I don't like t'do."

"But that's what chure gettin' paid for. You've got t'do what Melissa woants you to, Honey. Don't chu see that? Come on now, we're gonna eat supper pretty soon."

It was only then that Dulcie looked directly at Annie Lois. She felt better. *She ain't found the note.*

Knowing, or rather believing, that Annie Lois had not found the note was, after all, small comfort. She began wondering if she had lost it somewhere else. Trying to decide where else it could be was a monumental undertaking which kept her preoccupied for the rest of the evening, so much so that the pleasant smell and consequent taste of fried chicken later proved to be, at best, minimally distracting.

The possibility that somebody who did not know her or Tyler might have found the note was in some ways comforting. She failed to realize that the way the note was written could possibly be more incriminating than *what* she had written. While she was bathing, she tediously recalled as well as she could everywhere she had been and everything she had done the past several days. What she was not able to do was to remember when and how many times she had opened her purse.

When she pulled the bedspread back and saw the note, her first reaction was one of extreme joy and relief. As she opened it up, she suddenly realized her trouble had only begun. Since she had already decided Annie Lois had not seen it, she knew it had to have been Sophronie who found it and put it on her pillow. She turned around to make sure her door was closed, then sat on the edge of the bed, swinging her legs nervously, pressing the note between both hands as though afraid she might lose it again. How could she ever face Sophronie now, and even if she did, how could she be sure Sophronie would not tell Annie Lois? She chewed nervously on the side of her mouth as she tried to think of how she could lie herself out of the situation.

As soon as Annie Lois and Wanda Faye passed her room on their way to bed, she sat on the floor in front of the fireplace. The note, which she had struggled so hard to write and which for so long had been a source of guilty pleasure, all of a sudden had become something she hated with all her being. She wished she had never written it. She laid it beside her on the floor, crossed her legs under her and hunched forward with her hands cupping her face. When the heat began to burn her forehead and eyes, she straightened and laid her hands in her lap. She knew she wouldn't be able to sleep. She was too scared to cry, and she was more convinced than ever that praying wouldn't do a bit of good.

Slowly, as she stared at the waning flames, some of her anxiety abated and her thinking became a little less frantic. Maybe she could, after all, destroy the note and, if asked, say she never had any intention of giving it to Tyler, that she had just been practicing her writing the way Annie Lois had said she should always do. For a few moments, the purpose for which she had written the note became less important than the concern for saving herself or, at least, helping her get through it.

She sat on the floor until the last flame spit itself out in a weak burst of blue-orange sparks, then stayed a little longer, watching as the only remaining bit of charred wood crackled and dropped into the pile of embers and ashes, sending a spark onto the hearth directly in front of her. She finally felt the cold overtaking the room and chilling the back of her neck and arms. Not until the embers had greyed and their last weak smoke emissions had wafted feebly upward and out the chimney did she get up. She placed the note inside her purse, at the bottom under everything else, but only after she had fully decided that was the best place to put it, then crawled into bed.

She turned and twisted, trying to accustom herself to the extreme cold of the sheets and the pillow. She pulled the blanket and quilt up to her chin, then tucked them in around her neck, holding them in place. In a matter of minutes, the extreme congestion in her mind diffused imperceptibly and, in doing so, provided her with a degree of calm that gave her thoughts access to a remote corner of her brain where they could be filtered and she could think more clearly than before. In a way, it was like waking from a bad dream, and although she knew only too well that it was not a dream, she began to wonder if, and later to feel that she had probably blown the whole thing out of proportion. That was the way she had often dealt with matters too difficult to solve; it was one of the all-too-scarce items she carried daily in her survival kit.

It was while she was passing through this calmer and less congested state of mind that a thought suddenly occurred to her . . . *Sophronie can't read!* . . . Or *can* she? She tried to remember if she had ever seen Sophronie reading or having heard anybody say she could or could not read. This unexpected shift in her thinking caused her to become excited again, and it wasn't until an hour or so later that she finally went to sleep.

Even under normal conditions, Dulcie very likely would have failed to see that Sophronie would not have put the note where she put it if she had not been able to read it. If she were not able to read, she might have put it, rather, on the dresser or in the fireplace.

ANNIE LOIS SQUATTED in front of the fireplace in Dulcie's room until the flames from the kindling reached out and around the dry oak logs and started the fire. "It's time to get up, Dulcie," she said as she left the room.

Dulcie was already awake but didn't want Annie Lois to know it. All the bad things that had happened yesterday were lurking at the forefront of her brain, ready to assail her as soon as she opened her eyes. Normally, no matter how much she hated to get up, she felt something comforting about her room. It had been, up until yesterday, her cocoon, the place where she was able to indulge herself in strange and dangerous fantasies, where she had laboriously written the note which was able to stimulate her lust, no matter how far down in her purse she put it. It was where she could come when someone had laughed at or scolded her, where she could wish, as she often did, that she was black.

Even though Annie Lois had told her to get up immediately and get herself ready to eat breakfast, she did not. She pushed her body farther down between the bed clothes and listened to the crackling and hissing sounds coming from the fireplace. She remembered how, as a child, she used to enjoy waking up to those sounds. At some point since that time, however, her pleasure upon waking had changed as she had changed. She realized now that the comforting sounds of the fire had not changed as she had. She wished suddenly that she could stay in bed the rest of her life and listen to them.

The only reason she didn't make up an excuse to stay home was because she would have to face Sophronie. All the same, having to face Melissa again was almost as bad or maybe even worse. How nice it would be if Penny fired her and she could stay home all the time. But even staying at home was impossible as long as Sophronie was around five days a week.

"Dulcie, get chureself out of that bed this instant or I'm comin' in there and drag you out!"

As she slipped into her bathrobe, she tried to reconcile herself to what she had to do. It was always that way, she thought. Do right or be punished.

As she readied herself for work, her mind was on everything except what she was doing. Twice she had to go back to her room, first for her stockings and again for a belt for her skirt. Even as she made up her face and tried to force the spit curls into place, she was worrying about how she was going to get through the day. Usually, as she got ready every morning, she could think of something exciting that was going to happen and made it possible to bear the unpleasant hours she would have to spend with Melissa.

Always, too, there was the dark fantasy that, above all, gave her life meaning, and the note which, until yesterday, had the power to bring that fantasy to reality. Suddenly, because she had been in such a hurry to leave yesterday morning, she had put the fulfillment of the fantasy and, indeed, her whole life in direst jeopardy.

The longer she struggled with her hair and makeup, the more irritable she became. She stomped her feet in frustration. Annie Lois heard and came to the bathroom door to warn her again about being late.

"You're goana fool around and get chureself fired for sure," she warned, "and your breakfast is gettin' cold."

She wanted to shout back that she didn't want any breakfast and, yes, she didn't care if she did get fired. She was so upset by now that anything seemed preferable to another day with Melissa.

Later, at the table, she had so many questions she wanted to ask, that she felt her head was going to explode. She ate a biscuit with some molasses and two or three spoons of oatmeal and pushed the other things around on her plate as she wondered how to find out something she needed to know. Annie Lois helped Wanda Faye with her oatmeal and Dulcie watched. She seemed to notice for the first time a certain feature of Annie Lois' face, a slight dip of the eyebrows toward her nose, giving her a constant appearance of slight worry and unhappiness. Had she always looked like that, or had she changed only since Herschel died? Can Annie Lois tell what I'm thinkin'?

She thought of the many times she had peeped through the keyhole at night, wondering what they were feeling and how they would look at each other next morning after what they had done. Although she herself had never done it, she knew it had to be something wonderful, and she knew, too, that Annie Lois must be extremely unhappy now that she had nobody to do it with. All of a sudden, she realized how ugly she was being and ate another spoonful of oatmeal.

Annie Lois pointed to the clock. Dulcie shifted, stood, then sat down again. "Annie Lois, do you make up my bed like you used to or does Sophronie do it?" She had to look away for fear of showing more than she wanted to show.

"Sophronie does. Why?"

"Oh, nothin'. I was just wonderin'." She stood and straightened her skirt, then drank the rest of her orange juice.

"I wish you didn't have to go to work so early so you and Sophronie could visit," Annie Lois said. "You'd like that, wouldn't chu, Honey?"

She said she surely would, though she had a hard time making it sound right. It seemed to give her enough courage to ask the next question, however. "You know what, Annie Lois? I got t'thinkin' yesterday comin' home on the streetcar. Does Sophronie know how to read?"

Annie Lois laughed. "Now what brought that up?"

"I don't know. I just started wonderin' if she could. I ain't never seen her readin' anything."

"You mean you *haven't ever* seen her readin'."

"That's what I said."

"No, you said *ain't*. You're not supposed to use that word. You know that."

"Oh, yeah. Well, anyway, can she?"

Annie Lois laughed again. "Of course she can. She's one of the few niggers who can."

"SOPHRONIE, YOU'VE DONE enough," Annie Lois said. "Come on'n sit down'n have a cup of coffee with me."

"Is dey any mo' left?"

"Just enough for one cup apiece."

Sophronie seemed to take longer to get around, Annie Lois noticed. Or had she just not noticed before? Sophronie was eighty or older, she knew, yet she had not realized until now how remarkable it was that the old woman could still do so much and move as well as she did. Annie Lois realized, also, how much she enjoyed having Sophronie around, and how much their little visits over coffee and at lunchtime had come to mean to her. She didn't know her pleasure was showing on her face until Sophronie reacted to it.

"What chu smilin' 'bout, Miss Annie Lois?"

"D'you really woana know?"

"I sho' does."

"Well, to tell you the truth, I've been lookin' at you and thinkin' just how much you mean to me. I'm so happy to have you workin' for me. Just bein' with you makes me feel good. I suppose that's partly because I've known you so long. You bring back memories of my childhood."

"I s'pose so. Jis lak me bein' wit' chu'n Miss Dulcie make me feel good too."

"You know, in some ways it's like we're a family. You know what I mean. Oh, that reminds me of somethin' Dulcie asked me just this mornin'. She said, 'Annie Lois, does Sophronie know how to read?' At first I wondered what ever made her ask that, but then I realized she was still a little girl when you used to work for us and didn't know you as well as I did."

"An' what chu tell 'er, Miss Annie Lois?"

"Why, I said, 'of course Sophronie can read, and how come you t'ask me if she could anyway?' "

Sophronie squirmed, leaned a little forward, and looked directly into Annie Lois' eyes. "What she say?"

"She just laughed and said she got to wonderin' about it comin' home yesterday."

Sophronie made a soft nervous sound in her throat, pulled herself rigidly erect, and slowly drank the rest of her coffee.

Annie Lois leaned forward with her elbows on the table, holding the cup of coffee with both hands, her face having solemned and her eyes looking at nothing in particular. As her eyebrows contracted slightly downward, little creases formed just above her nose.

Sophronie reached over and touched Annie Lois' shoulder. "What be botherin' you, Honey?"

Without moving, she smiled sadly. "I don't know. I keep gettin' this funny feelin' that you can read my mind and already know what I'm thinkin'."

"No'm, I cain't read jo mine, but I can sho tell when you's got problems. Tell me what be botherin' you, Miss Annie Lois. Maybe I can hep you."

She had to think ahead before answering, then finally, "Well, naturally, it's Dulcie. She's been actin' so strange lately it's got me worried."

Sophronie listened with no visible expression of what she was feeling. When Annie Lois had told her everything, she sat stiffly upright but said nothing.

Annie Lois finally asked, "What do you think could be the trouble, Sophronie? D'you think as she gets older her mind'll get worse?"

"I don' know 'bout dat, Miss Annie Lois, but could be. If'n you woants t'know de God's truth, I been wuh'rd 'bout Miss Dulcie myself." With that, she got up slowly and put her coffee cup on the stove, then, obviously preoccupied, carefully eased herself back onto the chair. "Miss Annie Lois, you mine if'n I say sumpn I been thinkin' 'bout lately?"

"Of course not, Sophronie. I want chu to. Please."

"Well, first of all, I don' know 'zackly how t'say what I been thinkin', so I hopes you unnerstan' I means well."

"Yes, Sophronie. Go on."

"Well, I been wonderin', has Miss Dulcie evuh say anythang 'bout wantin' to have chirren?"

"No, not that I know of. Oh, for heaven's sake! You're not tryin' t'tell me . . ." She couldn't bring herself to say it. She had never felt free enough to talk about things of such a personal nature and had for a long time tried consciously to keep thoughts about such things out of her mind. She knew from her own standpoint how disruptive concerns of this kind could be, and as for the effect they might have on Dulcie's life, she felt as strongly if not even more so. Like Dulcie, she carried with her everywhere she went a survival kit in which she kept a collection of mental devises she had invented and accumulated over the years, various forms of thought control for the many times when she stood alone and defenseless and some of life's adversities had assailed and threatened to overpower her.

"But, Miss Annie Lois, you know she be thinkin' 'bout dat. Dat's God's doin', Miss Annie Lois. You know dat as well as I does, an' you know Miss Dulcie be feelin' it, no mattuh how huh mind be. Dat don't make no nevuh mind in Miss Dulcie's case. Dat mean she woana do it like evuhbody else."

"Oh, dear God, Sophronie! How is that possible? You know nobody in his right mind'd woana marry Dulcie."

"How you know dat? Dey mus' be somebody in Ellisville what sees de good in dat sweet li'l ol' girl an' woana marry 'er. She got mo' sense dan some a d'udder people in Ellisville what's married."

Annie Lois felt faint. She pressed both hands to her head, propping her elbows on the table, leaned forward and closed her eyes. She thought about the times when she had talked to Dulcie about such things, and, for some unclear reason, she thought about Bo Arthur Bilbo. How I detest him! She knew what Sophronie said was true, yet it had suddenly sent light to a spot in her mind which she wanted to keep dark. She knew, too, that the anxiety she was feeling right now would only intensify. She quickly prayed silently.

She removed her hands from her head and smoothed her hair back in place, then ran them over her face and shoulders as if to restore the circulation that had been momentarily impeded. "Sophronie," she said finally with a determined effort to control her emotions, "I don't know if you've ever noticed, but most of the people in this town don't woana have anything t'do with Dulcie. I couldn't tell you how many times Dulcie has come home cryin' and tellin' me some of the mean things folks have said or done to 'er. She's often told me she likes black people better than white ones. I've known that for a long time. I'm afraid I have to put some of the blame for that on Mamma. You know how she mistreated Dulcie. I've come to the conclusion that Dulcie developed this feeling as a child when she used to play with Kat and Roscoe. And she's always loved you. You know that, don't chu?"

"Yass'm, I sho does."

"I've thought about that a lot. I think I know why Dulcie feels so strongly about black people. It's because they've always been kinder and better to 'er than white folks have."

Sophronie was leaning forward on her elbows now with her eyes closed. From time to time she would give a little grunt at something Annie Lois said.

DURING THE DAY, Dulcie managed to deal with both of her problems. She was able to pretend she was having fun when she and Melissa played hopscotch in the back yard and, at the same time, to think about the note in her purse. Her thoughts about the note usually got just so far, then it was her turn to throw the marker and she never seemed to reach a decision about what to do. Sometimes she would be concentrating so hard Melissa would have to holler at her or slap her arm. By the time she had to go home, she felt she'd done a little better in getting along with Melissa, so maybe Penny wouldn't fuss at her anymore.

As she hurried to the streetcar station, she felt relieved enough to pursue the matter of the note. She kept wondering why the situation did not seem so scary now. She did not understand that being in Laurel instead of at home made some difference, and that her conscious efforts to keep Melissa entertained had tempered to some degree the urgency she had felt earlier. The longer she thought about it, the more able she was to rationalize matters to a point where it seemed, almost, that nothing had actually changed the way she used to feel or her determination to carry out the plan of somehow getting the note to Tyler. *Tomorrow I'm goana get up real early so I'll have plenty of time to go to the ice house and give Tyler the note.*

— f o u r t e e n —

WHEN DULCIE WENT into the kitchen next morning, she told Annie Lois she didn't want any breakfast. Annie Lois insisted she sit down, then laid the plate of eggs and bacon in front of her.

"I don't know what's gotten into you lately, Dulcie," she said. "If something's botherin' you, why don't chu tell me about it. You always have before."

"It ain't nothin', Annie Lois," she said with a mouthful of food. "I wish you'd leave me alone." She looked at her watch, hurriedly poured some molasses over a biscuit, stuffed the whole thing in her mouth, then, licking her fingers, got up from the table.

No matter how she tried, Annie Lois could not imagine Dulcie in an intimate relationship with anybody in Ellisville. The very idea was repugnant. She knew, though, that she must learn to deal with that possibility, no matter how remote it seemed. Although what Sophronie said yesterday had upset her, she now realized it was true and that she would have to come to grips with it. Before Sophronie talked with her yesterday, her single most serious concern for Dulcie was the possibility that her mental retardation would worsen.

Because Annie Lois had succeeded to some extent in suppressing her own sexual cravings, she had tried with some success until yesterday to suppress Dulcie's, too. If she had been honest with herself all this time, she would have known better. She was too intelligent not to know. She probably had never been consciously aware at the time that she was fortifying herself, building walls between herself and that possibility, the reality of what was on the other side.

Annie Lois followed Dulcie up the hall to the front door, and, as Dulcie started out, took one of the umbrellas standing in the corner and gave it to her. "Here," she said, "you might need this today."

Even when she could no longer see Dulcie, she stood at the

front door, holding the gathered sheer panel back, looking out but registering nothing she saw. With his satchel in one hand and a big black umbrella in the other, Hays Younger came out of the house across the street. He took the steps slowly, looked from side to side and finally over to where Annie Lois was standing. After closing the wrought iron gate behind him, he looked once more in her direction. He usually sprang out of the house as though he thought the world could not turn until he got to the bank. She couldn't help feeling sorry for him. She knew how alone and unhappy he was since his wife Hannah died. He possibly might never again walk with a spring in his step.

Dulcie, in the meantime, was walking as fast as she could to the ice house. The sky was covered with low-hanging, sooty clouds that moved nervously to the east, and the temperature had risen to nearly eighty degrees. The humidity wrapped itself cloyingly around her, adding to the difficulty of breathing, causing her to tug her clothes from time to time away from her body. The bright red and white striped umbrella, which she normally enjoyed using more for the attention it got rather than for the protection it offered, was fast becoming an added burden as she neared the ice house. At one point, when she was forced to stop long enough to catch her breath, she looked up ahead to see if Tyler was outside where she could talk to him. She was greatly relieved when she saw two men, as before, alternately retrieving the blocks of ice and loading them onto the wagon. She wished she could call him and tell him to wait until she got there, but she knew better. She was nervous enough already, in spite of the fact that she had tried so hard to control herself.

As she neared the platform where the men were working, she looked around to see if she was being watched. One of the men was bent over the block of ice and the other had his back turned to her. She was so out of breath she had to try three times before the words came out. "Hey, Tyler!"

The one bent over the ice, whose face she could see, either hadn't heard or was too busy to look up. The other one turned slightly at the sound of her voice.

It was not Tyler.

"Yassum," he said. "What chu want, m'am?"

"Where's Tyler? I thought he'd be here."

After guiding the block of ice onto the wagon, John Riley Carmichael straightened, pulled a rag from his back pocket and ran it over his face and arms. "Miss Dulcie," he said, "Tyluh, he don't be· hyeanh no mo'." He stopped momentarily as though reluctant to say anything else, but then added, "He jes hep out while Charley hyeanh be sick."

"D'yall know where he is?"

"What chu say, m'am?"

She took a deep breath and tried to speak louder without her voice cracking. "I said do y'all know where he is?"

"No'm, I sho don't. Mos' likely he be home or be lookin' fo' a job."

Both men watched as Dulcie lowered her head and walked away. John Riley, still holding the ice tongs, was shaking his head. "Wha' chu make a dat, Charley?" he said.

"Who dat lady?"

"I hyeard Tyluh call 'er Miss Dulcie. You reck'n dey knows one anudder?"

"Hit sho soun' lak it."

They returned to their work but John Riley continued to wonder about what just happened. He and Tyler had been friends all their lives. He knew some things about Tyler that nobody else knew, things which all of a sudden gave him cause to worry. Later, while he and Charley were delivering ice, he kept thinking about what had happened, and the more he thought about it, the more concerned he became. He couldn't help remembering some things Tyler had said and done in the past and, at one point, he became so distracted that Charley had to remind him he'd passed up Mrs. Lucy Jordan's house.

WHEN DULCIE CAME home around four-thirty that afternoon, Sophronie was still there, sitting and napping at the kitchen table. "What chu doin' here?" Dulcie asked.

"I'm waitin' fo' somebody t'come pick me up. Kat, she call a little while ago'n said Jess Bynum come down sick and Mistuh Wallace caint find nobody t'take me'n her home."

"Well, where's Mattie Lois and Wanda Faye?"

"Dey be uptown, Miss Dulcie. Miss Mattie Lois, she lef dis note fo' you in case I wuddn't hyeanh when you come home."

Dulcie took the note, looked at it, frowning and muttering something to herself, then handed it back to Sophronie. "Here," she said, "you read it. I'm too tired."

Sophronie grunted as she reached across the table to take it. "I done read it, Miss Dulcie. Hit say Miss Mattie Lois'n Miss Wanda Faye be uptown shoppin', den she go'n' hab Miss Wanda Faye's pitchure took, an' dey be back fo' long."

"You can read ever' single word a that, caint chu, Sophronie?"

"Yassum. You didn't know dat, did ju, udderwise, how come you t'ax Miss Annie Lois if'n I could read?"

The nervousness started in the pit of her stomach and quickly went out in every direction, and especially to her hands. Without looking up, she could feel Sophronie looking at her with eyes that now seemed to have the power to penetrate into her head and know exactly what she was thinking. She clasped and unclasped her hands, thumping them up and down on the table without realizing the message they were sending.

Sophronie reached slowly over and put both of her hands on Dulcie's. "What's de mattuh, Miss Dulcie? You 'fraid I knows sumpn you don't woant me t'know?"

She took a long time to answer. Finally, with a gesture of her head, she seemed to have found the needed resources to answer. "I ain't done nothin' wrong. Don't chu b'lieve me?"

"Yassum, I b'lieves you, Miss Dulcie. But it ain't what chu done but wha' chu thinkin' 'bout doin' what bothers me."

Dulcie idled, until she felt she could speak, by sliding her fingers back and forth on the table top. Sophronie's piercing eyes, when she looked up, frightened her.

"What chu woana tell me, Miss Dulcie? You needn't be skeert. I won't tell Miss Annie Lois."

She looked up slowly. "I was only tryin' t'thank 'im for hepin' me up when I fell that time."

"Miss Dulcie, I done tol' ju, Tyluh, he know how you feel. Dey ain't no need fo' you t'be writin' him dat note. Dat ain't right, Honey. Don' chu know dat?"

She nodded her head.

"But Miss Dulcie, dat note say mo' 'n dat. If he ever read it, dey ain't no tellin' what he might do. An' Miss Dulcie, if dat ever happen, Tyluh be kilt and you be de one what kilt 'im. Now you don' woant dat t'happen, does ya?"

"No, of course I don't. But why is it, Sophronie?"

"Why's what?"

"Why would anybody kill 'im for that? Just 'cause he's black?"

Sophronie shook her head. "Miss Dulcie, you knows as well as I knows. You don' need me 'splain it to ya."

"I reck'n so. Me'n Annie Lois were talkin' about that one day, but I still don't understand why it's like that. Y'all ain't never done nothin' t'hurt white folks, so why should white folks hate chall? Why's that, Sophronie?"

"Miss Dulcie, I bettuh not talk 'bout dat right now. Dat's sumpn you go'n' haf t'figger out fo yo'self."

She was more confused now than before, when Annie Lois tried to explain why white folks were superior to black people. All her life she'd had to keep others from knowing how she felt and, in doing so, she'd withdrawn farther and farther into herself, in constant fear that one day she'd do something that would get her in trouble. In spite of that, though, her cravings for what was "wrong" had intensified to such an extent that she had sometimes yielded to momentary lapses of judgment, times when she had convinced herself that satisfying the hunger was sufficient justification for whatever and however severe the consequences might be.

Her thoughts went now to the note in her purse. After all the arduous effort that went into its making, after all the months it had sustained her hopes that something wonderful would come from it, it had become, in so short a time, an obsolete piece of paper with no more value than a check you've written when there's no more money in your bank account.

Sophronie had not realized up until now the extent and intensity of Dulcie's emotional involvement in the situation, the evidence of which was now clearly discernible in every feature of her normally fair and youthful face. Nonetheless, her own empathy could go just so far. As she watched the transformation in Dulcie's appearance, she wondered how she would feel in a similar situation and what recourse there might be for eliminating it. She loved Dulcie now more than ever and wanted with all her heart and soul to help her. She not only felt some of her pain but, most of all, she felt a compelling obligation to rid her of it.

"Miss Dulcie," she said, rubbing her hands gently over Dulcie's, "I want chu t'promise me sumpn."

"What?"

"I woant chu t'promise me you'll take dat note out a yo' purse right now'n tear it up."

"How come? It ain't hurtin' nobody."

"Miss Dulcie, if'n you don't tear it up, you's go'n' keep on tryin' t'give it t'Tyluh. An' when and if'n you does, he go'n' do sumpn bad wif you, den dem white folks what killed Joe David Armstrong's go'n' do de very same thang t'Tyluh. Now, is dat what chu woants t'happen?"

"No, you know I don't want that t'happen."

"Well, den, you go on'n tear it up?"

She lowered her head and bit her lips together as she thought about what might happen now. "Awright," she said softly. "I promise t'tear it up. But chu ain't go'n' tell Annie Lois, are you?"

"Miss Dulcie, you knows I wouldn't do nuttin' like dat. I's tryin' t'hep ya, Honey, not hurt chu."

Dulcie wanted to cry but felt she'd better wait until she was alone. She must at least make an effort to do what Sophronie had asked her to do. She pushed herself away from the table and stood. "I reck'n I better go change clothes." It sounded as though she were talking to herself.

Sophronie was still sitting at the kitchen table when Annie Lois and Wanda Faye returned.

An hour or so later, while Sophronie was helping Annie Lois get supper ready, somebody knocked at the back door. Annie Lois asked Sophronie to see who it was.

"Mamma, come on. We's fine'ly go'n' home." Kat stuck her head inside and spoke to Annie Lois.

"Who drivin'?" Sophronie asked as she grabbed her bag of left-overs from lunch.

"I woant chu t'see fo' yo'self. You ain't go'n' b'lieve it."

As soon as they left, Annie Lois hurried up the front hall to see who it was. Dulcie heard and came out of her room.

"What is it, Annie Lois?" she asked.

"I don't know. Kat said Sophronie was goana be surprised to see who Mr. Wallace got to drive 'em home."

"Sophronie!" Annie Lois called from the open door, "who is it?"

Sophronie squeezed herself inside, then, before closing the door, said *"Holy Jesus!* I dittn' eben know he knowed how t'drive!"

"Who is it, Sophronie?"

"It be Tyluh, Miss Annie Lois!"

"Let me see!" Dulcie said, wedging her body between Annie Lois and the door facing.

"You cain't see 'im, Dulcie, it's too dark."

After Annie Lois closed the door and went back to the kitchen, Dulcie continued to look and listen until she could no longer hear the sound of the truck. Knowing how near he was just now was enough to forfeit everything Sophronie had just told her. It had been, after all, a false alarm, a reality-distorting nightmare. Her relief was instantaneous and overwhelming. Now she was fully awake again and able to resume her briefly aborted fantasy.

That night, after taking her bath and readying herself for bed, she took her purse from the dresser and, after lying down, put it beside her, outside the covers. Much to her surprise, doing so made the whole experience with Sophronie return with force enough to jeopardize the resolve she'd just made to ignore it. Her misgivings about the note returned with new fears, enough to realize she had no choice but to do what she'd promised Sophronie she would do. She got up, took the note out of the purse, opened it once more, then walked to the fireplace. Standing there suddenly reminded her of long ago, one time in particular when her mamma gave her a tall glass of castor oil, told her to drink it, *"Right this very minute, or get the beatin' of your life!"* Even then she waited. After her mamma left the room, she placed the glass of castor oil on the mantel and stared at it, hoping it would miraculously disappear.

Now, finally, she got up, walked to the dresser to get her purse. As she pulled it closer to her, she remembered and visualized the black rag doll burning under the black washpot, and what her mamma had said about black babies. Or was it Sophronie? Never mind, she would do it. As she stood in front of the fireplace, she opened the note once more, read it, folded it again, then dropped it inside her purse.

Next morning at breakfast, she was too excited to eat. Annie Lois reminded her that she must eat quickly or she'd miss the streetcar.

"Annie Lois," she said, trying to control her anxiety, " 'bout what time does Sophronie come every mornin'?"

"Oh, 'round eight o'clock or so. Why?"

"Nothin'. I was just wonderin'."

"Well, you better stop wonderin' and eat chure breakfast."

Between fast bites and swallows, she kept wondering. Finally, she asked, "What time does she usually go home?"

"You oughta know. Around four or four-thirty. That is, as long as ol' Jess was bringing' 'er. Why all of a sudden are you so interested in what time Sophronie gets here and goes home every day?"

"Oh, nothin'. I just wish I could get to see 'er and talk to 'er more'n I do." She had no intention of saying that but was glad she did, because she still wasn't sure about how to ask the next question without making Annie Lois suspicious. She propped her left elbow on the table and leaned her body over on it, taking big spoonsful of oatmeal, letting them stay on the back of her tongue before swallowing them as she wondered if she should ask anything else or just let it go at that.

Abruptly, she sat erect and pretended she had everything under control. So much so, that, before she asked her question, she thought it a good idea to compliment Annie Lois on the breakfast.

"Thanks, Honey. I'm glad you enjoyed it," Annie Lois said as she put the dishes in the sink.

Dulcie stood up and straightened the back of her dress. "By the

way, Annie Lois," she said as though something had just occurred
to her, "is Tyler go'n bring Sophronie and Kat from now on?"

"I'm not sure. I guess that'll depend on Jess, how bad off he
is. From what Sophronie told me, Mr. Wallace doesn't even know
what Jess's trouble is. It's possible that he might never be able to
go back to work."

What Annie Lois just said would determine Dulcie's emotional
state for a long time to come.

WHEN TYLER PULLED up in front of the house that same
morning, Sophronie, instead of getting out, kept sitting. She'd been
deep in thought even before she got in the truck earlier. She turned
her head and looked at Tyler for a while without saying anything.

"What chu got on yo' min', Miss Sophronie?"

She seemed as unsure about how to say what she was thinking
as Dulcie had been earlier. Once she knew how to begin, she took
a deep breath and let it out slowly and audibly. "Tyluh," she said,
"how much chu know 'bout Miss Dulcie?"

"I don't know much a nothin', Miss Sophronie, 'cept'n what
chu tol' me'n Mamma dat day out at cho place. I tol' you 'bout
seein' 'er at de streetcar station in Laurel."

"Dat all?"

He looked puzzled. "Yassum, I b'lieve dat's all. Oh, no," he
said, suddenly, squinting his eyes as he remembered. "I seed 'er
one day when Miss Dulcie be sick an' Miss Annie Lois ax me
t'stay wid 'er so she could call de doctuh."

"You mean you was in de same room wit Miss Dulcie?"

"Why, yessum. She be sick, you know, an' Miss Annie Lois be
real upset 'cause she feared Miss Dulcie was go'n' die."

"Did Miss Dulcie see you or know you was dere?"

"Why no, Miss Sophronie. I done tol' you, she be passed out
an' Miss Annie Lois be cryin', den come back sayin' she couldn't
git holt a de doctuh. Dat's all it was."

Sophronie knew she should get out but wasn't satisfied yet.

"Tyluh, you sho dey ain't nuttin' else? Now you think real hard."

"Well," he said, rubbing his chin and closing his eyes, "dey was
de time she fall down runnin' t'catch de streetcar an' I pick her

up. Dat's when de driver, he come out dere an' say he go'n' kill me if'n he ever see me touch her or any udder white woman. Dat's all, Miss Sophronie. You think I done wrong pickin' 'er up?"

"You done right, Tyluh, but chu oughta know white folks ain't go'n' put up wid nuttin' like dat. You seed what dey did t'Joe David, dittn't chu?"

"I ditt't see it, but I hyeard 'bout it."

"I's really wuhr'ed 'bout sumpn, Tyluh. I's so 'fraid Miss Dulcie's goan git chu in a heap a trouble. Right now you's in a bad, bad sit'chasion. I mean *real* bad, like you be kilt b'fo' you eben know what happened."

She could see he wanted to say something but seemed afraid. He kept running his hands around the steering wheel with his eyes closed, nodding his head back and forth.

"You got sumpn else you woana tell me?"

"Yessum, I does,'cause it be botherin' me lately."

"And what's dat, Tyluh?"

"Well," he said, "some a de fellows what wuhks up at de ice house say Miss Dulcie be comin' up dere sometime an' ax about me. Dey tell me I bettuh make huh stop doin' it, but I don't know how, Miss Sophronie. I know it be dangerous. How come she do dat, you reck'n?"

"I s'peck fo' a whole lot a reasons. She don't have no white friends. You know dat. Dey mostly makes fun of 'er. Dey always has. Dat's one reason why she likes us 'cause we unnerstands an' sympathizes wid 'er. You 'member what I tol' you 'bout de time huh'n Roscoe be playin' under dey house buck-skin nekkid, don't chu?"

"Yessum, an' how huh mamma beat 'er so bad."

"Po' little ol' thang, I don't know how she live t'be dis old. But Tyluh, you gotta think about cho'self an' yo' po' ol' mamma if'n you got choself mixed up in sumpn lak dat. Dat's why I want chu t'promise me right now dat chu'll keep away fum Miss Dulcie, no matter how much she try t'see ya. Will you promise me dat? I ain't go'n' have no peace a mine whatsoever 'till you does. Will you, Tyluh?"

"Yessum, I promise. Don't chu worry 'bout me. I knows bettuh."

* * *

ANNIE LOIS HAD just finished giving Wanda Faye her bath when Sophronie trudged up the back steps and into the kitchen.

"I saw you and Tyler talkin' out there," Annie Lois said. "Did you find out anything else about Jess? What his trouble might be?"

"No'm, Tyluh, he don' know. He just be glad he got a job."

Annie Lois poured herself and Sophronie a cup of coffee, then sat down with a smile on her face.

"You looks happy, Miss Annie Lois."

"I am, Sophronie, I really am. I don't know why exactly, but chu know how little things sometimes can make you feel good."

"Yassum."

"For instance, Dulcie surprised me a while ago. She asked me all about what time you come every mornin' and leave every evenin', and when I asked 'er why she was so curious, she said she wished she could get to talk with you more. Did you and Dulcie have a good visit yesterday before Wanda Faye and I got home?"

Little did Annie Lois know that what she said, instead of making Sophronie feel good, made her feel worse. "Yassum," she said finally, "we really did. We talk about evuhthang, you might say."

"She loves you so much, Sophronie. You know that, don't chu?"

"I sho does. An' I loves huh, too, Miss Annie Lois. I has t'be honest wif you, though, Miss Annie Lois. I cain't hep feelin' sorry fo' that po' chile. She's had such a bad time all huh life, it seem."

"I understand. I appreciate that very much. Anyway, maybe one of these days things'll work out so y'all can spend more time together."

Sophronie did not answer. Her face belied the sudden change in her feelings, the reactivated concern and fear. Distractedly, she put the coffee cup down, then, with both hands pushing with all her strength against the table, stood up. As she tried to brace herself against the chair, she gave a long, low moan, which Annie Lois might easily have construed as simply an expression of the pain in her body rather than the pain in her soul.

— f i f t e e n —

IT TOOK MARCUS Tatum only two weeks to convince the city officials that Bo Arthur Bilbo should be committed to the regional reformatory at Collinsville. After reminding them of some of the offenses they already knew about, he told them what he had just learned from Bo Arthur's grandma. Some of them seemed shocked, others did not. "Bo Arthur needs the strictest kind of discipline and Eula Bilbo isn't able to give it to 'im. As far as I'm concerned, we have no other choice. The Collinsville Reformatory is the only place he's goin' to get it."

After having rescued Dulcie that day and taking her home later, Marcus Tatum suggested to Annie Lois that she file an official complaint against Bo Arthur, and, although she dreaded doing it, she knew some drastic means of preventing further assaults on Dulcie were necessary and said she would do it.

Later that same evening, after talking with Annie Lois, Superintendent Tatum drove out to Eula Bilbo's place. They sat in the lamp-lit living room, she with a handkerchief that she dabbed from time to time at her eyes or her nose and a drawn and weary look on her face. When he told her Annie Lois was going to file the complaint against Bo Arthur, she put her hands to her face and cried.

"Bo Arthur needs to be in the reformatory, Miss Eula. You've done your best but it's gonna take more than that. It's not like being jailed, you know. Whenever the folks at Collinsville think he's ready to be a decent member of society, they'll let 'im out. It won't be forever. At least I hope not."

Eula wiped her eyes and stood up. "When are they plannin' on comin' t'git 'im?"

"I'm not sure yet, Miss Eula, but I'll let you know in plenty of time."

At ten o'clock next morning, Marcus Tatum told his secretary he had some important business to take care of at City Hall. Mayor Guy Bailey listened but appeared to be less than disturbed or even interested in what the school superintendent was telling him, but promised he would take the matter up with the city council next week.

The superintendent, in the meantime, called a hasty meeting of the school board. Three of the members raised questions and expressed concern that sending Bo Arthur to Collinsville would be disproportionate punishment for what they considered nothing more than "youthful, good-natured teasing" on Bo Arthur's part.

Chairman Frank Haley Bankston, visually and orally noncommittal except when someone asked for permission to speak, listened as he did in court, head lowered and eyes closed, while his mind sifted and gauged the emotional tenor of each member in order to assess his chances at any particular moment to get the majority of them to see things his way.

Marcus Tatum had already given his report of the assault on Dulcie Dykes which he witnessed and of his visit yesterday with Eula Bilbo. As soon as he sat down, several of the members voiced their outrage while others continued to justify and condone what they had just heard, suggesting that Bo Arthur was not really to blame for the way he was, and pleading with the committee as a whole to find some kinder way of punishing him.

Frank Haley straightened and thumped a few times on the table top. "Before we have a motion, I think I should say a few things that are on my mind. I realize this isn't strict parliamentary custom, but I think we all agree that our sessions need not be." He stood and walked around to the front of the table. "You might like to know that I had a long and revealing conversation with Bo Arthur only yesterday afternoon. Without telling you everything that was said, I would like you to know that, as a result of that conversation, I am deeply concerned and troubled about Bo Arthur. I had heard on several previous occasions some of the strange and inhumane things he's done since he's been living with his grandmother Bilbo, and, more seriously, the way his behavior has turned most of the young girls against him. As I talked with him yesterday, I was convinced that he is a malicious young man with a total disregard for other people and an intense and alarming inclination toward violence of the worst sort. He is, I can confirm, a liar of highly developed skill, and I am convinced, as some of you seem to be, that he is not the kind of person he pretends to be."

He stopped and walked back around the table, then leaned over it and looked directly at one and then another of the members before continuing. "We realize that all we can do today is to recommend to the city and county officials that Bo Arthur, for his own good and for the good of this community, be committed to the Collinsville Reformatory as soon as possible."

He waited for the audible reaction to subside. "I have only this to say to each and every one of you. Either you choose to commit Bo Arthur to the reformatory now, or expect to see him in the very near future committed, instead, to prison for life or possibly for execution. That's all I have to say. Is anybody ready to make a motion on this matter?"

The show of only one more hand would have made the decision unanimous.

Six days later, with Annis Lois' complaint in hand, Marcus Tatum presented the matter, along with the school board's recommendation, to members of both the city and the county governments. After over two hours of embittered debate, only six of the eighteen members had been convinced that the proposal was a just and appropriate solution for the Bo Arthur problem. Frank Haley Bankston, county attorney, asked that he might be permitted to speak. Granted the permission, he told the committee that he alone had some vital and pertinent information which he felt they should know about.

At three-thirty p.m., the matter was settled. Bo Arthur would be committed to Collinsville Reformatory on Monday, the second day of February, 1924. The legal finalization of the process would be left to Frank Haley Bankston.

MID-MORNING OF THE following day, when he knew Bo Arthur was in school, Marcus Tatum drove out again to see Eula Bilbo. When he told her Bo Arthur would be committed to

Collinsville on February the second, she collapsed into a chair. "Dear God," she cried into the palms of her hands, "why has it come to this? Why, why, O God?"

Marcus bent down and put his arm around her shoulder. "Everybody knows you did all you could to help Bo Arthur, but I'm afraid it was too late. Nobody will blame you for what's happened and neither will God. I hope you will find some comfort in knowing Bo Arthur will be a better person when he comes out."

She dried her eyes, then sat silent for a while, wondering if this were really happening and, if so, how she would ever live through it. She thought of her son Brandon and wished with all her heart and soul that he were here, that he had never left.

"I wish I could do somethin' to help, Miss Eula. You can be sure all of those who know and love you will be prayin' for you and for Bo Arthur. I can assure you I will."

Her eyes were fixed on something across the room, then suddenly she straightened, took a deep breath, drew her shoulders back and laid her clasped hands slowly and firmly on her knees. "Who's go'n' come git 'im?"

"It'll either be Sheriff Lee Anderson or one of his deputies."

"An' when d'you reck'n he'll git' chere? An' how can I make sure Bo Arthur'll be t'home?"

"What we'll do is this, Miss Eula. The day before, when Bo Arthur's in school, Sheriff Anderson or somebody else'll come out here to let you know exactly when to expect 'em next mornin'."

"But what if Bo Arthur finds out in the meantime what's go'n on?"

"I don't believe he will, Miss Eula. Everybody who knows has been warned not to say anything to anybody else. Now do you have any more questions? Are you goana be all right?"

She covered her mouth with the handkerchief, closed her eyes, and slowly and repeatedly nodded her head.

EULA BILBO PULLED the bed clothes up to her face and listened to the rain hitting the tin roof, hoping that, by God's intervention, she might be able to go to sleep for only a little while. She had managed by the hardest effort to get through the long day without

falling apart emotionally, though she felt that Bo Arthur had sometimes sensed that something was wrong. It was at such times that
she forced herself, as well as she could, to look and act normally.

All day he had seemed distracted and frequently went outside
and disappeared. She kept wondering where he might be, yet she
was glad to have the house to herself for a while so she could
begin learning how to be alone again. At other times he lay on a
quilt in front of the fireplace in his room, reading *The Adventures
of Tom Sawyer*, a required reading assignment in his English class.
On the way to her room that night, she stopped at his door and
told him he should be in bed.

The loud ticking of the alarm clock on the other side of the bed
seemed at times to be trying to outdo the metallic patter on the
roof and, at others, to be in perfect synchronization and harmony
with it. She had learned long ago that if you try to force sleep on
yourself you will only repel it and, also, that you can get through
a whole day without sleep if you have to. She had lived alone for
many years and had grown accustomed to it, had even convinced
herself that living alone had some distinct advantages, but now, in
the space of a few years, she had come to rely on someone else's
presence in her house and in her life. She faced the fact long ago
that one's aloneness becomes more acute with age and, for that
very reason, yields more easily and quickly to another person's
presence, even if for only a short time.

She wondered now if she had done the right thing by telling
Myrtis and others about how Bo Arthur was acting and, in
unfailing sequence, if she could and should have been more understanding of his problems and less strict in the way she had treated
him. Now that things had reached this irreversible stage, her
deepest concern and sorrow was for the guilt she felt for the way
things had turned out. No matter how much Bo Arthur deserved
the punishment of being committed to the reformatory, she could
feel only the severest anguish at having him taken away.

She eased out of bed, put her robe on, then tip-toed down
to Bo Arthur's room. The door was slightly ajar, so she gently
pushed it open a little farther to see him better. He was lying on
his right side, facing the window, with the covers pushed down to

his feet. He looked so innocent, so peaceful and unsuspecting. As she watched, she thought about all the unhappiness he had felt in his lifetime, all of the unparented loneliness, and all the things that had turned him into a wild and dangerous young man. She wanted to go over and wrap her arms around him and tell him how much she loved him, no matter what he'd done, to tell him how sorry she was for what she had done to hurt him, to assure him that he was going to be a better and happier person later, and that she would do everything in her power to make it so. She closed her eyes and tried to keep from crying, knowing there was nothing she could do to prevent what was about to happen.

No use to go back to bed. She might as well get dressed and be about her normal chores, to begin the hard job of strengthening herself against seven o'clock, when the deputy said he would come to get Bo Arthur, and the still harder job of trying not to show in any way that she knew what was going to happen. A sudden pain hit somewhere around her heart, suggesting to her that she was indisputably, in every respect, a traitor.

With lamp in hand, she went quietly to the kitchen and started a fire in the stove, made the coffee, then sat down at the table with her Bible to do some reading and praying. In a few minutes, she heard Bo Arthur stirring in his room. When he walked into the kitchen, she was surprised.

"Did I wake you up?"

"No m'am. I just decided t'git on up. An' why you up so early?"

She marked her place in the Bible. "Well, I just figgered it'd done all the rainin' it was go'n do, so I might as well do the wash as usual. You want some coffee, or your breakfast?" she asked. It was so hard to do, she felt he must have noticed.

"Naw. You go on with your readin'. I think I'll go outside for a while."

The first faint signs of dawn were comforting, something of the good and normal world which had not been affected in any way by what was about to happen. How remarkable, she thought, that the coming of dawn, like other of God's wonders, assumed increased meaning and beauty inversely to the emptiness and hopelessness she was feeling.

She read, but she did not perceive. Her thoughts were with him, wherever he was out there and whatever he was doing. She closed her Bible, prayed, then stood up and stretched. She couldn't resist. She wanted to see where he was. She walked slowly and softly to the back door and saw him sitting under the pecan tree. He had his right arm around Dodger, and Dodger had his head resting on Bo Arthur's shoulder. Her hands went quickly over her mouth and she cried convulsively.

Later, while Bo Arthur pumped the clothes-washing water and set the fire under the washpot, Eula cooked their breakfast. Her first impulse was to cook Bo Arthur's favorite fried pork sausage and pancakes, but decided to have, instead, the usual bacon, scrambled eggs, grits, and biscuits. The feeble effort in the direction of making things seem normal suggested, also, that she prepare the usual paper bag lunch for Bo Arthur, even though she knew she would have to eat it later. As she did so, the ticking of the big alarm clock on the window sill swam in and out of her consciousness, causing her heart to beat faster and her hands to shake and a growing tightness to press the walls of her chest.

It was a quarter past six when she finished with the breakfast dishes. She wondered what to do next. Bo Arthur had walked outside to stoke the fire around the washpot. He stopped momentarily in the kitchen as he came back in and looked at her as though he sensed something unusual. Her instant reaction was to point to the clock.

"You best clean yourself up now," she said, taking the bagged lunch from the stove and laying it on the table. "As soon as I'm finished in hyere, I'm goan'n'git started on the wash out chonder."

LEANING FORWARD OVER the rub-board, Eula drew the overalls back and forth against the raised metal furrows, her knuckles red and sore, and stopped from time to time just long enough to run the big bar of Octagon soap over them for more lather. At other times, she straightened, wiped the back of her soap-lathered wrist across her forehead and looked out at the road. The built-in clock inside her mind told her it was time for the deputy to come, and the gnawing emptiness inside her body told her that what was about to happen would be as bad as, and maybe worse than, what she had feared.

Bo Arthur came out the back door with his books and lunch. "I'm go'n on t'school, Granny."

"No, no!" She couldn't help the way it came out. "It's not time t'go, is it, Bo Arthur?"

"Yessum."

She felt he must suspect something. She had feared so long that something might go wrong. "Well, ain't chu got time t'draw me some more rinse water?

"I done drawed it, Granny."

"But I need some more. I spilt some a while ago. Would ju pump me two or three more buckets?"

He laid his books and lunch on the step. As he pumped the water, Dodger tried to get his attention by pulling on his shoe laces. At one point, he stopped, knelt down to play with Dodger, then suddenly jumped up as he heard the truck coming up the gravel road to the house. Dodger took off around the house to the front yard.

The sharp pain at the base of her spine, when she tried to straighten suddenly, reminded Eula that she had been bent over too long in one position. Wiping her hands distractedly with the end of her apron, she limped around the house, stopping when she saw the short, stocky man getting out of the truck.

Bo Arthur, as though forewarned, stood still and listened without seeing. "Good-mornin', Miss Eula," the man said.

She nodded slowly, wiping her forehead with the back of her hand. "What can I do for you?"

He opened the gate and smiled as he took off his hat. "Miss Eula, I'm Deputy Tracy Brand from the county sheriff's office. I've come t'git Bo Arthur."

"How come?"

He seemed surprised that she should ask. "Miss Eula, I thought you knew awready."

She closed her eyes and waited a few moments before nodding her head in the direction of the back yard.

As the deputy started in that direction, she reached out and grabbed his arm. "You won't hurt 'im, will you? Please, please don't hurt 'im!"

He put his other hand on her shoulder. "No, m'am, I ain't go'n' hurt 'im. My orders are just t'bring 'im down town."

She suddenly went rigid, straightening in spite of the pain, bracing herself.

Dodger, his curiosity apparently satisfied, suddenly darted off around the back of the house and beyond.

Tracy Brand knew about young boys and dogs. No need to hurry. He knew Dodger would let him know where Bo Arthur was. The privy was set back amongst a grove of oak and sweet gum trees, just beyond a narrow, bridge-covered ditch, which Dodger ignored in his haste. As soon as he reached the privy, he jumped upright against the door and barked and whined without stopping.

Deputy Tracy Brand crossed the bridge and motioned Dodger aside. "Come on out, Bo Arthur," he said, pulling on the door handle just enough to see that it was locked. He knocked. "I ain't go'n' hurt chu, Bo Arthur. All I'm s'posed t'do is take you t'town with me."

"What for?"

"I really don't know, Bo Arthur. But whatever it is, they ain't go'n' hurt chu."

Bo Arthur opened the door just far enough to wedge himself cautiously out of it.

Tracy grabbed Bo Arthur's right wrist with one hand and shut the privy door with the other. "We best be goin', Son. Now, you ain't go'n' try nothin' funny, are you?"

Bo Arthur shook his head and leaned over to rub Dodger's head. He was already trying to decide how to handle the situation.

When they approached the back yard, Eula was still sitting on the step. When Tracy felt the muscle in Bo Arthur's arm constrict, he tightened his hand and pulled him closer to him.

"What's go'n' happen now?" Eula asked, getting slowly up as they neared. "He's go'n' take me t'town, Granny," Bo Arthur said, trying to sound unconcerned. "Don't chu worry. I'll be back d'reckly."

She held the sack lunch out to him. "Here, you better take sumpn t'eat." As he reached for it, Tracy pulled him back. "He won't be needin' that, Miss Eula. They'll give 'im sumpn t'eat later."

She wanted to hug his neck and hold him close, but she knew it would only make matters worse. As they walked out to the truck, Dodger ran beside them, close to Bo Arthur's legs, then stood looking for a long time after they drove away.

"TRACY, THE SHERIFF said t'tell you he won't be comin' in till later this mornin'," Paula Prine, the receptionist, said. "Somebody else is comin' over after a while, he said, t'take care of everything. Bo Arthur, you go on in the office and wait till he comes. That door right chonder. That's it. It'll only be a few minutes."

"I better check the doors," Tracy said to Paula with a wink.

When he came back out, Paula stopped what she was doing, lit up a cigarette, and leaned forward on her elbows. "I'll swanee," she said, "Just t'look at 'im, you'd never guess he had a bad bone in his body."

"Just between me'n you, I don't think he needs t'be put in the reformatory. He didn't give me a bit a trouble bringin' 'im in."

"How long you reck'n he'll have t'stay?"

"I really don't know. I think that's up to Bo Arthur. If he does right and don't cause no trouble, they might not keep 'im very long."

Bo Arthur examined everything on the sheriff's desk and read all the notices on the bulletin board, then sat down and rested his head against the wall behind him. He wasn't afraid or, at least, he told himself he wasn't. Although he didn't know what was going to happen, the uncertainty and mystery of it excited him and made him feel important and liberated. Removed now from home and school, he realized how closely confined he'd been kept, how watched-over, forced to do things he didn't want to do, threatened constantly by the fear that a sudden, unexpected mental lapse might make him say or do something or look a certain way that would let people know what he was really thinking.

Tom Sawyer suddenly came to mind. He laughed as he recalled some of what he'd read last night in front of the fireplace. Even as he'd read, he'd longed to be with Tom, and now, more than ever. He closed his eyes and pretended he was there, lying face-up on a raft, a warped, worn-out straw hat covering his eyes, and, from over on and below the wooded bank, the incessant sound of birds, frogs, and crickets, and of people working, and talking, and laughing like none of the people he'd ever heard talk and laugh before.

The sound of the slow opening of the door and the talking just beyond dispelled the reverie. The shock was too sudden and severe for him to put on his other face. His hands, tightened around the arm rests of the chair, suddenly became more expressive than his face.

"Well, Bo Arthur," Frank Haley Bankston said as he slowly shut the door behind him, "seems your sins have found you out."

Bo Arthur heard but didn't perceive. He was in transition. The rickety raft was now his lumpy childhood bed, and the muddy river water was the hollow boarded floor of the hall leading back and forth to his mamma's bedroom. Remembering what he had seen and heard was one thing; now he did what he had tried consciously to avoid doing heretofore. He pictured this despicable man in bed with his mamma and imagined what transpired on those nights when they were together. Now he could feel the full force of his anger setting fire to his insides.

"We're goana take you to Collinsville and put chu in the Reformatory. You've had every opportunity to . . ."

Bo Arthur jumped out of the chair. "An' who the hell d'you think you are to do that?"

"I'm the county attorney and have been given full authority to do what I'm doin'. You've deliberately defied authority heretofore, so now we're putting you in a place where you'll be made to do right. And until you do, you will stay there. Do you understand?"

"An' I s'pose you ain't never done nothin' wrong."

"Yes, young man, I have done wrong things in my lifetime, but I stopped doin' 'em when I asked God to forgive me and He did."

"How long ago was that?"

"A long time ago. That's when I accepted Jesus as my savior and changed my whole life."

"How old were you?"

"I had just celebrated my twenty-second birthday. Some time ago, you see."

Once Bo Arthur had figured it out, he said, "You mean t'tell me you ain't done nothin' wrong since then?"

"No, that's not what I mean at all. I mean I haven't done anything seriously wrong since I accepted Jesus as my savior. You see, that's where you and I are different. I promised God I'd change the way I lived, but you've never done that. That's why you're being sent to Collinsville, where you'll have to change your ways if you ever want to get out."

Bo Arthur pushed himself up and out of the chair, then crossed his arms over his chest. "Man, I've been wantin' t'tell you sumpn ever since I seen you over at the courthouse. From the moment you said the very first word, I knew I'd heard that voice before. An' then when I seen one a your legs was shorter'n th' other'n, I knew I was right."

"Right about what, Bo Arthur?" Frank Haley asked, putting the papers back in his briefcase and shuffling the other things on the desk as though looking for something.

Bo Arthur walked to the front of the desk and leaned over it, a malicious, gloating look on his face. "I knew I'd seen and heard you before."

Frank Haley's smile seemed to say he thought Bo Arthur was kidding and that he was amused by it. "Of course you've seen me before. I'm seen in public all the time. After all, I am a lawyer, and you know lawyers are everywhere."

"That ain't what I mean. What I mean is that you been preachin' t'me about how bad I am and how I oughta be saved, when you're just as bad as I am. Naw, you're worser than I am. You know why?"

"Because I'm the one sendin' you to Collinsville? Is that why I'm so bad?"

"Naw it ain't. But let me ask you sumpn. Have you ever been t'my house?"

"You mean to Miss Eula's?"

"No. I mean to the house where I used t'live?"

"To the best of my knowledge, I was never in your house, Bo Arthur."

"That's a lie, Mister, and you know it!"

"It is not a lie. I was never in your house and that's the end of the story."

"Not quite, it ain't. It don't end till I tell you the rest of it. And the rest of it is that you just lied again. You was in my house 'cause I seen you. You was walkin' back up the hall from my mamma's bedroom late one night. And Mister, you were a lot older'n twenty-two!"

Frank Haley threw the briefcase onto a chair, grabbed Bo Arthur with both hands around the neck, shook him violently, then kicked on the door with his elevator shoe. Bo Arthur tried to get free by running his arms between Frank Haley's, found he couldn't do it, then started kicking and spitting out obscenities one after the other.

Tracy Brand, who, with Paula Prine, had been listening at the door, finally got it open. "Mr. Bankston," he said, "Take it easy! You don't woana hurt 'im. Let me have 'im."

Frank Haley pushed Bo Arthur through the door. "Take this no-good, low-down scoundrel outside and shackle 'im if you have to. As soon as I get all the paperwork together, you'll be ready to go."

Paula hurried over to the desk and started assembling all the documents that would be sent to Collinsville. Frank Haley went back inside the office for his briefcase and stopped long enough to steady his nerves. He realized he had almost lost total control. When he came out a few minutes later, he told Paula he needed one more document to send to Collinsville. "I want chu to write a short note to Wendell Wansley, the warden of the reformatory."

Paula uncovered the typewriter, inserted a piece of paper and waited.

"Better do it in triplicate," Frank Haley said.

"Is that two l's in Wendell or one?" she asked.

"Two. Simply say that henceforth all correspondence having to do with Bo Arthur Bilbo should be sent directly and only to me. Sign it, Frank Haley Bankston, County Attorney, Jones in parenthesis, post office box 248, etc., etc."

When Paula finished, she handed it to Frank Haley to sign, then slipped it inside the manila envelope with the other documents.

"I'd appreciate it if you'd take 'em out there," he said. "I need to get back to my office."

As she handed Tracy the documents, she gently touched Bo Arthur's right shoulder. He looked surprised. "Good luck, Bo Arthur," she said hoarsely.

He shook his head and smiled as though nothing unusual had happened.

— s i x t e e n —

EACH FRIDAY, WHEN Dulcie and Melissa went to Voncille's house, they passed in front of Sacred Heart Catholic Church. On this particular Friday, as they passed, they noticed that one of the heavy double doors to the sanctuary was slightly open. Although they'd often passed the church, they had never had any desire to go inside.

Melissa had run ahead of Dulcie and, upon seeing the open door, ran up the steps, stopping at the top to see if Dulcie was coming too.

"Melissa!" Dulcie hollered as loud as she could. "Don't chu go in there! You ain't s'posed t'go in there."

Melissa ignored the warning, walked slowly up to the open door and peeped in. The first thing she felt was the cool air from inside and the heavy smell of incense. When she heard and felt Dulcie's heavy breathing behind her, she turned around.

"Look in there, Dulcie, how pretty it is."

"We ain't s'posed t'be lookin' in there, Melissa. Now you come on out a there this minute."

"But I woana see what it looks like inside. Come on, Dulcie, let's go on in."

"Melissa! I done tol' ju we ain't s'posed t'go inside a catholic church."

"That ain't so! Mother said it's all right t'go to any church you woanted to."

"No, Melissa, that ain't so, and d'you know why?"

"Why?"

" 'Cause them catholics worship statues, that's why. And that ain't right, Annie Lois said." She tried to pull Melissa back.

Melissa resisted. "But we ain't goin' in there t'go t'church. An' stop pullin' on me!"

That sounded right, Dulcie thought. She shoved Melissa out of her way, then opened the door a little farther so she could slide through.

"What's that funny odor?" Melissa whispered as she came inside.

"I don't know, but ain't it pretty!"

Melissa gave a hasty look around, then tugged at Dulcie's arm. "Dulcie, I don't like it in here," she said irritably. "Let's go."

"Shhhh!" Dulcie signaled with a finger over her mouth. "No," she said aloud, then leaned over and whispered in Melissa's ear, "I tell you what. You go on over to Aunt Cille's house an' play with the goldfish, then I'll come over there in a few minutes. You hear?"

"No, I ain't! I ain't goin' unless you go too. And if you don't, I'm go'n' tell Mother when we get home."

Dulcie pushed her outside. "Melissa, why is it you always get mad about ever'thing I do? Now, it ain't go'n' kill you t'walk to Aunt Cille's house by yourself. My Lord, it's just over yonder 'cross the street."

Melissa looked around to make sure but still seemed reluctant to give in "Well, how long b'fore you go'n' come?"

"Just a few minutes. I promise, Melissa. I won't be long."

"Well, you sure better come on over real soon or I'm go'n' tell Mother on you."

After Melissa left, Dulcie leaned forward against the back of the last pew in the middle section and looked from one window to another where the stations of the cross were depicted in brilliant colors, not at all sure about what they meant, then to the domed ceiling, a mosaic representation of the birth of Christ in pale shades, primarily of green, blue, and yellow. She strained her eyes so hard to see and stood so long that her neck began to hurt. She needed to sit down. As she tried to slip into the pew, she tripped over the prayer rail and almost fell. She brushed her skirt down around her legs and held her purse tightly against her stomach.

The overall effect was incomprehensible. At first, she sat stiffly erect, tense all over, holding her purse, which had now become the common denominator, something to touch and, by touching, to know she was still awake, still alive. She thought of the Baptist church she'd gone to all of her life, how simple it was and how like a place of fear it had always been. She had dreaded every Sunday of her life, knowing that she would be made to feel even more different to other people than she normally felt. Every time the preacher flung his arms in the air as he described the fires of hell awaiting every sinner in the world, she felt he was looking right at her. Not without cause, too, because she usually unintentionally did something that displeased her mamma, and if it displeased her mamma, it more than likely displeased God. She felt sometimes that God had actually singled her out as an example to others who were trying to be good.

One Sunday morning, when she was feeling relatively at peace with the world, and the preacher asked the congregation to stand and sing hymn number 114, *Softly and Tenderly, Jesus is Calling*, she suddenly wanted to sing as she'd never been brave enough to sing before. It was a hymn she had always loved, even though for reasons she couldn't put into words. When the refrain came, she suddenly felt something so wonderful and personal that she instinctively needed to express it. "Come home, come home, ye who are weary, come home." The sound of Dulcie's strident and unwieldy voice alarmed Dora Dykes. She laid her hymnal down with one hand, then pushed Dulcie onto the seat with the other, pinched her arm and said, loud enough for everybody to hear, "Don't chu *dare* make another sound!"

She thought about how much she disliked Brother Stanwell, who'd been their preacher for as long as she could remember. Often, as she, Annie Lois, and her mother were leaving the church after Sunday morning service, he would put a heavy hand on her shoulder and shake her a few times while saying, without exception and so everybody could hear, "Dulcie, your Mamma tells me you've been a bad little girl. Don' chu think you oughta stop lettin' the devil tell you what t'do?"

Her dislike for Brother Stanwell increased with every passing Sunday. Most of all she remembered her baptism at the age of ten. The night following a beautiful Saturday in late April, the weather had changed from mild to unseasonably cold. She and eleven other children were taken in wagons out to Beaver Dam, where they were mercilessly baptized in the icy, murky water. She had stood at her mother's side, trembling in fear and from the cold as she watched the first six children immersed, then dried off. They all wore white sheets sewn together for the special ceremony, over which they wore coats to protect themselves from the cold before and after being baptized. When Dulcie would pull the collar of her coat closer around her neck, her mamma, thinking she was trying to break away, would roughly pull her back and shake her.

Brother Stanwell's hands were ghostly white from the cold water, but he didn't seem to mind. Every time he pushed another of the unwilling charges under, he threw his shoulders back and turned his closed eyes skyward as though he expected at any moment to hear God speak from a cloud, commending him for the wonderful work he was doing for the Kingdom, then he'd say, at the top of his raspy voice for all to hear, "*Satan, I command you now, in the name of Jesus Christ, let go of this sinner!*" Every time he said it, Dulcie hated him more and more.

Brother Stanwell walked deliberately over to where she and Dora Dykes were standing, reached out and grabbed her right hand and pulled her to him. "All right, Dulcie," he said, "it's your turn."

When Dulcie resisted, screaming and kicking, trying to pull away from him, her mamma grabbed her, squeezed her sharp fingertips into both of her shoulders, then shoved her forward to where Brother Stanwell was waiting with open arms. He pulled her all the way into the water, then pushed her head down and under. When she tried to come up, he sent her under again, then, finally, while she struggled and almost drowned, he threw his head back and gave an exultant cry, "*I baptize thee, Dulcie Dykes, in the name of Jesus Christ; Satan, let her go!*"

Dulcie, having forgotten in her fear to hold her breath when pushed under the last time, had strangled, then had to be carried bodily over to where her mamma was waiting, towel in hand. As Dora Dykes walked her over behind the wagon, where the drying took place, the other children laughed, pointing their fingers and making faces at Dulcie. Dora made her get back in the wagon, then handed her her coat. "Now put this on and button it up b'fore you catch cold. *And stop that whinin'!*"

* * *

DULCIE KNEW SHE should leave but didn't want to. Even though she did not understand most of what she saw, the quietness and beauty of the little chapel made her feel good all over. From time to time, when she took a deep breath in order to smell the wonderful incense, she felt as though nothing existed just beyond those closed doors out front. This must be the way Heaven looks and feels, she thought. She looked up again at the ceiling. It might as well have been God sitting up there for all she knew.

Suddenly she wanted to pray but didn't know how. She closed her eyes and tried as hard as she could to say something God would hear, but to no avail. Cautiously she turned her head in all directions to see if maybe somebody had come in without her knowing it, then eased out of the pew into the aisle. She must be careful, she must not make a sound, because she was doing something wrong, she shouldn't even be here. It felt as though the thick red carpet sank a full inch every time she put a foot down, and the smell of the incense seemed to get stronger as she neared the altar. Every few steps, she stopped and checked to see if she was still alone. That's when she realized just how scared she was and that her whole body had become so light she could fly right up to the ceiling.

She tip-toed over to the front of the altar and looked with squinted eyes at the huge cross with Jesus on it. He looked so real! She knew about Him and, from what she'd been told all her life, He knew about her. How wonderful that made her feel! Then she realized that He might possibly be the only one who knew about her and how she really felt. Her eyes began to burn. Still not sure about how to pray, she brought both hands up, with her purse on her right arm, and pressed them close to her body, then, looking up at the huge crucifix, with a small, timid movement of her right hand, she waved.

"Hey, Jesus!"

FATHER MICHAEL SERANNO, at the age of fifty-six, with twenty-seven of those years having been spent in the priesthood, had developed a keen intuitive sense about many things in general and one thing in particular. If someone were praying inside the chapel, he could feel that person's presence, even though he might be doing something somewhere else at the time. He had been working on a requisition to be submitted to the board next week when he gradually became aware that someone was in the chapel. If the acoustics in the chapel had not been so excellent, he might not have heard Dulcie speaking to Jesus. As soon as he heard her leave, he pushed the door to the chapel open just enough to see the other door close. He would later wonder about and ask himself why he was so concerned to see who it had been. He made sure she had gone before he walked out to the front of the church.

Dulcie was walking with her head down, holding her purse with both hands in front of her.

Dulcie stayed on Father Seranno's mind the rest of the day. He wondered where he'd seen her before. That evening, as he was walking from the Rectory to the Church, Dulcie and Melissa walked by. He stopped abruptly and watched. The older girl was the one. But there was something different about her. She was troubled. He knew instinctively, just as he had known earlier that she was in the sanctuary.

In Cefalu', Sicily, he was born into, had been brought up in, and was surrounded on all sides by unmitigated human suffering. Even before he joined the priesthood, he had made the elimination of human suffering the singular purpose of his life, knowing that he would need to live more than a thousand lifetimes to make any difference at all, and realizing further that, no matter what he did, the suffering would never end. At the age of seventeen, after a full week of fasting, he made a vow to God that he would, from that day forward, dedicate his life to the alleviation and, if possible, the elimination of whatever part of human suffering he would encounter as long as he lived, tending to those who needed it the full measure of his love and concern in ways materialistic as well as spiritual.

THINGS WERE DIFFERENT when Dulcie and Melissa got to Voncille's house the following Friday. First of all, Voncille greeted them both at the back door, looking fresher than usual, even gently patting Dulcie's shoulder as she came in. Next, she gave Melissa a big hug and a kiss, then reached over on the kitchen table and picked up the Sears, Roebuck catalog.

"Guess what, little lady?" she said, fumbling through the pages. Having found what she was looking for, she held the book so Melissa could see. "Looka there!" she said, pointing to a little girl in a pinafore dress with puff sleeves and ribbons around the collar.

Melissa looked at the picture, then at Voncille. "I don't know what chu mean, Aunt Cille."

"Well, don't chu like it? That's the dress I'm go'n' make you for your birthday. Ain't it pretty?"

"Are you really? When, Aunt Cille?"

"Right this minute!" she said, laying the catalog on the table. "Come on in my bedroom where my machine is so I can get chu measured."

Dulcie watched as the measuring was done and the figures written on a piece of tablet paper, and suddenly decided it was a good time to slip away and go to the church.

SHE SLOWLY PULLED the door open and tiptoed inside, then stood behind the back pew, remembering and still wondering what it all meant and why she felt so good just being there. She wedged and grunted her body into the back pew, wincing when her left ankle bumped into the prayer rail. She was overwhelmed by how different this church was from the Baptist church in Ellisville, the place she secretly hated but was too scared to let anybody know it.

Suddenly a lady came out of the confessional at the front of the church, walked over to the altar, knelt, bowed her head, made the sign of the cross, then, with whispered words intended for God's ears alone, yet audible enough to punctuate the silence, sought ablution of her sins. From time to time she put a handkerchief to her eyes, waited, then resumed her prayers.

Dulcie was too surprised and scared to know what to do. She knew if she tried to leave she would make a lot of noise which would not only disturb the lady but might also bring somebody else out to see what was happening. When the woman finally rose and turned around to leave, Dulcie knew she had been seen.

"Hello," the woman whispered and smiled as she walked by.

Dulcie was too scared to say anything. She turned around to

see the lady dipping her fingers into the holy water and crossing herself as she left.

FATHER SERANNA HAD seen Dulcie on the way back to his office after hearing the lady's confession and now had to decide which was more important, pondering and praying about the lady's sins or going out to the chapel to talk with Dulcie. The lady's sins would be on his mind later, but Dulcie might slip away again. He didn't want that to happen. His interest in her had intensified to a point of urgency, even though, as yet, he knew nothing about her.

With the door to the chapel slightly ajar, he watched her for a while, sensing even from a distance how different she was. In the incensed space and silence of the chapel she looked lost, extraneous, bewildered. He knew, too, that she was sad but as yet did not know why. He sensed something of what was inside her which gave the appearance of being undisclosed to everybody else, even to herself, maybe. He may not have been born with this special sensibility, but he could never remember when he didn't have it. Before he opened the door fully, he felt an aching emptiness and a compulsion beyond his control to know her. He opened the door again, softly, a little at a time until he knew she had seen him.

"Hello, young lady," he said in his slightly altered English. Seeing the effect his sudden appearance had had on her, he waited a short distance away while she struggled to free her feet from beneath the prayer rail. Seeing her increased frustration, he hurried over. "Please don't be afraid," he said gently, lifting the prayer rail "I'm not going to hurt you."

He could see how scared she was, how near to crying. He held his arms out to her, then gently took her hands in his. "You need not be afraid of me. I came in here only because I've seen you before and wanted to visit with you."

When she tried to leave, he gently pulled her back. "Please don't run away. Here," he said, helping her back into the pew, "sit down."

He could see that she was feeling a little less nervous, though she continued to fidget with her purse and slide her feet around under the prayer rail.

"Now," he said as he again took her hands in his. "I'm Father Seranno. What's your name?"

"Dulcie," she said timidly.

"I'm sorry, I didn't hear you."

"Dulcie. Dulcie Dykes."

"That's a lovely name, Dulcie. Now, would you please tell me something about yourself, where you live, who the little girl is who's with you every Friday afternoon when you walk past the church?"

"I ain't done nothin' wrong," she said, ignoring his question. "I know I ain't s'posed t'be in here."

"Why not, Dulcie? Why shouldn't you be in here?"

"'Cause I ain't a Catholic."

"Oh, my dear Child," he said, "you don't have to be a Catholic to go inside a Catholic church. Didn't you know that?"

"Nossir."

"Dulcie, this is God's house, where everybody is welcome."

"Even if I ain't a member of the church?"

"Yes, even if you're not a member of the church." He felt her arms relax, reassuring him that what he now saw in her eyes was calm and trust. But he saw something else, something which confirmed his earlier suspicions, that day when he watched her and Melissa pass by. He must accept the fact that her mind and her body were existing side by side at disparate levels, one several years behind the other, but he knew, also, that if he accepted that fact, he would have to accept also the responsibility of making her life better than it now seemed to be.

He was surprised by what she said next. "What'd you say your name was ag'in?"

"My name is Seranno." He spelled it slowly. "I'm a priest, Father Michael Seranno."

"D'you have any children?"

He laughed. "No, I don't."

"You don't? Then how come you're a father if you don't have no children?"

"Because in the Catholic Church a priest is called Father, and a priest can't marry."

"You mean they really won't let chu marry?"

"Yes, really. That's the way it is. When we become priests, we make a vow, that's like promising, that we won't ever marry."

He knew by the puzzled look on her face that she did not understand. "So now, Dulcie," he said. "I want to know more about you. First of all, where is the little friend I see you with every Friday?"

"She ain't my friend," she said quickly with a fierce look in her eyes.

"Not your friend. Then who is she?"

"She's Melissa. I take care of her so her mamma can work at the bank."

"Where is she now, then?"

"Over yonder at Miz Martin's. That's her aunt and she's makin' Melissa a dress. That's why I came on over here." Suddenly her eyes widened and she tightened her hands around the purse handle. "Lord have mercy!" she cried, jumping up. "I better get myself on over yonder 'fore she gets mad'n tells her mamma on me." She started to the front door when he pulled her back.

"Then what? What will her mamma do?"

She seemed shocked that he didn't already know. "Why, she'll raise hail Columbia, that's what! An' then she'll fire me. I know she will, 'cause she's already said so."

He held the door so she couldn't leave. "Dulcie, I'm sure Melissa won't mind if you stay a little longer. I hardly know anything about you, and I'd like to know more."

"You would? You really would?"

"I surely would. For instance, where do you live, and do you have any brothers and sisters, and . . . and what do you and Melissa do all day long? Surely you've got time to visit a little longer, haven't you? I promise I won't keep you too long."

She stood as though stunned, looking down at her feet and swinging her purse back and forth.

"Will you stay a little longer, please? I want to be your friend."

Her eyes looked quickly up into his, then lowered again. He could see that she was about to cry.

"I'd really like to be your friend, Dulcie. Will you let me?"

Without looking up, she nodded her head.

He wanted to put his arms around her but, instead, lightly laid his hand on her head. "Come on. Let's go outside."

"Now," he said as he pushed the door closed. "Tell me about yourself. Where do you live? Tell me about your family, your mamma and papa. And I especially would like to know how you and Melissa spend your time together. I want to know everything! I want you to be my friend, too."

"D'you really mean that?"

"Mean *what*?"

"You know, 'bout me bein' your friend?"

"Does that surprise you, Dulcie?"

She nodded her head.

He put his hand under her chin and raised her head. "Now look at me, Dulcie. If I'm going to be your friend, I want and need to know everything about you. Come on, now. Tell me."

Her face suddenly aglow, she answered his questions in gasping, broken and often incongruous fragments, bouncing her purse up and down against her legs and crossing and uncrossing her ankles when she thought something she said was funny. All of that changed suddenly as she said, "Mamma didn't like me." With that, she pulled the wicker purse as tightly as she could against her body and lowered her head. He had observed by now that the purse was a better gauge of what she was feeling than her outward appearance was, even though it, too, had changed drastically.

"And what about your friends?" he asked. "You do have friends, don't you?"

"No, un unh."

"And why not?"

"Why not what?"

"Why don't you have friends?"

It took a while to answer. "You know awready."

He did, of course, but didn't want her to know it. "I'm not sure I do. I wish you'd tell me."

She swung the purse back and forth against her legs and closed her eyes, as though waiting for something bad to happen.

He said again, "Please, Dulcie, tell me why you say you don't have any friends."

He saw the change that came over her, the earlier look of joy that abruptly turned to hurt and the lips held quiveringly together, and she, like someone standing before the door of a private compartment of her life, too afraid of what might come out if she opened it.

He could see the tears in her eyes as she turned slightly away with her hands over her mouth, causing him to feel he'd said the wrong thing.

" 'Cause a the way I am," she said finally between her fingers.

He couldn't trust himself to speak. What he wanted most was to put his arms around her, but knew he mustn't. Instead, he lifted her chin gently so he could see her eyes. "Dulcie," he said, "I know how you feel. You may not believe me, but I really do. Come," he said, "let's sit here on the steps. I want to talk some more with you. Is that all right?"

She wiped her eyes with the back of her hand and nodded her head. He pulled out his handkerchief and wiped off a part of the top step, then helped her sit down. "Now, Dulcie, I'd like to find out why you are sad. May I? Is that all right?"

She turned her head slightly without looking directly at him, nodding her head as though she really meant it.

As she waited for him to continue, she made a big to-do about straightening her dress over her knees, then put her purse in her lap and pulled it close to her body.

His first few words seemed to come from far away, as though he were still wondering what to say but had somehow let his amorphous thoughts take audible form before he wanted them to.

"Dulcie," he said, gently touching her hand, "I'd like to tell you what I think. I want you to stop me at any time if you don't understand what I'm saying. Will you promise me you'll do that?"

"Un hunh."

"All right, then. First of all, I want you to think about this. If people don't want to have anything to do with you, try not to get upset about it. I know that will be very hard to do. But Dulcie, it's not your fault that they feel that way. It's their fault. They are to blame, and I'll tell you why." He stopped momentarily to wave at someone passing by. "What I'm going to say now will probably surprise you. Just listen, then think about it. *Nobody* knows *anybody*, Dear Child. The way somebody looks on the outside is not the way they look on the inside. I think you already know, Dulcie, that God is not interested in what somebody looks like. Do you know what I'm saying, Dulcie?"

He was not convinced by the way she said she did.

"You do believe in God, don't you?"

"Yeah, sure I do!"

"And you do believe in Jesus, don't you? Have you been baptized?"

"Un hunh."

"Then I want to tell you something. One day a blind man asked Jesus if He would heal him and let him see for the first time in his life. Jesus spit on his hand and touched the blind man, then asked him if he could see. And do you know what the blind man said?"

She turned with a surprised look on her face. "No, un unh."

"Well, the blind man said, 'I see men as trees walking'."

He stopped long enough to see her reaction. He knew she was confused.

"You see, Dulcie, the blind man still couldn't really see. Just a little bit. So Jesus touched him again, and when He did, the man could see as clearly as you and I can see."

He saw that she still had not understood.

"Dulcie, this is what it means. Even though we can see, all of us are blind in a certain way. Like the man was before Jesus touched him the second time. No matter how good our eyes are, we simply cannot see what's inside a person. So, in a sense, we see men and everything else, as a matter of fact, as trees walking. Now, do you know what I mean?"

"Yessir."

"So you see, other people don't really know you, do they?"

"I guess not."

"But God knows, Dulcie. God alone knows who you really are. And God alone knows who I am, too. So, God is the only one who really knows what a person is inside."

The expression on her face now was more revealing, more comforting. "Do you understand now what I mean, Dulcie?"

"Yessir, I b'lieve so."

"That's fine. Now, Dulcie, do you know how to pray?"

Her face flushed. "No, un unh."

"Do you ever ask God to help you?"

"Yeah, but it don't do no good. He don't never give me what I ask for."

"What do you ask for, Dulcie? Do you ask Him to forgive you your sins? Do you ask Him to help you when you need help and there's nobody else you can ask? Do you ever just talk to Him, thank Him for all your blessings?"

Seeing that she had retreated inside herself, he reached over and laid his hand on hers. "Dulcie, do you really want God to help you? Do you really need Him?"

Even as he asked the question, he saw the tears forming in the corners of her eyes. She raised her knees, letting the purse fall, leaned forward and cried into her hands. Even though he had expected it, he was surprised that it had happened so quickly. Now the door was open. Now he could see what was inside.

He realized he was taking too much time away from other things he had to do, yet he still wanted to say something else before letting her go. "Dulcie," he said softly, "have you ever whispered something in somebody's ear so nobody else could hear it?"

She nodded her head, keeping her eyes closed.

"That's the way you should pray. But there's something else you must remember when you pray. You must make sure that what you're praying for is something you need, not just something you want. Also, you must be patient and willing to wait for God to answer your prayers. Just because God doesn't give you what you ask for right away doesn't mean He won't give them to you later on. Do you understand?"

She turned her head slightly to him and nodded again. The expression in her eyes told him that he had finally said something she understood.

"Very good! Now, Dulcie, I know you have to go, and I also have some things I need to do, but before you go, I want to tell you one more thing. When you pray, it doesn't matter what words you use when you talk to God. And remember, you must mean everything you say. Really mean it, Dulcie. Put all of your heart and soul in everything you say. Now, will you promise me you'll do that?"

"Yessir," she said.

SHE HAD WATCHED as Voncille took a pin now and then from several she was holding between her teeth, then used them to secure the newspaper pattern pieces onto the pale blue cloth that was to be Melissa's birthday dress. She knew she must show some excitement, too, though her mind was still on Father Seranno. She was glad when it was time to go and eager to get home so she could practice praying.

As she waited for the streetcar, she tried to remember everything Father Seranno had said, especially about how to pray. When she was sure nobody was watching, she closed her eyes and tried to say something without being heard. She couldn't do it. Her thoughts kept coming back to what Father Seranno had said about wanting her to be his friend and his wanting to be hers, and about wanting her to be happy. She remembered, too, about the blind man, but couldn't remember what it was that the blind man said to Jesus. All she could remember was that it was something about trees. Maybe she'd remember it when she got home.

Though the change was relatively insignificant, Dulcie was happier now than she had been in a long time. Anticipating her next visit with Father Seranno gave her something to look forward to. It helped to try remembering what he had told her, much of which, at the time, had passed fleetingly through her mind and now had returned in illuminated fragments that lingered long enough for her to think about them. Why, for instance, would he not be allowed to marry and have children? And why, then, would he be called Father? Father! She had never really thought about what the word meant. Yes, she knew God was Father, and she was aware, also, that other children had fathers, even though she didn't.

She had never seriously thought about how a real father might have changed her life. In fact, her father had seldom been mentioned, at least insofar as she could remember. She was never told why he was not there when she was born. What did he look like, and what kind of father would he have been? Now, suddenly she was sad, and the longer she thought about it, the lonelier she became. Why now, after all those years, was she getting upset about that? She had never missed him before.

Now she did.

Why? Because of Father Seranno. No matter what she did or where she was, she thought about him and longed to see him again, wondered if he could really help her to be happy. As she lay awake at night, she tried to pray without being heard, but she couldn't. So far, all of her praying had been in vain. Or so she thought. But strangely enough, though discouraged, she was determined to keep trying. She felt Father Seranno would want her to. How, she wondered, would God change her life when and if He ever heard her? It was hard to imagine, since, up to this point, she had never felt close to Him. Or was it that He was not close to her? Maybe He was disappointed that she was not what He had wanted her to be, and that's why He wouldn't listen when she tried to talk to him. What other reason could there be? Each time, she came to the same conclusion, one which, incidentally, she had reached many times before in her life. He wished He'd never made her in the first place.

The confusion she felt on Friday evening and Saturday was nothing compared to what she felt after being forced to go to church on Sunday. She had used every excuse she could think of, and Annie Lois had heard all of them. Never before had she given much or any thought to what the church auditorium looked like. Heretofore, when she wasn't thinking ugly thoughts about Brother Stanwell, she was most often thinking of things somewhere else that had nothing whatsoever to do with religion. Now she made a point of singling out some of the things that were different, which she didn't like . . . the plain white plastered walls and ceiling, the simple altar and its scant trappings, the big, heavy chairs on either side of the altar which always scared her, and the solemn, mean-looking people who sat there, the chattering and noise the people made before and even during the service, and the way so many of them looked, as though they didn't like being there any more than she did. She had never felt here the way she felt in the Catholic church. From the very moment she entered the church every Sunday she felt nothing but fear. It could hardly be otherwise, since for all of her life she had been made to think God hated her and, if she didn't change her ways, the devil himself would come out of nowhere one day and take her straight to hell. When Brother Stanwell stood up to preach, she closed her eyes and wished she could also stop up her ears.

DULCIE, FOR REASONS she didn't want to talk about, had not told Annie Lois that she had gone into the Catholic church in Laurel, and she surely didn't want her to know about her visit with Father Seranno. As soon as she left the church that first time, she started wondering about some of the things Annie Lois and others had said about Catholics, that they worshipped statues, they didn't eat meat on Fridays, and they had to confess their sins to the priest in order to be forgiven. At least for the time-being, she was not capable of determining whether any of that was right or wrong. What she had felt immediately that first time was the peaceful silence inside the sanctuary. She had been awed, too, by the beauty of everything she saw, but it was still the silence and peace which made everything else look so beautiful. She probably would never realize that it was the peaceful silence which would stir and continue to feed her discontent with the Baptist church in Ellisville. Now, two weeks later, she was purposefully looking for places in and around the house or wherever she could close her eyes and keep trying to get God's attention.

While eating lunch and later, while helping Annie Lois wash and put away the dishes, Dulcie had been preoccupied by the Lord's Prayer. Rarely, if ever, since Mattie Lois taught it to her years ago, had she been curious and interested enough to wonder about what the words really meant. She remembered how guilty she felt when Father Seranno had asked her if she knew the Lord's Prayer. As she repeated it with the congregation in church this morning, the guilt returned. The more she thought about it, the guiltier she felt. On the way home, she promised herself that she would learn what every word meant. It was an obligation she felt strongly, because it would please Father Seranno. And if it pleased Father Seranno, it would please God.

That night, with the lights out and a light cool breeze coming through her screened bedroom windows, Dulcie felt better than she'd felt all day. Before going to bed, she kneeled at the window and let the cool air touch her face and arms as she peered into the darkness, wondering what everybody up the street was doing. She watched the stars, especially the one that flickered on and off, wondering where God was. If He were up there, how could she ever reach Him? This suddenly added another dimension to her frustration, and she wanted to cry.

After getting into bed, she lay awake and wondered if it would do any good to try praying once more. She still waited, remembering all the times she had tried before and the disappointment that always followed. Something was different now, it seemed. She lay as still as she could, remembering how she felt the first time she sat in the sanctuary of the Catholic church. As she lay awake, she gradually sensed the quiet stillness everywhere; it seemed something beyond her control had transformed her thinking. Normally by this time she would be deeply asleep, but now, instead of burning eyes that refused to stay open, she felt an uncommon alertness, an enlivening expectation. Suddenly, without forethought, she pulled herself up, put a pillow behind her back, then clasped her hands together under her chin. It was a wonderful feeling, yet she felt more like crying than praying. She closed her eyes as tightly as she could and bowed her head. She tried three times before the first words came out. "Our Father, who art in Heaven . . ." She stopped, covered her face with her hands and cried. As the tears flowed, a feeling of warmth and lightness dispelled what only moments before had been fear and frustration, causing her to feel that a remote and hidden part of her brain had been accessed for the very first time in her life. It was then that she remembered what Father Seranno had said, to pray so nobody else could hear her. She slid farther down and pulled the sheet up to her chin. "Our Father . . ." It was too loud. She said it again, more softly, then again until she could feel rather than hear the words coming out of her mouth. "Our Father, Who art in Heaven . . ." She covered her face and let the tears flow between her fingers and down onto the sheet. "Hep me!"

— s e v e n t e e n —

MR. SAM BARRANCO always looked forward to Saturdays. That's when most folks from the country came to town to buy their groceries and meat. At a little after six o'clock the morning of February 23, 1924, he was sharpening his knives on a pedal-operated emery wheel just behind the store. From time to time he stopped pedaling long enough to sprinkle the emery wheel with water and rest his short legs. Not all his thoughts were pleasant ones, however. Lately, he had become increasingly concerned about all the people who had bought groceries and meat on credit but had not yet paid their bills. He had begun to wonder how he could tell them he needed money. He was always reluctant to ask them outright for fear they would stop trading with him, a failure for which his wife Rosa often berated him. She wasn't afraid to ask them point-blank to pay what they owed, nor was she in the least afraid to tell customers what she thought if they insulted or offended her or her family in any way.

Mr. Sam took great pride in his knives, and justly so. They were made of the finest steel by the Hussman Manufacturers of Erie, Pennsylvania, all, except one, with finely carved wooden handles that fit the hand comfortably. The exception was the smallest one of the knives. Its handle was made of slick white bone with an inset figure of an Indian chief on both sides. Because it was the prettiest one of the knives, and because it felt so good in Mr. Sam's hand, it had quickly become his favorite from the beginning.

After sharpening them, always the smaller ones first, he would wash and dry them, then lay them neatly off to one side of the meat cutting block, with the bone-handled one nearest the edge for quick and easy use.

On this particular Saturday morning, while he was drying the smaller knives, he heard someone enter the store. Since Rosa was still taking care of things back in the living quarters, Mr. Sam must take care of the customers. As he walked into the meat market section, still wiping one of the knives, he strained to see who was standing on the other side of the meat counter. Since the space from the top of the meat counter to the ceiling was screened in for sanitary purposes, it was even harder to know exactly who it was.

"Mornin', Mr. Sam."

Mr. Sam, without being consciously aware of what he was doing, laid the knives on the meat cutting block and walked through the door to the other side where the young fellow was standing.

"Good'a mornin', Boy Arthur," Mr. Sam said. "An'a what'a you doin'a here. I t'ought you was in'a Collinsaville."

Bo Arthur reached out to shake Mr. Sam's hand. "I am, Mr. Sam, but they let me come home for a few days."

"An' how come'a they do that?"

Bo Arthur laughed. " 'Cause I've been a good boy. You know I'm a good boy, Mr. Sam. I do right, so they treat me good. Like lettin' me come home like this."

"An' how long'a you be in a Collinsaville?"

"They told me if I keep doin' right, I pro'bly be out in another month or so."

"That's'a good, Boy Arthur. You be good boy an'a come'a back home t'take care a you grandmamma. Va bene, you go now, 'cause'a I'm'a busy, and I tank'a you very much for come'a by see me."

Bo Arthur reached out and shook hands again. "Thank you, Mr. Sam. If I get a chance, I'll run by later."

Bo Arthur started out the front door, then stopped momentarily, looked around as though he'd forgotten something, smiled and waved good-bye.

When Mr. Sam finished with the emery wheel later and went back inside, he was shocked and upset to see that one of the smaller knives was missing. It was the bone-handled one, his favorite. He hurried back outside just to make sure he hadn't left it there, even though he well remembered putting it on the meat block, in its special place. When he returned, Mr. Ben Rayburn had entered the store.

"Mornin', Sam," he said.

Mr. Sam hadn't heard.

"What's the matter, Sam? Sumpn' wrong?"

Mr. Sam looked up suddenly, his attention still mostly on the missing knife. "Yeah," he said finally and pointed to the knives on the block. "I'm'a miss'a one a my knives'a. I just'a sharpen it, brought it in'a here, an'a now it's'a no 'ere no more."

"You sure you brought 'em all back in here? Maybe you left it outside."

Mr. Sam looked straight at him. "Sure, I'm'a sure! I no leave'a nowhere but right 'ere," he said, shaking a finger at the meat block.

"Maybe somebody come in while you was chonder sharpenin' 'em. But who'd wanna steal one a your knives?"

Mr. Sam gave a little "humnph!" and quickly crossed himself. "Sure! Now I 'member. Boy Arthur! He come'a by while ago."

"Yeah, Sam, I seen 'im and was won'drin' how come he wuddn't over in Collinsville."

He put a hand to his forehead and thought about it, then threw both hands outward. "But'a he leave'a. I see 'im'a leave'a."

"He could've come back in without chu seein' 'im. All the same, Sam, I think I'd call Sheriff Lee Anderson and let him know, just in case. You never know what that boy's go'n' do. But anyway, Sam, I need 'bout ten pounds a hamburger meat, an' put a little bit more flour this time. If I can't come, I'll send somebody for it."

IT WAS WHILE Mr. Sam was sharpening the larger knives that Bo Arthur pulled two bananas from a bunch hanging out front and put one in each of his overall pockets, then slipped back inside the store, took the bone-handled knife, slid it behind the bib of his overalls and walked quietly out the front door, where he stood for a few moments, looking back inside and wondering how he could keep people from seeing what he had just stolen. If he ate one of the bananas and put the knife in that pocket, it would cut through the pocket and the handle would stick out where people could see it.

Looking around to see if anybody was watching, he walked south down the block, then stopped, looked around again before slipping into a narrow alley separating Creel's Mattress Works from City Barber Shop. While walking, he had thought of a way to hide the knife. Checking once more to see that he had not been seen, he took the banana out of his left pocket, broke the top of the peeling slightly, then pulled the knife out from behind the bib of his overalls, shoved the blade slowly, carefully to the bottom of the banana, leaving the handle out, then waited until he could decide how best to keep the handle from being seen. He soon had the solution. He put the handle down in the pocket first, leaving the end of the banana exposed. Fine, he thought, nobody will ever know the difference. He felt good for being so clever.

Now, what to do? He wanted to stay in town so he could let people see him and ask how he'd been doing at Collinsville. Knowing that he had been allowed to come home for a few days would convince them that he'd been unjustly sent there in the first place. He tried to remember what Saturdays were like downtown. He knew already that Dulcie didn't go to Laurel on the weekend. He knew her schedule well. What about the one person he wanted to see most of all, the one he'd never stopped thinking about with rage, the one who sent him to Collinsville? What would he likely be doing today?

It didn't take long before he realized he couldn't keep walking around town with that knife in his pocket, no matter if it did look like a regular banana. The more he walked, the more he could smell the banana and feel that it had gotten soft. Soon it would break open and then he'd be in trouble. What to do? To make matters worse, he realized now what he'd not considered earlier, that Mr. Sam would miss the knife and start looking for it. This made him uneasy. He suddenly felt the need to sit down, to think. Some ugly thoughts were threatening to ruin his day.

He was walking north now, away from Mr. Sam's store, wondering how and where to hide the knife until he was ready to go back to the farm. As he neared Dixie Department Store, he had a good feeling. Mr. Wiley Courtney, who owned the store, had been in the same infantry regiment in France that Brandon was in, and he liked to tell Bo Arthur some of the things he and his daddy had done together, always making sure he told him about the time he saw General Pershing up close. Bo Arthur always listened to the stories with an intense absorption and usually, afterwards, felt as though he was not where he was but over there where his daddy was. He enjoyed most the one about the time when his daddy and Mr. Courtney surprised three German soldiers who had been separated from their outfit, lined them up, shot them, and then shot them again to make sure they were dead. It was like being there, having a rifle of his own and being able to kill whenever and wherever he could or wanted to. Not only did Bo Arthur show an extreme interest in hearing about his daddy's death, but Mr. Courtney got the feeling the boy enjoyed it and finally decided not to mention it again.

Afterwards, his mind was all astir. As he walked aimlessly up the street, some of the people spoke to him and said how good it was to see him, but others, most, in fact, showed surprise and repulsion. He reacted passively to all of them. He needed to get rid of the knife. Without realizing it, he found himself walking east across the streetcar tracks toward the Confederate Monument. The closer he got, the greater his agitation. During his stay at Collinsville, the monument had become a symbol of intense, unabated hate, and as yet unfulfilled revenge. For a few moments as he stood there, remembering his first encounter with Frank Haley Bankston, he forgot about the knife in his pocket. It was the smell of the banana which brought him back.

As soon as he sat down and felt the banana break loose in his pocket, he stood up, looked first across the street to see if he was being watched, then looked on all sides of the monument to see if he could find a place to hide the knife. Good, he thought as he found a place where the grass had thinned out and rain, over time, had formed a short, narrow depression into and under the base of the monument. Standing behind the base of the gully, he took the banana and knife out, wiped the knife on the grass until it was clean, then slid it out of sight. He made a special effort to remember the exact spot where the knife was before going back around the monument and up to the top step, where he sat down, waiting to see who was stirring and trying to decide how to spend the rest of the day. In a few moments, he realized he was still holding the banana where the knife had been. Looking around to see that nobody was watching, he threw it as far as he could across the bright green courthouse lawn.

Mr. Sam was finding it hard to console himself about the knife. Whatever he did after Ben Rayburn left, his conscious thoughts were more on losing the knife than cutting up meat to be ground for hamburgers, especially since the knife he always used to do this was the one somebody had taken. When other customers came later, he was still upset, no matter how politely he greeted and served them.

At some later point his concern deepened. Not for the knife only, but for knowing who would take it and for what reasons. The more he thought about what Ben Rayburn had said, the more he was beginning to believe it. He kept remembering what different ones had said about Bo Arthur before and even after he had been committed to Collinsville. He had also heard in a roundabout way about what happened between Bo Arthur and Lawyer Bankston. If the truth be known, his friendliness with Bo Arthur had been less than sincere, although what he actually felt for the errant boy was the genuine kindness for and understanding of people in need, no matter what the need was. So much so that often, especially on Saturday nights, he gave leftover vegetables, fruit, and, in some cases, even meat to poor people he felt sorry for. It was this special quality, more than any other, which had endeared Mr. Sam to most of the folks who knew him.

Mr. Sam was fully aware, also, that what shows on somebody's face isn't always a reflection of what's inside. For that reason, his thinking finally settled on Bo Arthur, what he'd heard about him and what he, himself, had deduced over the years. He had suspected for a long time that Bo Arthur could not be trusted. He knew, in fact, that Bo Arthur often stole bananas, but he didn't really care. Anyway, bananas were good for the boy! Now, as he was ready to grind the meat for Ben Rayburn, he began to remember other times when Bo Arthur had stood on the other side of the counter, watching as though transfixed, as he had cut meat. Yet, maybe the boy wanted the knife for the same reasons many young boys want knives. It might be a source of pride when he showed it to others. Nevertheless, as he fed the cubes of meat into the grinder, his thinking took a dark turn.

As soon as Mr. Sam finished grinding the hamburger meat for Ben Rayburn, he called Rosa and told her what had happened. Since she knew how to talk on the phone better than he did, he asked her to call the sheriff and tell him about the knife.

"You don't think the sheriff or anybody else cares whether you've lost a knife or not, do you?" Rosa asked. "You've got plenty more knives. That's prob'ly what the sheriff's goana say when he hears about it."

Mr. Sam threw his arms out in a frustrated gesture. "Woman'a, I know what'a he say, but I no care 'bout that. I'm'a worry 'bout what'a that boy goana do with'a my knife. Don' chu understand'a me?"

"So, you still want me to call the sheriff?"

"Sure, I'ma woana you call'a the sheriff. Let him'a know just in'a case."

She hesitated long enough to realize that this time he was right. The clerk at the sheriff's office said Mr. Anderson hadn't come in yet, but she'd tell him what happened when he got there.

No matter what else he had to do or how hard he consciously tried, Mr. Sam couldn't stop thinking about his favorite knife. He knew, though, that he shouldn't keep talking about it, because very few people, if any, could understand his concern. It was shortly after lunch that he remembered something Bo Arthur had said this morning as he was leaving, that he might come back later so they could visit. Though Mr. Sam did not expect him to, he kept pondering the matter and wondering what would happen if he really did.

MOST MORNINGS DURING the week, when business had slacked up enough that his wife Addie could take care of things, Ben Rayburn would walk next door to Fletcher's Drug Store to join the group of men who every day except Sunday sat around one of the big, glass-topped tables, talking, drinking coffee, and smoking, and, when Ward Fletcher wasn't waiting on a customer, telling dirty jokes.

For someone entering the drug store for the first time, the smell and atmosphere were less than pleasant. Two big fans, one at each end of the ceiling, with unbalanced blades, squeaked and whirred lazily, producing a minimal amount of cool air, just enough to combine the extraneous odors of cigarette smoke and coffee with the intrinsic drug store odors of milk, ice cream, and medicine, sometimes in combination, sometimes separately. On hot, humid days, like today, the odors were stronger than usual, not as much to those who often frequented the drug store as to those who came less often or for the first time. Even the elaborately tiled floor, no matter how often or how thoroughly it was scrubbed, smelled of milk and medicine.

Wiley Courtney, owner of Dixie Department Store, was recounting his meeting with General Pershing during the war. The others had heard the story so many times they stopped listening and let their minds go off in different directions. Then, suddenly, before Wiley got to the best part, he stopped abruptly and turned around to see who was coming in the front door. The others turned around also.

Frank Haley Bankston walked in, nodded in their direction, then gave Ward Fletcher a prescription. As he walked to the table, three different men got up to make a place for him. He wasn't surprised, but he must pretend he was. He had already sensed the change that took place as soon as he entered the drug store, and noted immediately how each of them was trying to give the impression that he was just another one of them. He must not let them know he knew how they felt; moreover, he must not let them know how good it made him feel. Feeling one thing and showing another was a rudimentary guise he learned early in the practice of law as well as in the practice of everyday living.

As soon as he was settled in the chair, Maureen Turner, the clerk behind the counter, poured another cup of coffee and took it to him. He thanked her, then leaned back with the cup of coffee in one hand and the other lightly tapping Ben Rayburn's shoulder in a gesture of friendship, giving himself time to become one of them.

The others, in deference to Frank Haley, discontinued their discussion to give him a chance to say something. He was never at a loss for something to say and was able to talk of things he knew others would find interesting. He knew, also, how far to go in any direction a discussion might take or even suggest, and was able to circumvent what part of his information was not for public consumption by traipsing around and sometimes all but saying what he knew others were wanting and waiting to hear. Most people understood why and how skillfully he talked this way, yet they were always eager to hear what he had to say, even if it left a lot of their questions unanswered or, in some cases, angered them.

Ben Rayburn, taking a cue from Frank Haley's tap on his shoulder, suddenly, before giving it enough thought, said, "Frank, did you know Bo Arthur's home?"

It would have been better if Frank Haley had not been taking the cup of coffee to his mouth. As he brought his hand down, some of the coffee spilled out onto the table top. He slowly reached for a paper napkin, meticulously wiped the spill up, then put the wadded up napkin inside the cup. "No. And furthermore I don't believe it," he said.

"What d'you mean, you don't believe it, Frank?" Ben asked.

"I don't believe it because nobody at Collinsville has mentioned it to me," he said confidently. "And even if they had, I wouldn't have agreed to it."

Ben and Wiley exchanged questioning glances.

"Frank," Ben said, "I seen Bo Arthur not more'n two hours ago comin' outa Sam's with a banana in each pocket of his overalls."

"And I saw 'im, too," Wiley said. "Why, he even came by the store to pay me a little visit. Just like he used to."

Frank Haley's skill at keeping what was inside from showing was most effective when the people around him were more than an arm's length away. Even at close range he was able better than most others to keep all but the most subtle expressions from showing, especially when the people around him were not very discerning.

Now he was at a distinct disadvantage for at least two reasons. In the first place, learning that Bo Arthur had been allowed to leave the reformatory was too sudden and devastating a shock on his system, and, furthermore, he was surrounded on all sides by people who already knew him and knew him well, sitting so close they could almost hear his heart exceeding the speed limit.

His mind and insides were in turmoil, and all he could do was to sit very still, keep his eyes lowered and riveted on his folded hands, and say nothing until he was able to. He stirred finally and looked over at Wiley. "Did they release him?"

"Oh no, he said they just let 'im come home for the weekend on good behavior. He's goin' back tomorrow some time, he said, with a fellow from Ovett that works at Collinsville. He's the one that brought 'im."

"Good behavior!" Frank echoed. "That scoundrel doesn't know what good behavior is. Do you have any idea, Wiley, where he might be right now?"

"Naw, I don't. I didn't notice which way he went after he left the store. But Frank, I don't understand wha' chu meant when you said you wouldn't've agreed to let Bo Arthur come home. Why would you or anybody else have anything to say about that? I thought when they put chu in a place like that you had to do what they said you were go'n' do and not what somebody else said. Not even you, Frank."

"You're right, Wiley, and that's the way it should be. But Bo Arthur is a special case, so I felt duty-bound to retain certain restraints on his behavior, even though he's legally a charge of the Collinsville Reformatory system."

Wiley leaned further forward so he could see the reaction. "Frank, you don't really think what you say in the long run's gonna have any effect on how Bo Arthur's treated, do you?"

"As a matter of fact, Wiley, I do, and for a very good reason," he said, straightening his back against the chair. "As of February the eighteenth, I'm Bo Arthur's guardian."

Each face registered the shock simultaneously. Luke Wallace, hardware store owner, leaned forward assertively, with his arms crossed over his chest, and looked directly and unintimidatedly at Frank Haley. "I don't believe it, Frank," he said. "When Brandon died and Lily Ruth ran off, Eula Bilbo automatically became Bo Arthur's guardian. I know that for a fact, and you surely must know it as well."

"Yes, Luke, up until a few months ago Eula was his guardian," he said calmly with a half smile. "But now I am."

"What d'you mean?" Wiley asked. "How could that be?"

"Look," he said, leaning forward, turning his eyes from one to the other to reassure them that, no matter what they thought, he was still one of them, "I know this will come as something of a shock to all of you, but I assure you it's all perfectly legal, and what I have done I've done only after giving a lot of serious thought to it and asking God for His guidance and approval. So, a few weeks after Bo Arthur was committed to Collinsville, I went out to see Miss Eula. I knew how distraught she was so I thought I'd just go out'n talk'n pray with 'er, and ask if there was anything I could do to help 'er. She started cryin' and told me how much trouble she'd had with Bo Arthur while he was livin' with 'er and said she simply was no longer physically able to be responsible for 'im. I told 'er I understood perfectly how she felt and that I wished I could help her some way. That's when she asked me if there was any way I could be Bo Arthur's guardian instead. I told 'er there was a way, and that I'd try to arrange it for her. On February eighteenth, I took the papers out to 'er, we prayed together, and she signed them, relinquishing Bo Arthur's guardianship to me until he reaches the age of eighteen."

Luke drew limply back in the chair with a hand gesture of shock and frustration.

It took a while for the others to comprehend it. Wally Post, of Ellisville Seed and Feed, was the first to break the silence. "Frank," said, "I still don't understand what you just said. I know you're a mighty fine lawyer, but there ain't no way you can convince me that them folks at Collinsville are go'n' do what chu tell 'em to do when it comes to the way they treat Bo Arthur. I hate to disagree with you, but you or somebody else's gonna have t'convince me if I'm wrong."

"It won't be somebody else, Wally, it'll be me. Just wait a little longer and see." Then he turned slightly to face Ben. "When you saw Sam, did he mention Bo Arthur?"

"Yeah. As a matter of fact, he said Bo Arthur'd been by, then left. When I got there a little later, Sam was standin' by the meat block, lookin' like he'd lost his best friend."

Up until now, Ben had not realized the seriousness of what Mr. Sam had told him. Should he let Frank Haley and the others know?

"Well, Ben?" Frank Haley's concern was evident. "Then what?"

Ben looked from one to the other, as though asking for their approval. It was obvious that they were as curious as Frank Haley was. It took a while for him to decide how to do it, then he resumed, falteringly at first, as if afraid the next word would be the wrong one or one too many. "Well, Sam said he'd been sharpening knives in the back of the store when he heard somebody come in. When he went to see who it was, he laid the knives he'd just sharpened on the meat block. After Bo Arthur left, he went back and finished sharpenin' th' other knives. He'd just come back inside when I got there and said he noticed one a his knives was missing . . ."

Another of Frank Haley's skills was the ability to listen to what was being said while planning, at the same time, for when they would be needed or asked for. Although on rare occasions he lost control of his physical responses, he was almost always able to rein in his emotions before they got out of control. Shameful to admit, he would never forget the bitter confrontation with Bo Arthur in the sheriff's office the morning of February 4, his loss of control and the extent of his anger and, most of all, the actual physical contact with Bo Arthur that resulted. That's what he was thinking about now, recalling the rage and hate in Bo Arthur's eyes, the face which, at that moment, lost forever the affected, beguiling look of innocence that had fooled and was still fooling most of the people who knew him. There was no doubt in his mind that Bo Arthur had stolen the knife, and that he planned to use it for something other than whittling or playing mumbledy-peg. *I've got to find it. Where do I start?* The answer came fast. Mr. Sam. He must talk with him right away.

"What d'you think, Frank?" Ben asked. "If Bo Arthur didn't take the knife, who d'you think did?"

In spite of his capacity to appear calm on the outside, Frank Haley's face remained tense and severe. When he finally opened his eyes, he turned them sternly from one to the other, then, with some difficulty, cleared his throat. Gradually he assumed his confident courtroom demeanor. "What do I think?" he said, tapping both hands repeatedly against his chest. "I'll tell you what I think. Bo Arthur Bilbo is a potential criminal, and if he continues to get preferential treatment at a place where he's supposed to be rehabilitated, he will very soon prove to all of you that my assessment of him is absolutely correct. I b'lieve I know 'im better than any of y'all do. In fact, I know 'im even better than he knows himself. And mark my words, he's a deceitful, sick, immoral and malicious scoundrel!"

In the meantime, Ward Fletcher had filled Frank's prescription and was standing behind the counter, listening intently, with a grave expression on his normally cheerful face.

"CAN YOU DESCRIBE the knife, Mr. Sam?" Frank Haley asked.

Mr. Sam wrinkled his brow. "Non capisco. I no understand'a."

"Can you tell me what the knife looks like? Is it like this one?" he said, picking up one of the larger knives.

"No, no, no, like'a questo, this'a one. See?" He picked up a small knife he used for trimming.

It was a good first clue. "Tell me more about it, Mr. Sam. What does it look like? Tell me everything you can about it."

Mr. Sam walked over to the big roll of wrapping paper secured on a cast-iron, footed frame, pulled and tore off a piece of it, then took a pencil, laid the paper on the counter and proceeded to draw the knife. On the handle, he drew a small figure of the Indian chief's head, then surrounded it with an oval ring. "Questo," he said, pointing with the pencil, "this'a 'andle'a made a bone'a."

"Yeah, Sam, I see. And this thing on the handle. A figure of a man?"

"Si, si! Like Indian, his'a head'a." Then he raised a finger above and across the figure, shaking his head and clicking his tongue because he couldn't say what he wanted to say.

"You mean the Indian head was carved into the handle?"

"Si, si! On'a both'a sides'a, tutti i due. I no able'a talk'a very good, but I make'a you understand'a. Buono, buono."

WHEN FRANK HALEY left home earlier, he'd promised his wife Gayle that he'd come back as soon as possible with her medicine, but now he had changed his mind. Even though her coughing seizures the last few days had become more frequent and more severe than before, he rationalized that the medicine was probably not doing its job anyway, so no need to hurry home now that an urgent situation requiring his full attention had developed. His conscience, however weakened it had become during the past fifteen years or so of his marriage, still retained just enough of itself to be felt. No matter, even if it took all day, even if Gayle's seizures worsened still, he had to find Bo Arthur.

He was on his way to his office when Ben Rayburn stopped him. "Frank," he said, "Birdie Buinside was in the cafe a while ago and said she'd just seen Bo Arthur."

"Where 'bouts?"

"Sittin' on the courthouse monument."

"How long ago?"

"I don't know exactly, prob'ly an hour or so."

Frank Haley pulled out his watch and flipped it open. "Thanks, Ben," he said, then went to his office, where he called Collinsville several times but never got an answer. As he waited between calls, he pondered the situation and questioned the wisdom of what he was trying to do. He knew that his guardianship of Bo Arthur would not reverse or change in any way whatever decision the officials at Collinsville made, yet he refused to concede on the matter. On several previous occasions he had been successful in convincing a judge to change a verdict or even a sentence, though there was no law or legal precedent for doing so, by using every means, legal and otherwise, and, on one or two occasions, to create a loophole where one did not exist. Maybe it would work again.

On the other hand, he was now forced to consider the extent of his increased vulnerability, the serious ramifications of doing battle with Bo Arthur. He swiveled his chair around to face the wall of framed diplomas, certificates, awards, notable successes documented with pictures and stories from newspapers throughout the South, and, separated by a bronze replica of the Scales of Justice, an assortment of photographs, all elegantly framed, of himself and his family. It was something he did on occasion, less often merely for egotistical reasons than for reassurance in times of misgiving, something he was feeling now. His office was figuratively the scene and source of his pride, the womb where so many notable legal victories had been plotted and rehearsed, where he had pored late into many a night over various volumes from the extensive law library surrounding him on three sides, where he had consulted with and counseled hundreds of people in trouble who were willing to pay any fee he asked, knowing he would get them exactly what they wanted in return, and where, after each court victory, he would come alone, to exult in the win and the ensuing accolades, and, though reluctant to admit it publicly, his inflated celebrity. Without fail, the final gesture was to get clumsily down on his knees to thank God for making it all possible.

Studying the framed records of his illustrious past did not now have the exhilarating effect it had always had before. For one thing, he was tired and dulled by a lack of sleep. Although the hall and a closed door separated him and Gayle, her continuous coughing last night had kept him awake for hours, and now he had a hard time keeping his eyes open. He had always prided himself on being able to go without sleep for long periods of time and still be able to deal with any situation, no matter how challenging. Now, if something that promised sufficient professional and financial reward needed his attention and energies, he could stay awake. What he was feeling now promised none of that. Finally, he swiveled the chair around and willed himself back to be what people thought he was.

He reached across the desk and picked up the little sack of bronchitis medicine, then left, still wondering what to do, where to go. It would be easier to decide once he had put Gayle and her coughing seizures out of his mind. He stopped just before getting into the car, threw the little bag of medicine onto the front seat, then stood for a while, head down, wondering how to do what he suddenly decided was more important than easing Gayle's bronchitis, even though the alternative to easing her bronchitis was, by all legal assessments, a relatively inconsequential matter of a small trimming knife thought to be stolen from a Sicilian immigrant's meat market earlier that day.

The needed response came, fully equipped, with commensurate urgency to justify what he planned to do. Enough of coddling himself because he hadn't slept well last night, no need to be concerned about what Bo Arthur might do. Some folks might feel inclined and curious enough to wonder about the validity of Bo Arthur's public accusation, but most, Frank Haley felt, would simply discredit it as a youthful attempt to get revenge on the one responsible for his having been sent to Collinsville. There had been other times when his reputation had been questioned, yet each attempt had failed. After all, Frank Haley Bankston was a man of God. Nobody in his right mind would dispute that. He had proved consistently, no matter how great the challenge to his integrity, to be as good or even better than he was normally reputed to be.

BO ARTHUR HAD tired of sitting alone on the Confederate monument and was getting ready to walk across the street to talk with Mr. Elmo Poole at the ice house when Miss Ida Belle Bustin, who had taught him in the eighth grade, saw him and walked over to where he was.

"Why, Bo Arthur," she said, putting an arm around his shoulder, "are you home to stay?"

"No'm, Miss Bustin," he said, moving away from her. "I gotta go back t'morrow."

His sudden moving away caused her to remember something unpleasant. Ida Belle Bustin had been teaching eighth grade since returning seven years ago from China, where she'd sought, but failed to find, solace from the anger and shame of having been left waiting in her wedding dress at Tula Rosa's altar by Joe Dale Milner.

The religious fervor that had motivated the missionary experience had come late in life and was minimal at best. Unendowed from birth with less than laudable talents or physical appeal, she felt the likeliest recourse at this juncture of her life was to serve God, even though, in sleepless nights before applying for and receiving the commission for China service, she often had to do battle with her conscience, which more and more, lately, had made itself felt, in spite of all the ways she had tried to assuage or ignore it.

The long ocean voyage to China was almost more than she could bear. It was the first time she had been away from home. Everything was unfamiliar; it neither held nor promised anything in the way of consolation or fulfillment once the arduous getting there was done. She made repeated soul-searching appeals to God to strengthen her faith and help her cut the umbilical cord which still connected her to her anguished past.

With special interest and motivation, she had learned to read and speak Chinese sufficiently well to qualify for the missionary job. Little did she realize how insufficient her language skills or the Chinese culture lessons were until she debarked from the ship and came face-to-face for the very first time with the overwhelming world where she now found herself. As a missionary, she failed because she refused or simply could not adjust to the drastic change of physical and cultural environment. Nothing which she'd read about or was taught to expect had prepared her for the strenuous, demanding job she had been given. Each time she was brought before the mission board she had been less and less gently reprimanded and then, finally, asked to leave.

By the time she returned, she was well on the way to becoming the typical old-maid, having inventoried and congealed, during her missionary years, all the resentments she felt for people in general and men in particular, and, in spite of the fact that she was in no way qualified to do so, she now took advantage of and pleasure in every opportunity to offer advice to anyone having marital problems, and in every instance to suggest divorce as the only sensible and permanent solution.

Of all the men she hated, the one she hated most was Frank Haley Bankston. He had insulted her, often in public, more times than she could count. When she had stubbornly refused to agree to sending Bo Arthur to Collinsville, he had virtually accused her of having private, unnatural feelings for the young boy. She was still seething about that and was determined to be avenged, even though she knew that to do so would require abundant skill and discretion, both of which, she was forced to admit, were now in short supply.

"How're they treatin' you, Bo Arthur?" she said, moving a little farther away. "I hope they're not being mean to you. Are they?"

He took a few moments to think, then said, "Oh no, m'am, they like me. That's why they let me come home."

She pulled her fleshy chin in and shook her head up and down a few times, her way of confirming to herself what she'd believed all along. "Well, I'm not the least bit surprised," she said. "As far as I'm concerned, you never should've been sent there in the first place." She was tempted to tell Bo Arthur everything she knew about the situation but faltered just before doing so, realizing she was, after all, a teacher, which meant exercising restraint in such matters. On the other hand, she had learned the hard way that too much concern for professional ethics could, and usually did, have reverse consequences. More and more, when she decided to air her true feelings about a situation, especially a volatile one, and people listened without arguing with her, usually because they understood and pitied her, she had misconstrued the strained silence as a sign of agreement, and was encouraged by it to go the limit in saying what she thought. She had so often stepped over the ethical boundary that now, when her emotions were kindled out of control, she could cross over and not give it a second thought.

"You know who's responsible for sendin' you to Collinsville, don't you, Bo Arthur?"

"I don't know what chu talkin' 'bout, Miss Bustin."

"Well of course you do, and stop actin' like you don't. Surely you remember the trouble you got into about Dulcie Dykes."

She leaned over toward him, her squinted eyes fixed on his, waiting for an answer.

He lowered his head and shuffled his feet, then looked up but away from her. "Yessum."

"Well," she said more confidently, "that's when a lot of folks in town decided you needed to be put away. Remember that?"

"No'm, I don't know nothin' 'bout that."

As if to herself, she said, "I'm certainly surprised to hear that!" Then, to him directly, "The school board had a meetin' to decide whether you should be sent to Collinsville or punished some other way."

She could see he was shocked by that. "You know who the chairman of the board is, don't chu?"

He shook his head. "No'm."

"Well," she said, "it's Frank Haley Bankston, that's who! Now don't tell me you don't know who he is!"

"No m'am, I know 'im. I sure do."

She hesitated for a moment, not in misgiving, but in trying to calm what had already become an internal rage and, at the same time, without thinking, tugged with both hands at the strained corset that kept sliding up over her broad hips. The words seemed to halt briefly behind and between the clenched dentures, then spewed out vengefully, carrying with them a faintly discernible medicinal smell. Every muscle in her face seemed to have atrophied in a hideous expression of all the hate she felt for Frank Haley Bankston, then, in a sweeping, dramatic gesture, taking up what little slack was left in her thin lips, she beat her clinched right fist as hard as she could against her breasts and gasped out the words with emphatic jerks of her head, "I hate the bastard! And if I ever get half a chance I'm goana kill 'im, so help me God!"

Something about the way Bo Arthur looked and the way she felt about him had sapped what little was left of her restraint and brought on the tears. Still crying, she pulled the handkerchief from her purse and wiped her eyes, stopped, turned slightly toward him and said hoarsely and softly, "I'm sorry, Bo Arthur. I didn't mean to say that. God forgive me!"

Bo Arthur had started across the street to the ice house but stopped suddenly, distracted to the point of not knowing where he was, aware only of some of what Ida Belle Bustin had told him, those special words that, unlike most of the others, had gone directly into his hearing where they had adhered with suctioned feet in unrelenting agitation. Alternately, his conscious mind remembered the knife, where he had put it, and when, how, or if he should retrieve it. He turned and looked over to the Confederate

Memorial, as if to convince himself that the knife was still there, then took two or three steps in that direction before he realized the obvious danger of trying to get it now.

Elmo Poole had seen Ida Belle Bustin talking, then raising her voice as she leaned close to Bo Arthur's face, even the crying that followed, the handkerchief. He was better able than Bo Arthur to understand why she had become enraged, because he had known, even before he heard her say it, that she hated Frank Haley Bankston. He knew, also, why she hated him.

Many years earlier, Ida Belle had been in love with Frank Haley and had resorted to every means possible to get him, but he did not love her. Elmo knew from what others had told him that, in spite of Frank Haley's disinterest in Ida Belle, he had encouraged her obliquely in such a way that she finally believed he loved her. Several months later, when he began to avoid her, she barely escaped a complete mental breakdown. At about the same time, a rumor began circulating around town that what Ida Belle had barely escaped was not a mental breakdown but unintended motherhood. After recovering, she directed all her energy and attention in spiteful retribution to the pursuit of Joe Dale Minter, whom she hardly knew but for whom she had allowed, even forced herself, to develop a strong physical attraction, and who finally agreed to the marriage, then decided at the last minute to avoid it by leaving town and finally ending up among the poppies in Flanders Field.

Elmo knew, also, that Bo Arthur was carrying around more hate than a normal boy his age should be carrying, and he knew why, just as he knew why Ida Belle was carrying hers. As he watched from the ice house porch, he could see the look of total distraction on Bo Arthur's face, a look he'd often seen and wondered about, the look which could change in an instant for purposes of deception, for hiding the latent evil waiting to come out.

Bo Arthur hardly heard when Elmo called him, then came suddenly out of his trance and tried to see who it was. He didn't want to see Mr. Poole. He wanted to see Mr. Sam. He turned around once more and looked in the direction of the Confederate Monument, wishing he could somehow get it out without being seen.

He realized suddenly that he had to leave it where it was if he planned on going to see Mr. Sam.

He still felt reluctant to go, but he did, cutting diagonally across the street in front of the ice house, waving slightly at Elmo as he passed. Though he knew where he wanted to go, he still stopped now and then to decide what he should do after visiting with Mr. Sam. It was a long time before dark, and he had by now decided it would have to be dark before he could get the knife.

That made him feel a little better. Looking from side to side to see if he was being watched, and hoping that he was, he assumed a confident demeanor, slid his hands down to the bottom of his pockets, stirring up the latent banana smell and reminding him of how hungry he was, then walked jauntily down the street, speaking to everyone he met, pulling his hands out of his pockets only to wave at someone up ahead or across the street, and smiling the smile for which he was often complimented, and seeing the effect was still the same. Boy, it really made him feel good, as though nothing had changed at all and folks still liked him. Remembering something, he stopped and pulled from the bib of his overalls the money his grandma had given him and the list of things she wanted him to buy, making him promise he would bring back every cent of what was left over. He had no idea how much he would need to buy what she wanted, but figured she wouldn't mind if he bought himself a hamburger or two and a Nehi grape soda pop. And looka there! Mr. Ben's City Café was just down the street a ways, where you could buy the best hamburgers anywhere in Mississippi. He could just taste 'em! Even before he opened the front door, he could smell the familiar odors, hamburgers, chili, onions, and coffee, all afloat on a dense undercurrent of cigarette smoke, only slightly displaced by the weak blades of the two overhead fans, that made his mouth water, reminding him of the few times in his life when he was happy.

The afternoon sun, partially shaded by the big oak tree on the street outside, was filtering its way through the front windows of the café, defining not only the thick layer of smoke hovering just above the customers' heads, but sneaking into corners and under tables where dust and dust balls had accumulated, where someone had discarded a used toothpick just under the foot rail on the counter, the scant remains of a hand-made cigarette snuffed out and pushed off to one side under a table, a crumpled-up mustard-stained napkin left on the cane-bottomed seat of one of the chairs, and bringing a weak shine to those parts of the linoleum-covered floor which had not so far been scratched or worn through to the wooden surface below.

Ben Rayburn, wiping off the top of the counter with a wet rag, stopped the moment Bo Arthur came in, then made another distracted sweep or two before stopping and trying to get used to what was happening. Immediately an alarm went off in his head, the same one that had earlier made him so eager to tell the men in the drug store about what Mr. Sam had told him. He tried to look normal, even raising the hand with the wet rag to wave a welcome to Bo Arthur, but he couldn't keep what he was feeling from showing on his face and in the way he said, as his eyes went directly to the bib of Bo Arthur's overalls, then to his pockets. "Hello, Bo Arthur! Welcome home!" He felt he ought to do something, maybe go back to the kitchen and call Frank Haley. No, that wouldn't do; he'd better think of something else.

Everyone's eyes were on Bo Arthur. Nola Newell, doing what Lily Ruth Bilbo used to do, turned around so fast to see him that the coffee she was pouring into a customer's cup ran onto the table instead. One or two of the customers, after just overhearing part of a muted conversation between Ben Rayburn and Postmaster Allen Aiken, seemed to be especially interested in what Bo Arthur was wearing. Alone at a corner table, Ida Belle Bustin was about to take the last bite of her hamburger when Bo Arthur walked in. She quickly swallowed what was in her mouth, dabbed the wadded up napkin repeatedly against her thin lips with one hand and, with the other, made a slight, ineffective gesture in his direction.

He acknowledged every greeting with a slight turn of his head in one direction, then another, smiling buoyantly, reaching over to give someone at a table a hand-shake, and answering the obvious question the same way every time it was asked, that he was home only for the weekend but would soon be home for good.

"He should never have been sent there in the first place," Ida Belle Bustin said, rising slightly from the table, then sitting back down.

Bo Arthur seemed to be surprised, though he wasn't. He already knew how Miss Ida Belle felt about him and about Frank Hayley. In fact, it was common knowledge, as soon as that crucial meeting adjourned back in February, that she was the only one to cast a dissenting vote on Bo Arthur's behalf. Yet Bo Arthur had some concern as to what Miss Ida Belle might later decide to do.

"What'll you have, Bo Arthur?" Ben asked.

"Oh," he said, coming to, "gimme two hamburgers and a Nehi grape soda."

Still a little preoccupied, he crossed his arms on the counter and leaned forward to watch Mr. Ben fry the hamburgers on the gas griddle, turning them at just the right moment, rubbing the two open-faced buns across the griddle to soak up the juices, then putting on his own special sauce, his well-kept secret. He straightened as Mr. Ben laid the plate of hamburgers in front of him, then waited. "Mr. Ben," he said, laughing, "where's my Nehi soda pop?"

Ben snapped to. "Oh, that's right, Bo Arthur. You did want a soda pop, didn't chu?" As he reached into the ice box, he looked around and said, "What kind, Bo Arthur?"

"I said grape, Mr. Ben."

As he opened the soda pop bottle, he leaned a little farther across the counter, thinking he might be able to see behind the bib of Bo Arthur's overalls. If the knife was there, he couldn't see it.

Bo Arthur took another big bite and looked up suddenly.

Ben watched, distracted, wondering what he should do or say. There'd never be a better chance and if he didn't at least mention the knife, and his friends later found out about it, he'd have a hard time explaining why he hadn't.

"Bo Arthur," he said, picking up the wet towel again, aimlessly wiping off the end of the counter, "have you been t'see Mr. Sam since you got home?"

Bo Arthur's mouth was too full to answer. When he finished eating the first hamburger, he sat back, smacked his lips and took a deep swallow of the grape soda pop, looking happy. "Yeah," he said, lifting the top of the other hamburger, then putting it back, "I saw 'im first thing this mornin' as soon as I got t'town."

"Say you did?"

"Yeah, me'n him had a good visit. I always like t'talk with Mr. Sam, even though I cain't understan' half a what he says." He laughed and took another big bite.

"Hmmh," Ben said.

Ida Belle Bustin wiped her mouth as she looked around to see if she was being watched, then reached inside her purse and pulled out a little bottle of Tischner's antiseptic. Turning toward the wall, she slowly and quietly unscrewed the metal top, held the napkin over her mouth with one hand, leaned forward and took a quick swallow. Before getting up, she fumbled until she felt the end of her corset, gave it a few jerks and managed with some difficulty to stand and walk toward the door, unaware that she had caught part of the back of her skirt under the girdle. She had already opened the door to go outside when she suddenly turned and walked up to the counter where Bo Arthur was sitting. Forgetting for the moment, she put one of her hands on his shoulder. He turned around, surprised and visibly irritated.

"You'd better watch out, Bo Arthur," she said, leaning against the counter, looking around and waving her arm in circles to include all of the customers. "They're out to get chu," she said. "You better be careful! They think you've been a bad boy." She was on her way to the front door again when she suddenly stopped at one of the tables, grabbed the top of it with one hand, leaned over and whispered loudly enough for everyone to hear, "Y'all better watch out, too. I hope y'all are ready, 'cause Christ is comin' soon."

Ben had never witnessed one, though others had told him that lately Miss Ida Belle had been experiencing sudden but momentary lapses of memory, believing she was still a missionary in China.

"Why d'you say that, Miss Ida Belle?" Ben asked.

She started to answer but decided not to. She had just opened the screen door and stepped outside when she saw Frank Haley. "Look!" she said, sticking her head back inside and pointing her finger in his direction. "See! What'd I tell you? Didn't I tell you Jesus was comin'?"

"I see you've been nipping the bottle again, Ida Belle," he said, walking past her into the café.

She shrugged her shoulders, threw her head back, still laughing, and walked past him out to the street, stopping suddenly, wondering where she was supposed to go.

Bo Arthur, turning around, seeing Frank Haley, started to leave. He was still trying to put the change Ben had given him back in his bib pocket when one of the dimes fell on the floor and rolled over close to where Frank Haley was standing. As he stooped down to pick it up, he felt Frank Haley's hand on his left shoulder. He straightened in an instant, wiping his shoulder off as though it had been contaminated, livid and snarling through his teeth. "Don't chu touch me!" he said, taking a rigid fighting stance, keeping the distance between them with his extended left arm in Frank Haley's direction and his thick fisted right hand, held in unwilling restraint close to his chest.

Bo Arthur and Frank Haley were now the center of attention. Everybody was watching, arrested momentarily in varying degrees of animation like figures in a still-life painting, with eating utensils at different heights and angles between table and teeth, mouths agape, either in curiosity and shock, in anticipation of the next bite, or suddenly immobilized in the process of chewing. Ben, showing signs of increased concern for what was about to happen, knowing, as he did, certain things, serious and incriminating things which none of the others knew, was wondering when or if he should put a stop to it. He thought he should, but he didn't want to.

Frank Haley feigned a smile. "I can see that bein' at Collinsville hasn't done you one bit of good. You're still the same scoundrel you always were, and it looks like we may have to keep you there until you learn how to live like a civilized human bein'."

"That's right, mister!" Bo Arthur sneered. "They ain't changed me none, 'cause they said there wuddn't nothin' that needed changin' in the first place."

"That's a defenseless lie and you know it," he said deliberately, looking deeply into Bo Arthur's eyes for some sign of a private reaction. "So don't be stupid enough to think that I believe a word of it."

He recalled their first encounter at the Confederate Memorial and his suppressed surprise at seeing how, at such an early age,

Bo Arthur was able to misrepresent visibly what he was feeling. What was even more illuminating was their confrontation in the sheriff's office the morning Bo Arthur left for Collinsville.

It was at some quiet and pensive point shortly afterwards that he realized that, whereas he had acquired his skills at deception by years of training and practice in courts of law, Bo Arthur's skills had come with him at birth, like a lion cub that knows instinctively that all that he immediately sees represents a threat to his very existence, no matter how short-lived it is at any given time.

Bo Arthur was pleased to see that Frank Haley's face had reddened and all the muscles around his eyes and mouth were tight. "Well, I don't give a damn whether you b'lieve it or not. But if you don't b'lieve it, why don't chu go over there and see for yourself. And be sure an' ask 'em what I tol' 'em that day they called me in an' asked why I was over there in the first place and who was it responsible for me bein' there. But just in case you ain't able to go over there, I'll tell you myself what I tol' 'em. I tol' 'em the one that sent me there was some two-bit lawyer who thought he was Jesus but had some bad secrets nobody but me knew about."

The grown-up mean and wily lion cub saw the clenched fist coming in his direction and jumped aside just in time to avoid it. He had seen it the moment it started, while he was still talking, the amassed forces normally held in reserve for special occasions, breaking loose out of control. It made him feel better to hear and feel his heart bumping against his chest while he waited in high expectancy to vent the rest of his rage on the one person he hated most in the world.

Embarrassment was something Frank Haley almost never felt. Failing in his first attempt to down Bo Arthur was one of those rare occasions, and having it happen in a public place of business, witnessed by friends who knew and respected him, was having a bad effect on his pride. At some later point he might be able to sift through the rage he was feeling now and find some solace by remembering that Bo Arthur had not been specific about the secrets he said he was privy to, and even if he had, nobody who knew him would believe what he said. Furthermore, those who saw what happened probably didn't believe what Bo Arthur had said, that Frank Haley thought of himself as Jesus, but, if they did, it wasn't against the law.

Bo Arthur was standing a little more than arm's length from Frank Haley, pulling his overall straps back and forth with his thumbs, gloating, ready to spring at any moment.

The repeated action of the overall straps triggered all the rage and anger Frank Haley had been able, so far, to hold back. He made a sudden, frantic attempt to reach far enough across to grab Bo Arthur's hands, to stop him and see if the knife might be hidden behind the bib, and, in any case, to knock him backward onto the floor. As he put his right foot forward and tried to grab one of Bo Arthur's arms, his left foot, the one with the elevator shoe, stayed behind.

That's when Ben Rayburn stopped enjoying what he'd been watching. He ran over to where they were, helped Frank Haley get to his feet, then got between them and pushed them as far apart as he could. "Hey, now, that's enough!" he said. "I ain't go'n' have none a this in my place a business. You both gotta' put a stop to this nonsense right this minute! One or both of you's go'n have t'go." Then, turning, "Now Bo Arthur, whatever it was you was plannin' on doin', you get on out a here and do it."

Even after they got him back on his feet, Frank Haley made another attempt to grab one of Bo Arthur's arms but could not reach him. Bo Arthur taunted him by jumping father away, crossing his arms and laughing.

"You better hope they keep you in Collinsville the rest of your life, you low-down good-for-nothin' savage, because, if you ever come back, you're goana belong to me and I'm go'n' do whatever I need to do to make your life miserable."

Bo Arthur, holding the front door open, stopped. "You done made my life miserable, you two-faced, lyin' so-called man a God, but when I come back it'll be my turn. And, yessir, I *am* comin' back! I done made up my mind. I got my plans awready made."

— eighteen —

IT TOOK BO Arthur a few minutes to realize that the light that followed the long blackout had brought something besides relief. There were several things he would have to think about and work out now that he had possession of the knife. The bag that contained Granny's things had provided the clever solution to the problem of keeping the knife out of sight. That same bag now presented another challenge. What could he do with it until he decided to go home? He surely didn't want to carry it around all day. It would look silly and it would be risky, too. After thinking back on what had happened today, he didn't see any reason why he should stay in town any longer. The way he was feeling now, he didn't care if he never came back.

He didn't even want to walk down main street to go home, but went directly three blocks east and turned right on Augusta Road, which led to within a mile of Granny's house. He didn't care how far it was. By the time he reached Tula Rosa Church, the sun had set and a winter twilight of blue and grey was already chilling the air. He looked around as he passed the quaint little church, then stopped long enough to remember some of what he used to feel when he was taken there as a little boy. Remembering helped, it was encouraging. It displaced any misgivings he had had earlier about what he wanted to do. He felt better as he continued on his way to Granny's.

Dodger ran out from under the house as soon as he heard Bo Arthur and welcomed him by jumping all over him with his dusty paws, trying to lick his face, slobbering all over him and barking at the same time. Bo Arthur laid the bag on one of the steps, bent down and hugged him as hard as he could, for a long time, feeling warm and comfortable. He took the knife out of the bag, crawled under the house a short distance to the first brick pillar, with Dodger close behind and watching as he laid the knife on top of it, making sure it could be easily gotten to but hard to see.

The pressure in Eula's chest, which had begun earlier in the day, now suddenly intensified at the sound of Dodger's barking. She was heating some leftover rutabagas from lunch when it happened. She shoved the pot of rutabagas to the back of the stove and sat down, wondering how to deal with what was about to happen.

As soon as Bo Arthur came inside, he felt something was different, though everything looked the same. Eula was standing in the doorway to the kitchen, wiping her hands on a flour sack towel and trying to look normal.

"Did you have a good time in town, Bo Arthur?" she asked.

"Naw, I didn't."

"You didn't? Why not?"

"Oh, I don't know. I guess everything's different now."

"I'm sorry you was disappointed, Son. I was hopin' bein' in town again would lift your spirits." She walked back into the kitchen to hang the towel up and stood for a while, looking out the window, wondering how to tell him what had happened. She said softly, "O God, please hep me."

She didn't realize Bo Arthur had followed her and was still wondering what was different, why she looked the way she did. Was she sick and didn't want to let him know, or was she just worn out and maybe had lost interest in living? He handed her the bag, hoping it would make a difference.

She looked inside. "Was you able to find evuhthing?"

"Yessum. One of the clerks helped me 'cause she knew I didn't know how t'buy stuff like that. Is everything all right? Did I do good?"

"You did just fine, Bo Arthur." She laid each item out on the table, then picked up the skein of yarn and smelled it. "Why, Bo Arthur, evuhthing smells like bananas."

"Well, yeah. That's 'cause Mr. Sam gave me some bananas and I put the one I didn't want in the sack with your stuff. Did it hurt anything?"

"Oh, I don't think so. As soon as they git a little air they'll be awright. Don't worry, Son."

"Oh, I forgot," Bo Arthur said, reaching inside his bib pocket. "Here's the change. I spent some of it on some hamburgers."

"Is that all you've eat all day?"

"Yeah. I wuddn't very hungry."

"Then you must be mighty hungry now. Let me fix you sumpn."

"Wha' chu got, Granny?"

She opened the oven door. "Why, I've got some leftover fried chicken, a little bit of creamed potatoes, and some rutabagas I was just heatin' over. You want some?"

"Yeah, but I don't want no rutabagas."

"They're mighty good and they're good for you, too. You sure you don't want none?"

"No'm. Just some chicken and potatoes."

He was leaning against the door facing, still trying to decide why she didn't seem the same. "Granny," he said, sitting down, "are you all right?"

"Why of course, I am. What makes you ask such a question?"

"I don't know. Sumpn 'bout chu don't look the same."

She handed him the plate of chicken, then sat down to watch him eat it. "That's yore 'magination workin' overtime, Son. Why, they ain't a thang wrong with me, but they prob'ly will be if you keep on saying they is. Now you go on'n eat the chicken. The taters'll be warmed up d'reckly."

He had just taken a big bite out of a chicken leg when he heard something. Still holding the chicken leg, he turned his head in the direction of the sound, then looked at Granny. "What was that?"

"What was what?"

"I thought I heard sumpn. Sounded like it was close by."

She got up. "I think I know what it is," she said. "I'll be right back."

"What was it?" he asked when she returned. "Sounded like you were talkin' to somebody."

"I was."

"You ain't takin' in boarders, are you?"

"Why no, Son, it's just some pore ol' woman what come knockin' on the front door this mornin'. You hadn't been gone more'n twenty minutes, an' I'd just started doin' a little house cleanin'. When I opened the door, there stood the most pitifulest sight I ever seen in my life. She looked t'be evuh bit a ninety years old an' was totin' a ol' beat-up suitcase what looked like it was gonna bust wide open just any minute. The pore ol' thang had on a ol' raggedy coat what looked like sumpn she taken out of a Salvation Army box som'ers."

"Did you know who she was?"

"Why, not right off. But she knowed me. She called me Miss Eula and asked if I knowed who she was. I tol' 'er I dittn't have the slightest idear."

"You felt sorry for 'er, dittn't chu, Granny?"

"Why, of course I did, Bo Arthur. Wouldn't chu have?"

"Naw, I don't reck'n I would. You'n me are different, Granny."

"Well, I don't know 'bout that, but I knowed as soon as I seen her that I dittn't have no choice in the matter. I felt I had to do whatever I could t'hep 'er. I shore wuddn't go'n' leave 'er standin' out there in the cold. Jest as soon as I let 'er inside the house she started cryin' an' said she was bad off sick an' hungry an' just give out from walkin' so far. She said she'd been tryin' t'find my house all night long. Now, Bo Arthur, wouldn't chu've done the same thang?"

"Maybe," he said, laughing.

She ran her hand across her forehead and pushed some loose hair back, securing it with one of her big bone hairpins, then got up, took the creamed potatoes out of the oven and laid the bowl in front of him. "Now eat, Son. I know you ain't full enough yet."

It seemed he wasn't ready to eat. He pulled the bowl closer, holding it with both hands, looking, no, staring at it as though it had suddenly turned into something beyond his comprehension. She saw the sudden meager change on his face and wondered what it meant. She knew now as she had always known that the expression on his face and even in the way he moved his body could and often did belie something ugly taking place inside his head. She hoped prayerfully, now, that this was not one of those times and, because she wanted him to be better than she knew he was, she construed the look as something beautiful stirring weakly inside him. She wondered if now was the best time. His expression changed, he looked up at her as he scooped the potatoes onto his plate. "How long you goan let 'er stay, Granny?"

"Why, as long as it takes, I reck'n." She knew it wouldn't take long. She started to tell him about the ugly brown splotches on the woman's face and hands but thought better of it.

She watched him eat, trying to decide when to tell him, wondering how he would react when he finally knew who the woman was. A sound down the hall got her attention. "No, stop!" Eula said, jumping out of the chair and moving as fast as she could into the hall. "You can't do that! Get back t'bed, Lily Ruth, 'fore you fall down an' break yo' neck."

If it had been a bolt of lightning instead of the sound of her name, it couldn't have affected Bo Arthur any differently. He jumped up, pushed the chair out of his way, knocking the plate of unfinished creamed potatoes onto the floor. The first sight of her was like opening the lid of a garbage can that had been put out of sight and forgotten. All the rot and stink that had formed since he killed her in his mind years ago reeked out in thick spastic gusts that wrapped itself around him, bringing back to life all the dead and ugly forms, the long and restless nights of wondering what she was doing and why, and ultimately, of knowing, visualizing, and hating her with all his heart, mind, and soul.

There she was, with Eula's arm around her to keep her from falling, drained and warped into something not even he would have been able to recognize if asked to. He didn't want to see her, yet he looked. Just thinking of where she had been and what she had done since she ran away brought the knife to mind.

Lily Ruth thrust her head forward, straining to see through eyes that had dimmed beyond seeing years ago. She tried to speak but there wasn't enough strength in her lungs to make it happen. Looking around at Eula, she mumbled, pointing to Bo Arthur, "Wh . . . who . . . is that?"

"Why, that's Bo Arthur, Lily Ruth."

Lily Ruth covered her mouth with both hands and cried.

"Bo Arthur," Eula said, "come on over hyere an' see yo' mamma!"

He kicked the chair all the way across the room. "She ain't my mamma, goddammit! She ain't never been and she never *will* be. I ain't got no mamma and I ain't got no daddy. I'm a orphan, and glad of it. I'd rather be a orphan than to have t'call her my mamma. She ain't nothin' but a sorry, run-down whore!"

"Bo Arthur Bilbo," Eula shouted back at him. "You shut yo' filthy mouth or I'll take my shotgun to you. Now this is yo' mamma, no matter what chu thank or what chu say, an' if she won't tell you why she's come back, then I will. The onliest reason she come was so she could see you one more time 'fore she dies. Yo mamma is dyin', Bo Arthur, an' you ain't man enough to forgive 'er. You ought'a be ashamed of yoself. I never knowed you could be so mean."

"Are you go'n' stand there and listen to what she's sayin'. Don' chu know she's lyin'? Don' chu know that ain't why she came back," he said, looking like he was about to explode. "Th' only reason she came back was 'cause there ain't no more men that'll have anything t'do with 'er and she ain't got nowhere else t'go."

"Oh, Bo Arthur," Lily Ruth cried, straining to be heard. "I'm so sorry, Son. I don't blame you for feelin' the way you do. I know I done wrong and I don't blame you for hatin' me. But please, Son, please forgive me. I would'na ever come back if I didn't love you as much as I do. Don't chu understand, Bo Arthur?"

"I don't give a damn whether you love me or not. I'll never forgive you, an' the sooner you die the happier I'll be."

"Bo Arthur," Eula said, "I never thought I'd hear you say such mean an' ugly thangs to yore mamma or nobody else. I knowed for a long time that you was troubled, but I never knowed you was this bad off. Yo' mamma's always loved you an' she still does, no matter what chu think or what she's done, and I'm just as heartsick as I can be that you feel the way you do."

Lily Ruth laid a frail, trembling hand on Eula's and made a weak attempt to show her appreciation. She seemed to have gotten a little control over her emotions. "Miss Eula," she said, "d'you think you could git me a chair t'sit on?"

"Well, I'd be glad to, Lily Ruth, but d'you think you're strong enough t'stand up while I go git it?"

"I think maybe I am."

After Eula brought the chair and helped Lily Ruth sit down, she went to her bedroom and came out with the shotgun.

"D'you plan on usin' that on me, ol woman?" Bo Arthur asked with a sneer.

"I hope t'God I don't have to, but if I do, I shore will."

Lily Ruth reached out again, gesturing with both hands in what looked like a sign language attempt to prevent what she feared was about to happen. "Miss Eula," she said, "I need t'tell you'n Bo Arthur sumpn but don't know 'xactly how to do it." She stopped and tried to take a deep breath, but the effort brought on another coughing seizure. Finally, she leaned back in the chair, closed her eyes, and tried to steady her hands by putting one on top of the other over her heart.

"What is it you woana tell me'n Bo Arthur, Lily Ruth? Take yo' time, Honey. Wait till you feel up to it."

"Well," she finally said weakly, taking a short, shallow breath, "first of all, I woant Bo Arthur t'know he ain't a orphan yet. An' furthermore, after I'm dead'n gone he still won't be a orphan." Then, after another effort to breathe, she added, "An' not even after you're gone, Miss Eula."

Eula looked over at Bo Arthur, wondering with her eyes if he was thinking what she was thinking, that Lily Ruth had lost her mind. "Lily Ruth, what in the world are you talkin' about? Surely you ain't forgot that Brandon's dead, have you?"

"No, Miss Eula, I ain't forgot. I know Brandon's dead." She looked down sadly as she put her hands in her lap and closed her eyes.

"Well, then, you tell me how can somebody we don't even know keep Bo Arthur from bein' a orphan after you've gone?"

She suddenly came to as if out of a short but deep and disorienting sleep, moving her faded and near-sightless eyes from one to the other. "What was it I was sayin'? I forgot."

"You was 'bout t'tell me'n Bo Arthur 'bout some man what was go'n' take care a him after you'n me's gone. Do you 'member that, Lily Ruth?"

She still hadn't made the transition, and even after it was apparent that she had, she seemed unsure about how to get the rest of it said.

Eula prodded her on. "Then what is it you tryin' t'say, Lily Ruth?"

"Well, I reck'n all I was go'n' say was that he ain't never go'n' woant for nothin'. They's a friend a mine that promised me some years ago that he'd look after Bo Arthur if he ever needed 'im to. That was just b'fore I had to leave."

"Lily Ruth, you done tol' us that. What I woana know is why d' you keep talkin' 'bout that man? An' how come him t'tell you he'd be willin' t'do that in the first place? What possible reason could he have 'less'n he figured he stood t'gain sumpn from it? It just don't make no sense t'me. What I'm won'drin' now, Lily Ruth, and I wish you'd tell us, just what kind'a relationship was it y'all was havin'?"

Even as she was asking Lily Ruth about the relationship, she realized she shouldn't be doing it. It was like the time she decided to get rid of a hornet's nest that had been stuck on the back of the privy for a long time. She never had felt the need to get rid of it because it wasn't bothering anybody and, also, because she knew she might get stung if she did. But on that particular day, she figured she'd left it there long enough and, also, she didn't like the idea of hornets or anything else like that taking over the place. She picked up a stick and punctured it, then stumbled over the stick and fell to the ground with hornets all over her.

So far, she had not been inclined to go beyond what she was hearing. The man, whoever and however generous he was, could have been any one of many men in Lily Ruth's life, and it was only his generosity which caused Eula to wonder, and to wonder was to ask the question, how could he keep Bo Arthur from being an orphan? Wondering was taking her farther than she wanted to go. All too soon she'd come face-to-face with it. Of course! *He was Bo Arthur's daddy!* What followed was another question: which is it . . . *was or is?*

She realized too late that she had punched a hole in the hornet's nest Lily Ruth had brought with her. My God! My God! That means Bo Arthur ain't my gran'son, an', oh dear Jesus, Brandon ain't his daddy. She soon realized that, having verbalized these thoughts to herself, she had answered the questions Lily Ruth had either been reluctant or unable to answer. Yet she refused to believe it; there was still the faintest possibility that she had not answered them correctly. The possibility, however, was too unlikely to soothe or in any other way temper the way Miss Eula was feeling.

When she turned around to see how Bo Arthur was taking it, she considered the possibility that he might at any moment become the somebody else who was in no way related to her. It caused the pain to return to her chest. In a way, she felt she was the one who was out of place, out of the picture for all time remaining.

She could see that Bo Arthur was boiling over inside. She moved over just enough to where she could see both of them. Her thoughts were in conflict, pulling her in two opposite directions. Did she really want to know who Lily Ruth's rich friend was, or would she rather not know now or ever, so she could die, believing that she still belonged to both of them? To keep from knowing, she must not ask the same question she'd asked before, even though it was right behind her dentures, waiting to come out. She couldn't possibly sort out of her tangled thoughts any particular one, so, consequently, she lost control of her tongue. Curiosity got the best of her. "An' who *is* that man, Lily Ruth? What's his name?" It sounded as though somebody else had said it.

Bo Arthur started toward Lily Ruth. Eula braced her feet against the floor and stood directly in front of her, defiant, determined and ready to do whatever she had to do. When she saw that Lily Ruth seemed to have passed out and was leaning forward in the chair, she grabbed both of her shoulders while, at the same time, trying to shield her from Bo Arthur. "Lily Ruth," she said, "are you aw right? Lily Ruth, can you hyear me?"

Lily Ruth struggled to lift her head, looked up pleadingly at Eula and tried to speak. Nothing came out. What little life there had been a few moments before seemed to have been used up.

Eula looked around just in time to see and hear Bo Arthur running out the front door. "Where you goin'?" she asked. He didn't answer. She knew by the way he slammed the door that he was going to do something bad. She couldn't help feeling a little relief to have him outside, yet she knew he'd be back, and things would get worse. She realized for the first time how scared she was, and how defenseless. Bo Arthur was going to get revenge, she knew, and Lily Ruth seemed to be dying in front of her and she couldn't do a thing about it. She closed her eyes. *"Precious Jesus, hep me!"*

Lily Ruth's head by now was resting on her chest and her limp and scarred hands had fallen into her lap. With one hand Eula tried to keep her from falling onto the floor and, with the other, tried to feel a pulse in her neck, then in her left wrist. It was slow, weak, and erratic. "Lily Ruth, can you hyear me? Nod yore head if you can."

She had to do something soon. Could she possibly get her back to bed? Still holding Lily Ruth's left shoulder, she got behind the chair, leaned it back toward herself, then began pulling her down the hall to the bedroom. Inside the bedroom, she pulled the chair as close to the bed as she could, then staightened it and tried to lift Lily Ruth up and onto it. The first attempt exhausted her, making her wonder if she would be able to do it. She knew she had to, even if she died doing it. After all, Lily Ruth didn't look any heavier than the old well bucket she'd pulled up full of water a million or more times. She straightened with a grunt, then reached both hands behind her back and tried to rub away some of the pain the trip down the hall had caused. Lily Ruth seemed to be trying to say something. Eula leaned over as close as she could. "You wanna tell me sumpn, Lily Ruth? Lily Ruth, can you hyear me?"

BO ARTHUR WAS so riled up and preoccupied as he bolted down the steps that he failed to see in the darkness that Dodger was waiting for him. "Get the hell out'a the way," he said with a kick and a yelp in return. At first he thought he might need the lantern or a flashlight, but the longer he stood, the more he could see. He felt the effects of the colder than usual night, rubbing his hands together, feeling and hearing his insides churning and his hands and arm shaking as he reached up to get it. For the moment, he could put to the back of his head what he'd just seen and heard. Remembering how he'd stolen the knife and managed to get home with it made him feel clever and brave. He knew exactly where he'd put the knife on the pillar. The remaining faint scent of bananas was the only reassurance he needed. His hand went right to the spot as if of its own volition, but what it felt was only the cold pillar bricks where the knife was supposed to be. He knew instantly what had happened. He turned around to feel and see Dodger sitting just behind him, looking innocent and unperturbed, as though he knew already that something exciting that included him was about to happen. Bo Arthur drove his right foot into Dodger's side. Dodger swung around to bite back but, instead, took off as fast as he could, limping and still whining, to the farthest and darkest corner, where he drew himself tightly together, turning his head around to lick where Bo Arthur had hit him.

"Bo Arthur!" Eula was standing in the door, holding the shotgun in one hand and a lantern in the other. She had gotten two more cartridges from the box in her bedroom closet and had them in her apron pocket. "Wha' chu doin' up under the house? Wha'd'you do t'Dodger t'cause'im to holler like that?" When Bo Arthur didn't answer, she leaned the shotgun against the door facing and started down the steps with the lantern. She stopped at the bottom and swung the lantern around, wondering where he was. She had to bend her weary body down low enough to get a glimpse of him. He was bent over with his head close to the ground. She could tell he was looking for something. "Bo Arthur, what in the worl' are you lookin' for under there? Come on out'a there and say good-bye t'yo mamma 'fore she dies."

He had found the knife and was rubbing it against his leg, too engrossed to hear or pay any attention to what Eula had said.

She felt strange, her mind was trying to go several places at once. Something told her she should go back inside and make sure the shotgun was close at hand. Bo Arthur emerged, holding the knife in front of him, causing her fears to deepen. "What's that chu got there? That thang you're holdin'? What is it, Bo Arthur?"

"It ain't none a yore damn business, old woman. You better get back inside b'fore I decide to use it on you."

"Hit looks like a knife? Is that what it is? An' if it is, what chu plannin' on doin' with it?"

"This is how I'm go'n' tell 'er good-bye."

Instead of answering, she trudged back up the steps, laid the lantern down and picked up the shotgun. When she saw that he was planning on coming inside, she lifted the shotgun to her shoulder and aimed it at his feet. "You take one more step with that there knife an' I'm go'n' shoot it right out'a yo' hand. I don't know where it come from, but chu ain't bringin' that thang inside this house. Now you throw it down right this minute!"

"You don't scare me, ol woman. I'm goin' in and if you try to stop me I'll use it on you. Now get the hell out'a my way!"

He was only a few feet away. She aimed the shotgun above his head, shot, then quickly reloaded. "Now, Bo Arthur Bilbo, you take one more step with that knife and I'm goan shoot cho' toes off."

Before she knew what was happening, he had jumped up the next two steps and was trying to take the shotgun away from her. She pulled it away, then swung it around as hard as she could, knocking him off balance and causing him to fall backwards down to the ground. The knife had fallen out of his hand and was lying on the bottom step. As soon as she saw it she laid the shotgun down on the stoop, went down and picked it up. She smelted the banana odor and for an instant tried to connect it to something else, then threw it as far as she could out into the weeds and bushes behind the privy, making the chest pains come back. *"Oh, my God!"* she cried when she saw he was not moving. Had she killed him? *"Merciful God! Please don't let'im be dead!"*

She didn't notice that Dodger had taken off into the woods as soon as he heard the shot. She set the lantern down on the other side of Bo Arthur, then bent down as far as she could and tried to pull him over on his back. As soon as she touched him, he opened his eyes and sat up. "Wha'd ju mean, pushin' me down the steps like that? Were you tryin' t'kill me, ol' woman?"

"No, I wuddn't tryin' t'kill you, an' I didn't push you down the steps. You nyear bout kilt cho'self when you tried t'take the shotgun away from me. Now, git on up from there if you can. Then I woant chu t'promise me you'll go inside and let cho mamma know you love 'er and tell 'er good-bye, cause she ain't go'n' last much longer."

He stood up and looked around. "Wha'd you do with my knife?"

"I chunked it out chonder somers. Come on, you can git it later."

"You go on inside, ol' woman, 'fore you catch cold and I'll have t'bury both of you."

"Then will you come on inside and do what I tol' you?"

He didn't answer. He wanted her to leave. Was Lily Ruth crazy or not? The only thing that sounded crazy was what she'd said about some man that promised to take care of him after she died. What man would ever promise anybody such a thing? Could it be somebody he didn't know, maybe one of her "customers"? Which one? The only one he knew was the lame-legged lawyer, and he knew it wuddn't him. That low-down bastard would be the last person on earth who'd do sumpn' that stupid. He took him off the list right away, but he couldn't get him off his mind. He tried to think of somebody else that might've said it. His thoughts took a sharp, brief detour: could it possibly be Wiley Courtney? Not after what had just happened today. Ben Rayburn? Maybe he tol' 'er that one day when they were just sittin' 'round after all the customers were gone and they just started talkin' 'bout things like that. He knew folks sometimes did. He remembered hearin' Granny talkin' one day 'bout some pore ol' young'uns that were left orphans when their mamma and papa died and some fellow that had lots a money promised t'take care of 'em. No, not Ben Rayburn. He didn't have that much money in the first place, and also, when Lily Ruth ran off, he let her have it with both barrels and told her he never wanted to see her again as long as he lived. That's what somebody'd told him later. Something kept coming back to mind: whoever it was had to be one of her "customers." Just thinkin' it might be made him sick to his stomach. All the same, one thought led to another, some getting so close to one another he had trouble trying to keep them apart. Always at the head of the pack was Frank Haley Bankston. The more he thought about it, the madder he got.

As Eula went back inside, she was wondering what had come over Bo Arthur. He seemed to have calmed down a little. Maybe things would work out right after all. She decided, however, to take

222 | GEORGE IMBRAGULIO

the shotgun with her. She leaned it against the chest of drawers, then put her ear as near Lily Ruth's mouth as she could and listened. The first thing she heard could have been a throat-clearing, followed by the ominous sounds she'd heard so many times before, the death rattle. She put her fingers once more to Lily Ruth's neck and wrist, then shook her shoulders again and again, hoping still to feel even the weakest pulse that would let her hear what she wanted, needed but dreaded to hear, and never would.

She straightened with effort, causing the pain in her chest to return, this time stronger and longer than before. She knew she ought to sit down. She knew, also, that she should keep the shotgun close by. She eased herself slowly down into the old rocker, one hand holding the shotgun and the other over her heart, pressing down and wincing, hoping and praying she wouldn't die. She tried to take a few deep breaths but the effort was extreme and the hoped for effects negligible. She slowly, cautiously lifted her feet onto the little tree-trunk stool Brandon had made many years ago, then lay back, still holding the shotgun. She must not fall asleep. She needed to decide what to do about Lily Ruth. It was Saturday evening. How could she possibly do what had to be done?

The pain in her chest abated somewhat, she felt a little better but she'd better stay put, just in case. She looked over to where Lily Ruth lay, wondering if, as folks usually said when they saw somebody dead, if she was at peace. She didn't seem to be. Had she ever been? Would she ever be? She thought about the way Lily Ruth had lived, the disrespect she had for herself, the feeling that she was never any good, that nobody ever really loved her, and the way she tried to make up for it by giving herself to any- and everybody in sinful disregard for what anybody thought, cared, or said. And now there she is, gone forever, and I don't know an' prob'ly won't never know if she made me a grandma or not. She couldn't bear to think she wasn't. Her own life was and had been barren for so long, she needed to believe she had not been completely lobbed off the tree like a dead limb. She eased out of the chair. She needed to see if there was anything in the suitcase suitable for burying her daughter-in-law.

She was saddened to see the meager and unattractive things in the suitcase. It looked as though every one of the dresses needed something done to it. There was one that might do, but it needed a belt which wasn't there. She pulled everything else out onto the bed and went through the items one by one. The missing belt was at the bottom. As she lifted it out, she saw something else on the bottom of the suitcase, an envelope, dirty and wrinkled, with Bo Arthur's name on it. Her curiosity made her forget the lingering chest pain. She turned it over. It was not sealed. She laid it down firmly on the other side of the suitcase, determined not to read it. She reconstructed in her mind what had happened outside a while ago.

Bo Arthur's sudden change, instead of being comforting, had stirred up some dark fears that brought to mind similar situations, particularly the one when he was going to kill Dodger that time and she went out with the iron pipe and threatened to hit him with it. He had suddenly turned from violence to tears. She, too, cried and tried later to reconcile the two reactions. She wondered what he was doing out there now but figured she'd better wait a while before going to see. Maybe, too, if she sat still long enough her heart would calm down. Surely he couldn't have changed in that short time? No. It was Bo Arthur, she knew. She pushed herself out of the chair, walked over to the door as quickly as she could and waited.

Slamming the door reminded Bo Arthur of what he'd been thinking outside. This time he would have to do things differently. He slid the knife behind the bib of his overalls. He made sure she heard him, then stopped in the doorway, waiting for her to see the change.

Eula noted the change and felt a little better, though feeling better was not the same as feeling relieved. She had been made amply aware of the difference between the two almost as soon as Bo Arthur came to live with her. From the beginning, she was afraid of him. During the first anxious days and sleepless nights she had determined that he was not going to take charge of her life and home. With each attempt on his part to control her, her

resolve intensified. When things finally went from bad to worse and she wasn't able to deal with them, she asked Frank Haley Bankston if he would assume Bo Arthur's guardianship. He agreed with one reservation: Bo Arthur was never to know about it.

MYRTIS PARKER HAD supper cooked and was waiting for Jason, her husband, and daughter Lorice to get back. They had said they were going to stop by for a few minutes on their way home from town to see Virginia Wallace's new baby. She put the food in the oven in the meantime and was adding some wood to the fire in the dining room when she heard the shot. She wondered about it. Had it been a shot or a log popping in the bedroom fireplace as it sometimes did? She went from room to room and saw nothing wrong. Maybe it hadn't been a shot at all.

Later, when they were eating supper, Myrtis mentioned having heard what she thought was a gun shot.

"Where'd it sound like it come from?" Jason asked.

"Hit sounded t'me like it come from Eula's," Myrtis said.

"You reck'n maybe she was shootin' at a squirrel?" Lorice asked.

Jason lifted the bowl and let the warm, tasty pot liquor slide down his throat. "I don't s'pect she'd be shootin' squirrels this late at night."

"But I seen 'er out there 'fore that with a lantern," Myrtis added. "Like she might'a been lookin' for sumpn or other."

"Oh, I bet I know what it was," Lorice said. "I bet it was Bo Arthur. Miss Eula said he was comin' home for the weekend. I bet he was the one out there shootin' squirrels."

Myrtis and Jason exchanged knowing glances, each waiting for the other to say something.

"Jason," Myrtis said, "d'you reck'n you might ought'a go over there anyway just t'see what's goin' on? Hit might not be nothin' a'tall, but you don't never know what's go'n' happen when Bo Arthur's aroun'."

"I guess maybe I ought'a. Let me finish my coffee."

"Here," she said, giving him a flashlight. "You might better take this."

Dodger, recognizing the neighbor, followed him to the top of the steps. Jason gave a few knocks, something he didn't usually have to do in the daytime. When Eula didn't show up, he walked in, turning the flashlight off as he walked slowly and softly into the hall, feeling a little uncomfortable.

"Is she dead yet?" Bo Arthur asked, making himself look at her without seeing her.

"Yes, Bo Arthur, she died just a little while ago. While you was still out chonder refusin' t'come see 'er 'fore she went."

"What chu go'n' do with 'er?"

"God only knows, Son. Maybe t'morrow I can git word to Dr. Cranford an' see if'n he can come out chere."

"I see you opened the suitcase. Wha'd you find?"

"A few clothes an' a little a this an' a little a that . . . Oh, by the way," she said, reaching across the bed to get the letter. "This h'yere's yore'n." She offered it to him.

He drew back. "I don't want it. You read it."

"She didn't write it t'me. She wrote it t'you."

"I said I aint go'n' read it, so, if you wanna know what's in it, you go'n' have t'read it yo'self."

"Here! You read it like I tol' you to. There may be sumpn in there we need t'know." He still refused to take the note. She pulled the letter out of the envelope and stuck it in his face. He grabbed it and was about to tear it up when she put the barrel of the shotgun against his right shoulder. "Don't you dare tear that up! Read it! Go on! I said read it or I'll shoot yore hand off!"

"Ol' woman," he said between his teeth, "I'm go'n' get even with you if it's the last thing I do. Maybe we'll put chu'n her in the same grave." His eyes moved quickly across the scribbled note, not comprehending, just looking for something that might interest him. There were only seven lines, poorly written, apologizing for her life and how it had affected him and begging him to forgive her and try to think kindly of her after she was gone.

Eula saw the effect the note was having on him. When he started to tear it up, she reached over, jerked it out of his hands and stuck it inside her apron pocket, realizing, as she did so, that there were no more shells. Almost before she knew what was happening, he was standing on the other side of the bed, leaning forward with the knife in his right hand, just over Lily Ruth's head, in such a rage as she had never seen before. He spit several times on Lily Ruth's face and shook the bed fiercely, as though expecting it to bring her back to life long enough to see what he was about to do, then leaned down as far as he could. "It's a lie, a goddam lie," he yelled, close to her face. "You ain't nothin' but a low-down, lyin' stinkin' bitch whore, and I'm go'n' whittle you t'pieces!"

Eula tried once again to knock the knife out of his hand but was so scared she couldn't do it. The exertion ignited the already glowing coals in the cauldron of her chest and spread the fire and scorching heat into every part of her body. She had to stop him. If she died doing it, she would be vindicated. She tried to raise the shotgun with both weak, trembling hands, trying at the same time to steady her legs by leaning against the bed. She felt her legs weakening. Fearing that she was going to fall, she made one last effort to raise the shotgun, unaware that the two middle fingers of her right hand were still on the trigger. The shotgun fired. The bullet barely missed Bo Arthur's head and burrowed itself in the wall behind him. He came at her. She stepped back into the doorway as fast as she could, still aiming the shaking, empty shotgun at him. He grabbed the barrel of the shotgun, pulled it away from her, threw the knife onto the bed, then pounced on her, spitting out every obscenity he could think of. "Ol' witch, I've been wantin' t'do this for a long time," he said, as he grabbed her around the neck. Two of her bone hairpins fell to the floor, letting her long grey hair fall over her shoulders.

LOOKING FROM DOOR to door as he walked down the hall, Jason heard. "Eula," he called. "Eula, it's me, Jason. Where are you?"

Tugging at Bo Arthur's hands, trying to drive her fingernails into them, she managed to say, *"Jason, hurry! Bo Arthur's tryin' t'kill me!"*

Jason tossed the flashlight onto the bed as he came up from behind, wrapped his left arm around Bo Arthur's neck and pulled him away, then dropped him to the floor. He motioned for Eula to give him the gun.

"It ain't loaded, Jason."

"You got any more shells?"

She shook her head.

"Give it to me anyway."

He poked the barrel into Bo Arthur's back and forced him to get up. "Git on yore feet, you low-down no-good bum, 'fore I put a bullet through that sorry, mixed-up brain a yore'n."

Bo Arthur grabbed both of Jason's legs and tried to pull him down. Jason reached over, got the flashlight and came down on the top of Bo Arthur's head. "Now, Eula, we gotta decide what t'do with 'im. You got a key to the door of his bedroom?"

"Yeah. It's hangin' on a nail on th'inside door facin'. I'll git it."

"No, you stay here."

He grabbed Bo Arthur's overall straps and pulled him down the hall, then picked him up and threw him across the bed, leaning over to see if he'd come to in the meantime. He locked the door and left.

"Now tell me, Eula, what's this all about. An' that woman over there. She looks like she's dead. Is she?"

"Yeah, Jason, she is. That's Bo Arthur's mamma."

"You mean t'tell me that's Lily Ruth?"

She told him how it came about, but she didn't tell him everything. She could see he was concerned and still wondering about something.

"What d'you plan t'do with 'er?"

"God only knows," she said. "I ain't never had t'deal with nothin' like this. There was allus Brandon or his papa t'take care of such thangs. What d'you think I ought'a do, Jason?"

"I don't know right offhand, Eula, but I'll figger out sumpn. In the meantime, try not t'worry. You know I'll do whatever I can t'hep you."

"I know you will, Jason, and I'll be in yore debt the rest a my life. But oddly enough," she added, "I'm more worried right now 'bout Bo Arthur than 'bout gittin' Lily Ruth buried. He ain't hurt too bad, is he, Jason? He'll be comin' to pretty soon, won't he?"

"Yeah, I didn't hurt 'im too bad. Just enough to put 'im out a action for a while. You say you ain't got no more shotgun shells?"

"Nairn. But at least he ain't got the knife no more. What I keep wondrin', Jason, is where in the worl' he ever got that knife in the first place."

Jason's expression changed. "I think I know, Eula."

"You do? Where?"

"I b'lieve that's the very knife Mr. Sam said somebody stole from him this mornin'. When me'n Lorice was in town t'day, I hyeard different ones taikin' about what happened. They said Mr. Sam'd just laid some of the knives he'd sharpened on the block and was back behind the store sharpnin' the rest of 'em when somebody come in an' stole one of 'em. He said Bo Arthur'd been in t'see 'im earlier. Ben Rayburn said he even seen Bo Arthur comin' out a Mr. Sam's 'bout that same time. Him'n some a th'other fellers seem t'think it was Bo Arthur that stole it."

"Now why would he do sumpn like that?"

"Eula, you know better'n I do how much hate Bo Arthur's got in 'im. Look what he was tryin' t'do t'you a while ago. He used to like t'play with knives for the fun of it but now he's got other idears in his head. Eula, you know what I'm sayin' is true, don' chu?"

She looked so forlorn, so desperate. "Yes," she said softly, as if to herself. "I do. I really do."

"Well," he said after a while, "I think we go'n' need a gun a some sort, so I'm wondrin' if you'd be willin' t'go over to my place an' ask Myrtis to give you my pistol. It's in the drawer of that little ol' table by our bed. I'll stay hyear an' keep my eyes and ears open, just in case Bo Arthur tries sumpn. Here, you might better take the flashlight."

Jason was sitting in the kitchen when Eula returned with the pistol. "Sit down, Eula'n let's talk about gittin' Lily Ruth buried. But first, how 'bout making us a pot a coffee? I'm plannin' on stayin' with you tonight."

"Oh, Jason, you don't need t'do that. I can manage somehow."

"Eula, you know you ain't able t'handle this thang by yoreself, an' anyway, I been thinkin' while you was gone an' b'lieve

I know how t'take care of it. You go on, put on the coffee. We go'n' need it."

"I think what I'll do in the mornin' is drop Myrtis and Lorice off at Tula Rosa'n then go up town and see if I can find Dr. Cranford. I need t'find Sheriff Anderson, too, 'cause he's the one what's gonna have t'take care a Bo Arthur. By the way, didn't chu say he was s'posed t'go back to Collinsville t'morrow?"

"Yeah, he shore is."

"Well, don't chu think they'll give 'im one or two more days so he can see his mamma buried?"

"I reck'n they would, but I don't b'lieve Bo Arthur plans to see his mamma buried."

"If I was you, I'd tell Sheriff Anderson t'make 'im go."

Her mind was on something else. Should she say what she was thinking? If she did, she'd be betraying someone's trust. If she didn't, what was already a situation beyond her control would get worse instead of better. She hardly realized she'd made the choice. "Jason," she said, trying to keep each sluggish thought ahead of her tongue, "I been wondrin' 'bout sumpn else."

"What's that?"

"I been wondrin if maybe Bo Arthur's guardian shouldn't oughta be the one t'talk to about what t'do."

"Why, Eula, I thought you was Bo Arthur's guardian."

"Well yes, I was at first, but several months ago, when I was havin' so much trouble with Bo Arthur, I asked Frank Haley Bankston if he'd agree t'bein' Bo Arthur's guardian. He said he would on one condition."

"And what was that?"

"He said he'd be Bo Arthur's guardian till he's eighteen years old, but Bo Arthur weren't s'posed t'know 'bout it."

She could tell Jason was mulling this bit of information over before saying anything.

"What d'you think, Jason?"

He was remembering what he'd heard earlier about the run-in Frank Haley had with Bo Arthur. "I don't know, Eula. I need t'give it some more thought. On the surface, hit sounds like the right thang t'do, but I'm not sure."

"What d'you mean? You mean maybe since Bo Arthur b'longs over at Collinsville that maybe Sheriff Anderson oughta be the one t'talk to?"

"Yes, that's what I think. On th' other han', though, since you say Frank Haley's now Bo Arthur's guardian, maybe he oughta at least know about what's happened. I'll think some more 'bout it. Maybe by mornin' I'll have a better idear 'bout what t'do."

That made her feel a little better. Then, suddenly, she remembered. "Oh, by the way, Jason, don't chu think you better check on Bo Arthur? We ain't go'n' leave 'im in there all night, are we?"

"Naw. I'll go check on 'im as soon as I finish my coffee."

He noticed that Eula was rubbing her neck with both hands and wincing. "Eula, I think you oughta go lay down a bit. I'll take care a thangs. You need some rest. You need some sleep, too, but I doubt chu go'n' git any a that tonight."

"I'll be awright d'reckly. I'll stay up a little longer."

Jason got up, reached over and got the pistol. "I'm goan look in on Bo Arthur. Have you hyeard anythang since I locked 'im up?"

"No, I ain't, an' that don't seem nat'ral. Jason, I'm gittin' a little worried. You might'a hit 'im harder than you intended to."

"I might have at that, but I don't think so."

He tiptoed down the hall, put his ear close to the door, then opened it. The room was cold. Clothes were strewn all around, on the floor and on the bed. One of the dresser drawers had been pulled out and left sagging. The window was shoved to the top and the outside screen hung loose on one of its hinges. Bo Arthur was gone. In the kitchen, Eula was standing with both hands to her mouth, scared of what was going to happen. When Jason started to the front door, she asked where he was going.

"Bo Arthur ain't in his room. He got out through the winder. I'm goan see if I can find 'im."

"Oh, my God! What's goan happen now?"

"You stay put. I'll be back d'reckly."

She sat down and covered her face with her hands, feeling again the pain in her chest. Why had things reached such a point? What was there in the note that could have caused him to go wild all of a sudden? Then she remembered. The note was in her apron

MEN AS TREES WALKING | 231

pocket. This was no time to be conscientious, she had to know what was in it. She opened and flattened it out on the table. The last few lines more than sated her curiosity.

> *Bo Arthur I been wanting to tell you something for a long time but was to scared to I know how much you loved Brandon and Brandon loved you I loved him to but you seen how mean he was to me one time I tole him I was going to get even with him and went to town after he was sleeping and met a nice man he seen I was upset and said I could stay with him that night after you was homed and big enuff to understand I was afraid to tell you who the man was I'm sorry I done waited so long to tell you I want you to know who he is cause hes your real daddy his name is mister Frank Haley Bankston I hope you will forgive me son, I done ask God to forgive me I love you Bo Arthur mamma.*

The minimal effort of getting the note back in her pocket triggered a quick succession of severe chest pains.

— n i n e t e e n —

IT WAS WHILE Lily Ruth was being laid to rest on Monday after-noon that the icy winds and sleet began and continued throughout most of the following week. Eula had hoped the members of Tula Rosa would allow Lily Ruth to be buried there, but they would not. Jason Parker and several of the other neighbors put together a simple pine coffin, then dug the grave in the leafy and secluded southwest corner of Eula's land. It was while the men were cov-ering the coffin that the first cold winds came, to be followed shortly thereafter by continuous, chilling sleet.

Dr. Cranford had come out on Sunday afternoon, but Frank Haley Bankston had not. When Jason told Frank Haley that Bo Arthur's mamma had died and that he thought that he, Frank Haley, being as how he was Bo Arthur's guardian, might need to run out to Eula's and see if he could be of some help, Frank Haley underlined with several quick shakes of his head that he had an important trial beginning next week in Meridian and didn't have time to be looking for or after Bo Arthur. When Sheriff Anderson learned that Bo Arthur had run away, he called Collinsville to let them know. When he mentioned that Bo Arthur's mamma had died, the official on duty said that Bo Arthur would be permitted to remain at home until the following Sunday, when a sheriff's deputy would take him back.

Ida Belle Bustin had just finished her sponge bath on the previous Saturday evening and was shuffling from one room to another in her bathrobe and high-top bedroom slippers, wondering whether to read her Bible or take another swig of Dr. Tischner's. She took the little vial from a dresser drawer, sipped it, put it back, making sure it could not be seen if anybody happened to be looking for it (always a suppressed suspicion and concern), poked at the nearly spent logs in the fireplace to rekindle the tired, timid flames, then sat down in the old cane-bottomed rocker that had become one of the few constant and comforting factors remaining in her otherwise erratic and unhappy life.

She liked reading Luke's version of things, especially the chapters where Jesus sends his disciples forth to spread the word, then the later account of their experiences and accomplishments. It was odd that she would enjoy reading those particular verses, especially since it always reminded her of her own being sent forth and her own returning in failure and total disillusionment. Doing so was a very personal way of repenting for her sins and her failure as a missionary. It always hurt in a strange way, a sore spot that felt good whenever she touched it.

As the scant, exhausted remains in the fireplace went from luminous orange to sooty black and the room went icy cold, she felt the discomfort, yet lacked the energy or the desire to get up and go to bed. Each time a dying ember was spit out onto the hearth, she heard it, then went back to sleep. It was many years ago that she had learned the special quality Dr. Tischner's had for inducing and maintaining sleep.

At about nine-thirty, she was fully wakened by the repeated knocking at the back door. She rocked herself out of the chair and stood for a few moments, slightly disoriented, wondering if someone were really at the back door and, if so, who could it be, and why would anybody be bothering her at this time of night.

It was too dark to see who it was. "Who are you, an' what d'you want?"

"It's me, Miss Bustin. Bo Arthur. I've got t'talk to you."

"Why, Bo Arthur? Don't chu know you're not s'posed to be here at my house? You're goana get churself into a lot more trouble if anybody finds out you've been here. Why don't chu go back home?"

"I cain't, Miss Bustin. I need t'talk with you about sumpn very important."

"Like what? You ain't had another run-in with Frank Haley Bankston, have you?"

"I'd rather not say out here. Cain't I please come inside?"

"Don't chu realize I could get in a lot of trouble if I let chu in my house? Why cain't chu just tell me out here?"

" 'Cause I just cain't. I gotta talk t'you about what's just happened. You're the only person that can help me an' tell me what to do."

"Have you been home since I saw you this afternoon?"

"Yeah, and sumpn bad happened. You've just got to help me."

"Dear Jesus!" she exclaimed, as she stood aside to let him in. She could see how distraught he was and how difficult it was for him to look directly at her.

"What's the matter, Bo Arthur? Go on, sit down and tell me all about it."

"Sumpn very bad's happened out at Granny's."

"You've already said that, Bo Arthur. What has happened?"

"My mamma died."

"Your *mamma?* Where'd she come from?"

He told her most of the story, avoiding the part about the letter and what had followed.

As she listened, she remembered Lily Ruth and had often wondered what had happened to her. She could tell Bo Arthur was having a hard time trying to decide what to say next. "You still haven't said why you've come to see me. I don't know how I could possibly be of help to you. That is, unless there's still somethin' you're not tellin' me. Is there, Bo Arthur?"

He shook his head. "Yessum. Granny found a letter Mamma had wrote me an' made me read it. I didn't want to, but she made me."

She cringed at the wrong verb form and waited until he could clear his way forward. He looked up briefly and seemed not to know what to do with his hands. "She said my daddy Brandon wuddn't really my daddy."

"What! Say that again."

"She said my daddy was somebody else."

"That sounds ridiculous, Bo Arthur. I don't believe it. Did she happen to say who that somebody else was?"

He nodded his head first, then softly said, "Yessum."

She waited, thinking he would continue. "Well, who is it, Bo Arthur?"

"I bet chu know already."

"I suppose by that you mean it's somebody 'round here that I know."

"Yessum. And you hate 'im as bad as I do."

"Do you mean to sit there and tell me she said that low-down bastard Frank Haley Bankston was your daddy?"

He shook his head.

"And you believe it?"

"No, I don't, but she said so in the letter."

While he waited for her to respond, she leaned forward, closed her eyes and left him for a while. She was not thinking of Lily Ruth; she was thinking about herself, about the hungry, lustful, and unfulfilled time of her life when she, too, might have as easily become Bo Arthur's mother. She realized suddenly that the few sordid moments of retrogression had done her in. She should have known better than to throw a lighted match into a fireplace full of gas-laced logs.

She made a conscious effort to bring her thoughts back to Bo Arthur's situation but had trouble doing so. "The letter," she said, as though to herself alone. "Bo Arthur, I'd like to see that letter your mamma wrote. Have you got it with you?

"No'm. I left it at the house."

"Can't chu go get it and let me read it?"

"I wuddn't plannin' on goin' back there."

"Why not?"

"Well . . . Mr. Jason Parker came over when he heard about Mamma and me'n him got in a fight."

"For God's sake, Bo Arthur, you're *always* gettin' into a fight. I'm warnin' you, if you don't change the way you react to people, you're goana end up spendin' the rest of your life behind bars. This is certainly no time for you to go off the deep end and make a jackass of yourself. If you want me to help you, you've got to do as I tell you to. I have some premature thoughts about the situation, but I'm not yet ready to tell you what they are. For the time-being, all I'm askin' you to do is bring me that letter your mamma wrote. Everything depends on it."

"But I'd have t'go back home t'get it."

"Well, of course you would."

"But I don't woana go back, Miss Bustin. I don't never woana see that place again as long as I live."

She threw up her hands in a gesture of futility. "Very well! If that's the way you feel, then don't expect any help from me. And I certainly hope you don't think I'm goan let chu stay here with me. So, why don't chu go back home? Right now. And don't ever come back until and unless you're willin' and ready t'do things my way. In the meantime, regardless of whether you come back or not, you've simply got to get hold of that letter. And when you do, don't chu dare let anybody else see it. I mean *nobody*. And you've got to do it as soon as possible. Right now. Do you understand, Bo Arthur?"

She could see he was having a hard time deciding what to do.

"Well?" she prodded.

"Miss Bustin, I don't know if I can. I'm afraid I might run into ol' man Parker again, an' he's got a pistol. I heard 'im tell Granny t'go to his house and get it."

"The only way Jason Parker would try to hurt chu is if you'd start smart-talkin' the way you do sometimes and makin' him mad. You'd better think of a way to go back home, even if you have to pretend you're sorry for what chu've done. I know you better than you think I do, Bo Arthur. I know you can put on a false front as easily as you can run off at the mouth. Now, once more, I'm go'n' tell you what chu've got t'do if you woant me to help you, and if you think you just cain't do it, then say so right now and that'll be the end of it."

It took a long time for him to nod his head.

She sat down again and clasped her hands together on the table. "All right! You've got to go back home and pretend you never intended to stay gone. Miss Eula needs you. You must tell her you've come back to help her get things worked out about chure mamma. In the mornin', after she goes to church, you can look for the letter. Now, didn't chu tell me you have to go back to Collinsville tomorrow afternoon?"

"Yeah, but I ain't plannin' to."

"What d'you mean, you ain't plannin' to? You've got to go back. You don't have any choice in the matter, so you might as well make up your mind right now that that's what you're gonna do. Remember, I'm doin' this for your benefit, not mine. Will you promise me you'll do right, Bo Arthur?"

"Yessum," he said just above a whisper, without looking at her. "I'll try."

"Tryin' isn't good enough, Bo Arthur. You've *got* t'do better than that."

"Awright. I promise."

She still wasn't convinced, but there was nothing to be gained by further coercion. "All right, now. You'd better go on home."

LONG BEFORE HE got home, Bo Arthur had made up his mind. He didn't intend to do anything Miss Bustin suggested except to get the letter and keep anybody else from seeing it. Other than that, he was setting his own course, as always, whether she liked it or not. There was only one reason why he had condescended to ask for her help in the first place. He knew she hated Frank Haley Bankston as much as he did.

He stood at the gate and tried to determine if Granny was still up. He could see some lamp light in the kitchen, so decided she must be. He could see, also, that the customary lamp for the dead was burning in the back room where his mamma was. Was ol' man Parker still inside, too? Maybe he was, and that meant he had to think of some way to get inside without being seen. He couldn't tell if the screen to his bedroom window was still hanging loose, so he moved over in that direction. The screen and window were both just as he had left them. It would be harder getting back in than it had been getting out, but he knew he could do it, even though he couldn't see very well. He took the screen completely off and laid it aside, then stood on his toes, reached inside and grabbed the window sill with both hands and pulled himself up, pushing the window farther up with his back as he did so.

He was by now shivering from the cold, though he wouldn't want anybody to know it. Better not light the lamp. He didn't need it, anyway. Without taking off his clothes or socks, he jumped into bed and pulled all three quilts and blankets up to his chin, slid his feet around to warm up some space for them, then lay still and quietly for a few moments, trying to plan what he was going to do in the morning when Granny was at church. He fell asleep without having reached any conclusions.

During the night, while Granny and Jason were talking, she kept hoping he couldn't see that her mind was somewhere else. She continued to think about Bo Arthur, how all of this was going to affect him and, also, how much her own life was going to be, and already had been changed. Sometimes her thoughts were so painful, she felt Jason must have noticed. More than anything else, though, she worried about Bo Arthur. She didn't want him to be somebody else's grandson. How strange, she thought, that she should have already designated Frank Haley Bankston as his guardian. She felt some small comfort in knowing, or thinking, that she might still be able to take care of Bo Arthur, and oh, how she hoped that she could. Where was he now? Where had he gone, and would he come back?

When Jason went home briefly to tell Myrtis what his plans were for tomorrow, Eula, holding a lamp, went up the hall and stood for a few moments behind Bo Arthur's door, wanting to look in but not wanting to see that he was not there. She turned the knob as quietly as she could, then stuck her head inside. He was sound asleep. He had come home. No matter how mean and dangerous he was, no matter whose grandson he really was, he had come back!

It was a little while later, when Eula and Jason were talking in the hall, just outside his door, that Bo Arthur awoke for the first time.

"No, Eula," Jason said, "you go on'n eat chure breakfast. I'm goin' home now, 'cause Mrytis said a while ago that she was goan fix breakfast for me'n Lorice. We're goan come by a little b'fore nine'n git chu and take you t'church with us."

"Oh, no, Jason, that's too much sugar for a dime. I can make it up there awright."

"I don't want chu t'have t' walk that far, Eula, not after stayin' up all night, so I'm goan insist on you goin' with us. It won't cause us one bit a inconvenience."

"Well, thank you, Jason. That's mighty kind of you."

"By the way, Eula. I'm leavin' the pistol on the kitchen table just in case you need it. I don't think you will, but better t'be safe than sorry."

Bo Arthur decided he'd better get some more sleep. He knew he was going to need it.

Jason had been gone only a few minutes before he came back. "By the way, Eula, I got t'thinkin' 'bout Mr. Sam's knife and decided I might as well take it to 'im since I'll be in town anyway." But as soon as he started home with the knife, he was more concerned with how best to do the different things he'd promised Eula he'd do, whether to do them before or after church. It was while Brother Gaylon Beard was exhorting the divine obligation and earthly rewards of tithing by citing at least a dozen evidentiary verses of Scripture, that Jason remembered the knife. He was trying to remember where he'd put it when Myrtis nudged him to take the offertory plate.

Bo Arthur woke up later when he heard Eula leaving for church, but decided to stay in bed a little longer, long enough to plan what he would do later. Usually upon waking, either during the night or next morning, his first thoughts were about what his mamma had written. This meant that he had to wrestle with the idea, hoping and trying to believe it was not true, but being made to consider, at least, that it was. Still unconvinced either way, he knew the first thing he had to do was find Lily Ruth's letter. Also, where was the knife? When had he last seen it? Where could he go, where could he hide long enough later today to avoid being found and taken back to Collinsville? The solution to that problem, like all the others, seemed to involve Miss Bustin, even though he knew she didn't like him and he surely didn't like her. Yet, maybe she did like him. After all, she'd told him she was the only one on the school board who said he should not be sent to Collinsville. He tried to remember something else she had said in that regard, something he hadn't thought about until now, and even now he couldn't remember exactly what it was. Something Frank Haley Bankston had said, something that made her angry. He started remembering other things, too, how she seemed to like him, how she even had put her arm around him when she'd seen him yesterday, when she told him some things he didn't want to hear and thought she shouldn't have said. But the fact that she had told him those things meant that she really did care about him, even to the point of trying to keep him out of trouble.

He remembered that he had dropped the knife on the bed just before Jason came in. He tried to open the door to the back room where Lily Ruth was but it was locked. The key, then, had to be somewhere this side of the door.

Granny's apron was hanging on a nail to the right of the stove. The letter was still in the pocket. When he touched it, he felt more like tearing it up now than he had before, but he knew he'd better not. He still couldn't figure out why Miss Bustin was so interested in seeing it. What did she plan to do with it? He had spent most of his time wondering about it as he walked home last night.

He saw that Granny had left some food on the heat shelf of the stove. It was when he sat down to eat that he saw a key lying on top of the flour canister. It must be the one he needed. When he opened the door later, he saw that the knife was not there, yet he stood without wanting to, letting his eyes shift from one place to another, trying not to see Lily Ruth. He started toward the door but stopped suddenly, just long enough to look back. She looked peaceful. He didn't want her to. He wanted her to suffer the way he'd made believe she was suffering every time he cut her up on the back steps.

When he went out onto the back porch, he saw that Granny had washed his Collinsville uniform and had hung it up to dry. That reminded him of something else he had to think about. He stood at the foot of the back steps, looking over at the Parker house, remembering the fight with Jason yesterday evening. The longer he thought about it, the more likely became the possibility that Jason had taken the knife home with him. He suddenly remembered what he had heard Jason say about the pistol, but he let it pass. A pistol wasn't a part of his scheme.

He knew that the Parkers never locked their doors unless they were going to be gone for a long time. Most people, especially those living in the country, felt no need to lock their doors. A knock was usually all that was needed before entering, and sometimes not even that. He pushed his hands deeper into his pockets and turned his head from side to side, trying to look normal, just outside for some fresh air as he edged his way closer to the house. He hesitated before opening the back door, still a little uneasy about what he was going to do, but a deep breath or two restored his confidence.

Renewed confidence notwithstanding, he still felt a little uncomfortable as he tiptoed into the kitchen, where he stopped long enough to get used to the new surroundings. The embers in the stove had turned to dust and the kitchen was cold, but it wasn't the cold that was making him feel different. He would not know until after the deed was done that it was the guilty thrill and personal satisfaction of having done something he had never done before, something unlawful that gave him more of what he knew he needed, a stronger assurance that he could do something else, something more serious, that had to be done. But for now he had to find the knife. It was only when he reached the front bedroom, where Myrtis and Jason slept, that he saw it, open to view on the seat of a rocker on the other side of the wardrobe. He could still smell the banana as he ran his fingers over and around it. He felt good.

He must now make up his mind about what to do next. It was too early to go back to Miss Bustin's house, church was not over yet. Yet, it might be by the time he got there and, if she wasn't home yet and had left her house open, he could wait for her inside. Otherwise, he could go sit in the depot, where a fire was usually burning in the little pot-bellied stove. But what was more important than that was what he would finally do, after giving Miss Bustin the letter. The letter! Yes! That's what would determine what he would do afterwards. He would not give her the letter! He would make her do what he wanted her to do, because he knew how much the letter meant to her. After all, if the letter meant so much to her, and it certainly seemed that way, then he could make her do anything he wanted her to do. Yes, she would have to let him stay in her house until he did what he was planning on doing. She couldn't refuse. The longer he thought about it, the better he felt. Suddenly, he knew why she wanted the letter. She wanted the letter as much as he wanted to kill Frank Haley Bankston.

It was important that he do everything he needed to do at Granny's before leaving, even though he had not worked his plans out completely. It was better to have more than he might likely need, like the Collinsville uniform already dried out on the back porch. As he took it down, he tried to think far enough ahead to justify taking it with him. The uniform was made of light blue cotton fabric, with Collinsville, Boys made Men embroidered in darker blue on the left pocket. He saw that Granny had mended where he had ripped it loose the other day.

In his room, while stuffing one of the pillowcases from his bed with the things he thought he might need, he realized he had to have some money. He knew Granny kept the money she made from sewing and doing alterations in the bottom left hand drawer of the sewing machine. Heretofore, he had never stolen any of it, but now it didn't matter. He took two folded dollar bills and slid them into his bib pocket, then left, stopping long enough to give Dodger a big hug.

IDA BELLE BUSTIN lay sleepless between the warm blankets and quilts all night long without having fully made up her mind what she was going to do. The two Tischner attempts to fall asleep had been ineffective and had, in fact, made her more fully awake than before. The longer and harder she tried to go to sleep, the more agitated she became. That's the way she had felt years ago, knowing she was about to leave everything she had ever known and needed in order to bring faceless masses of strange people to Jesus, throwing out the short, limp life-line on which she herself had never had a firm enough grip.

The present situation, however, was different in a very significant way; she was in no sense of the word planning to save *anybody!* She had a firm grip on this line, even though the person at the other end of it was, in some striking ways, faceless, also.

She dreaded the thought of having to go to church, yet she knew from past experience that she would feel worse if she stayed home. Her own personal preferences must yield now, as always, to God's will and glory, no matter how inconvenient it would be to do so. She readily and often acknowledged to herself that she was a hypocrite, as much so as were some of the other church members whom she had often condemned for the same reason, but she knew she had to retain at any cost the meager part of the charade that remained or go under completely and hate herself more than she already did. Too early in life, as soon as the seeds were planted, she had failed to till the soil of her soul sufficiently and often enough to deter the tares from taking a firm, deep hold on her spiritual garden. The aborted missionary attempt that was intended to be the turning point of her Christian life forced her to face up to just how limited her faith and convictions were. Physician, heal thyself, she admonished herself time and time again, but the cure never came.

As she had expected, her physical self was the only part of her that went to church later. She had resolved before leaving home that she would put out of her mind the matter that had kept her awake all night, but she was finding it more difficult than she had expected it to be. Just the thought of having Lily Ruth's letter in her own hands excited her. She must decide the best way to use it. Bo Arthur must give it to her, not permanently, but long enough for her to put it to good use.

IDA BELLE WAS one of the few people who always locked their doors before going anywhere. Bo Arthur half expected that to be the case when he got there. The screen door to the back porch, though, was not locked. He would go to the depot, but he first had to do something with the pillowcase full of his belongings. If it were not for the knife, he could just leave it on the back porch. Looking around to see that nobody was watching, he took the knife out and laid it on the cool, moist ground behind the first step, then stood back to make sure nobody could see it. He felt good and confident now as he walked toward the depot. He was getting ready to cross the street when he heard somebody calling him. It was Tracy Brand, the deputy who had taken him to Collinsville the first time.

"I got sumpn' t'tell you, Bo Arthur," he said, as he neared.

"What is it?"

"The sheriff told me if I saw you t'let chu know that the folks at Collinsville said you could stay home till next Sunday on account a yo' mamma."

"They really did?"

"Yep. I'll prob'ly be the one t'take you back. I'll try t'see you b'fore then t'let chu know 'bout what time I'll pick you up."

That made him wonder, now, about whether he really needed to stay at Miss Bustin's house instead of going back to Granny's. He knew it would be better for Granny if he did, but this was no time to get tender-hearted. No, he needed to be somewhere else, a place from which he could plot and carry out what he had in mind. He knew she was planning to do something serious and he wanted to see what it was. He was pretty sure that whatever she had in mind involved him. That was something he must never forget! What he was trying not to think about was how much he was going to need her. He must never let her know. If he did, she would have the upper hand. He was damn sure that would never happen!

IDA BELLE WAS surprised to see the stuffed pillowcase on the top step as she went to the back porch to get some firewood. She knew right away what it meant, and she knew, too, that she was not going to let Bo Arthur stay in her house. Under no circumstances! She started back inside, then stopped, laid the logs down so she could see what was in the pillowcase. Yes, it looked as though he planned to stay a while. Where was he now? She reminded herself that it would require all of her common sense and extreme caution to persuade him to do things the way she thought they should be done. And she knew it was not going to be easy. They were too much alike. Yes, she had known that for a long time, and it did not make her feel any better.

She was warming some leftovers from yesterday when he came, bringing the pillowcase of things in with him. "Are you hungry?" she asked, fearing he might say he was.

"No, un-unh, I done ate at Granny's 'fore I left."

"You say you *done ate?*"

"Yessum."

"I see you've brought you some clothes and things. You're not thinkin' about stayin' here, are you?"

"Yessum," he said confidently.

"Well, you'd better stop thinkin' about it, because you're not!" she said, turning from the stove to see his reaction.

"Yessum, I am."

She didn't like the way that sounded. "And what excuse are you goan give the folks at Collinsville for not returnin' like you're supposed to?"

"I don't need no excuses. I do things the way I want to'n if I don't woana go back, then I won't go back."

She got as close to him as she could, leaned over and glared into his eyes. "And I suppose you think they're not goin' to do anything about it. Well, you can rest assured that they most certainly will, and don't be surprised if they send you on up to Parchman."

"I don't think so. In the meantime, I plan to stay here. An' anyway, you need me too much for me to go back and leave you t'do things by yourself. No ma'm, Miss Bustin, *I'm stayin' here with you.*"

"And just how do you know what I plan to do, if anything? You don't know and you never will, and no matter what my plans are, they don't require your presence in my house." She leaned over again and looked him straight in the eye. "I repeat, *you are not goin' t'stay here and that's that!* So don't give it another thought."

She had never seen that look on his face before. "I done tol' you, Miss Bustin, I'm goan stay here in this house, or you ain't goan see the letter. I done decided that's the way it's goan be. So what d'you say now?"

She wasn't ready for that. Back at the stove, she distractedly stirred the pot of peas, wondering what to say and praying that she would be able to control herself. She leaned against the stove, facing him, breathing deeply and slowly, wiping her hands on the apron, making sure she said the right thing. "I can now see for myself that you are every bit as evil as everybody but me, it seems, has said you were. Now, I'm goin' to say it one more time, and you'd better listen carefully. *You are not goin' to stay in this house!* If you continue to believe you are, I have ways to see that you don't. And as for the letter, I don't need to see it. And furthermore, just in case you've forgotten, there's Mr. Sam's knife that you stole. Yes, I knew all along that you'd stolen it. So you make up your mind now." She opened the kitchen door and stood aside. "Now you get chure belongin's an' be on your way. I said, *be on your way!*"

He laughed. "You don't scare me, you frustrated ol' maid. I knew all about chu long b'fore I was in yore class. An' I know how much you hate Frank Haley Bankston, an' that's why you wanted to see the letter my mamma wrote. Well, now you ain't *never* go'n' see it! And yes m'am, I was the one that stole the knife from Mr. Sam, and if you don't change yore mind about me stayin' here, I'll use it on you. And don't think I won't!"

As soon as he walked out the door, onto the porch and down the steps to where the knife was, she locked the screen door and the kitchen door as quickly as she could, then ran into her bedroom. When he started back inside and found that the screen door was locked, he shredded the screen with the knife. Ida Belle, not aware that he had the knife, opened the door just enough to see him reaching for the latch. He threw the knife at her but it hit the door and landed just beyond where she was standing. Realizing he would try to come inside to get it, she threw the door open wide and pointed the pistol at him as he started inside. Now she knew he was defenseless. She kicked the knife off to one side, then stepped forward with the pistol pointed at his head. "You move one more inch in my direction, you demented bastard, and I'll blow your brains out! Now move!" She got closer to him and he backed up. She could tell he was scared, even though he was laughing.

"*Keep movin'!*"

As soon as he fumbled the door open, she pushed him down

the steps and watched as he tried to get up. She kept the pistol aimed at him, even though her hands were shaking so much she was afraid she was going to drop it. She would never forget what he said as he left.

WIDOW MYRA MACINTOSH had just eaten lunch and was letting her dog Reno out when she saw Bo Arthur shredding the screen on Ida Belle's porch door. She didn't recognize at first that it was Bo Arthur. What was he doing, in the first place, at Ida Belle's house, and why was he ruining her screen door? As soon as he could open the door, he started inside, then stopped suddenly. If she had not been so fascinated, she might have asked him why he was trying to get into Miss Bustin's house. Then she remembered having been told by two or three of her friends on the school board that Ida Belle Bustin had been the only one who objected to Bo Arthur's being sent to Collinsville. Why would she be the only one to dissent? Could it be true, as rumor had it, that Ida Belle had certain feelings for Bo Arthur that blinded her to his faults and influenced the way she voted?

A little later, Myra called V. Allison Coats, who had worked as an operator in the telephone exchange until she was dismissed three years ago for improper conduct in the exercise of her duties. During the course of her employ, however, she had been privy to countless phone calls to, from, and about Ida Belle.

V. Allison had taught second grade since losing her job at the telephone exchange. She would be the first to admit that she had no background in teaching and, furthermore, had not acquired during her fifty-four years even the minimal educational requirements for the job. As a matter of fact, she had found getting through high school one of the most daunting and in every other way difficult challenges of her life. For as long as she worked at the telephone exchange she had been able to acquire and maintain friendships which she might not have been able to do otherwise. She was usually the most popular guest at any get-together and often remarked that you didn't need to be a young social butterfly or even a wife in order to be popular. She was fortunate in another way, as well. She was Frank Haley Bankston's sister-in-law.

V. Allison lay down for a few minutes to think about what Myra had just told her. She was reminded once again of how drastically her life had changed since she was no longer a telephone operator, how uninformed she was, how desperate she sometimes felt to learn that there were others who knew more about what was going on in Ellisville than she did.

She called her sister. "Were you asleep?" she asked as she struggled to get another pillow behind her head.

"No, just readin'. "

"You by yourself?"

"Yes."

"Where's Frank Haley?"

"He's down at the office, Vee. He's workin' on some big court case next week in Meridian. He went down there as soon as we ate lunch. What's the matter?"

"Oh, nothin', really. Well, anyway, how're you feelin'? Is your bronchitis any better?"

"A little, I think. Frank didn't bring my medicine until late yesterday evenin'."

"D'you know what the lawsuit in Meridian is all about?"

"Of course not. He never tells me anything. In fact, something's been botherin' him ever since yesterday. I knew the moment he walked in the front door he was mad. He chunked the bottle of medicine on the bed, then went off by himself. I never bother anymore to ask what's wrong. It only makes 'im madder. I cain't help wonderin', though, what happened yesterday to upset 'im so much. Do you have any idea what it could be?"

"No, I sure don't. Me'n Sue Sellers spent all day yesterday shoppin' in Laurel. I tell you what. I'm go'n' do some phonin' aroun' n if I learn anything, I'll call you back."

Admittedly, getting information these days was certainly harder than it used to be, but V. Allison was still better at it than most other people were. Though she complained endlessly about having to be on a party line where other people could hear everything she said, she adamantly refused to concede, either to herself or to others, that the party line was her most valuable source of information.

The afternoon of phoning proved profitable. When she called Gayle again around three-thirty, she had a long two-page list of information to report. "Well, first of all," she said, clearing her throat as she scanned the first page, "I can now tell you why Frank Haley was so upset yesterday. Do you want to know?"

"Well, of course I do."

"All right. Here's what happened. The word had been going aroun' town yesterday that Bo Arthur had stole one of Mr. Sam's knives and when Frank Haley heard about it, he promised Mr. Sam that he was go'n' find it. So, he goes in Ben Rayburn's and what d'you know! There's Bo Arthur, just gettin' ready t'leave. When Frank Haley asked 'im about the knife, Bo Arthur got all riled up and said sumpn real bad that got Frank Haley hot under the collar, so he tried to knock Bo Arthur down but wuddn't able to on account'a that lame leg. Instead, he lost his balance and fell down right there in front of all them customers. You know how that must've made 'im feel. Well, anyway, when somebody hep'd Frank Haley up, he tol' Bo Arthur he was go'n' get even with 'im if it was the last thang he ever did. They never did find the knife, though."

"What was it Bo Arthur said that made him so mad? Did you ever find out?"

"Well, bless patty, I couldn't get heads nor tails out of Irene Lott. She was in there at the time, but she's so deaf she couldn't hear it thunder, let alone what people were sayin'. Never mind. That's when I decided t'do what I should'a done t'start with. I called Ben Rayburn. Well, I don't need t'tell you how Ben loves t'talk, 'specially if he's got sumpn bad t'say about somebody. Anyway, I didn't have t'wait long b'fore he tol' me evuhthang. He said Frank Haley asked Bo Arthur sumpn 'bout bein' home instead a Collinsville an' Bo Arthur, smart alec that he is, walked right up t' Frank Haley an' said sumpn like he wuddn't s'posed t'be there in the first place. An' then he went on t'say that when he first got to Collinsville, they asked him why he was there and who was responsible for him bein' sent there in the first place. He said he tol' 'em he was sent there by a two-bit lawyer that thought he was Jesus but wuddn't, an' that he knew sumpn' 'bout 'im, Frank Haley, that is, that nobody else but him knew and when he got ready he was go'n' tell evuhbody. That's when Frank Haley lost his temper'n tried to knock 'im down but wuddn't able to."

Every Sunday morning for forty-four years, Shelley Ruth Shannon had walked the four miles from Ellisville to Tula Rosa Church. The only times she did not go were when she was either bed-ridden or too afraid to challenge what was serious, and imminently threatening weather. She was a sixty-four-year-old spinster without any living relatives. Up until the time tuberculosis killed her father, they had ridden to church together. She could not drive and often said she wouldn't drive even if she could. When asked why she chose to walk that far, she usually said that the walk was a part of her religious experience.

This morning after church, she was visiting with Eula Bilbo, Jason, Myrtis, and Lorice Parker out front under one of the giant water oaks. Jason said he needed to go to town to take care of Eula's business, so he asked Shelley Ruth if he could take her home. She thanked him but said she'd rather walk. In the meantime, Jason suggested they all go back inside and visit until he could come back for them. The main topic of conversation, of course, was Lily Ruth's return, her death, and the funeral needs and plans.

Each Sunday, before going home, Miss Shelley Ruth stopped at Ben's City Café for the Sunday Special that most often consisted of two pieces of southern fried chicken, mashed potatoes with gravy, green beans, peas, or cabbage, and either lemon or apple pie, chocolate or banana pudding, and coffee or iced tea. The place was crowded when she finally got there, but Ben made sure there was a special table for her, off to one side up front. When he asked how things were going, how she was feeling, and if she'd heard anything interesting out Tula Rosa way, she seemed to perk up more than usual, then told him about Lily Ruth. At his prodding, she told him almost everything she had learned earlier.

V. ALLISON'S DISTRESSING account of things involving her brother-in-law had a debilitating effect on Gayle, which was precisely what had prompted the call in the first place. The two sisters had not grown up ideally like two oak trees, side by side, existing on the same soil, sharing life in similar ways, or letting their leafy arms touch and even cling to each other from time to time. They were, instead, two side-by-side slim loblolly pines with scant and high needled arms that rarely even touched and, if they did, the touch was neither gentle, nor did it last long.

V. Allison called Gayle again around five o'clock to report the latest information Ben Rayburn had given her. Lily Ruth Bilbo had died at Eula Bilbo's home. Shelley Ruth Shannon had not said more than that about Lily Ruth, but it was enough to stimulate Ben's suspicions and enough for him to speculate, conclude, and suggest to V. Allison that Lily Ruth had died of syphilis, a word he tried to find a substitute for but couldn't. He didn't need to. V. Allison was already ahead of him. "Gayle, you know as well as I do that she was a cheap, no-good whore. There's no tellin' how many men in this town learned about it first-hand, if you know what I mean, and I bet chu I could name at least a dozen of 'em right now if I was asked to."

"Well, don't. I don't care to know who they are."

"Well, yeah, I guess not. Well, anyway, that's all the news for t'day. Take care a yourself. Bye."

In her eagerness to tell Gayle the things she'd heard about Frank Haley, she had forgotten what Myra Macintosh had told her about Bo Arthur. The longer she thought about it, the more important it became. *Why, of course,* she thought, *he was trying to break into Ida Belle Bustin's house. But why?* She should have gotten the answer to that one before she called Gayle. Why did she call Gayle first? *Oh well, it don't matter nohow.* She fidgeted with the phone, waiting to be connected.

Ida Belle was washing some undergarments in the sink when, after seven rings, she heard the phone and decided to answer it, drying her hands on her apron and still lost in thought as she picked up the phone. "Hello, Ida Belle, this is V. Allison."

"Yes? What's the matter?"

V. Allison laughed. "Why, nothin's the matter, Ida Belle. I just thought I'd give you a call t'find out how you're doin'."

Ida Belle knew better than that. Normally, she would find some way to break the connection, but this time she felt different.

"I'm doin' just fine, Vee. So what d'you know that's worth talkin' about? Heard anything lately?"

V. Allison was trying to control her curiosity, but Ida Belle could tell that the real purpose of the call was to find out why Bo Arthur had been seen at her back door. "Well, I've been concerned about chu ever since Myra Macintosh told me she'd seen Bo Arthur ripping the screen off a your back door. We're very concerned for you, Ida Belle. Why would he be doin' sumpn like that?"

Ida Belle decided to sit down. It gave her a chance to weigh what she had just heard and to decide how much she wanted or even dared to tell her. She had never liked V. Allison and, at times, had even been intimidated by her. She was ashamed to admit even to herself that she was actually afraid of her. Her shame was such that she would figuratively thrash herself every time she came close to saying why. Now, though, while V. Allison prated on and on about this and that, she had time to disconnect mentally long enough to consider that there might be some legitimate justification for changing the way she felt about her. Even as she listened, her thoughts were bumping into one another, sometimes causing her not to hear and to have to say, "I'm sorry, Vee, what was that?"

She started off slowly and cautiously, believing she could cut her way through the clutter in her head as she went, just so long as she could keep her mind a word or thought or two ahead of her tongue. She took a deep breath. "I don't blame you and Myra for wondering why Bo Arthur was cuttin' up my screen door, but the truth of the matter is that he had run away from Granny's for some reason or other and had the crazy idea that I'd let him stay here with me. When I told him he most certainly could not, he got mad and for some reason or other acted like he was leavin', but instead, he had gone out there where he'd hidden the knife he stole from Mr. Sam and was plannin' on usin' it on me. Can you believe that!"

"Why, Ida Belle, I cain't b'lieve it! He must a gone crazy. Wuddn't you scared t'death?"

"Well, of course, I was. But I'd already decided when he started outside that I was goan lock my doors, and that's just what I did." She stopped long enough to detect, if she could, V. Allison's reactions to that much of the story. Whatever the reactions were, she was not making them known. "I cain't believe he would try sumpn like that on me, the one person who's been on his side all along. What do you think, Vee? D'you think I did the right thing?"

She seemed not to have heard. "Oh, what? Oh, yeah, of course you did."

After a few moments, V. Allison surprised Ida Belle by asking, "But d'you think he'd do such a thang unless he was really upset about sumpn? We know Bo Arthur's always had a mean streak a mile wide down his backside, but he's never done nothin' like that before, has he? . . . Has he, Ida Belle?"

Was this the time? What would happen if she said what she was thinking, something she wished with all her being that others knew without her having to tell them. If V. Allison had not called, she would not now be doing battle with her conscience, her weak, exhausted, vengeful conscience.

She waited long enough to give some cursory thought to what she had already said and to consider to what extent she might have already incriminated herself. When she had hitherto faced similar situations that required the full measure of her intelligence, faith, and will, she had managed somehow to survive and even, in some instances, to prosper. This one was different, however. She knew that to tell V. Allison or anyone else everything she knew about the present situation would be her undoing. It would obliterate the last remnants of the facade she had hoped to retain; it might possibly be the last of all her battles, so she must decide now if she wanted to fight it. Oddly enough, the decision had already been made long ago. All she could do now, all that she really wanted to do was to start it. To fight it would require more armor than she had at her disposal. There was no more faith, no more interest, wisdom, courage or willpower to resist. Let it begin!

"Well, I'll tell you what I think," V. Allison was saying. "I b'lieve seein' his mamma after all this time, 'specially bein' full of that you-know-what-I-mean disease, must'a had a lot t'do with it. I've heard time an' time again how much he hated 'er, otherwise, why would he be tryin' t'run away from home just when he ought'a be there. No matter how much he hated Lily Ruth, he surely ought'a have the decency to see her buried. Don' chu think so, Ida Belle?"

"Well, yes, of course, he should. But . . . but it was what happened later that made the difference."

"What d'you mean, sumpn that happened later. Later than what?"

"Vee, I don't know if I should tell you or not."

"What d'you mean? You can tell me, no matter how bad it is. Why are you afraid t'tell me?"

"Because it's extremely bad, that's why. And . . . and it involves somebody you know."

"So, that makes it even more important that I know. Tell me, for God's sakes, or I'm goana have a stroke!"

"You may have one anyway if I do, Vee."

"All right, all right! I'll risk it! Tell me, Ida Belle. *Tell* me!"

"Vee, I find this extremely difficult to do. Do you understand that if I tell you, there may be some very serious repercussions. Do you want to take that risk?"

"Anything, Ida Belle. Tell me!"

"All right. The reason Bo Arthur left home and the only reason he refuses to go back and attend the funeral is because Eula found a note in Lily Ruth's suitcase, written to Bo Arthur. She told him that Brandon was not his father, that somebody else was."

"Good God! Who? Who, Ida Belle? Is it anybody we know?"

"Yes, it's a person we all know, Vee, though some of us know 'im better than others do. It's somebody who's very cruel, somebody who's very mean and evil inside the saintly shell he wears whenever he's around other people. Vee, he's your brother-in-law."

— t w e n t y —

IT WAS A little after midnight when Frank Haley Bankston went home. He had spent more than seven hours doing some last-minute research and documentation in preparation for the beginning of the murder trial in Meridian. Next morning, he was on his way shortly after breakfast, having told Gayle he might decide to spend the night in Meridian rather than drive home so late.

It was going to be a hard case to win. He would be defending his friend Jacob Morgenstein, owner of numerous men's wear stores throughout the south, who is alleged to have killed his wife in self-defense when he learned she had been spending more nights with Casey Bruno than with him. He had had misgivings about this case from the moment he accepted it as a favor for his friend, but as soon as he learned that the presiding judge would be Mark Allen Carruthers, his misgivings multiplied. In his younger days, he had tried several cases with Judge Carruthers on the bench, and each one had been an uncommon failure in his otherwise astonishing list of successes.

As he drove north on Highway 11, he was thinking more about his early failures than about the brilliant others that followed. He normally went at every new case with exuberance, manic determination, and unwithering confidence, feeling and knowing that each one would further enhance his already enviable reputation. As much as he was trying now as he had tried many times before to put Judge Carruthers out of his mind, he was unable to. Carruthers had warned him time and time again to stop using Bible references in his defense arguments. "Mr. Bankston," he had said repeatedly, "you will stop this form of defense or I'll cite you for contempt of court if I have to. This is a court of law, Mr. Bankston, not a house of worship."

In an attempt to put Carruthers out of his mind, he practiced the opening statement he wrote last night. It made him feel better. He thought what he had written was good, even brilliant, with enough allowable scriptural references to have the usual effect of bonding himself from the beginning with the jurors.

The good feeling did not last long. Having Lily Ruth come to mind was the last thing he needed. He had kept her locked up in one of the file drawers in a vault at the back of his office. As one might expect, he was meticulous in the way he labeled and filed legal documents as well as certain other ones of a personal nature. Filing was a job secretaries normally did for their bosses, but not for Frank Haley. Some of the files were not identified by labels but by special marks or symbols which he alone could interpret. One of them came to mind now. Lily Ruth was dead. He would no longer be obligated to help support her. He would destroy it as soon as he finished the Morgenstein case. But he knew that destroying Lily Ruth's file would not remove her completely from his consciousness. What he had feared hitherto and now realized was that she would always be present in some capacity like a lesion that would never heal.

What was wrong? What was happening to him? Except for feeling good about his opening statement, he realized that virtually every thought he'd had since leaving home had been a negative one. Was it because he had not slept well or very long last night? Not likely. He had always prided himself in knowing and letting others know that he was always ready for battle, whether he had slept much or not at all the night before.

AFTER TELLING V. ALLISON everything she had wanted to know, Ida Belle went into an emotional slump. Sunday night was restless, sleepless, and many hours too long. She recalled time and time again everything she had said, everything she had intended not to say. Her intentions lately had been nothing more than broken promises. All of her shortcomings made their separate appearances like ghosts coming single-file out of her closet, and stayed long enough to remind her of each of her failings, each one of her feeble, false attempts to be Godly when, in truth, she was not Godly at all and never had been.

She learned while very young that something strange and wonderful happened every morning when she awoke and got out of bed. Her ghosts were gone, and there were lots of good and happy things to look forward to, to live for. But when this present one of Ida Belle's mornings came, the ghosts got out of bed with her. Even as she trudged her way around the house, getting ready for school, she felt as though her feet as well as her mind were still asleep.

Her altered state of mind continued throughout the day. The younger students in her freshman English class had not seemed to notice anything different. It was during the third period class of senior English that the students realized something was wrong. In school, as around town, her more obvious peculiarities had long ago been recognized and accepted as common side effects of spinsterhood. There were still enough parents and school children who recognized and valued her considerable knowledge and teaching skills to such an extent that her eccentricities went unnoticed.

On that particular Monday morning, instead of asking her students to open their textbooks and prepare to answer some random questions regarding the use of the subjunctive mood, she asked them to bow their heads while she prayed. She prayed so intently that she failed to see how many of them were turning their heads and asking one another with knitted brows what this could mean. When she finished, she said, "Now, let's all repeat the Lord's Prayer."

"Today, students," she said, laying the English book down and taking a Bible out of the desk drawer, "we're going to consider and explore the presence and proliferation of evil in the world."

There was a rare, lingering silence in the classroom.

"I'm going to tell you somethin' now that may surprise you. I hope you will understand. I hope, also, that it will not upset any of you." She waited long enough to make sure she had their full attention and was encouraged to see, by the expectancy in their eyes and on their faces, that she did. She continued. "Today is goin' to be a day unlike any other day of your lives. Something wonderful, which will affect you and the lives of all people in the world, is going to happen."

Finally, after thinking and hoping somebody else would say

something, Joyce Bailey Jennings seemed to have lost her patience but had found her tongue, instead. "What is it you woant to tell us, Miss Butin?"

She closed her eyes briefly, then crossed her arms over the Bible and pressed it close to her breast, but still waited. "Last night," she said, finally, "I was awakened from a sound sleep by the Holy Spirit and was told that something wonderful was going to happen today, something that would drastically affect your young lives and the lives of all the people in the world." Her voice sounded unnatural, not at all like her own, because it was not her voice. It was the Holy Spirit speaking through her. She had departed her own body; she was transformed! "What is goin' to happen? I'll tell you what's goin' to happen." She threw her arms out and over her head, holding the Bible up for them to see, then threw her head back and shouted to the ceiling, *"Jesus is comin'! Jesus is comin'! Come, Lord Jesus, come!"* The Bible fell from her hands. She collapsed into the chair, laid her head on the desk and cried convulsively.

"I'm goan get Mr. Tatum," Joyce Bailey said.

Mr. Tatum came immediately.

"Miss Bustin," he said, putting his hand gently on her shoulder, "let's go home."

She looked up as though she had never seen him before. "No, no, I'm not through. Class is not over yet."

"Yes, Miss Bustin, class is over," then, to the students, "you may go now. I'll talk with you later. Would one of you please tell my secretary Betty to come as soon as she can t'help me get Miss Bustin home?"

Now that she was at home, she wondered why. She lay down for a while, trying to understand what had happened earlier in class and trying to remember, even, what exactly she had done, why she was now at home when she should be teaching. She remembered yesterday with shame and wished now that she could run it all through her head again and feel a little better. She couldn't deny that she had said more than she should have, even after making a spineless effort not to.

She was hungry but did not want to eat. She seemed to be thawing out, feeling different parts of her body coming alive again as though her blood had only now begun to flow through her. She was cold, also. She could hear and feel the cold air sneaking in through the windows where the caulking had fallen out long ago. It was a problem she had never cared enough about to remedy. It was like the brooch her mother wore as a bride, which she now kept in a little chest on her dresser to remind her always of the time when she was happy and loved and aspiring.

She kept all the rooms closed except her bedroom, the bathroom, and the kitchen. From time to time, when she was weary with the world, her own and the larger one, she would open the closed door to each room, stand for a few moments while the heartache made her wish she were dead. That's what she was doing now. She stayed long enough in each room to let the pain consume her, but she refused to cry. Each room was a walled sanctuary that kept the ugliness outside and beyond from gaining access to what was left, what was good and beautiful. In her mother's bedroom, she sat on the edge of the bed, smoothed her hands over the quilt she had helped her mother make, then lay back for a few moments. There was no longer the merest suggestion of the sweet lilac smell that always used to scent the whole room, the same smell her mother seemed to carry with her everywhere she went. But the bed was there, just as it used to be, and, in the dark closet off to the left, her mother's clothes still hung, food enough yet for the moths she had never been able to get rid of. She visited each of the other rooms, also, waiting a few minutes in each of them until she was able to feel something of what she used to feel. As she went to the kitchen to build the fire in the stove, she felt as she always did after revisiting her past, that she had left part of herself there. By now, after many years, she sometimes wondered just how much of it was left.

That night, before going to bed, she had two swigs of Dr. Tischener's, hoping it would get her through the night. It used to, but things were different then. She had even planned to have a few more sips if tonight was as bad as last night was. In the meantime, she decided to make her daily entry in her diary. She had a hard time remembering what she needed to write. Fortunately, she fell asleep even before she finished reading her Bible. She knew it was going to be extremely cold, so she put extra blankets on the chair by the bed just in case she needed them. She did, actually, but she never consciously realized it. She slept soundly for several hours before the dream came:

> *Someone was knocking on the front door and she was afraid to see who it was, The knocking continued intermittently until she finally decided she should get up, Normally, she would not answer the door unless somebody called her name, meaning that it was someone she knew. Now she had no alternative. She tip-toed up to the front door and raised the shade slightly. Someone was standing on the other side, someone who looked familiar. Yes, of course, it had happened as she had said it would. She cupped her hands over her face to keep from screaming. He should not be coming to her house. He had made a mistake.*
>
> *She stepped back, still covering her face and crying.*
>
> *He tapped lightly on the glass. "Ida Belle," he said, "will you let me come in?"*

THE COLD WET tears woke her up. She was shaking, holding the bed clothes up to her chin, trying to decide what had happened, wondering where she was.

The ringing telephone shocked her fully awake and rational enough to realize that ten o'clock meant she should be in her classroom but wasn't. Furthermore, she felt no compulsion to get up and go there. She told Marcus Tatum she was not able to come back yet. While she was eating breakfast, she thought of the knife Bo Arthur had thrown at her. Where had she put it? She had been too upset at the time to remember. She sat back and recalled what had happened and why. What alarmed her most now was that she had pointed a pistol at him. She actually intended to kill him. *What's happening to me? What's wrong?*

BY THE END of court Tuesday, Frank Haley realized he was in trouble. So far, he had found that none of the stratagems that had paid off before was having its usual desirable effect and, furthermore, since he could no longer depend on his knowledge and skillful use of Biblical references to reinforce what might otherwise be ineffective, he had gradually become aware that his frustration was showing. As soon as court recessed, he drove back to Ellisville. He would have to do more research. There must be something he had overlooked, some legal maneuver, though he thought he knew them all, or some precedent that might possibly change the course of the trial.

"How's the trial goin'?" Gayle asked.

"Not very well."

"I'm sorry, Frank. Are you hungry? You must be. If I'd known you were comin' home, I wouldn't have let Ella Jane have the leftovers from lunch. You woant me to fix you somthin'?"

"No, I need to get back to my office."

BO ARTHUR FELT he had in his own way attended his mamma's funeral, even though he had watched from behind an oak tree some distance away. What he felt during and following the simple ceremony was neither sadness nor relief. During the past day or so he had been planning what he would do now that he had a few more days away from Collinsville. Whatever he planned or needed to do, getting the knife back was high on the list. The longer he thought about Frank Haley Bankston, the madder he got, sometimes even, when out of sight of others, he would plan how he would use it. He even practiced doing it, bringing the knife up and behind his right shoulder, then bringing it down, to the face, first, then the chest and his ribs, closing his eyes and visualizing how it would look. Mr. Sam always came to mind at such times.

Miss Bustin would be teaching, he thought. That meant his only concern was getting inside the house without being seen, especially by old lady Macintosh. He'd better act like he was just walking for the fun of it, throw rocks at squirrels, bend over, pretending he was tying his shoe laces. On his way to the back of the house he stopped all of a sudden and started wondering if he was doing the right thing. He remembered what had happened back there. He could still see Miss Bustin picking the knife up off of the floor and shutting the door with a bang. Maybe he ought to try the front door instead, especially since he couldn't see anybody outside anywhere.

He didn't see her, but Vayda Baygents had just raised the shade on her front door and was looking out, wondering what Bo Arthur Bilbo was doing over on this side of town and why her married daughter Barbara was so late coming by to cook breakfast for her. Vayda had just survived a restless night of leg cramps and was far from being ready to cope with another day on an empty stomach. And seeing Bo Arthur Bilbo didn't help matters, either. She was one of the few folks who didn't like him and often predicted that he would one day do something bad enough to put him in Parchman for the rest of his life or on the end of a hangman's rope. She watched him walk up to Ida Belle's front door, where he stopped, looked around, then knocked and waited.

Well, for Pete's sake, why couldn't Barbara have waited a little longer? I'm not all that hungry.

The screen door was unlatched. That's because Miss Bustin had come out that way to go to school, he reasoned. As soon as he tried the doorknob and found the door was locked, he thought that, also, was the way it should be.

Even so, he felt something was wrong. It was the shade. It didn't seem right that it was not raised the way it usually was. He put his hand on the doorknob, turned it back and forth, then pushed against it.

Ida Belle heard. She raised the shade just enough to see who it was. He's come back! She was trying to remember when He came the first time, when He asked if He could come inside, had she let Him? Had she? *Oh, it was so hard to remember. No matter, He's back, and I'm glad. I need Him.*

"Come in, Lord," she said," stepping back to curtsy with one hand under her chin and the other stretched out, motioning him inside.

Bo Arthur was surprised to see that she was still in her nightgown and that the long, matted hair hanging over her shoulders looked greyer than it did the last time he saw her. He didn't know whether to go in or not. Something was not right. He had never seen her look that way. And what was it she just said, didn't she say 'Lord'? He remembered now what folks had been saying about her lately, that she always carried a little bottle of Tischener's antiseptic wherever she went and, if anybody asked her about it, she would say it was only for keeping her breath fresh. Nobody believed her. He knew it could make you drunk, too, because he had tried it once, and it worked. Was she drunk now? *Her? A teacher?*

She grabbed both of his hands and tried to kiss them, but he pulled away and stepped back as far as he could, trying to find the doorknob. She moved closer, pressed him against the door, then cupped her hands around his face.

He pushed her away with one hand and reached around for the doorknob with the other. When she reached out again to touch him, he stepped back outside and watched to see what she was going to do.

Thinking he was following her, she stumbled down the hall in her stockinged feet, removing her nightgown as she went, until she reached her bedroom door. When she saw that he was still standing in the open doorway, she said, "No," motioning him to follow her. *"Come back, Lord! Please don't leave! Come in here with me. Please!"*

By now, she had gotten out of her nightgown and was holding it in one hand and holding the door to her bedroom open with the other, standing, waiting for him, completely naked.

During the brief time it took for each of them to look at the other a hall's distance apart, an extraordinary something happened. He had become Jesus to her and she had become Lily Ruth to him. He was eight years old, holding the bedroom door open slightly, quietly, hoping to see the man come out of his mamma's bedroom at the end of the hall. Up until now he had been too scared to do so, even though he had wanted to many times before. *Doan'chu ever come out'a yore room at night less'n you're sick or you gotta pee-pee!*

No matter how often or for how long he watched as he got older, he never saw anything more than his mamma's hand or forearm extended just far enough to give the visitor a gentle touch, a simple, thoughtless gesture, meaning only that the deed, was done, the visit was over, time to go home. Later, on this particular night, unable to go back to sleep, he lay awake, trying to imagine how the man and his mamma looked as they were doing it. He could get just so far, then his insides seemed to roll over and he felt like throwing up. Up until that time, he had never seen a naked woman, and later in life he often got tangled up in his thinking, wondering how it would be when and if he did and how would he know what to do. He would have to if he wanted to have children, and he knew for sure that he did. On that particular night, though, as he lay in a puddle of confusion, he finally put both pillows over his head and cried.

By daylight next morning, he had decided how he was going to live his life. In the first place, as far as he was concerned, he didn't have a mamma. He recalled some of the times when Brandon waited up for his mamma to come home, then knocked her around and all but killed her. Remembering those times made him feel better. If that's the way his daddy treated her, then why shouldn't he? After all, like father, like son. The only problem was that he did not yet know that he was not Brandon's son, nor did he yet know that *whoever* his father was would have as much meanness in him as Brandon had, enough, even, to pass some of it down to him and still have a lot left over. By the time Lily Ruth left town with the salesman, Bo Arthur had made his own appraisal of the world and the people in it.

He and a number of his friends reached and dealt with puberty about the same time and in the same way, until they realized that sexual fulfillment meant being with girls, playing around and, sometimes even, marrying by choice or of necessity.

That's when the trouble began, that's when he realized he disliked girls. Up until then, before his *libido* went into action, he had no definite feeling for them at all. Now, all of them without exception represented his mamma, not in the way they looked, but how and to what extent they would go to satisfy their own cravings. What surprised and, in some cases, bothered him most was that his own cravings were out-distancing his convictions, propelling him in their direction, forcing him to make risky attempts to find out for himself whether each girl was or was not what he thought she was. After several fumbled attempts, he decided all of them were the same and all of them deserved to be punished.

Some of the fellows had already been wondering if Bo Arthur was telling the truth and had decided he wasn't. They knew from their own experiences that a little stretching of the truth is normal, but three of the girls he thought should be punished had given similar accounts of what their experiences with Bo Arthur had been. Each of them said he had lost his temper immediately and had cursed and abused them. There would be yet another instance that would leave no doubt about whether or not he was telling the truth.

Last year in midsummer, he and a group of other high school girls and boys were swimming at Beaver Dam, about three miles north of town, when, still wet and not yet fully exhausted, some of the couples took to the woods. Next day at recess, when each of the fellows told the others how he had made out the night before and one of them asked Bo Arthur what he and Prissy Phillips had done, he laughed louder and longer than any of the others and told them the story he had made up on his way home last night.

On Monday morning, Prissy Phillips told a far different story and was not surprised when several of her friends said they had had similar experiences and refused to have anything to do with him afterwards. A few days later, when Austin Anderson and Lee Butler asked Bo Arthur if Prissy's story was true, he went into a rage and denied it. When they asked if he would go with them and let Prissy tell her side of the story, he blew up, spitting obscenities into their faces, then turned and huffed off. After that, none of his so-called friends would have anything to do with him.

It was a few days later, following his first encounter with Frank Haley at the Confederate Memorial and, later, watching Mr. Sam cut meat, that he suddenly blew up, determined to find and lay Dulcie if it took all day. He was going to prove that he was as normal as anybody else, too mad to consider that the normal anybody else would never think of doing such a thing. It was that failed attempt that sent him to Collinsville.

As soon as court was dismissed on Thursday, Frank Haley left for home. He was exhausted from a day full of futile attempts to defend his client while his own witnesses either forgot what they were supposed to say or said it in such a way that the prosecution's case profited from it. Furthermore, Judge Carruthers seemed pleased that such was the case, or so Frank Haley felt. By now he had badgered Frank Haley to the point of not knowing what to do, something no other judge had been able to do. Lurking constantly at the back of Frank Haley's mind was an uncommon fear that he was losing the case in spite of anything he could do. Even during the few times when he was able to think clearly, he could not remember some of the maneuvers he had used in order to win cases that had been even more challenging than this one. What was even more disturbing, his relatively clear moments brought forth matters he thought he had fully stifled long ago.

The rain seemed to intensify as soon as he started home. Lightning flashes followed by explosive thunder bursts came in rapid succession, sometimes obscuring the road ahead, making it necessary to slow down, which was not what he wanted to do. Whenever possible, he lowered the window on his side and let the cool, moist air touch his face and hands. It reminded him of his childhood, playing in the rain, being baptized. He was often reminded of his childhood but that was as far as it went. Reliving one's past, he felt, was like looking at a pine tree covered with cones, yet feeling it still needed additional ornaments in order to look like a real Christmas tree.

He had intended to make good use of the time it took to get home by recalling everything he had said and done during the day, hoping he could decide what he had done wrong, but the rain was affecting him in a strange way. He actually was eager to be at home again, hearing the rain on the roof, eating something other than restaurant food, enjoying the feel of his own bed and the comfort of things well known and long enjoyed. Even so, thinking of those things now did not have the soothing effect he had hoped for and thought it would. Each of the would-be happy thoughts came reluctantly to mind like mischievous children taught to keep their distance because of the trouble they always caused if they didn't.

Even so, he seemed to realize for the first time that going home had never been as fulfilling as it seemed to be for other people. His mind started in that direction but he resisted with only partial success. His home itself had never been like other homes. He was never reluctant to leave home for any length of time, just as he normally was never really happy to return. He refused to go much farther, he had done what he had done for good reasons, or at least he had deemed them to be so at the time. He thought about some of their friends who always seemed to be getting along well. They always invited him and Gayle and asked them to share other social affairs with them, yet he and Gayle had never reciprocated in even the slightest way. His excuse was always the same, Gayle didn't enjoy such things.

Frank Haley came physically flawed into the world, but by the time he was three years old he was used to it, he knew how to walk and climb stairs without difficulty, and he rarely considered it a hindrance to whatever he wanted to do with his life. As a matter of fact, at some early point in his youth, he had vowed that his physical defect was going to be the steam that would power his engine for the rest of his life.

There was another flaw that came with him at birth, but it did not require special attention until about the time he started shaving. He alone knew what it was and he alone would do with it whatever he wanted. Fortunately, people could not see it. It was somewhat like the wind, one can feel it without seeing it, though also, like the wind, there may be visible signs of the effect it has had after it passes over. To satiate the first few years of his sexual appetite, he indulged whenever and wherever he could, indiscriminately, always telling himself and trying to believe that what he was doing was not wrong. Later, even, while assuming the visage and lifestyle he knew he would need to show publicly, he was able to reconcile all the licentious liaisons as legitimate workings of the human body, whether the intent was to procreate or not.

As a result, his ultimate sexual preference was for women who either had never had misgivings about whether what they were doing was morally right or wrong and who seemed to possess some rare gift for making the experience more enjoyable than the experiences he had on occasion tried and found unfulfilling.

When and if one of the Bible verses about adultery ever slipped into his consciousness, he willed it killed instantly and the door to that part of his brain slammed shut and locked.

DURING FRANK HALEY'S frequent absence, Gayle had plenty of time to think about what V. Allison had told her. Being alone had become her normal marital state. It was an always accessible, invisible and easily applied adhesive that held the pieces of her fragmented marriage together so well that most people were never aware that there was a break anywhere. Before marrying him, she had not been aware of Frank Haley's dallyings. She felt sure that he was an honest and honorable man and would be an ideal husband. He had been born into an honorable and highly respected family, he had inherited at birth the obligation to maintain his father's reputation as lawyer and preacher of the Gospel. She had had a secret crush on Frank Haley for a long time before they started dating, so much so that she began to feel, at one early point in their relationship, that both of them had been among the multitude Jesus succored with bread and fish. The fact that one of Frank Haley's legs was shorter than the other never seemed to concern her. She was so enamored of him that she had learned by constant practice not to look down that far.

She was only eighteen when she married Frank Haley, too young to know how reality can differ from dreams and how unreliable advice and yes, even warnings from married others would prove to be after the deed was done. The first indication that married life would be vastly different than she had expected came as soon as they returned home after the elaborate and extravagant ceremony at the First Baptist Church and, later, the gala reception at the home of Mr. and Mrs. Harold Hepling, owners of the Jones County Sawmill and Cotton Gin. If she had seriously expected to be carried over the threshold, as she was led to believe she would be, she was gravely disappointed. He did not carry her over the threshold, he even walked into the house before she did.

On Thursday, day four of the Morgenstein trial, the rain had started early that morning and continued all day, with brief periods of low thunder rolls to the east and an occasional break in the clouds, just enough for a ray of sunshine to sneak out, causing some to hope the rain would stop, but causing others, like Gayle, to hope it never would. As soon as Ella Jane left, Gayle retired to her bedroom with a book of Emerson's Essays. For a while she stood at the window, watching the rolling clouds and quick, bright lightning strikes miles to the east, then pulled the pillows out and lay down with the book at her side. The pelting rain against the window panes comforted her, though she did not know why. Somehow the sound gave her the feeling that there was something better outside than inside the house where she and Frank Haley lived.

The steady rain lulled her to sleep. When she awoke later, she was still holding the book of essays. She felt a little better and decided to sit up and read some more. But she couldn't read. She kept remembering what she had tried so hard to forget. Not only what V. Allison had told her, but other things, as well, things she had to some degree been able to keep at bay. She had to. She realized her life would never change. She knew also that if she were to have any peace of mind at all, it would have to be of her own making. She would have to block as much of the ugliness from her consciousness as she could, and, to some extent until now, she had been able to do so.

Her thoughts went far back to those first times when she and Frank Haley were together at parties, civic functions, funerals, and the like, how he introduced her with feigned pride and even put his arm around her shoulder, compelling her to act her part as well by pretending they were deeply in love and happily married. What surprised and sickened her more than anything else he ever did was when, on two or three occasions, he had leaned over to whisper in several ears that they were trying to have a baby but things were not going very well. It was all she could do to keep from adding on each occasion that things for having a baby would never go well as long as they slept in separate rooms and separate beds. As time passed, she dreaded more and more to be with him in public and often developed sudden physical disabilities too severe to risk being away from home for any length of time.

She had just begun to read when she heard Frank Haley come

in. He neither called her name nor did he seem at all concerned where she might be or what she might be doing. Even at this late stage of their disparate marriage, she thought he might at least tell her something about how things had gone in court today. He went directly to his room, laid his valise on the bed, then went to the bathroom. "Is that you, Frank?" she asked, knowing how foolish it sounded, but she wanted him to know where she was in any case.

"Yeah. I'm exhausted. Is there anything left over from lunch?"

"Yes, but I don't think you'd want it. It's some salmon croquettes and some broccoli."

"Oh well, that's alright. I'd rather have a bowl of Ben's chili. I'm also goan need to do some work in my office later. Don't wait up for me."

After so long, she still felt guilty for not getting up to be with him, even though she knew he did not expect her to and did not care that she hadn't done so, and she knew he did not really expect her to wait up for him, either. She still remembered and would never forget how he entered the house ahead of her when they returned home after the wedding. It was like a plaque hanging on the wall of every room with large letters burned into the wood to remind her, since they were married, that she was an unwilling accomplice in the charade.

A little after midnight, a sequence of lightning flashes followed by ear-splitting thunder that rattled the window panes scared her awake. She looked at the bedside clock, wondering if Frank had come home yet. She was too afraid to get out of bed to see if he had. She had so many times before lain fully awake, wondering why he hadn't come home yet and finding, when she called his office, that he was not there or didn't answer the phone. It took a while before she realized there was nothing she could do to change things. They had mutually agreed long ago to sleep in separate rooms and separate beds.

But tonight something bothered her, she was scared of the weather and of a strange, unsettling feeling inside her head and body that she could not dispel, no matter how hard she tried. She slipped out of bed and tip-toed up the hall to his room. The door was still open, the valise was exactly where it had been before, and there was no sign that he had been in the house since leaving earlier that evening. She leaned against the door facing, trying to understand and wondering if she should call the office anyway. She did but there was no answer. Did that mean he was not there?

When she was young and naive, she took her wedding vows seriously and devoted her time and energy selflessly to making him comfortable and happy, even when it became apparent that he considered wedding vows to be nothing more than a time-honored ritual that normally lasted only as long as the wedding ceremony did. When she decided he would never love her, no matter how much of herself she gave, she performed a private ritual of her own, one that would help to retain some of what remained of her dignity and self-respect. She did it subtly, little by little, even though she knew he would not have noticed if she had done otherwise.

She was standing now in the doorway, holding the phone and wondering if she should call Ben Rayburn. It was a little before five o'clock. She knew Ben and Abbie would be busy in the kitchen, getting things ready for opening at six. But why did she feel uneasy, why give a second thought to whether calling Ben would be an imposition? She started dialing, then stopped suddenly and hung up the receiver, having suddenly convinced herself, for some reason or other, that not knowing was better than knowing. That would suffice for the time being.

NEXT MORNING, WHEN Ben Rayburn was turning the hanging sign on the front door from closed to open, he was surprised to see that Frank Haley's car was parked out front. He hadn't even noticed last night that Frank had come in his car and had parked out front. He lost no time checking it out. The car doors were locked and Frank Haley was not inside. Now what did that mean?

"You reck'n he could'a had trouble with the car'n decided t'walk home?" Addie asked.

"Naw, I don't think so. Maybe I better call Gayle?"

"It's mighty early. She more'n likely's still in bed."

"That don't matter."

"Gayle, this is Ben Rayburn callin'. Listen, Gayle, I jus' seen

Frank Haley's car still sittin' out chonder and I'm wond'rin if he's home an' maybe couldn't get his car started. Might'a flooded'r sumpn."

"He's not here, Ben. He didn't come home last night. Where d'you think he could be? What d'you think might've happened?"

"I ain't got no idear. If I find out sumpn, I'll call you back."

Night-watchman Eustis Saul, just coming off duty, was ready for his first cup of coffee before going home to sleep. "What d'you make a that, Ben?" he asked.

"Beats the livin' hell out'a me. I figger he couldn't git it started'n just decided t'walk home instead."

"You might be right, but you'd just closed up when I come aroun' the corner last night'n seen 'im jes sittin' in the car'n then, after a little while, he got out an' locked it, then started walkin' up the street. He looked t'me like he was mad or real upset about sumpn."

"You said he looked upset?"

"He looked that'a way t'me. I spoke to 'im, but he dittn't answer."

That was not what Ben wanted to hear. He had thought Frank Haley would want to know that V. Allison was only repeating what Ida Belle had told her earlier, about the note Lily Ruth had written to Bo Arthur. Distractedly, he walked back to the kitchen, trying to remember everything he had said to Frank Haley. The longer he thought about it, the more he worried.

"You better have a look at that chili," Addie said. "It smells t'me like it's startin' t'scorch."

Several early customers, seeing the change, asked Ben if he was sick. He had a hard time trying to convince them that he wasn't. Then, as he was on his way back to the kitchen, he thought about something. Why, of course! Frank Haley was worried about something, he really was mad! He said so, he said he was madder'n hell because Judge Carruthers "is on my back and won't get off," he remembered. It was only a few minutes later, when he was telling others why he thought Frank Haley was so mad, that Eustis Saul said, "But Ben, why would gettin' mad at the judge make 'im leave 'is car out chonder an' then, in the middle'a the night go walkin' Lord knows where?"

Ben couldn't think of a good answer. He wished he could.

Hanging from the ceiling of Ida Belle Bustin's screened back porch was a forty-watt light bulb on a black, bug-crusted cord. At seven o'clock Friday morning, Myra Macintosh noticed as soon as she got up that the light was still on, swinging back and forth as it had done all night. It bothered her. It wasn't like Ida Belle to leave a light burning like that. Now she would wonder about it every few minutes as she prepared her breakfast. She even got up one time between bites to see if, perhaps, it had been turned off. Even when and if she tried to put it out of her mind, she was unable to. Making mountains out of molehills had helped her through many of the long days and nights she spent alone.

— t w e n t y - o n e —

THE USUAL CALM that follows a storm was, in this instance, meager and short-lived. Folks in Ellisville woke up Friday morning relieved that the storm had passed without having caused any serious damage. All that remained above were a few abandoned clouds against the otherwise clear sky, hurrying in fast-changing forms as though they had a rain to catch.

Lee Anderson called Judge Carruthers in Meridian to tell him that Frank Haley was missing, then appointed and dispatched four new deputies, warning them that they'd better not come back unless and until they had found Frank Haley. By day's end, they had not found him. Clay Hinton and Marvin Meadows learned about Frank Haley's disappearance while they were eating breakfast at Ben's Café, and by eight o'clock the news had been spread all over town. Folks were crowding the sidewalks on both sides of the street and between the streetcar tracks, all of them curious for one reason or another, some trying to imagine how things would be if Frank Haley were not found and some, who for a long time had wanted to see Frank Haley's fancy automobile up close but had been afraid to, now had a chance to do so, even though Sheriff Anderson kept chasing them away.

While Dulcie was waiting for the streetcar, she listened to what people were saying about Frank Haley Bankston, that he had disappeared. She didn't know much about him except that one of his legs was shorter than the other. Up until now, she had rarely thought of him unless she happened to see him, and every time she did she couldn't keep her eyes off of the elevator shoe he was wearing on his left foot, and she would try to imagine how he felt about being crippled. She bet his mamma had to keep telling him when he was little that he wasn't any different than anybody else, no matter if one of his legs was shorter than the other. She wondered when he had first found out that he was crippled and different. How long did it take him to stop thinking about it? How old was he when he finally made up his mind that being lame in the leg had nothing to do with either his mentality or his ambition and determination to do anything he wanted to do. She bet his mamma had to tell him all the time for him to believe it. Now she wondered if his mamma had lived long enough to see that everything she did to help him had paid off.

It reminded her of what Father Seranno had told her. Nobody really knows anybody else completely, ever. He had already helped her so much, yet she realized that he could never do for her what Frank Haley's mamma had done for him. She pondered that for a while until she saddened. There was nothing wrong with her feet; she could walk as well as anybody else could.

Thinking about Frank Haley Bankston had distracted her and made her sad, but knowing it was Friday made her feel better. That meant she would see Father Seranno again. She had been able to visit with him several times when Melissa wanted to stay with Voncille. Otherwise, when Father Seranno saw her and Melissa playing outside, he would come over to watch, pretending he was interested in what they were doing. He had even planned his Friday schedule in such a way that he could be with them. He was always gratified to see in what small but significant ways Dulcie had changed. He realized he was better able to see the difference than she was.

She was much more patient with Melissa than she had been before. She seemed to have learned how to minimize Melissa's anger by distracting her and suggesting they do something else. Sometimes on the way to Laurel, she would try to think of ways either to keep Melissa happy or how to divert her attention long enough so she could run to the church and see Father Seranno.

Voncille had a platter of freshly baked oatmeal cookies on the kitchen table when Dulcie and Melissa arrived that afternoon. She seemed calmer than usual, somewhat detached and sad. She had privately been trying to overcome her craving for bourbon. She had reached a point when she needed to talk with somebody about the problem but did not know who it would be. Penny came to mind, but just as soon left it. How absurd! The blind leading the blind.

After Dulcie and Melissa left the week before, Voncille kept remembering something Dulcie had said Father Seranno told her when they first began their friendship, that, unless he had things to do for the church, she could stop by and talk with him whenever she wanted to, even though she was not a member of the Catholic church. Voncille had more than her share of prejudices. Like many other people, she believed that Catholics worshipped idols and, although her knowledge of the Bible was scant, she either had read or heard that idol worship was the devil's doing. Lately, however, she had been made aware that to be helped in any way by anyone, Catholic or otherwise, she would have to reconcile idol worship with bourbon-drinking.

As Dulcie and Melissa ate the oatmeal cookies, Voncille leaned over the table on her elbows and watched them, not as she usually did, but with a sad, tender look in her eyes. Softly, she started telling them about how she and Penny used to play dolls when they were little, how they even started drawing and cutting out their own clothes for the dolls, and how she had gradually become interested in sewing on their mamma's old Singer. From then on, she would make the dolls' dresses on the machine, then she and Penny would have the time of their lives dressing the dolls in all kinds of pretty, fancy outfits.

"Why don't chu make some for me'n Melissa?" Dulcie asked before swallowing what she had in her mouth.

"Yeah," Melissa said, "why don't chu, Aunt Cil? That would be so much fun, wouldn't it, Dulcie?"

Dulcie had just put another cookie in her mouth and could only shake her head up and down.

"Well, if y'all want me t'do that, you'll have t'bring your dolls next time. In the meantime, why don't we pick out some pretty dresses from the Sears, Roebuck catalog? Woana do that?"

Melissa looked at Dulcie. "Yeah, we do, don't we, Dulcie?"

"Maybe after a while, Miz Martin. Y'all go on and start an' I'll be back d'reckiy."

"You plannin' on goin' t'see Father Seranno, Dulcie?" Voncille asked.

"Yessum, Is that awright?"

Voncille looked at Melissa. "You think we need Dulcie t'hep us decide? Is it awright if she does?"

"I reck'n. But chu better not stay over there too long or I'm go'n' tell Mamma."

"No, now, M'lissa, don't be like that. Me'n you'll pick out the dresses while Dulcie runs over t'see Father Seranno. Then, when she comes back, we'll let 'er see which ones we've decided on."

When Dulcie returned, Voncille asked how her visit with Father Seranno had been. "Oh, him'n me just talked a little while. Oh yeah, he said he saw you walkin' in front of the church one day and you stopped and kept lookin' like you was goana go inside."

"Why, I wuddn't go'n' do no such of a thang, Dulcie. After all, it ain't against the law to walk by the Catholic church. And if I woanted t'go in, I would surely do so. That don't mean I would, though."

"I know that, Miz Martin, but he dittn't mean nothin' by sayin' that. Why, I tol' 'im you were Melissa's aunt when me'n her first started comin' over here."

"Well, nohow, be that as it may. I have t'admit, though, I am a little curious. I been wonderin' what it is he talks about that makes you feel so good. He's not tryin' to get chu to join the Catholic church, is he?"

"Why, for goodness' sake, Miz Martin, he wouldn't do nothin' like that. He tol' me the first time we talked that all he wanted t'do was hep me."

"Hep you do what?"

"Why, I don't know. He asked me if I was happy'n I jus' tol' im I wuddn't'n he asked me why not an' I tol' im. I dittn't want to, but he kept on askin' me till I did."

"I see. Well, if you think he's heppin' you, then I reck'n you ought'a keep on seein' 'im. As for as you not bein' a Catholic, why if he don't think that makes any difference, then I don't think I'd bother about it."

"I don't, Miz Martin. I done made up my mind, he's the best friend I ever had in the whole wide world."

Later, after Dulcie and Melissa had gone, Voncille lay down and did some serious thinking. It surprised her to know that

Father Seranno had even recognized her. It was true, though, she had stopped momentarily the other day on her way from town and tried to imagine what the church looked like inside. She had often wondered before but always put it out of her mind as something strange that she wanted no part of. She turned from side to side, got up a time or two, wondering if she should weaken and go finish the bottle of bourbon in the kitchen cabinet. Before she even realized it, she was crying.

SEVERAL OF IDA Belle's best students had made repeated visits to Mr. Tatum's office to complain about Annie Pearl Potts, who had been substituting for Miss Bustin. He had called Ida Belle several days ago and she told him she still wasn't well enough to come back. When he called her again on Friday morning, there was no answer. He decided it was time to do something about it. Maybe some of the neighbors had seen her or had also kept in touch with her by phone. Myra Macintosh came to mind first.

"Marcus, I'm beginnin' t'think sumpn's wrong over there. When I talked with 'er yesterday mornin' she sounded real strange, like she might'a been out a her mind."

He was not surprised. "Myra," he said cautiously, "would you mind goin' over t'her house and seein' if you can get her to come to the door?"

"Why no, Marcus, I don't mind a'tall. I'll go over there right now if you woant me to. I'll call you as soon as I get back'n let chu know what I find out."

It wouldn't hurt to try callin' Ida Belle one more time, she thought. Later, as she started down the back steps, holding onto the banister with both hands, she was reminded of what had transpired during the night, the ferocious wind and rain and the ear-splitting lightning bursts that kept her awake. One in particular had scared her so much she decided to get up and build a fire in the fireplace, then sat there until daylight. Her first thought was that the lightning had struck something on or just outside her house.

The back screen door of Ida Belle's house was open, lodged on a swollen floor board. She pulled it back in place as she tip-toed to the back door of the kitchen, calling, "Ida Belle, are you awright in there?" She waited long enough to listen for any sounds from inside. "Ida Belle," she called again, "are you awright?" The only sounds were the irregular ones her heart was making, the ones she'd been worrying about the past two years. She stepped back, wondering what to do. Was her curiosity aroused enough to lessen her fear? It had been on other occasions, so why not now? Before touching the doorknob she knocked three times and waited, then touched and held it for a few seconds. Even before she intended to, she pushed the door open. The deflected light and sunshine that flooded the kitchen, though bright, was not able to mask either the sight or the smell of the fireplace smoke that was trapped inside. Even so, it cleared the air below enough to make it possible for her to see what was on the floor, just a few feet away from where she was standing.

"My God!" she screamed, *"Oh, my God, what has happened!"* She nearly stumbled and fell as she stepped down onto the porch floor and struggled her way down to the ground and over to her house. But now there was something else getting the greater part of her attention, causing her to fear that the occasional chest pains that were now more acute, frequent, and fire-like than before would keep her from completing her mission. She simply must not let it happen. She must get to the phone as fast as possible, even if it killed her.

She dropped the receiver twice before calling. Marcus Tatum's secretary Donna answered, said Mr. Tatum was out of the office but would be back shortly, please hold on. She did but wondered if she'd be able to much longer.

"Hello, Myra," she heard finally. "What have you found out?"

"Oh, Marcus!" she cried, "it's Frank Haley!"

"What d'you mean, Frank Haley?"

"He's dead! Somebody killed 'im. He's layin' on Ida Belle's kitchen floor right this minute with a knife stuck in 'im!"

"Good God! You don't mean it."

"I most certainly do."

"But what about Ida Belle?"

"I never saw 'er. She wuddn't nowhere t'be seen. I called and called but she never did answer."

"Wonder where she is. My God, she had t'be the one that killed 'im. Look, I'd better let Lee Anderson know what's happened. Thank you, Myra. I know how this has upset you. I'll let chu know later what I find out. In the meantime, take care of yourself."

Marcus then called Lee Anderson. "When I asked about Ida Belle, Myra said she didn't see 'er and she never answered when she called 'er. She's been out'a her mind lately and I had to take her home the other day and get a substitute teacher t'take her place."

"Then where d'you reck'n'she could be?"

"There's no tellin'. She certainly couldn't go too far away."

"I know, but I ain't go'n' be satisfied till I see for myself. I'm goin' over there right now."

Marcus Tatum was standing on Ida Belle's back porch when Lee got there. "I cannot figure this thing out t'save my life. I've looked high and low, and there's no sign of Ida Belle. I'm pretty sure she left after doin' what she did."

"Anyway, I'm glad you're here, Marcus, 'cause we goan need t'find out if she's got any kinfolks close by an', if so, where they are. You know of any?"

"Not right off the top of my head, but I've got some personal information about her in my office files. Seems I've heard her mention a cousin, I b'lieve, a nephew, maybe, somewhere on the coast. I'll find out what I can. Right now I need t'get back t'my office as soon as possible."

Marcus had gone just a little ways when he came back. "Oh, I just thought of Ida Belle's nephew. His name is Schyler. Schyler Bustin. I'll see what I can find out."

As he was getting into his car, Vayda Baygents saw him and told him she wanted to talk with him.

"Good-mornin', Vayda. What's the matter?"

"That's what *I'd* like t'know. What's all the commotion over at Ida Belle's house?"

"I thought you already knew."

"Well, what makes you think that? I wouldn't've asked if I did."

"Frank Haley Bankston has been killed."

"In *there?* You mean *Frank Haley Bankston? Dead?* What in

the worl' was he doin' in Ida Belle's house in the first place? Did she kill 'im?"

"We have no way of knowin'."

"What d'you mean, you have no way of knowin'? Did ju ask 'er?"

"Vayda, Ida Belle's gone. We don't know where she is."

"Well, then, if she didn't do it, then who did?"

"Vayda, like I said, we don't have any idea who else could have done it. That's for Lee Anderson t'find out, not me or you."

"Maybe Lee Anderson ain't got sense enough t'find out. Maybe I awready know more'n he does, so maybe me'n him oughta have a little talk."

"And what is it you know that we don't know?"

"I just happen t'know who it was that killed Frank Haley, an' furthermore, the one that did it had every good reason for doin' so."

"You're not talkin' about Bo Arthur, are you?"

"I most certainly am."

"And why are you so sure it was him?"

She drew her head back and crossed her arms. "B'cause yesterday mornin' I saw him knockin' on Ida Belle's front door, and d'reckly she came and let 'im in."

"Do you *really* mean that?"

"I would'na said it if I didn't. I saw it with my own two eyes. I saw her open the door for 'im t'go inside. Now, what d'you think he was doin' over there in the first place? You know how sorry an' no-count'n mean he is an' how much trouble he's caused. An' what about when him and Frank Haley locked horns in Ben's café? Alice Mae Minter said he even tol' Frank Haley he was go'n get even with 'im, no matter what it took. Remember that?"

"Yes, I wasn't there but I heard about it. But Vayda, you've overlooked one very important matter. At the time you said you saw Bo Arthur goin' in Ida Belle's house, Frank Haley was in Meridian. He was in court there."

"I dittn't say I saw Bo Arhur comin' out, did I?"

"No, you didn't."

"Well, then," she huffed, "put *that* in your pipe'n smoke it!"

He disliked Vayda Baygents now more than ever, but what she said stayed on his mind for a long time.

When he called Lee Anderson later, Paula Prine told him Lee was out but would call him as soon as he got back, and he did. When Marcus told him about Vayda Bagents, he said, "Now, ain't that funny! I never even thought about that, but now, after what chu jus' tol' me, thangs look a little different."

It was getting close to twelve o'clock and Ben and Abbie Rayburn were busy getting lunch ready. Ben was mixing some more flour in the chili pot when he heard somebody out front holler, *"They've found Frank Haley! He's been stabbed t'death!"*

Ben put the flour can on the table and started to the front of the café as fast as he could, wiping his hands on his apron, remembering how Frank Haley looked last night. Lee Anderson and one of the new deputies were looking inside Frank Haley's car. Ben walked over to where they were.

"I cain't b'lieve it, Lee," Ben said. "I cain't make myself b'lieve it. Why, me'n him talked for over a hour just last night. It just don't seem possible."

"Yeah, but chu don't know the half of it. That's the goddamnest sight I ever seen in my life, an' now we gotta try t'find Miss Ida Belle."

"You mean she killed 'im an' then left?"

"That's the way it looks right now. You have any idear where she might be? Miz Macintosh mentioned that the light on Ida Belle's back porch had burned all night, an' that makes me wonder if she might've left after she killed 'im."

"Where in the world would she go? She ain't got no livin' relatives in this part a the state. At least as far as I know she ain't."

When Lee returned later that afternoon, he suggested they go to the back of the cafe to talk. "Ben, I promised Gayle this mornin' that I'd find out as much as I could about what happened last night. I mean, when Frank Haley was here. How did he look an' how did he act? An' what did he say that might've give you some idear of what he was thinkin'."

From the moment he heard that Ida Belle had killed Frank Haley, Ben had been trying to remember everything Frank Haley had said and done, recalling most of all how he looked when he first came into the café. He still wondered, also, why Frank Haley decided to walk to Ida Belle's house instead of driving. What he wished he did not know was why Frank Haley suddenly decided to go there.

"By the way, how did Gayle take it?" Ben asked.

"Pretty bad. But Gayle's a strong and sensible woman. She cried a while but then calmed down and started askin' a lot a questions I couldn't answer. That's why I told 'er I'd find out as much as I could and then call 'er back or go see 'er."

"Lee," Ben said, "I knew the minute Frank Haley came in the cafe that sumpn was wrong. He said he'd awready gone home but decided he woanted sumpn t'eat, an' he also said he needed to be 'roun' people he knew'n liked. I asked 'im what was botherin' 'im an' how was the trial goin'. He said the trial was goin' real bad, that he didn't like the judge and the judge didn't like him and was makin' things real hard for 'im. He said he was afraid he was go'n' lose the case an' he needed t'come home for the night an' maybe that would hep his feelin's."

Lee nodded his head. "Keep talkin'."

"Well, while he was eatin' his bananer puddin', he asked me how things were goin' in Ellisville. I didn't know at first whether he knew Lily Ruth had come back and was out at Eula's when she died. So I mentioned it and he sorta nodded t'let me know he already knew about it. Then, when I told 'im she'd been buried out at Eula's Monday, he nodded again."

"I better see if I got a customer," Ben said as he got up. When he came back, as he sat down he closed his eyes and leaned over, squeezed his fingertips around his knees as if both fingers and legs had gone to sleep, then cleared his throat and looked up. "That's when I should've stopped," he said hoarsely. "Right then and there, an' not said another word." Shaking his head from side to side, he said, "But I didn't."

"I know, Ben," Lee said. "Sumpn you said made 'im mad enough to go t'Ida Belle's house. What was it, Ben? What was it you said that made 'im so mad? Did ju by any chance mention Ida Belle's name?"

"Yeah, I sure did."

"Why, and what did ju say?"

"I just asked 'im if he knew folks were talkin' 'bout 'im, sayin' bad things about him an' Lily Ruth, an' he said he didn't and why were they sayin' bad things about him and her. I tol' 'im that his sister-in-law had been tellin' folks that he was Bo Arthur's real daddy. That's when he really boiled over. I could tell he was really losin' his temper. He woanted t'know why V. Allison was spreadin' such lies about him an' who started it in the first place. I tol' 'im V. Allison said Ida Belle Bustin had told 'er, an' said she even had a letter Lily Ruth wrote to Bo Arthur, tellin' him he was Bo Arthur's real daddy."

"*Good God a'mighty!* D'you b'lieve that?"

"Yeah, I sure do."

"Why d'you say that?"

"Well, because I knew what kind a woman Lily Ruth was. As a matter a fact, lots a men in Ellisville knew, too, and first hand, if you know what I mean."

"Yeah, I knew that. But chu don't mean t'tell me Frank Haley was one of 'em, do you?"

"Why, Lee, I would'a thought you'd be one of the first ones t'know that. Well, anyway, I can tell you for sure that he was. And more than a few times at that."

"*Good God!* I always thought Frank Haley Bankston was one of the finest and most upright men I've ever known." Lee closed his eyes, as if having trouble dealing with what Ben had just said, then, looking up, he seemed more puzzled than before. "Ben, what about Ida Belle Bustin?"

"What d'you mean?"

"I mean, how does she figure in all this?"

"All I know is that she's hated Frank Haley for years. Before she went to China as a missionary, she and Frank Haley had been goin' t'gether. I don't know for sure what happened, but he broke it off and she never got over it. When she came back from China, they seemed t'be at each other's throats all the time. And that's the way it's been ever since."

Lee sat back and thought it over. "Now I'm wondrin' how much that had t'do with her killin' 'im."

"I'd say it had a lot t'do with it. But, by the way, I forgot t'ask you earlier, what kind'a knife did she use, one a her kitchen knives?"

"No, it ain't a kitchen knife. At least not like none I ever saw. It sorta reminded me of sumpn you'd see in a pawn shop. It even had what looked like a ivory handle and sumpn carved on it."

"Hey, wait a minute! That sounds like the very knife Bo Arthur stole from Sam. I remember now."

"Well, how can we tell? Did ju ever see it?"

"I prob'ly did but I never paid no 'tention to which knife he was usin' but Frank Haley did. That sounds just like the way he described it."

"Well, if it is the same knife, how'd she ever get a holt of it?"

"Beats the hell out a me. By the way, where is it now?"

"In a bag with evuhthang else in my office. It's been cleaned up."

"Why don' chu show it to Sam'n let 'im tell you whether that's his knife or not?"

"You reck'n it'll upset 'im?"

"Prob'ly will, but that's the only way we go'n' ever know for sure. You woant me t'do it?"

"Naw, I better do it. I don't mind. I better go get it right now." He started to leave, then stopped. "Oh, by the way, Ben, 'bout what time did Frank Haley leave last night?"

"As well as I rmember, it was 'roun' 'lebben o'clock."

"Awright. I'll prob'ly be back d'reckly."

"But wait now. What if Sam says this is the knife Bo Arthur stole?"

"Good God amighty! That means it had t'be Bo Arthur."

He came back in a matter of minutes, red-faced and out of breath. "Ben, my men said they jus' found Miss Ida Belle."

"Where?"

"In one of the clawsets. One a the men said he used t'go there'n that it was the clawset in Miss Ida Belle's mamma's room. She'd probly shot herself and had been layin' there ever since with the pistol right by 'er side. They said they just happened to notice that the door of the clawset wuddn't shut all the way. They said they was almost no blood nowhere 'cept a little trickle down the right side'a her head an' a little bit in her hair."

"*Good God!* Why d'you reck'n she'd do a thang like that?"

"I don't know. I don't guess we'll ever know. So, here," he said, handing Ben the bag with the knife, "if you got time to t'do it, you might as well go see Sam yourself. I gotta git over t'Ida Belle's as soon as I can. I'll call you later t'find out 'bout the knife."

Though Ben wasn't yet sure if the knife he was holding was the one Bo Arthur had stolen, he readily assumed it was. "Well, Sam," he said as he entered, "now we know where yore knife is."

Mr. Sam was cleaning the butcher block with a metal-toothed brush. He looked up and wiped his hands on his apron. "What'a you say? *Che dice?*"

"I said, Sam, that the knife you was missin's fine'ly been found."

Mr. Sam smiled. "You no telly me lie, do you?"

Ben laughed. "Naw, Sam, I ain't lyin', but chu're gonna be surprised when I tell you where it's been."

"An'a where's it been? Who got it?"

Ben figured he'd better get serious, because Mr. Sam was expecting some good news and certainly not what he was about to tell him. "Well, Sam, you heard that Frank Haley Bankston'd been killed, dittn' chu?"

"Yeah, I heard'a. *Che peccato!*"

"Well, Sam, in this h'yere bag I've got what I b'lieve is the knife Bo Arthur stole. Here, have a look and tell me if it is."

"*Oh, good 'a God!*"

"*Is* it, Sam?"

He cupped his hands over his face and moaned. "*Si, si, veramente. Oh, my God'a!*"

"I'm sorry, Sam. Somehow Miss Ida Belle Bustin must'a got a hold a yore knife an' used it t'kill Frank Haley. D'you know 'er, Sam? Miss Ida Belle, I mean?"

"*Si, si*, I know 'er. But a you mean'a she kill 'im with *my* knife'a? She no steal'a my knife'a. How come'a she get it?"

"We don't really know, Sam."

He solemned suddenly, closed his eyes, and made the sign of the cross, then clasped his hands together prayer-like and shook them back and forth, muttering in Italian.

"I'm real sorry, Sam," Ben said again.

Mr. Sam opened his eyes but continued to shake his hands back and forth. "I'm a sorry, too," he said, removing the brush and wiping the block off. "What'a can I do for you, Ben?" he said, wiping his hands again on the apron.

"Naw, I don't need nuttin, Sam. I just come t'make sure this was yore knife. I gotta git back to the café."

In the meantime, Lee Anderson called Marcus to let him know what was happening. "By the way, Marcus, a little while ago I sent two'a my deputies back over to Ida Belle's house t'get Frank Haley'n take 'im t'Doc Cranford's place. An' I tol' 'em b'fore they did that t'give the house one more good goin' over. I'll let chu know if they find anythang."

And they did. "We seen blood comin' out from under a clawset door in what must'a been her bedroom, an' she was curled up on the floor with a bullet hole in the right side of her head'n the pistol layin' right b'side 'er on the floor."

"How ironic," Marcus said after Lee told him. "I just talked with her nephew in Pascagoula, Schyler Bustin. I mentioned 'im a while ago. You might be interested in some of what he said."

"I hope it was sumpn we need to know."

"It is. Definitely. He said he'd received a letter from Ida Belle about a week ago. He said he figured she was out of her mind, because she wrote some things that didn't make sense. But he said some of what she wrote did. For instance, she told him where everything was in her house and that she had deeded everything to him a long time ago. But this is the part that shocked me the most. She said she didn't want t'live anymore and planned to kill herself. She tol' 'im not to be sad, that that's what she'd been woantin' t'do for a long time."

"Good God! Can you imagine sumpn like that hap'nin' in Ellisville, of all places?"

"I know what chu mean. But more to our interest and needs, he said he would come up as soon as possible. By the way, he works an' cain't come any sooner. He asked if I thought somebody up here could do whatever needed to be done for buryin' Ida Belle, you know, whatever's necessary, an' he said he'd pay whatever it costs."

"I reck'n we'll have to. They's no other way, as far as I can tell. It ain't go'n' be easy."

"I realize that, an' I'll do all I can t' help. After all, she was a fine teacher, no matter how odd she was at times. But Lee, I've got sumpn else t'tell you, sumpn you might find even more interestin' than what I've just tol' you."

"I hope it's sumpn good."

"Well, I wouldn't say that, but it's sumpn I think might change the whole situation drastically."

"And what's that?"

"Remember when me'n you were over at Ida Belle's house'n I said I needed t'get back to school?"

"Yeah."

"Well, just as I was leavin', Vayda Baygents saw me'n came over, wantin' t'know what was goin' on over at Ida Belle's house. I told her what had happened, and the asked if Ida Belle had killed Frank Haley, an' I said we didn't know, but she said *she* did, that it was Bo Arthur. She said she'd seen 'im go into Ida Belle's front door, but she never saw him come out. Now, who would believe she stayed out there all day to see if he did?"

Lee was listening, but he was thinking of something else. "Marcus," he said, "now I'm go'n' tell *you* sumpn. You know the knife that killed Frank Haley?"

"Yes."

"Well, Ben Rayburn tol' me that it was the knife Bo Arthur had stole from Sam several weeks ago. In fact, he's just about right now talkin' with Sam and showin' him the knife. When my deputy called'n said they'd found Miss Ida Belle, I asked Ben t'take it to Sam and see if it really was the knife Bo Arthur'd stole."

"Why don' chu call 'im an' find out? He's probably back at the café by now."

He did. Ben had just returned and was eager to talk.

Marcus knew, without being told, what the answer was.

"Sam said it's his knife. The one Bo Arthur stole a while back. I gotta git out t'Eula Bilbo's as soon as possible. Talk with you later."

* * *

EULA HAD JUST finished cooking figs and was sealing the lids on the jars of preserves when Lee Anderson knocked on the back door.

"Miz Eula, I hope I ain't come at a bad time. Are you busy? Can me'n you talk a while?"

She wiped her hands on her apron, then opened the door. "No, I'm not busy. I've jes' got through doin' a little cannin'. Come on in, Lee. I'll be with you as soon as I seal these last two jars'a figs. I figgered I'd better make some preserves out of 'em 'fore the birds did away with the few what was left."

Lee fidgeted with his hat as he waited, then followed Eula into the dining room, where she motioned for him to sit down. "Miz Eula, I guess you're wondrin' why I'm here. Well, it's about sumpn what's just happened uptown. Have you heard about Frank Haley Bankston?"

"Why no, what about Frank Haley?"

"Frank Haley's been killed, Miz Eula. Somebody killed 'im over at Miss Ida Belle Bustin's house last night."

She covered her face with her hands. "No! You don't mean it. Who in the worl' would do a thang like that? *My God in Heaven!*"

"Is Bo Arthur t'home?"

"Yeah, he come home last night, soakin' wet."

"What time did he git home? You remember? An' was there any blood on his clothes?"

"What d'you mean, was there any blood on his clothes? Of course there weren't. Why should they be?"

"I was jes' wonderin', Miz Eula. I'll explain later. But I'm concerned about when he got home. D'you remember?"

"Well, of course I remember. Hit was a few minutes after nine o'clock. He was soakin' wet. Lee, why you askin' all these questions 'bout Bo Arthur? He ain't got 'is self into some more trouble, has he?"

"I'm 'fraid so, Miz Eula. I hate t'be the one t'tell you, but this time Bo Arthur's done sumpn real bad. I mean *real* bad."

"Well, for God's sakes, what is it?"

"He's killed Frank Haley Bankston."

"*What? Killed Frank Haley?* Lee Anderson, that's a lie! He

ain't done no such of a thang. He wouldn't do such a thang. You know that."

"No, m'am, I *don't* know that, Miz Eula. All I know for sure is that all the evidence points to Bo Arthur. It's true. He did it."

"No! No! That ain't so! I know it ain't so!"

"I'm sorry, Miz Eula, but it is."

"How d'you know? Tell me! Go on, *tell me*, cause I don't b'lieve one word a what chu're sayin'. I *know* it ain't so."

"D'you know 'bout the knife he stole from Mr. Sam a while back?"

"Yes, I knowed that, but what's that got t'do with killin' Frank Haley?"

"Miz Eula, that's the knife that killed 'im. An' I don't know if you knew 'bout this, but one day him'n Bo Arthur had a fight in Ben Rayburn's café, an' he swore in front a all them people that he was goan get even, no matter how long it took, an' he even said he'd awready planned how he was goan do it. Now, d'you see what I mean?"

"No, I shore don't know what chu mean. Tell me, what time did all this happen?"

"We don't know for sure, but we figger it was somewhere b'tween ten o'clock'n midnight."

"Well, then, how come you think it was Bo Arthur when he was awready home b'fore that?"

She slumped into a chair, beat her fists against the table and cried.

Lee waited a while. "I'm real sorry, Miz Eula. I hate for you t'have t'go through all this, but I can assure you that ain't none a this your fault. Bo Arthur just growed up the wrong way, an' there wuddn't nothin' you could do about it."

She arduously straightened and cupped her face in her hands, looking into the distance, shaking her head slowly from side to side, unable to speak.

"Where is he right now, Miz Eula? I gotta take 'im t'town."

"What chu go'n' do with 'im?"

"I'm go'n' lock 'im up."

"In jail, you mean?"

"Yessum. They ain't no other choice."

"Out chonder," she said finally, motioning with her hand, "with his BB gun, shootin' squirrels."

Bo Arthur was sitting under a big sweet gum tree with his BB gun across his legs, unaware that somebody was approaching.

"Bo Arthur," Lee said a few feet away. "Let's go. We got some serious talkin' t'do. Git up."

"An' who in hell d'you think you are t'come here on private property'n tell me what t'do. I ain't goin' with you nowhere."

"You know who I am? I'm Lee Anderson, the sheriff of Ellisville, an' when somebody commits a crime, they ain't no such thang as private property. I've come out chere t'let chu know you're bein' charged with the murder of Frank Haley Bankstson. Now, does that gi' me the right t'be here?"

He watched closely to see the effect on Bo Arthur's face. It was not what he had expected, it was genuine shock, and it gave him a quick, odd feeling that his suspicions might be less than reliable. But Lee Anderson had been sheriff long enough to have accumulated what was still a sufficient and dependable store of willpower and courage to ignore as quickly as possible any sign that he might be going down the wrong road as well as after the wrong person. Finding the one who killed Frank Haley Bankston was a challenge unlike any he'd ever had before, and he was not about to let doubts or anything else keep him from winning that prize.

"Man, I don't care who you are, you ain't goan pin that on me. I dittn't even know he was dead, but I'm sure's hell glad t'know he is. But chu or nobody else can prove that I done it. I don't even know when it happened an' I don't know where it happened. So you better find somebody else t' blame."

"They ain't nobody else that could'a done it but chu, 'cause it was that knife you stole from Mr. Sam that killed 'im. You *had* t'be the one. Mr. Sam's awready said that was the knife you stole."

"I don't care what Mr. Sam said, I dittn't have that knife no more. I gave it to Miss Ida Belle Bustin, so why don't chu go see her? I reck'n you decided it was me just because a that knife. Or maybe you ain't got sense enough t'think maybe somebody else did it. Well, Mr. Sheriff, you got a big surprise in store for you, and I caint hardly wait t'see it."

"You know, for a sorry feller your age, you're a real smartass. I've always heard you was, but now I can see for myself. But chu're not as smart as you think you are. I happen t'know that you went t'see Miss Ida Belle jes' yesterday mornin' an' nobody ever seen you come out. Now what was you doin' over there in the first place?"

"What I was doin' over there ain't none a yore goddamn business, an' that's the same answer you'll get for evuh other question you ask."

Lee quickly reached around and pulled the handcuffs off of his belt. When Bo Arthur saw what he was doing, he brought his BB gun down across Lee's arms. Lee took the gun and threw it away, then grabbed Bo Arthur's collar, pulled him closer, then slapped him three times on each cheek. Bo Arthur, raging wild, spitting out obscenities, raised his right leg up as far as he could into Lee's crotch. Lee groaned, then threw Bo Arthur to the ground, kicked him, then sat on his legs as he put the handcuffs on, then pulled Bo Arthur back up. "Git movin', you sorry bastard, I'm lockin' yo' ass up!"

EULA HAD WATCHED from the kitchen window and was now slumped over at the table, more angry than sad about what had just happened. She knew, she had not a doubt, that Bo Arthur had not killed Frank Haley Bankston, and that Lee Anderson had made up his mind even before he came out there that he was going to put the blame on him, no matter who beyond Lee's awareness might know more than he did or possibly what bit of evidence yet unfound might contradict or in some other way make it possible to know definitely who the killer was. She began wondering what she could do. She felt deep down inside that there was something she could do, so she prayed.

Marcus Tatum listened distractedly as Lee Anderson told him about arresting Bo Arthur. Since he and Lee talked earlier, he had been having misgivings about the situation and how Lee was handling it. He decided to talk with Ben Rayburn, and that's what started him thinking that something needed to be done. Ben said he'd already told Lee about how Frank Haley reacted to some of what he told him, but that Lee didn't seem to think it was some-thing important enough to follow up. That's when Marcus decided something had to be done. It was obvious that Frank Haley went in his rage, in the rain, to settle things with Ida Belle, since she had been the one who reported to some friends that Frank Haley was Bo Arthur's father and that he had been paying Lily Ruth monthly payments to stay out of town. Maybe Lee thought it best not to mention that since Frank Haley was so well thought of.

Shortly after lunch, Marcus paid Myra Mcintosh a visit. It proved helpful. She told him she had witnessed with her own two eyes that incident between Ida Belle and Bo Arthur recently, seeing Bo Arthur slashing the screen door and later throwing the knife at Ida Belle. At the time she said she wasn't quite sure what it was that Bo Arthur had thrown, so Ida Belle told her. She said Ida Belle had even threatened to kill Bo Arthur if he ever came back.

After talking with Myra, Marcus went to see Eula Bilbo. He could tell she had been crying, yet she seemed to transform when she saw him and, in the excitement, hugged him and motioned him to the couch. "Marcus, you don't know how happy I am t'see you. I ain't never been so upset in all my life as I am right now."

"I know how you must feel, Miz Eula, and that's why I woanted to come see you. I believe you are better able to help me than any-body else. I need to ask you some questions, do you mind?"

"No, no, Marcus, please do."

"Well, now, can you tell me about what time Bo Arthur came home last night?"

"It was about nine o'clock. He was soakin' wet."

"And how did he look, Miz Eula? Was there any blood any-where on him?"

"No, no, there weren't the first sign a blood nowhere."

"Did he tell you where he'd been all day, and what he'd done?"

"He said he was goin' t'town, but he never tells me 'xactly what he's goan do'n I don't ask 'im. He don't like for me to ask a lot a questions. But he said he spent several hours, sleeping on one of them benches in the depot. He's always liked t'go over there. Him an' Travis Turner are friends. Travis, he does all the baggage stuff, you know, when the trains come in."

"Yes, I know Travis. Did he mention goin' anywhere else before that?"

"Well, yes, he did. He said he went to see Miss Ida Belle Bustin. She'd asked him t'let her read a letter his mamma had wrote 'im."

"An' what kind a letter was that? What was special about it?" She waited, looking at her hands, wondering how to answer. "Well, Marcus, I 'magine you'n evuhbody else must know by now that his mamma come here a few days ago, on the verge a dyin', and she fine'ly did, a day or so later. Bo Arthur, he was real upset an' dittn't woana have nothin' t'do with 'er, no matter how hard I tried to get 'im to. When I was goin' through her thangs she had in a suitcase, I come across a letter she'd wrote to 'im, tellin' him how sorry she was for how she'd treated 'im an' said she woanted him t'know they'd always be somebody t'look after 'im, an' said it was Frank Haley."

"Did he give 'er the letter?"

"No, he said she scared 'im so bad he figgered he'd better git outa there. He said she acted real funny, like she was outa her mind."

"Yes, I know about that. Miss Ida Belle had lots of problems. So Bo Arthur didn't actually go inside, did he?"

"No, from what he tol' me he dittn't."

He stood up as though ready to leave but reluctant to.

"So, what's go'n' happen now?" she asked softly.

"I really don't know, Miz Eula, but I'm goana confide in you about a few things that've been botherin' me. Now when I say I'm a little worried about the way Sherriff Anderson is goin' about solvin' this matter, I don't mean to insult or belittle him in any way. But there's sumpn that keeps botherin' me. He seems t'think Bo Arthur actually killed Frank Haley, but I don't b'lieve it. Not in any way. First of all, Bo Arthur, accordin' t'what chu said, was at home at the time Frank Haley was killed. An' that bein' the case, the only person who could've had the knife was Miss Ida Belle. By the way, Eula, I don't s'pose you know, then, that Miss Ida Belle killed herself also. She used a pistol. We were fortunate enough to contact her only living relative on the coast, an' he tol' us she'd written him a letter an' said she was thinkin' about killin' herself. So we've lost a very fine teacher as well as a fine lawyer."

"Well, seein' as how you feel that way, what d'you plan t'do? Is they any way you could change the sheriff's mind. An' by the way, Marcus, Bo Arthur's due back at Collinsville day after t'morrow."

"I'm not sure that anybody can change his mind, but I'm goana try to as soon as I get back t'town. In the meantime, I'm go'n' tell Lee he needs to call Collinsville and see what they say."

LEE WAS STILL feeling the effects of Bo Arthur's knee in his crotch, and for that reason, if for no other, he was not inclined in the least to change his mind about who killed Frank Haley. His thinking was impaired to the point of maintaining that Bo Arthur was guilty, no matter what time he got home, or whether or not he had any blood on him. When Marcus mentioned these things to him, his quick answer was that Bo Arthur had stolen the knife, therefore he was responsible for Frank Haley's murder.

When Lee asked Gayle where she wanted to have the wake for Frank Haley, she said she had not decided yet. Lee Anderson, without having discussed the matter with anybody else, suggested it be in the foyer of the County Courthouse, "where he spent so much of his time."

"I don't know about that," she had said. "Don't chu think that would be goin' too far? I don't think he should be treated any differently than anybody else." She was surprised to hear the words coming out of her mouth, especially since she didn't care where it was held so long as it was not in their home. That would be more than she could take. The funeral would be held Monday morning

Marcus Tatum spent most of Saturday, trying to add substance to his conviction that Bo Arthur was not the person who killed Frank Haley Bankston. He had visited Eula Bilbo the day before and had come away feeling he had enough good and solid evidence to clear Bo Arthur. In order to convince Lee Anderson, however, he knew he would have to come up with still more evidence. Shortly after eating lunch on Saturday, he told Elsie he was going to visit Bo Arthur at the jail.

His first surprise was to see that Bo Arthur was being kept apart, in leg chains, from the other prisoners. When he asked why he was being treated that way, Chester Sellers, the jailer, told him

Lee Anderson had ordered it to be done because Bo Arthur had killed Frank Haley.

"And do you b'lieve that?"

"I sure do. I ain't got no reason not to."

"Well, I've got a few reasons why you should, but I don't plan to waste my time an' breath tryin' to make you think otherwise. Right now, though, I need t'talk with Bo Arthur. *Privately.* Now, let me see 'im."

Marcus could tell right away that Bo Arthur was not happy to see him. "Bo Arthur, the last time we met was not very pleasant, was it?"

"No, it wuddn't. Wha' chu plannin' on doin' to me now?"

"Sumpn good, I hope, though you may not b'lieve me. Bo Arthur, I wonder if me'n you can talk a while. I have a lot of questions to ask you, and I'm hopin' I can prove that you didn't kill Lawyer Bankston. Are you willin' t'hep me?"

The answer was not forthcoming, not yet. "I dittn't even know he was dead."

"It seems he was killed around eleven o'clock last night. Where were you about that time?"

"By that time I was awready home in bed. I don't know what time it was when I left the depot. The rain slacked up a little'n I tol' Travis I was goan try to get home before it got worse."

"Did ju go to Miss Bustin's house yesterday mornin'?"

"Yeah."

"Why?"

"She woanted t'see a letter my mamma wrote me b'fore she died'n that's why I went over there."

"Was that the only reason?"

Hesitation. "Well, not exackly."

"What d'you mean by that?"

He studied his hands, as though waiting long enough to feel safe in answering. "No," he said finally, "I thought while I was there I could get Mr. Sam's knife that I left there one day."

"Did ju get it? Be careful, Bo Arthur. *Did you get it?*"

"No sir, I dittn't."

"Why not?"

" 'Cause she acted funny, like she'd lost her mind. As soon as I got there, she tried to get me t'follow her down the hall, then she stopped at her bedroom door and pulled off her nightgown'n motioned for me to come in there with her."

"And you wanted no part of that, did ju?"

"No sir, I sure dittn't!"

Marcus tried with his eyes to tell Bo Arthur not to say anything else, then turned and said, "Chester, you get back where you b'long. What me'n Bo Arthur say is none a your business. Now, Bo Arthur, I woant chu t'know that I'm tryin' to clear you of any suspicion about who killed Frank Haley Bankston. All I ask is that you behave while they've got chu here, b'cause, if you don't, it'll make my job even harder. Will you promise me that?"

Lowering his head, he said, "Yessir. Thank you."

Later that day, while Marcus and Elsie were having supper, Schyler Bustin arrived. He said he had planned to take a week off from work in order to take care of Miss Ida Belle's business.

"I'm greatly relieved, not only to meet chu Mr. Bustin, but to know you'll have time to help us do what we need to do to settle Miss Bustin's affairs properly. By the way, do you have a place to stay while you're here? If you don't, my wife'n I'll be happy to let chu stay with us."

"That's very kind, Mr. Tatum, but I've already got a room at Hotel Alice downtown."

"Fine! You couldn't do much better than that. But would you by any chance have some time to stay and visit with us a while? I wish you could."

"I'd be more than happy to do that, but I need to go back to the hotel for a few minutes. I'll be back as soon as I can."

BROTHER STANWELL WORKED until two-thirty Monday morning, March 30, revising the funeral eulogy he had written over forty years ago, making sure that Frank Haley's name replaced Gladys Miller Moser's wherever it appeared and that appropriately exalting adjectives and adverbs had been generously applied wherever possible. He either was not aware or, if he was he didn't care, that some of the faithful church members had heard the eulogy so many times they could probably fill in for him if there was ever a need to.

He was disappointed, next morning, that so few people had come for the funeral service. During the process of amending the eulogy last night, he realized that he would have to do everything he could to reconcile Frank Haley's private life with his public one. In the process of doing so, his feet figuratively stumbled over each other as he waded through the weeded paths of his own life and, even though he was convinced that God had forgiven him, he was forced to remember, at times like this, something he had heard so often as a child that now he hated to hear it or even to remember having heard it: *Physician, heal thyself.*

Somehow he would have to minimize Frank Haley's dallyings, and perhaps the best way would be by emphasizing some of the good things he had done, specific names and instances, his generous tithes to the church, his incredible success as a defense lawyer, the intense concern for the education of children which resulted in continuous contributions to the school system and other generous ones whenever the need for money was made known.

A New Testament reference to earthly riches came unbidden to mind. He pondered it, wondering how or if he could misconstrue it in any way to Frank Haley's benefit. Regardless of all the good things he could say about Frank Haley, there were those whose ears had suddenly gone deaf to anything good that was said about him. He had, in fact, often heard members of the congregation disparaging Frank Haley for being haughtily rich and extremely arrogant. That meant he would need to come up with an adequate rejoinder, something significant enough at least to cause some of them to reconsider. The only verse of Scripture that came to mind was one that intrigued him the first time he read it and had continued to intrigue him ever since.

Jesus had said it would be easier for a camel to go through the eye of a needle than for a rich man to enter into the kingdom of Heaven. Surely, most or all of those at the funeral service would know the Scripture and, moreover, some might recall it at the time even if he did not refer to it in the eulogy. It was while he was drinking a late night cup of coffee that the idea occurred to him. Frank Haley was a rich man, no doubt about that, but not all rich men were like him. He was different, he was rich but he was a generous man who loved to help others, and wasn't that essentially why Jesus had said what he said? Frank Haley had always given abundantly of his wealth. More to the point, Bryson Beech, who was Frank Haley's private attorney and executor of his will, had told Brother Stanwell only yesterday that Frank Haley had bequeathed twenty-five thousand dollars to the Baptist Church. There! That made the difference! He would have to convince the doubting Thomases that Frank Haley was an *exceptional* rich man and, for that reason alone, he could not only go through the needle's eye, but could do so without needing to be pushed.

Ironically, eulogies, whether they are "tailor-made" or revamped versions of the original, seldom sustain for very long the interest of any except the nearest of kin and, in some cases, even the nearest of kin are not listening but are, instead, trying to think of something or anything other than death and funerals, some happy event to anticipate, friends and family who are still well and happy and likely to stay that way.

Gayle was aware that she was being critically scrutinized but was able to project what she thought was an appropriate countenance by keeping her eyes on Brother Stanwell, though her thoughts were seldom on what he was saying. Only a few of those who were watching her knew she was acting, they had been front-row observers at many of her finest performances. Some, even, were aware of how she had become so skilled at it.

SCHYLER BUSTIN HAD lain awake Saturday night, trying to reconcile himself with what he had to do next day. It had been such a long time since he last visited his aunt, more than two years ago, and what he remembered of that visit was less than pleasant. Ida Belle had been loving and attentive, sometimes more, he felt, than was necessary. She had been clearheaded, in fact, extremely lucid and at times, even, jovial. They had spent most of the time remembering. He had noticed as soon as he arrived that she had not yet severed her ties with the past, yet never referred to her aborted missionary experience. He remembered but was still surprised that she was a good cook. She always seemed to come fully alive while she was at the stove, preparing some special food for which, as she would say at the time, "I was made to feel there was something the old girl could still do without the aid of Tischenor's antiseptic."

After eating Sunday lunch with the Tatums, Schyler felt a little better. Afterwards, he went back to the hotel, took a short nap, then decided it would be a good time to go back to Ida Belle's house. There was much he needed to do. Yesterday, he had spent his time primarily trying to find anything that might be needed or even of interest later on. He had asked Marcus Tatum yesterday if he could find somebody to do some cleaning, especially in the kitchen and in Ida Belle's bedroom. Marcus said he would see what he could do, but it might be a little difficult. Schyler, though not squeamish, had already set limits on how much of what needed to be done he was willing to do.

He raised as many of the windows as he could and hoped it wouldn't rain, then went from one room to another, trying to decide what needed to be done before putting the house up for sale, being distracted at every turn by something that stirred the faded and frayed fragments of his boyhood. He was an only child. His father, Ida Belle's younger brother, Stanley, died three years ago of peritonitis after an appendectomy.

He avoided going in her bedroom for the time being, though he knew he would find many things of interest when he did. He stopped at the door, however, and let his emotions do what they needed to do. Her bed was unmade, the alarm clock on the little bedside table had stopped at three-thirty-four. He wondered about the clock and tried to visualize what had already happened when it stopped. It had to be after she killed herself, because she was meticulous about keeping the right time and about a few other relatively minor matters, like having all the dishes washed, dried, and put back where they belonged, always in a certain order, lined up precisely. He had noticed all of that whenever he had visited in the past. He had decided she needed to be able to control everything in her life that she was able to control, because she was deeply distressed about all the things she had to bear. She hated people who seemed to feel they were better than others, and she hated cruelty of any kind. She cried at the slightest provocation. He remembered the last time he visited, when she talked tirelessly about Bo Arthur, and how she cried because she felt sorry for him and wanted to help him but was unable to. He walked up and down the hall, trying to decide which of the unpleasant jobs he should do first.

He had decided in the meantime that he would have only a graveside service for Ida Belle. When he told Marcus Tatum what he had planned, Marcus said he would ask as many of the teachers and students as he could to attend. Instead of having Brother Stanwell perform the brief ceremony, he asked if Marcus would be kind enough to say a few words. Seven of her best female students readily agreed not only to attend but to say a few words also. Each of them cried as she did so. By six o'clock Monday evening, Ida Belle had been interred.

Marcus Tatum decided to talk with Mayor Guy Bailey, who apparently had not yet heard the whole story from Lee Anderson.

"Guy," Marcus said, "I think we've got a problem. I've talked with Bo Arthur and am convinced that he had nothing to do with Frank Haley's death. I even went out to talk with Eula, and, from what she said, he was home and asleep at the time Frank Haley was killed."

"And what does Lee say?"

"He says he doesn't b'lieve any of it. He made up his mind that Bo Arthur did it, and after Bo Arthur put up a fight with 'im'n even kicked him in his groin, he seems determined to have him punished."

"You know Lee as well as I do, Marcus. Well, maybe not for as long. But Lee would rather die than admit he's wrong about anything. I remember even as a child, he was always into some kind'a mischief 'n when called on the carpet and asked if he'd started the trouble, he'd lie with a straight face an' even sometimes pretend he was cryin'. That got 'im off the hook many a time. I don't think he's changed one bit."

"But this isn't like breakin' somebody's window with a baseball'n then blamin' it on somebody else," Marcus said. "This is an extremely grave matter, and I think it's time to find out who's teliin' the truth. As for as I'm concerned, Bo Arthur didn't have a thing to do it."

"Well, how d'you think we ought'a do it? We'd certainly need to go about it the right way. We don't want it t'look like Lee's on trial."

"What if we had a town meetin', sorta hear what the folks think after we tell 'em what we know so far, especially about what Eula swore to and any other evidence."

"Then you think I ought'a call a town meetin'?"

"I surely do. We've got a mighty serious problem that's got t'be solved, no matter what Lee Anderson says or plans on sayin' later. As I see it, that's the only thing we can do short of havin' a regular court trial, and that's sumpn we don't need and cain't afford."

"How 'bout Saturday night. You think that'd be a good time?"

"As good as any."

FOLLOWING FRANK HALEY'S funeral, V. Allison spent most of Monday afternoon wondering whether or not to visit Gayle. It was like trying to decide whether or not to eat the collard greens that usually came with Ben Rayburn's Blue Plate Special. She had always hated them, no matter how nutritious folks said they were, and the greasy way Addie Rayburn cooked them only made them harder to swallow. As she pondered the advisability of doing the visit, she made a few weak attempts to convince herself that the purpose of the visit really was a genuine concern for Gayle's frame of mind and outlook. Maybe Gayle would be in one of her rare moods, willing and wanting to say exactly what she was thinking. That would be reason enough.

Ella Jane let her in. "Miz Bankston be layin' down a while."

"Is she asleep?"

"Yassum, I b'lieve so. Lemme see."

She came back, shaking her head up and down. "Yessum, she be sleepin'. She done tol' me 'fo she lay down she dittn't woana be woke up."

V. Allison shouldn't have been surprised, but she was. It would certainly seem that her older sister would want to have someone to talk to at a time like this. She had known a number of instances when the death of a family member had brought together brothers or sisters who had been separated and kept apart for many years because of envy and hate. That's what she was pondering as she walked back to her house. She failed to consider, however, that a death in the family, instead of healing a rift between members, can and often does make the rift deeper.

SCHYLER BUSTIN HOPED he could complete his work by Friday noon. Marcus Tatum had procured the services of four Negro women who did all the cleaning and also some of the other jobs they saw that Schyler either did not know how or want to do. He spent much of that time looking through Ida Belle's personal mail, lesson plans, and even the first ninety-five pages of a story she had begun, according to her own markings, in 1918. He was impressed by the writing and even the insight she seemed to have for the several characters. It was, not surprisingly, a sad story of unrequited love a Protestant missionary in Africa had for a handsome Catholic priest. Much of the missionary's musings was extremely poignant and even heart-wrenching at times.

When he finished, he put the story back in the cardboard box where he had found it, feeling, as he did so, that he was burying the writer herself. It saddened him more than he wanted to admit. He had also noticed earlier, when he opened the drawer of the bedside table, that there was what looked like a diary, its cover smudged from much use and several fragments of different colored ribbons marking special places in it. Before taking it out, he decided to check on the work crew. One of them had suddenly hollered and the others came running to where she was. She was standing in the door to the bathroom with both hands over her mouth and so scared she could hardly speak. She pointed to the clothes hamper in the far corner near the bathtub. The lid was down, but she kept pointing at it and screaming. When Schyler asked why she was hollering, she just pointed at the clothes hamper. "Over yander," she said, "in de clothes hamper."

"What is it?"

"Look inside!"

He lifted the lid. The hamper was full of towels and clothes, Ida Belle's nightgown, her slippers, and five or six bath towels, all soaked with blood. He took the hamper outside, wondering how to get rid of it. He should let the sheriff know about it. Or should he? Not until he had told Marcus Tatum, he decided as he went back inside.

Before opening the diary, he moved over to the window, trying to put together the scene involving what was in the clothes hamper. He knew how meticulous Ida Belle was about herself, her house, and everything else. She was fanatic to the point of absurdity, he knew, but was that an offense? If she knew she was going to kill herself, she would make sure she was as clean as she could be. He was conjecturing, he realized, yet everything suddenly seemed to make sense.

With equal amounts of curiosity and sadness, he held the diary before opening it. In so short a time when she was no longer present, he now felt that she was. He knew that what was inside would challenge his emotions. He knew, also, that what was inside was seldom if ever sensed outside by others. Yet he felt guilty. He and Ida Belle had never been close enough to justify his reading the outpourings of her most private feelings and experiences. Yet the diary was only one of her earthly possessions, and she had left them all to him.

He had often wondered why she or anyone else would want to keep a diary in the first place. Not for her own eyes, necessarily, but maybe for other eyes to see that here, in her own handwriting, was the tangible evidence that she was not who they *thought* she was, but who she *really* was, like being naked and, for the first time, not being embarrassed.

As soon as he opened it, a small, faded picture of her mother fell out. He laid it aside, remembering that he should put it back later. At first he randomly turned page after page, stopping when he saw something that interested him. Every entry had been written impeccably in her own distinguished style, some obviously done more hurriedly than others, then, realizing it would take too long to read all the entries, he turned to the last one.

March 27, 1925: For sixty-six years I have fought and lost the battle of Life. Tonight I have won the victory of death. There's no light at the end of the tunnel, only total and endless darkness, a long and painless sleep. I go there willingly on my own terms. I have loved, I have hated, but I've hated more than I've loved. Now, after killing the one I've loved and hated most, I feel vindicated, ready to rid myself of this ugly world and all the ugly and mean people in it. God, forgive me!

—twenty-two—

A LITTLE BEFORE seven o'clock Friday morning, Speck Barber and Denny Weems were drinking coffee in Ben's Café when the subject of frog-gigging came up.

"Have you done any giggin' lately?" Speck asked.

"No, I aint. I thought it was too early for frog-giggin'."

"Naw, it aint too early. Th'other day I heard Jim Parker say he'd gigged a whole gallon full."

"Where was that?"

"He said it was 'bout a mile east a town, out near where Bruce Evans lives. You know where that is, don't chu?"

"Yeah, but are you goan be able t'walk that far?"

"If I know they's that many frogs waitin' t'be gigged I can. Well, how 'bout it? Woana go?"

"What kind'a weather we goan have? It aint s'posed t'rain, is it?"

"Naw, I don't b'lieve."

"Well?"

"Well what? D'you woana gig or not?"

"Let me give it some more thought," Denny said, holding his cup out to Ben for a refill "What time?"

"I don't know. Roun' sebben?"

"Where we goan meet?"

"Why don't chu meet me in front a the court house?"

"Awright. Don't f'git."

Speck and Denny grew up together, liking and doing the same things. They had no way of knowing to what extent they were alike. That's something it takes a long time to realize. It so happened that both were members of large families, and had fathers who knocked them down to size anytime they did something wrong or didn't do something right. In the little country school out on the edge of Jones County, they had been poor students and mischievous kids, always in trouble, never able to meet even the meager requirements of that little country school. Their less-than-qualified teachers were always scolding or punishing them. Then, if their parents learned about it, they were punished again.

During puberty, they began to express themselves by causing trouble. At some undefinable point in their young lives, they had come to realize they were much alike and, also, that sometimes being mischievous and unlike others was fun. Oddly enough, even though almost all white people hated black people, Speck and Denny hated them more. That being the case, they often avoided punishment if they did something bad to somebody who was black and sometimes even publicly recognized for it, such as when they killed Joe David for drinking out of the white water fountain. You could count on the fingers of one hand how many people in Ellisville at that time did not feel the same way. Most people, it seemed, were not concerned that Speck and Denny were so mean. There were others who were concerned but were not persistent or honest enough to go all the way in trying to understand. Actually, Speck and Denny themselves didn't know why they were the way they were. It had never occurred to them that they hated others because they hated themselves even more.

It was during their early teens that they started frog gigging. It afforded them a moment of parental grace for bringing in all those frogs, the legs of which would be cut off, breaded, and fried for breakfast next day; their greater joy had come earlier, as they spotted and gigged the frogs and watched them squirm and die. They both often laughed about seeing the big eyes almost before they saw the rest of the frogs, then thrusting their homemade gigs into the frogs' bellies. Every time they went gigging, the thrill of killing became more intense and pleasing.

SOMETHING HAD BEEN bothering Lee Anderson ever since he went out to arrest Bo Arthur, and it was something most folks never thought about or, if they did, they never mentioned it. He could not get it off his mind, what Bo Arthur said about Ida Belle trying to get him into her bedroom. Even as Bo Arthur was telling him about it, Lee was feeling his own cravings, no matter that he was married and thought to be well-mated.

He sat in his office for a long time, thinking about what Marcus Tatum had told him after visiting with Eula Bilbo. He had heard but he had not listened. He could tell the moment Marcus started talking that he had come for one purpose only, to try to convince him that Bo Arthur was innocent. As a matter of fact, Lee had already been trying to think of something bad enough to discredit what he knew Marcus Tatum would say at the Saturday meeting. He kept thinking about some of the things Bo Arthur had said and the way he looked when he talked about Ida Belle bustin' their relationship. He realized that he had not listened carefully enough when Bo Arthur was telling him about it. Now that he was trying to find something in what Bo Arthur had said that could possibly be used against him, he suddenly came to a different conclusion.

Bo Arthur could very easily have found the knife the morning he went to Ida Belle's house, the morning when Vayda Baygents said she saw him going in but not coming out of the house. When he saw Ida Belle, he could either have done what she wanted him to do, or he could have ignored her and gone looking for the knife. In either case, he would have found it, then left by the back door. While he was visualizing the scene, the thought suddenly came: Ida Belle didn't recognize him; she thought he was somebody else! Sure! That's exactly what happened. He went out the back door with the knife.

Then, in case this version of what happened proved ineffectual, there was still another, something far out of the ordinary that would bring shame and condemnation on Bo Arthur, proof that he was a sexual deviant who should, by the nature of his crime, be removed from society and remanded either to Collinsville or Parchman for the rest of his life.

As a rule, Lee Anderson's job as sheriff rarely if ever required more mentality than he possessed. Unless Ben Rayborn had told him, he would possibly never have considered to what extent Lily Ruth's behavior had had on Bo Arthur. As far as he was concerned, when Bo Arthur saw Ida Belle motioning for him to come with her, he should have done so without giving it a second thought. That's simply what any normal young fellow his age would have done.

And of course Lee had never been anything but normal when it came to such matters. Swiveled back, with his feet on the desk, he called to mind some of the things he did as a kid, things with a woman, that is, the first time he and two other friends, after hearing about Daisy Daughdrill, decided to pay her a visit.

Daisy lived at Ovett, alone, far out in the middle of nowhere. He remembered how scared he was, and how accommodating she was, being gentle with a coarse laugh now and then, explaining in her own funny way what to do. Afterwards, he felt good, manly, and lost no time telling a revised version of it to all of his friends. He realized now that he hadn't seen Daisy in a long time. He had heard that her place was no longer open for business. What did she look like, he wondered. She must be sixty or older by now. But that didn't matter. He had a plan, and she figured in it.

The little town of Ovett had grown since the last time he was there. He was so interested in the new bank on the corner where he used to turn that he forgot where he was and had a hard time finding Daisy's place. He hardly recognized the old house and almost didn't recognize her when she finally came to the door.

He was surprised. She had put on weight, but otherwise she still looked like her old self. He could tell she was having a hard time recognizing him, and he could tell, also, that she was trying to make a good impression.

He laughed. "Hello, Daisy. D'you'member me?"

"Should I?"

"I don't know. I just thought chu might. Well, I shore do remember you."

"I bet chu do. Lots a fellers do," she said, laughing. "So, which one are you?"

"I'm Lee Anderson. I'm sheriff over at Ellisville."

"You don't say! Come on up a little closer."

As he came nearer, she blocked out the afternoon sun with her hand and watched as he came up the steps, holding onto the loose hand rail.

"Lord Jehovah!" she said, laughing and coughing at the same

time. "Yeah, I see. What can I do for you? Don't tell me you still don't know how t'do it!" She laughed again, so hard she almost strangled. "I'm sorry, Lee, I dittn't mean that. What can I do for you otherwise?"

She had thrown him off-course. Why had he come? Certainly not to be laughed at and made to look and feel foolish. "Daisy," he said, "I need yo' help. I really do. Could we go inside just for a few minutes? I promise I woant stay long."

"I really am busy, Lee. Couldn't we talk about this some other time?"

"No, Daisy, I need t'settle this matter now, as soon as possible. Before tonight."

"Why? Do all yo' prisoners have to prove they can lay a woman?"

"No, Daisy. This prisoner is different. I don't think he wants t'lay a woman. That's the problem. I b'lieve he's a pansy."

"Is that what they call 'em?"

"Yeah."

"Well, if he is, how in hell can I hep 'im?"

"Well, if I can prove he *is* a pansy, I stand a better chance a provin' he's the one that killed Frank Haley."

"I fail t'see even the slightest connection, Lee. It just don't make no sense t'me."

"I thought chu might be able to tell if he was. I need t'know ever'thang I can about 'im t'prove he's the one that killed Frank Haley."

"Good God a'mighty. Lee. What in hell are you talkin' 'bout? An' furthermore, I done tol' ju I don't do that no more."

"Yeah, I heard that, but I thought chu might be willin' t'do me a big favor."

"An' what's yo' idear of a big favor?"

She had derailed him to the point where he didn't know what to say. No matter he had one thing in mind, and he was going to let her know what it was, no matter how crazy it sounded. "Daisy, all I woant chu t'do is pretend you go'n' rape 'im just t'see what he does. I need to prove that he's not normal, and that's why he's been doing some'a the mean things he's been doin' all his life. I know it might sound crazy to you, but I know what I'm talkin' about. If you'll just promise t'do that, I'll make it well worth your time, an' I'll tell you more about it if you'll just promise to hep me now."

"Lee, how many more times I'm go'n' have t'tell you? I ain't in that kind'a business no more."

"I'll pay you well, Daisy."

"Well ain't good enough. I ain't innerested."

"How 'bout fifty dollars?"

"Lee, you must be deaf. I'm not go'n do it, and that's th' end of it!"

"I'll give you a hunderd."

"Lee, you ain't *got* a hunderd dollars. An', furthermore, they'd kick yo' ass out'a office as soon as they found out what chu'd done."

"Maybe I ain't got it right now, but I shore as hell can git it when I woant to."

"Money, you mean?" she said, laughing and coughing again.

"Oh, come on, Daisy, stop playin' 'roun' with me. I need yore help."

"It sounds t'me like you're go'n' need more'n my help, Lee."

"Naw, that ain't right. If you'll just do what I woant chu t'do, I'm pretty sure I can prove my case."

"Tell me, Lee, how were you plannin' t'do that? I mean, if I agreed to do it?"

"Like I said, Daisy, all I woant chu t'do is maybe take some a yo' clothes off'n I'll have 'im go in the room where you are. That might be pretty hard t'do, but I can do it. If my guess is right, time he sees you tryin' t'git out a yo' clothes, he's go'n' come out'a there like lightnin' struck 'im. An' that's exactly what I woant 'im t'do.

"An' that's all I have t'do?"

"I guarantee it. That's all."

She turned her head and seemed not to have been convinced yet. "An' you gimme a hunderd dollars for that?"

"Well, maybe."

"Like *maybe?* Like *hell!*" she said and started back up the steps. "You said a hunderd a while ago, and that's what it's goan' cost chu, or you can git back in that run-down fliver'n head back t'Ellisville,"

"Awright, Daisy. If that's what it takes, that's what I'll do."

"An' what if you decide on the way home that chu aint goan pay me a hunderd?"

"You have my word on it, Daisy. B'lieve me, I'll do what I said I'd do."

She shook a finger directly at him. "You will, or I'll tell the folks in Ellisville what you've done. Is that guarantee enough?"

"Yes, Daisy. If it's awright with you, I'll try t'have 'im here around six or so this evenin'."

As he drove away, she stood on the top step, looking over into the woods where some buzzards were feasting on the corpse of a newly killed deer. It had always bothered her, especially after she got old enough to start making a living the way she did. But she would never let anybody know. When, on certain occasions, she had sought help and forgiveness for her sins, she had never felt better to any extent afterwards. Sometimes at night, especially after the last customer had gone, she would feel as though she was of no more worth than the stuff buzzards eat. One day, maybe before long, they'd find her out there, and they wouldn't even notice that she wasn't like all the others.

Lee's trip back to Ellisville was certainly not what he had wanted and hoped it would be. He was disappointed, and he was scared, too. He shouldn't have expected Daisy to remember him, but even so, he had no idea she would treat him the way she did. After all, he was the sheriff of Ellisville. That was the disappointment. The worry, though, was harder to deal with. In the first place, he should have his tongue cut out for even suggesting he would pay her for what was nothing more than a small favor, and, to make matters worse, to have offered fifty dollars more! Where would he ever get that much money? If anybody knew what he planned to do with it, he'd never get it, and he knew only too well that he'd be kicked out of office. So, what chance did he have now? If this plan didn't work, how would he ever be able to get his revenge on Bo Arthur?

As soon as he got back to his office, he called Ben Rayburn.

"Lee, I'd like t'hep you," Ben said, "but I just caint do it. What' chu need it for?"

"I caint tell you, Ben. You go'n' have t'trust me."

"Caint do it, Lee. You'll have t'find somebody else."

"Ben, there ain't nobody else. I need it now!"

"I don't know why you cain't tell me what chu need it for. If you did, I might be willin' t'hep you."

"I'll be right over."

Lee's account of what he wanted to do got Ben's full attention immediately. "Lee, I don't know why you still b'lieve Bo Arthur's the one that killed Frank Haley. Nobody else b'lieves it."

"That's b'cause they don't know what I know. He ain't normal like other fellers his age."

"An' so you b'lieve that what chu plan t'do is goan prove it?"

"Absolutely! Now, how 'bout hep'n me do it?"

"You know, Lee, if I give you the money, you goan have t' pay me back as soon as you can."

"You can trust me, Ben. I will."

"B'fore next month, Lee. No longer, you hear?"

"Don' chu worry, Ben. I'm as good as my word."

ON HIS WAY back to the hotel, Schyler decided to stop by Marcus Tatum's house, to let him know about Ida Belle's diary. Elsie Tatum told him Marcus was still at school.

"Do you think he'd mind if I stopped by and talked with him a few minutes?"

"No, I'm sure he wouldn't. You must feel free to talk with 'im as long as you like."

Marcus was looking through a file on Ida Belle Bustin when Schyler got there. "Have you made any headway with the clean-up?" Marcus asked.

"Well, a little. It's not a pleasant job, as you know, and the women helping me don't like a lot of what they see."

"I don't think I would, either. But what about you? How much longer do you think it'll take to finish the job?"

"I can't really tell, but I'll probably have t'come back several more times. Every once in a while, though, we find something of interest and even sometimes something of value. Which reminds me of why I wanted to stop by and talk with you about something. Mrs. Tatum said you wouldn't mind."

"Of course not, what's on your mind?"

"Something I just found, something that should be of interest to you."

"Yes, yes, what is it?"

"It's Ida Belle's diary. I found it a while ago as I was going through one of her dresser drawers."

"Her diary? You don't mean it! Is that what chuve got in your hand?"

"Yes, and I do mean it, and I wanted you to read it. Would you like to?"

"Well, yes," Marcus said hesitantly, "but I'm not sure I should. Why don't you just tell me what it is?"

"But of course you should read it. I think she'd probably woant chu, more than anyone else, to know how and why she ended her life the way she did."

Schyler could see the effect Ida Belle's words were having on Marcus' face as he read the entry and, finally, the stiffened lips and the sad eyes looking but seeing nothing.

"It's shocking, isn't it?" Schyler said.

Marcus seemed not to have heard.

"What d'you think about it?"

"I'm too deeply affected to know for sure what I feel." He leaned over the desk, closed his eyes, then straightened, covered one hand with the other and looked up. "Well," he said softly, "that should leave no doubt in anybody's mind about who killed Frank Haley."

"Now, what will you do?"

"I don't really know. This may still raise some questions."

"What d'you mean?"

"Schyler, have a seat," he said. "You seem to be a very sensible man. You might be able to help me even more."

"I'd give anything if I could, but how?"

"By preventin' our sheriff from turning this thing into a free-for-all. I shouldn't say this, but he's a poor excuse for a sheriff in the first place. He wasn't elected. He's the sheriff because a few folks with lots of influence put him where he is. The election, like a lot of others, was rigged, but nobody seemed concerned enough to do anything about it. Would you b'lieve that on certain occasions the feeble-minded folks at FMI have been brought to town on election day and forced to vote? Think about that!"

"I would never have believed it if you hadn't told me."

"What it boils down to, I think, is that most folks in Ellisville don't think we even need a sheriff. Sometimes I get the feelin' I'm the only one who does."

"But why do you still anticipate trouble? Isn't the entry in Ida Belle's diary sufficient evidence to prove who killed Frank Haley?"

"Yes, of course, but only under normal circumstances. I might as well fill you in. I think you deserve to know."

Schyler nodded his head.

"Well, no matter what valid proof I can offer, Lee Anderson is going to ignore it and try his best to put Bo Arthur behind bars for the rest of his life. They both hate each other, and there's a good chance that one or the other of them is goanna do something really bad. For the time-bein', Bo Arthur is bein' held in the city jail. By rights, he should be discharged as soon as I prove his innocence. In this case, that is, because Bo Arthur's a violently mixed-up young man who has done and will probably continue to do things worthy of jail time either here or at Parchman." He closed his eyes and threw his head back for a few moments, then, tapping his fingers on the desktop, gave Schyler a long and serious look, then affected a smile. "I b'lieve it's time, Schyler, to take Lee Anderson on. Can you stay around a little longer? I may need your help."

"I don't know. Right now, though, I think I should get back to the hotel and freshen up a bit. May I come back later? Will you be here or at home?"

"There's no tellin'!" he said and laughed.

As soon as Schyler left, Marcus called the sheriff's office. "Paula," he said, "this is Paula, isn't it?"

"Yessir."

"This is Marcus Tatum. I need to talk with the sheriff. Is he in?"

"Nossir, he iddn't. But just a minute, let me ask Tracy. He might know where he is."

"This is Tracy, Mr. Tatum. What can I do for you?"

"Paula said you might know where Lee Anderson is. Do you?"

"Nossir, I sure don't."

"You mean he never lets you know where he's goin'?"

"Sometimes, yessir, but this time he didn't. Would ju like for me t'see if I can locate 'im?"

"I'd be mighty obliged if you would, Tracy. It's most urgent."

"Awright, Mr. Tatum. I'll let chu know as soon as I find 'im." Marcus then called Mayor Guy Bailey and told him to cancel the town meeting.

"Why, what's happened now?"

"I caint tell you now, Guy, but it's important enough to call off the meeting."

"How can I, Marcus? T'morrow's Saturday, you know."

"I know, but chu can do a little callin' or have some hand-written notices posted here and there downtown. And I'll let as many people know as I can."

EARLIER, BEFORE LEE Anderson came out of his office, Tracy called Marcus at his office but did not get an answer. He wanted to let him know what was about to happen. He then motioned Bo Arthur aside and whispered, "Aint nobody goan hurt chu, Bo Arthur. I'll see to that. But chu gotta do what the sheriff says. I promise, evahthang's goan be awright. I'll see to it."

As soon as he got in the car, Bo Arthur began wondering where they were going. What Tracy had said made him feel a little better, but he was convinced that what lay ahead was bound to be a challenge he must start preparing for now, this moment. He knew Lee Anderson was out to get him. He had to make sure that nothing between here and there lured him into believing otherwise. He would kill if he had to.

"Hello, Bo Arthur," Lee said. "Woana go for a little ride?"

"What kind'a ride?""

"Just a reg'lar ride. I've gotta go to Ovett on some business and thought chu might like to get out a that cell for a while. We won't be gone long. Woana go?"

"How come all of a sudden you tryin' t'be friendly? You ain't never been b'fore."

"I know, Bo Arthur. I realize me'n you ain't never been friends, an', in fact, me'n you might never be. But that don't mean I cain't do a little sumpn t'make you feel a little better, even if ain't but for a few minutes. What say? Woana go or not?"

Bo Arthur saw Lee slide the handcuffs under his seat as they got in the truck. Neither of them said anything for a few minutes, until Bo Arthur felt safe enough to say what he was thinking. "I still don't trust chu. I guess you know that, don' chu?"

"Yeah, I sure do."

"Would ju tell me if I asked sumpn else?"

"What's that?"

"Are you really doin' this t'make me feel good or for some other reason. I gotta tell you, I still don't trust you no more'n you trust me. Right now I don't feel too good, if you know what I mean." He could see out of the corners of his eyes that something was bothering Lee. "I don't b'lieve you're tellin' the truth, are you?" he said.

Lee seemed suddenly to come partially awake without having settled the matter he'd been pondering.

"So, maybe I was right all along, you done lied ag'in, ain't chu? You dittn't have no intention a takin' me for a ride t'make me feel good. You done made up yo mind long ago that chu aint go'n' be satisfied till you see me hangin' by my neck or spendin' the rest a my life in Parchman."

By the time they arrived at Daisy's house, Lee had decided it was time to level with Bo Arthur, even if he had to do some lying along the way. "Bo Arthur, a dear lady friend a mine lives here. I was tellin' her about chu just this mornin', an' she said she'd sure like to meet chu. I tol' 'er I'd see if I could get chu to come with me sometime an' maybe y'all could get acquainted. So, that's why I brung you here."

"Well, what in hell ever gave you the idea of doin' such a stupid thing? An' furthermore, I don't b'lieve a word of it. I think it's sumpn else you just made up, thinkin' you were goan make a fool a me. And also, you ought'a know I don't woana meet nobody, woman or otherwise, who likes you enough t'do such a stupid thing. So you can just turn this junk heap aroun' an' take me right back where I came from, and the sooner the better."

Daisy was slow coming to open the door.

"Let's go inside for a minute or two, Daisy. I been wondrin' how we oughta do this. I thought if me'n you could just have Bo Arthur come inside for a little visit, then maybe I could leave 'im in here with you. You think that'll work?"

MARCUS WAS ALMOST home when he suddenly decided to go to the jail. Chester Sellers, the jailer, told him Lee and Bo Arthur had gone for a ride.

"Where were they goin'?"

"I don't have no idear. What chu woant with 'im?"

"That's none of your business, Chester."

"Well, awright, Mr. Smart man. I aint goan tell you where he's takin' Bo Arthur, neither."

"I thought chu said you didn't know where they were goin'."

"Yeah, I did. That's what the sheriff said t'tell anybody what wanted t'know."

"Why wouldn't chu tell me, Chester. What chu scared of?"

"Shucks, man, I aint scared a nuttin'. I just haf t'do what the sheriff tells me t'do., that's all."

"Oh, I see. Which reminds me. Chester, I've been askin' different ones about how they felt about what happened to Frank Haley. Most of 'em seem to think it was Ida Belle who did it. I'd be interested to know what chu think. How do you feel, Chester?"

"I don't think, Mister, I know! It was Bo Arthur. None other."

"How come? I'd really like t'know why you believe he did it."

"B'cause he said hisself that he went t'Ida Belle's house that mornin', thinkin' she'd be teachin' an' he could go inside'n find the knife he thowed at 'er one day an' she kept it. Who else could it've been?"

"But he tol' Lee that he didn't go inside the house, that Ida Belle tried to get 'im t'come down the hall where she was, an' he didn't do it because she was actin' funny."

"Actin' funny, my hind leg," Chester said, snickering. "She was buck naked and wanted him to do her pleasure an' he wouldn't do it."

"Then how did he get the knife? He didn't even know where it was."

"I don't know 'bout that, but he still got it, just the same."

"That's absurd, Chester. You ought'a know it is, but chu still maintain that Bo Arthur got the knife in spite of that."

"That's right, an' you'n nobody else aint goan make me feel no different."

Marcus wondered what would happen if he asked the other question. Why not? "Alright, Chester, I won't say any more about that, but there's one other thing I'd like to hear your explanation for. It's about Ida Belle."

"What about Ida Belle?"

"You said Ida Belle was naked and tryin' t'get Bo Arthur to come down where she was. Why d'you think Bo Arthur wouldn't do it?"

Marcus saw the abrupt change in Chester's outward appearance. He had long ago assessed the fellow to be little more than sane, ready to make assertions about whatever was being discussed, yet tongue-tied whenever the matter being discussed was sexual in nature.

Chester avoided Marcus' eyes. "Lee says Bo Arthur's a pansy."

"A pansy! What's that?"

It took Chester a while to say it. "That's a feller what don't like girls."

"And Lee thinks Bo Arthur doesn't like girls?"

"That's right."

"But it's not right. Bo Arthur does like girls. He's just had a hard time growin' up without a father. And you probably know about his mother."

"Well, that don't matter. He ain't normal. That's what Lee says. That's why. . ." He stopped suddenly and lowered his eyes.

"That's why *what*, Chester? Is that why Lee's taken him for a ride, as you call it?"

"I done tol' ju all I'm goin' tell ya."

LEE HAD TO knock three times before Daisy opened the door. "Hey, Daisy. Could me'n you go inside for just a minute or two? We need t'think about how we goan do this."

"I would'a thought chu'd awreddy have evahthang planned. I should'a knowed better."

She stepped out onto the porch, holding the door open with her left hand and shading her eyes with the other, trying to get a good look at Bo Arthur, who was still sitting in the car. The deep shadows of the tall oak and sweet gum trees made it all but impossible to see him.

"Come on, Daisy! Let's go on inside the house. We need t'decide about the best way t'do this."

She chuckled as she went inside. "Lee, I never knew that."

"Knew what?"

"About which way was better'n another'n."

He didn't laugh.

She could tell he was nervous. As for herself, she planned to let things happen, the way she had usually done before when entertaining a visitor, even a new one. "I made some oatmeal cookies a while ago," she said. "You reck'n Bo Arthur'd like some?"

"What was that? Oh, cookies? Well, he might. He's not like most other fellers his age."

"I know. I gathered from what chu said this mornin' that he wuddn't. You reck'n he'd like some milk or a Nehi soda pop?"

"I don't know. Let me go git 'im."

WHEN SCHYLER RETURNED, Marcus was just finishing some notices he'd made about the town meeting cancellation. "How 'bout helpin' me put these out downtown? Would ju mind?"

"Not at all. I think I'd enjoy that."

A few minutes later, as they neared Ben Rayburn's Café, Marcus' stomach reminded him that he had missed his lunch earlier. "Say, by the way, Schyler, I just remembered I didn't go home for lunch and I'm hungry. Since we're going to Ben Rayburn's café in a minute or so, would you let me take you to supper? Well, not a real supper, but Ben and his wife Addie are rather famous for their good food. Their chili is about the best you go'n' find anywhere within driving distance, and his hamburgers are the best I've ever eaten. Will you let me treat chu to some of that good food? Are you hungry?"

Schyler laughed. "Yes, I am hungry. Let's stop and eat. I used to hear Ida Belle talk about the good chili. I'd like to try it."

"First, though, let me go inside'n ask Ben if it's alright to put one of these notices on his window. It'll only take a minute or two. You woana go on and get a seat?"

"No, I'll wait out here."

Ben had seen them and came out to where they were. "Well, if aint the professor his self," he said. "What's on your mind, Marcus. And who's this other young feller with you?"

After introducing Schyler, Marcus told Ben about the notice.

"What notice you talkin' about, Marcus?"

"The town meetin' we'd called for tomorrow night's been canceled."

"Why?"

"Because we know now who killed Frank Haley."

Ben's mouth dropped open. "What?"

"Yes, we really know. You don't b'lieve me, do you?"

"I don't know what t'b'lieve. When did this happen? How d' you know for sure?"

"Well, the murder, you know, happened a week ago last night, but Schyler just learned this morning who did it."

"An' how'd ju find out, Schyler?" Ben asked, leaning over as close as he could to keep from missing something.

"While I was going through one of the drawers in my aunt's dresser, I found her diary. The last thing she wrote was that she had killed Lawyer Bankston."

Ben threw his arms over his head and swung around so they couldn't see. "Good God a'mighty!" he moaned behind his hands. "Jesus Christ! What're we goan do now!"

"Ben, we're goanna let everybody know the truth, that's what. You still don't b'lieve it?"

"Naw, that ain't it. It's sumpn worse than that. Much worser."

"Well, for God's sakes, what is it." Marcus reached over and pulled Ben's hands away from his face. "Do you know sumpn we don't know? Sumpn we oughta know, maybe?"

"Yeah."

"Well, tell us, for God's sake!"

"I caint. Not out here. Let's go inside, to the back. I'll tell Addie t'take care a the customers."

"Marcus," Schyler said, "I think I'll just go on to the hotel.

You need to take care of this. Remember, if I can help you, let me know."

The fast walk to the back of the café had tired both of them. Ben, in fact, was out of breath. Add to that the increased fear about what was happening, he needed a few moments to catch his breath and do the best he could in choosing his words.

"Marcus, I've done it ag'in!" he said.

"Done what, Ben?"

"I let Lee have some money so he could take Bo Arthur t'Ovett to see if Daisy Daughdrill . . . you know who that is, don't chu?"

Marcus nodded his head.

". . . ell, t'see if she could find out if Bo Arthur was a pansy or not. Lee thinks that's why Bo Arthur's so mean. He even thinks that's why Bo Arthur killed Frank Haley."

"Good God! Ben, d'you realize what chu've done? D'you realize Bo Arthur might be tryin' t'kill Lee'n even Daisy right this minute? Why don't chu think before you do such crazy things? We'd better do somethin' and do it fast. Right this minute! Ben, you're goanna have t'get it done, no matter what it takes. You brought this on yourself, so now you've got to settle it. Now!"

"How? What can I do? Marcus, hep me!"

"Alright, first of all, right now, call Tracy over at the sheriffs office'n tell 'im to get over here as fast as he can with whatever car or truck he can get his hands on. No, no, wait! That's not right. Ovett's outside Lee's jurisdiction. Maybe you better still call Tracy'n let him tell Sheriff Eubanks what t'do. Tell 'im we got a real bad situation in the makin' and we need 'im t'help us as soon as possible and, if he cain't come, send a deputy. And soon. Tell 'im, also, t'stop at Ben's Café to pick me up so I can let 'im know what the trouble is. I only hope'n pray it's not too late to stop what I'm sure is goan be a number-one disaster."

Eustis Eubanks was familiar with the whole Jones County area, including the unpainted, tree-shrouded house where Daisy Daughdrill conducted her business without dissent, warnings, or other deterrents for about thirty years. He also had learned some time ago that she had, as she was heard to say, "closed shop." He also knew a lot about Lee Anderson and had, on several occasions, locked horns with him about a few matters not mentioned in the last five editions of CODE OF ETHICS FOR LOCAL GOVERNMENTS IN MISSISSIPPI.

KNOWING THAT EUSTIS was on his way to Ellisville gave Marcus a sense of optimism. He knew what kind of sheriff Eustis was and had been for the twelve years he'd held that position. Eustis was known to be severe, honest, and humane, qualities not normally found or reputed to be found in other defenders of the law. He wanted to know exactly what Lee was up to. Marcus let him know.

"I'm glad ju tol' me that, Marcus. Now I have sumpn t'go on. Now I'm I more convinced than ever that it's time to put Lee where he b'longs. I mean by that, anywhere except where he is now."

Though Marcus felt a little better, a little more confident, knowing that Eustis would handle the present situation the right way, the extent of his anxiety and fear had abated only minimally, and he suddenly became aware of the faster than normal heart-beat as the two of them turned off of Highway 15, onto the winding dirt and deep-rutted road to Daisy's house.

Bo Arthur, during his short lifetime, had not been made aware of some of society's demands. Even if he had been, he most likely would have ignored them deliberately in order to assert his convictions that such things were unnecessary, even absurd. For instance, except in the case of Ida Belle Bustin, he had almost never been invited to visit others in their homes. Such being the case, he felt out of place and more self-conscious than he wanted Lee and Daisy to see. It would, and did make him feel alone, defenseless to the point of being vulnerable. Vulnerability had always been a dirty word.

Though Daisy tried to lessen his self-consciousness, she knew she was not succeeding. "Bo Arthur," she said, sitting down beside him on the dingy sofa, "how have you got to be sixteen years old and still single? You're a mighty handsome young man. Did ju know that? Has anybody ever told ju how good lookin' you are?"

"I never paid no attention to it," he said, slightly above a whisper, wishing he had stayed in jail.

She went to the kitchen and returned with the plate of oatmeal cookies. "Would ju like a cookie, Bo Arthur? They're oatmeal cookies."

"No M'am. I ain't hungry."

That was Lee's cue to leave. "Daisy, I'll be right back. I forgot sumpn in the car."

Daisy could see that her job was going to be a hard, a situation which she had almost always been able to handle. She got up and laid the cookies on a little table near Bo Arthur, then decided to sit in an old rocker on the other side of the room.

"Bo Arthur," Daisy said, pulling back on the rocker handles. "Have you got chu a girl?"

"Yeah, I got a lot of 'em."

"Is that right? Well, now, I s'pose that keeps you pretty busy, don't it?"

"It would if I let it," he said, crossing and uncrossing his legs.

"But Bo Arthur, that don't sound like what Lee told me. He said he don't think you're tellin' the truth."

"I don't give a damn what Lee Anderson thinks or says. An' anyway, I thought chu'n him had some business to talk over. Why ain't ch'all talkin' it over?"

"We will direckly, Bo Arthur, but right now, though, I'd rather talk with you. Now, gettin' back t'Lee, I don't b'lieve he meant nothin' bad, Bo Arthur. An' besides, he ain't got no room t'talk." She laughed. "I'll never forget the time him'n two of his buddies come out chere for me t'show 'em how t'do it. You know what I mean. Well, they was all beginners, but Lee, he was the most igrant one of 'em! I mean I had t'tell him evahthang! Why, if you asked him what side a the bed he got up on evah mornin', he couldn't tell ya. When I told 'im later, 'bout being so igrant, I mean, he nyilly split his side open!" She laughed so hard, she started choking.

By now, the low rage that began moving upward as soon as Daisy started talking had reached Bo Arthur's lungs and had settled there momentarily, as if to gain strength, just below his neck. If he didn't get rid of it soon, he knew he was going to do something bad, something he had vowed to do on the way over here.

He got up suddenly and stood a few moments, wondering if she knew what was about to happen, and hoping she didn't.

He walked over to where she was and looked directly at her face. The moment he saw the understanding in her faded grey eyes, he grabbed with both hands around her neck, squeezed hard, and held the pressure down until he finished talking. "So that's why he woanted me to come here. He thought I ought t'be showed how men screw women. He thought I was stupid enough not to know awready. He maybe even paid you t'teach me how it's done. Well, let me tell you now, while I've got yore throat between my hands, that I don't need t'be told how to screw a woman. And even if I didn't, I sure as hell wouldn't be out here tryin' to learn how t'do it from you. I could'a learned everything you know and a hell of a lot more than you know about it from my Mamma, b'cause she was just like you, a low-down, good-for-nothing bitch whore."

She tried to scream but couldn't. She tried to push her arms up between his to get him to stop choking her, but he only stiffened and pinned her in. There was a sound outside. He listened, wondering what it was, forgetting momentarily and giving Daisy just enough time and breath to holler. "Lee! Come in here and get this son-of-a-bitch out'a my house!"

He shook her back and forth and squeezed even harder. He wanted her dead.

Lee had been listening with his ear to the door and one hand on the doorknob, turning it a little at a time to hear better. Bo Arthur wasn't aware that Lee was just a step or two behind him. Before he knew what was happening, Lee had grabbed both of his arms from behind and was forcing him to turn around. Now they were face to face, the way they were once before. Lee remembered and was making every effort to prevent it happening again. He needed the handcuffs. During the remembering where they were, Bo Arthur had enough time to repeat the performance that had done him well before. He didn't consider, though, that Lee was also remembering and would do anything to keep Bo Arthur's knee where it belonged. Then it happened. As Bo Arthur lifted his knee toward Lee's groin, Lee grabbed it, held it a moment, then gripped Bo Arthur's ankle with both hands and lifted the leg as high as it would go. Bo Arthur staggered, lost his balance, and fell backwards onto the floor.

"Daisy! Hey, Daisy!" Lee hollered. "Go get the handcuffs! They're out chonder in the car, under the front seat. Hurry!"

Just as she opened the door, she heard the crunchy sound of gravel and saw the Jones County Sheriff car coming up the driveway. "Lee! You'd better get up from there, the county sheriff's here." She didn't know whether he heard or not. The muscles in her neck were still constricted and aching.

"Wud'ju say?"

"I said the county sheriff's out here. You better get up as fast as you can."

"I cain't, not now while I've got this bastard where I want 'im."

"You'd better forget about that. Here they come."

"Are you Daisy? Daisy Daughdrill?" Eustis asked as he got out of the car.

"Yes, I am. What's the matter?"

"That's what I woana know. I heard there was some kind'a unlawful activity goin' on out here, sumpn bad."

"Since when is it against the law t'entertain a visitor?"

"Is that what chu call 'em, Daisy? I heard you'd stopped doin' that kind'a entertainin'. By the way, who's the visitor inside. The one that came in that car over yonder. I woana see 'im. Right now, Daisy! Go tell 'im."

"Well, who's he?" she asked, nodding her head in Marcus' direction.

"That's Mr. Marcus Tatum. He's the Ellisville school superintendent. He's takin' care a Bo Aarthur since his mamma died, his actin' guardian. But come on now, Daisy, stop stallin'. Go tell Lee t'come out here or I'm comin' in there an' get 'im."

"Don't chu need some kind'a permit t'do that?"

"I sure do, Daisy, and I've got it, but I ain't got time t'show it to you. Go tell Lee Anderson t'come out here. Now!"

About five minutes ago, Lee had found that trying to hold Bo Arthur to the floor, knowing the sheriff was out there, ready to come and get him, was not working. He had Bo Arthur sprawled out, holding his arms to the floor and, at the same time, holding

Bo Arthur's legs by covering them with his own. It was a sudden and uncalculated plan he feared would not work, but he had no other choice. When, at one point, he raised his upper body in order to get a better hold on Bo Arthur's arms, Bo Arthur felt the slight lifting of weight on his right leg, wondered whether it would work, then, as fast as he could, raised that leg far enough up to do what he had done before. Lee hollered, then tried to kneel himself into a sitting position. It worked for just the length of time he needed to get revenge. Lee drew his cow-milking hand into a thick fist, then drove it onto the left side of Bo Arthur's face. Bo Arthur went out.

Before going outside, Lee made a few futile attempts to stand straight.

Eustis blew the horn and motioned him to come over.

Why? What's wrong? What's goin' on now?

"Lee," Eustis said, "what in the hell are you doin' out here?"

"I woanted t'take Bo Arthur for a little ride. I thought he needed to get out a his cell for a while,"

"And where's Bo Arthur right now?"

"He's inside, knocked out. Me'n him had a little scuffle a while ago."

"From what I've been told, you an' him have one of them about every day, don't chu?"

"Come on." Eustis motioned with one hand for Marcus to get out, and with the other for Lee to stay put.

"Now Lee, I've asked Marcus to do the talkin' first, since he obviously knows more about this situation than I do, and then, when he's finished, I may woant to ask you some questions, too."

"Lee," Marcus said, "you know good'n well you didn't bring Bo Arthur way out here because you felt sorry for 'im. I don't b'lieve you've ever felt sorry for anybody, Lee. You know, and we know that's a lie, so why don't chu tell Eustis'n me why you really brought 'im over here, of all places, to visit, as you say, with Daisy Daughdrill, a whore just like his own mamma was? How could you possibly do such a stupid thing, knowin' how Bo Arhur's whole life has been affected negatively because of how he was brought up? Don't chu know how he hated his mamma and even tried to kill 'er?"

Lee hung his head and closed his eyes, trying, it seemed, to push out the bottom of his pockets.

"Eustis," Marcus said, "I've got one or two more things to say to Lee, then you can have 'im."

"Take all the time you need. We might as well clear it all up now, before we decide what action needs t'be taken."

"Alright, then. Now, Lee, ever since Frank Haley was killed, you've accused Bo Arthur of killin' 'im. You've used every trick in the book t'make others think the way you do. That's why you put Bo Arthur in jail. You've even trained Chester Sellers to spread the same lie all over town. I suppose, when you hear the truth, you'll still say it's not true. This morning, on two occasions, I tried to contact you to give you a bit of important information, hoping you might finally be convinced enough to let Bo Arthur out of jail. You could not be found anywhere. Later, I learned you had gone to Ovett the first time to ask Daisy to play around with Bo Arthur long enough to decide if he was normal or not. But in order for you to do that, Daisy said you'd have to pay her a hundred dollars. Since you didn't have a hundred dollars, you begged Ben to lend it to you. He did, then he found out what a big mistake he'd made. Lee, this mornin', while Ida Belle Bustin's nephew Schyler was clearing out some things in her bedroom, he found her diary. You know what a diary is, don't chu?"

He nodded without looking up.

"Well, the very last entry in her diary was written the night after she killed Frank Haley. She admitted she killed 'im and, to some extent, said why she did it and why she was goan kill herself. Now, do you still b'lieve Bo Arthur killed Frank Haley?"

When Lee refused to comment, Marcus continued.

"Finally, Lee, Eustis has already told me I can tell you one more thing. It's extremely important, and Eustis has said he will back me up in case you think we've ganged up against you. I've suggested to him that he immediately set in motion the necessary legal process that will relieve you of your duties as sheriff of Ellisville."

They waited for Lee to say something. They saw the shocked reaction, but couldn't hear what he said.

"Marcus," Eustis added, "you said it better than I could, and I think you're right on the button about everything you said. Right now, though, I'm wonderin' where Bo Arthur is. Lee, have you seen 'im?"

"Yeah, I tol' ju a while ago me'n him had a fight'n I knocked him out. I don't know if he's still out or not. He might've awready done sumpn bad. A while ago, b'fore y'all got here, he nyilly choked Daisy t'death."

"My God, Marcus! Let's go see! Come on, Lee! Lee, I said, move!"

Daisy had been standing just outside the front door, trying to hear and see all she could. Two or three times she looked inside to see if Bo Arthur was still out. He was. Instead of being concerned, she felt safe. Now, though, they were coming in to see about him. She stepped aside, holding the door open, eager to see what the reaction was going to be. She could see how scared Lee was, and couldn't help feeling a little sorry for him. He still owed her a hundred dollars, whether or not she helped him prove anything or not. Shortly after he arrived at her place earlier, she sized him up, as she did all the others, and felt uneasy. She had seen his kind before. A few of them had had to be bodily removed from her premises.

"Good God, Lee, what'd ju do to 'im? " Marcus said, kneeling down, feeling Bo Arthur's forehead, his wrist pulse, and pushing his eyelids up. "Eustis, let's see if we can get 'im up. Let's see if we can pull 'im over to the couch."

"Daisy, could ju get us a towel or sumpn or other and run some hot water on it? I don't know if that'll do any good, but I don't know what else t'do."

"I got some smellin' salts. Sometimes that heps. You woant me t'git it?"

"Yes, Daisy. Anything, but hurry!"

"Eustis, let's see if we can get 'im up," Marcus said.

As soon as they lifted him up, they felt his arm muscles make an effort to assist. That was encouraging, but he was still out cold. They laid him gently down onto the fuzzy couch, then stood back and watched, hoping to see some movement somewhere on his body. Daisy brought the smelling salts. "It ain't goan do no good less'n he inhales it."

"Gimme the hot towel, Daisy. Let me wash his face with it before the heat's gone." He laid it across Bo Arthur's face the way a barber would do before a shave and left it until it was no longer useful. As he took it off, Bo Arthur twitched his nose and tried to open his eyes.

"Daisy, could you please heat up another towel in a hurry. This seems t'be helpin'."

Marcus leaned over to lift Bo Arthur's eyelids again, hoping to see any sign that they may open voluntarily soon.

Daisy brought another heated towel, but put the smelling salts under Bo Arthur's nose first. Then she laid the towel over his face, stood and prayed it would work. It did. Bo Arthur blinked his eyes and moved his feet simultaneously. She sobbed silently. Marcus and Eustis exchanged smiles of relief. Bo Arthur opened his eyes fully and looked from one to the other. There was no apparent appreciation for what they had done, or why they had done it. As usual, his awareness and his defense system came as a pair. He didn't realize that Daisy had helped him. He didn't know how concerned Marcus Tatum and Eustis Eubanks had been for his life and his safety. As thoughtlessly ugly as it might appear to each of them, Bo Arthur's concern was for survival and revenge.

When Marcus tried to help him get up, Bo Arthur pushed him away. When Daisy tried to put her arm around him and tell him she was sorry, he snarled and made an indecent gesture.

"Bo Arthur," Eustis said, "you goan ride home with me'n Marcus." Then he gave Lee a look that normally wouldn't need words but, on this occasion, did. "Lee, me'n you'll be talking in a few days, so be prepared."

Bo Arthur's hate and anger continued unabated all the way back to Ellisville. He didn't know that he was no longer a prisoner, nor that Lee Anderson would soon be without a job. Knowing that might have calmed him down somewhat, but it wasn't to be. He spent his time otherwise, trying to decide which of several plans of revenge he would use. He was so engrossed that he didn't hear when Marcus told him he was free now to do whatever he wanted to do, then added, "But Bo Arthur, you're not plannin' on doin' sumpn bad, are you?"

"Nossir, Mr. Tatum, I promise I woant."'

He could hardly believe what had happened. It didn't seem real. Nothing did, in fact. He watched as Eustis and Marcus drove away, feeling good that they had helped him and seemed sincerely concerned for his well-being and happiness. How often had he felt that way? What he felt, though he wasn't aware of it, was the need to celebrate, to put to use some of what had suddenly become an overabundance of energy, physical and mental. What to do? How?

He didn't know when it happened, he knew only that it had. He hollered as loud as he could, then, flailing his arms high above his head, started running as fast as he could, not knowing where he was going or why. He had never felt so wonderful!

AT ABOUT SEVEN o'clock that moonlit Friday evening, after Tyler had taken Sophronie and Kat home and was on his way back, he ran out of gas. Up until that time, he had been enjoying the ride. He had made two mistakes and was now paying for both of them. He shouldn't have let Sophronie talk him into staying a while and eating what she said she'd been craving all day, some pancakes covered with oodles of fresh-churned butter and molasses. The other was that he should have checked the gas level in the old Essex before leaving Ellisville. He usually did. Now he would have to walk the long way back to Mr. Wallace's house. Mr. Wallace always kept several cans of gas in the garage just for such purposes. He knew, too, that Mr. Wallace was going to lose his temper, not for running out of gas, but for being so late getting back.

Mr. Wallace was one of the few people who retire early and get up shortly thereafter. He didn't like being waked up during that time for any reason other than something of extreme urgency, like sickness or death. "Do you know what time'a night it is? It's almost eight o'clock, and here you come draggin' yo black ass in here this time'a night, sayin' you ran out'a gas. I ought'a fire you, but I ain't got nobody else sorry enough t'take your place. Now, go on! You know where the gas is. And don't make no noise doin' it."

* * *

WHEN DULCIE HAD not come home by eight o'clock that night, Annie Lois, whose earlier concern had turned to fear, called Marcus Tatum.

"Marcus, this is Annie Lois. I hope I'm not callin' at a bad time, but I just had to. I'm in trouble, Marcus. I need your help, now!"

"No, no, Annie Lois. What's the trouble?"

She cried. "Oh, Marcus, I don't know where Dulcie is. She hasn't come home yet. She always comes home at seven-thirty on Fridays, but she hasn't and I'm frantic. Can you please help me?"

"Well, of course I'll help you, Annie Lois. I'm so sorry to hear that. What d'you woant me t'do?"

"I wish you could find her. Maybe somebody saw her get off of the streetcar, or maybe somewhere else. I'm so scared sumpn bad has happened, Marcus. I've had a strange feelin' all day. Oh, my God! I simply don't know what t'do."

"I know, Annie Lois. Yes, I know. Now try not to worry. I know it'll be hard t'do, but try. I'll go t'town right now an' start lookin'."

With the can of gas in his right hand, Tyler was walking on the left side of the courthouse when he heard something that didn't sound like anything he could identify. It was coming from behind the court house, where for a block or more, there was a grove of cedar, mimosa, oak, and sweet gum trees that shaded the white benches and tables that were used for picnics, political rallies, band concerts, and other fetes, referred to as Powahatan Public Park in honor of Ellisville's founder.

He tried to make out what it was he'd heard but couldn't. He looked several times from one table or bench to another, without seeing anything else. He hadn't seen, however, that one of the tables farthest to his right looked different. He had been looking only at the tops of the chairs and the benches. Now he looked down to see what was under the table farthest to the right. The sounds had stopped momentarily, but he saw something moving. Only slightly, though, just enough for him to see it without knowing what it was. What was it?

Instinctively, he started walking as fast as he could in the direction of that table, but had to stop just long enough to put the can of gas down. Some of it spilled out. It didn't matter. He knew suffering, whether he saw or heard it. Who is it? Is she dead?

"Oh! Good God'a mighty! It's Miss Dulcie! Please, God, don't let 'er be dead!"

When he got close enough to see her, he whispered, "Miss Dulcie, is dat you?" He was shocked to see how she looked. Her face and arms were scratched, her dress was pulled up to her waist, and her bloomers had been removed and thrown off to one side. He knew she always carried the wicker purse, but he didn't see it.

When she didn't answer, he pulled her dress down over her legs and asked again.

She looked dead. "Miss Dulcie, dis is Tyler. Miss Dulcie, can you hyeanh me?" He heard the slow, soft sound as she tried to push the words through her lips and felt a little better when she made a weak effort to sit up, but couldn't.

He kneeled down on the grass and touched her forehead. She didn't move. He lightly touched her left hand and felt only the merest attempt to touch back. The fingers of her right hand were clutching something firmly, but he couldn't tell what it was.

He knew the first thing he had to do was let Miss Annie Lois know. "Oh, Jesus! I bettuh tell Mr. Wallace, too, no matter what he say. I gotta run!"

SPECK AND DENNY were walking back home on the other side of Free State Highway, their carbide lights burning, their frog gigs over their shoulders, and a big bucket of frogs they took turns carrying. A little way before they came to the crossroad at Dark Town, they both stopped at about the same time, looked at each other, wondering what it was they were smelling.

"What chu think that is, Denny?"

"I don't know nothin' else that smells like gas, d'you?"

"Is that what it is?"

"It's gotta be. It's comin' from the park over yonder."

"What chu reck'n it is?"

"What I awready said it was. Gas."

"Woana go see?"

"Yeah. We goan take our gear with us?"

"Yeah, we're in nigger quarters."

While they waited for a log truck to pass, they saw Tyler turning left in front of the courthouse. He seemed to be in a hurry.

WALKING BACK TO Mr. Wallace's house, Tyler told himself he ought not be the one to tell Annie Lois. He'd better tell Mr. Wallace first. He'd know what to do. Somebody better do something right away or she was going to die, if she hadn't already. He took a deep breath and rang the doorbell, then waited, dreading what was about to happen.

Mrs. Wallace opened the door, looking scared and angry. "Now what d'you need, Tyler. For God's sake, d'you realize what time it is? Go on! What's the matter now?"

"Miz Wallace, I hates t'do dis, but I got sumpn real bad t'tell ya."

"What, Tyler? What?"

"Well, M'am, when I was takin' some gas back t'where the truck was, I heard sumpn bad and when I went t'see what it was, it was Miss Dulcie Dykes. Miz Wallace, M'am, somebody'd done sumpn bad to 'er, an' if she don't git some hep real soon she goan die. Miz Wallace, please tell Mistuh.Wallace'n please M'am, 'splain 'im what I jes tole you. Please, M'am! Please!"

"Oh, my God in Heaven! Yes, Tyler, I will. You wait out there. I'll wake Mister Wallace up."

"Where 'bouts is she?" Mr. Wallace asked as he got into his clothes.

"In de park, Mistuh Wallace, b'hind the co'thouse. She be bad off. She aint goan las' much longer. I woants t'go wit' chu."

"You reck'n we goan need a flashlight?"

"I don't know, Mistuh Wallace. You might."

"Hey, Nell! Nell, we goan need one or two blankets an' a flashlight. Then you need t'let Annie Lois know as soon as possible. But wait! B'fore you call anybody else, you need t'call Doc Cranford'n let 'im know what's happened, an' tell 'im me' n Tyler are goan bring Dulcie over to his place as fast as we can. On second thought, I think it'd be better for you t'call Marcus and ask him to let 'er know. He can do it better'n we can."

* * *

SPECK AND DENNY found the can of gas.

"Wonder how this got here," Denny said.

"Somebody must'a left it there'n plans t'get it later."

Denny seemed more interested in something else. "Hey, Speck, take a look over yonder."

"Where?"

"Over yonder. Under that table over yonder. The last one on the right."

"I cain't tell. What chu think it is?"

"I don't know, but I could'a swore I seen sumpn movin'."

"Let's go'n over there an' see what it is."

As soon as they saw who it was, each knew what the other was thinking.

"We better let Lee know," Speck said. "Come on, Denny, leave your gear. Ain't nobody goan bother it."

Lee had retired early. It had been a bad day, and he needed to get some sleep. He'd be as good as new if he did. He still realized he was the sheriff, and he planned to go about his business as always. Tomorrow he would be back in harness. Going to sleep wasn't as easy as it usually was. He was still tossing and turning when Chester woke him up and told him Speck and Denny needed to talk with him.

"Don't chu two know I need some sleep now'n then? What's the matter? It better be good."

"I don't know if you'd call it that or not, but sumpn real bad's happened, and we figgered we ought'a let chu know."

"Like what, for instance?"

"Like somebody's raped Dulcie Dykes'n we know who it was."

"Wait a minute. Slow down. You say somebody's raped Dulcie?"

"That's what I just said, Lee," Speck said.

"Where'd it happen, and how come y'all t'know 'bout it?"

"Me'n Denny seen it with our own two eyes when we was comin' back from giggin'. Under one a them tables over yonder in the park."

"D'you have any idear who done it?"

"We got better'n a idear. We seen who did it. It was that black

son-of-a-bitch Tyler whatever his name is. We seen 'im runnin'
away right after he done it."

"Good God a'mighty!" Lee said. "What about Dulcie, how's
she? Is she hurt bad?

"She looked t'me like she was awready dead, but we couldn't
really tell, could we, Denny?"

"If she wuddn't, she wuddn't far from it."

"Gimme a minute t'git my clothes on." If Lee believed there
was a God in Heaven, he would have thought he was being lifted
up and put to the test. Jesus! What an opportunity this was!

FROM THE WAY Dulcie looked, Mr. Wallace wondered if she
had died before they got there. He picked up her bloomers and
threw them in the car, then leaned over and tried to determine
whether she was alive or not. Her face was drawn in what had
to be unabating pain. When he tried to lift her up, he felt her
trying to help him but unable to. He noticed that she was trying
to raise her right arm and was clutching something in her hand,
trying to get him to take whatever it was. As she opened her hand
slightly, there was a torn fragment of blue, linen-like cloth that
had something written on it. When he tried to put it in his shirt
pocket, Dulcie almost raised herself up, trying to speak but still
not able to. He could tell there was something about the piece of
cloth that was significant in some way, and that she wanted him
to see it. As soon as he did, he knew why. There were four words
embroidered with white thread. It took a few moments to make
the connection. "My God! She pulled it off of his shirt while he
was raping her."

MAKING MEN OF BOYS

Lee, Denny, and Speck were surprised to see Mr. Wallace and
Tyler Canfield putting Dulcie onto the back seat of the car when
they got there.

"Shep Wallace, what's goin' on here?" Lee asked as they got
out of the car. "What chu'n that black bastard doin'? Don't chu
know that's my job?"

When Mr. Wallace told Tyler to get in the front seat, Lee walked over and tried to hold him back. "You ain't goin' nowhere, you black son-of-a-bitch, until I tell you you can, an' that aint likely t'be anytime soon. Now git cho ass out'a there!"

Speck and Denny were having a good time watching.

Mr. Wallace walked around to the other side of the car and grabbed Lee's left arm and pulled him away.

"Now you lay another hand on him, an' I'll have you put away for the rest a yore life. Now move yore flat ass away from my car!"

"This black bastard is comin' with *me*! I'm goan haul him to the jail, where he's goan stay till we can get the chains t'hold 'im and the rope t'hang his goddam black neck!"

Mr. Wallace pushed Lee aside, then put his hands close to Lee's face and rubbed the dirt off and laughed. "Now I woana tell you just how stupid you are. If you had any sense at all, and nobody I know b'lieves you do, you would'a known that Tyler wouldn't be here with me, heppin' me put Dulcie in the car if he'd raped 'er. When I tell folks about this, you're goanna be the laughin' stock of Ellisville. We may even see what we can do to replace you. There's no excuse for anybody as mean and stupid as you are to be called sheriff in the first place." He walked to the other side of the car. Before getting in, he turned to Tyler. "Look, Tyler. The sheriff brought his posse with 'im. They must'a thought chu were goan try t'get away." He laughed as he shut the door.

Speck and Denny were surprised, too. They knew it was time to keep their mouths shut, pick up their gear and go home. Lee was red-faced, speechless, trembling and boiling over. This should have been his one last chance to redeem himself after what he'd been through at Ovett.

THE FEAR THAT Annie Lois began to feel shortly after seven-thirty that Friday night was now in total control of her mind. The thoughts, both good and bad, came alternately of their own voli-tion. The brief, good ones came less often than the bad ones; the bad ones, like unwanted guests, came and stayed too long, long enough for her to lose what little faith she had that Dulcie was safe and would soon be found.

As soon as she and Marcus got to the clinic, Dr. Cranford took Annie Lois's arm and went with her to see Dulcie, who was in one of the rooms of the little clinic at the back of Dr. Cranford's office. Before they went in, he put his arm around her waist and drew her slightly closer to him.

"Annie Lois," he said, "little Dulcie has had a most unfortunate accident. She apparently ran as fast as she could when she saw him comin' after her. "

"Bo Arthur, you mean?"

"Yes."

They went in together, but he stood to one side, waiting to see Annie Lois' first reaction. He had seen so many first reactions, yet this one was different in ways he couldn't discern as it was happening. Even to an untrained eye, it was obviously an attempt on Annie Lois' part to assess with all of her mental and physical wherewithal the state of Dulcie's life.

"Annie Lois," he whispered, "I'm goan leave you and Dulcie together, now. You take as long as you like, an' afterwards, I woant chu t'feel free to ask me any and every question you may be woanting to ask."

"Dulcie, can you hear me? It's Annie Lois, Honey. Can you move your head or your hand?"

There was the slightest indication that her eyebrows wrinkled for an instant. That was all.

She leaned over and kissed her, then ran her hands over her face and through her hair. She wanted to cry, but resisted. She took Dulcie's right hand and held it for a while, rubbing her own palm over and over it again, praying and hoping that Dulcie would open her eyes. It reminded her of something Dora Dykes told her long ago, about a young mother whose first baby was born dead. She thought and believed that rubbing the baby's hands long and hard enough would give it life. Annie Lois knew better; it only brought to mind pleasant times of long ago and an excruciating detachment from the then and the now.

Then followed the sharpest pains of all, the undeterred recall of all that was good, happy, and beautiful, the taken-for-granted times when each provided for the other, unsolicited and without awareness, whatever of life's intangible essentials was needed. Now would follow the unending sad moments of looking for and not finding, listening for and not hearing, seeing what was hers but not her.

Dr. Cranford checked from time to time to see when she came out. He knew she would be emotionally drained, and even though he had known Annie Lois for a long time, he couldn't remember ever having seen her lose control of her emotions. If she did now, though, he would be surprised, and glad.

When she came out, he could tell she was trying not to show all of what she was feeling. As a matter of fact, she had remembered something she planned to ask about earlier. "Dr. Cranford," she said, "d'you have any idea where Dulcie's purse is? I certainly woant to get it back if I can."

"I can understand, Annie Lois, but I feel sure somebody will have found it by now and will let chu know. If not, I'll see what I can do to hep you."

In the meantime, Shep Wallace and Tyler had gone, but Marcus stayed. He knew how she felt. Her grief was resonating inside his own mind and heart. He and Elsie had lost their only child some years ago. He hoped that Annie Lois would be able, whenever the two of them were together to hear the muted echo of what he and Elsie had experienced three years after their marriage. He had taken to teaching as the quickest and most promising surcease of his otherwise endless grief. He wondered what Annie Lois's would be.

It was almost ten o'clock p.m. when Marcus took Annie Lois home. He walked with her to the front door, then gave her a friendly hug and an unintended sob.

Saturday morning, at about eight-thirty, Marcus called Eustsis Eubanks and told him what had happened. He wanted to know who would arrest Bo Arthur.

"That's a horrible turn of events," he said. "Normally, Lee would be the one, but chu know what would happen if he did. I don't b'lieve there's any way I could do it, even though this seems to be one instance when there's nothin' else t'do and you hope in the long run that it'll be justified. Marcus, I tell you what. Let me think about it a while'n I'll call you back'n let chu know what t'do."

About thirty minutes later, he called and said he'd considered every angle and, as risky as it was, he thought Lee should be the one to arrest Bo Arthur. "I realize what the outcome might very likely be, but it's a chance we're goan have t'take. I'll call Lee in a few minutes. Let me know what happens."

Marcus called Lee as soon as he hung up. "Lee, this is Marcus. We know for sure now that it was Bo Arthur who raped Dulcie. I've just been talkin' with Eustis, and he said for you to arrest him and bring 'im back to the jail. He's more than likely out at Eula's. Let me know if I can help."

At the time, Lee was having trouble trying to figure things out. He had stayed awake last night after letting Denny and Speck make a fool of him. What they told him was just what he needed, though, after what had happened at Ovett. After some of the scare and worry of what Eustis had told him wore off, he realized how stupid he'd been to conceive such an unlikely scheme for paying Bo Arthur back. Now there'd be no need for another scheme. This was the best of all, and he didn't have anything to do with it. So he thought. His limited intelligence had not yet made him aware of what it was, nor to what extent he had contributed to it.

Bo Arthur had gone home after raping Dulcie. Granny was asleep. He was glad. He tiptoed slowly in the dark, wishing he could wash off but knowing he'd better not. He shut his bedroom door quietly, then lay down without taking off his clothes. He was angry at himself. It had not been successful. Instead, it had confirmed his direst suspicions about himself. He had hoped raping Dulcie would have rid him of what at first were doubts, but it hadn't. Now he realized his problem would stay with him as long as he lived. Nevertheless, he hated Dulcie. She should have been the one who would prove to himself and others later, that he was as normal below the belt as any other young man was.

BEFORE GETTING IN the car, Lee did a quick run-through of what he planned to do. The handcuffs were still under the seat and he had the pistol in the right pocket of his jacket. He knew Miss Eula was going to be hurt deeply. He would have to let her know exactly what happened, no matter how much it hurt.

Jason Parker and Eula were talking on the back porch steps when Lee drove up around ten o'clock Saturday morning. Jason had brought her some sweet potatoes and was telling her about the special church service planned for tomorrow at Tula Rosa.

"You got comp'ny, Eula," Jason said. "I better git back home." She reached over and touched his shoulder. "No, Jason, not yet. Stay hyere. Lee don't never come out chere less'n he's got sumpn bad t'tell me. O God, I wonder what it is this time."

"He might not woant me t'hear what he says."

"That don't make no never-mind. You stay hyere with me."

Lee thought it might be better to knock on the back door rather than the front one, even though he knew nothing about the layout of the house. It was a few minutes after ten o'clock a.m. "Good-mornin', Miss Eula," he said. "An good mornin' t'you, Jason. How you been?"

"Fine enough, Lee."

The tired frown on Eula's face gave Lee the impression that she was not happy to see him. "What now, Lee? What chu come out chere for? Sumpn else bad happen?"

"Yes m'am, it sure has, Miss Eula, an' I wish I didn't haf t'bother you ag'in like this."

"Well, what is it this time?"

"Mss Eula, the Jones County sheriff told me t'come'n git Bio Arthur. We goan haft put 'im back in jail."

"Why'd he tell you t'do that, Lee?"

Jason stepped down. "Miss Eula, I better git back to the house. Myrtis'll be wondrin' where I got off to. If you need me, call me."

"Oh, awright, Jason," she said hesitantly.

Lee told her why he'd come. He found it harder than usual, not because he was overly concerned about how she was going to react, but because he wasn't crafty enough with the English language to let her understand certain things in terms that were suggestive enough as replacements for the other, at which he was more adept. "Now, is Bo Arthur t'home?"

"Yes, he is, but he's still sleepin'. I s'pose you're goan woant me t'wake 'im up, ain't chu?"

"Yes m'am, an' I'm sorry. But I gotta see 'im right away. D'you mind?"

"I shore do, but I reck'n they aint nothin' I can do 'bout it. You wait out chere. I'll go git 'im up."

She didn't have to. As soon as she walked back into the kitchen, Bo Arthur was standing by the stove, looking like a hungry tiger. He had heard all of it. She had seen that look many times before, and she knew he was about to do something bad. He looked across at her for an instant before turning and running as fast as he could to her bedroom. He came out with her shotgun, the one she had used to protect herself against him while Lily Ruth was there, even though the gun was unloaded. She had run out of shells and hadn't yet bought any more. He didn't know that and she was not going to tell him. Now, no matter what happened out there, he wouldn't be able to kill Lee, and that provided only an ounce of comfort, no more. As Fate would have it, that ounce of so-called comfort was about to prove to be much more than a pound of pain. It was while she was experiencing that ounce of comfort that she forgot to remember that Lee Anderson had a pistol. He always carried a pistol, and it was always loaded.

Instead of going back through the kitchen, Bo Arthur sneaked out the front door, inched his way over to the corner of the house, then stopped and leaned against the side of the house to take a few deep breaths. He had to be sure that he and the shotgun were out of Lee's sight.

Eula was standing on the screened back porch, watching, knowing what was going to happen and wishing she was brave enough to go out there and put herself between the two of them. She felt better seeing Jason across the yard, pretending he was looking for something.

With the gun pointed at Lee's head, Bo Arthur put his right foot slightly forward and hollered, "Die, you no-good bastard, you sorry son-of-a-bitch!" He pulled the trigger. Nothing happened. He jumped back out of sight and shook the shotgun, once, twice. He leaned forward just enough to see Lee on the other side of the steps.

Lee had his pistol aimed at the corner of the house, waiting to see any part of Bo Arthur. On the way over, he had programmed his mind for whatever might happen. He had been at the job long enough to know how to act if his life was threatened. The survival instinct almost always took over, time passed in smaller segments, normal seconds came in four parts. On one or two occasions, especially when he was new at the job, he had come close to losing his life. The likelihood that it might happen the next time always made its presence felt.

Jason had been watching. He knew there was nothing Bo Arthur could do. His only chance of staying alive was left up to Lee. Lee knew now that the shotgun was empty. There was no way that Bo Arthur could kill him, but Lee did not put away his pistol. He leaned slightly forward to steady his arm on one of the steps, aimed and shot. Bo Arthur was too slow jumping back. He fell forward on his face, on top of the empty shotgun.

Dodger came running out from under the house. He stopped long enough to see what had happened, then ran to where Bo Arthur was and started licking his face. When Eula came out, he moved to the other side so she could cry, too.

Jason tore off across his yard, hoping he could get his hands on Lee Anderson before he left. When he saw he was too late, he stopped where Eula was, on her knees, bent over Bo Arthur, talking to him, hoping he could hear even though she knew he couldn't.

"What was it Lee said just now as he was leavin'?"

He could hardly hear her. "He said he was only doin' what he was tol' t'do."

The pain in her legs and back was more than she could bear much longer, but even in her weakened state of mind and body she was able to consider, even to conjecture about what was going to follow. If she survived, she might later wish she had died on her knees rather than on her feet.

"Eula," Jason said, tapping her shoulder, "let's get up now. We need t'think about what we goan do." He straightened and rubbed his back, trying to decide which of the things that needed to be done was most urgent. *Bo Arthur, take him inside right away. Help Eula get up, take her inside.* There was something else, the most urgent of all the others. He was thinking of Lee Anderson, on his way back to Ellisville, where he probably expected to be congratulated and made a lot over, especially since it was Saturday, and maybe even have something about him next Wednesday in Free State Tribune, the weekly news dispenser.

As soon as he got home, Myrtis and Lorice were waiting at the back door. He told them what had happened, then said he had to go to Ellisville. "Somebody with some authority's gotta t'do sumpn about Lee Anderson. I'll see what I can do. In the meantime, Myrtis, you better go over to Eula's. She's in a bad way'n she might not live through it. I hepped 'er git inside a while ago, but she needs lookin' after. An' Lorice, you go with 'e'n hep 'er. I gotta see that this murder ain't called sumpn else. I'll be back as soon as I can."

LEE HAD ACCOMPLISHED his mission. Now he could go back and call Eustis Eubanks. The longer he thought about what he had just done, the better he felt. The importance he was giving it, though, continued to take over his thoughts. Now there was a good chance that Eustis might be willing to forget about what happened yesterday. To have been made a fool of was bad enough. He could live that down, but not to be sheriff was something shameful that he would never be able to live down. The very idea made him so mad he was willing to do anything in his power to prevent it. Killing Bo Arthur might be exactly what he needed.

BEFORE LEAVING, JASON went back to Eula's to let her know what he was going to do. "Myrtis'n Lorice said they'd come over'n stay with you while I'm gone. You reck'n you goan be awright till I git back, Eula?"

"Yeah, Jason. Don't worry 'bout me. I'm g'on be awright. I jes need t'do some prayin'."

When he got to the police station, Tracy told him Lee had not come back yet. "Is there sumpn I can hep you with, Mister Parker?"

"Well, I don't know if you can or not. I was hopin' I could git in touch with Eustis Eubanks. He's the one what needs t'know they's been a murder out at Eula Bilbo's place."

"What happened, Mr. Parker?"

"Like I said, they's been a murder at Eula Bilbo's place. Lee Anderson shot'n kilt Bo Arthur, that's what happened."

"In that case, Eustis is the one who needs t'know. I'm goan see if I can get in touch with 'im. If and when I do, I promise you, Mr. Parker, I'm goan tell 'im what chu just tol' me. You woana stay aroun' an' see if I can get 'im?"

"Yes, I shore do, but I cain't wait too long. I need t'git back'n look after Miss Eula."

Eustis answered the phone. "Tracy, this is serious. Ask Jason if he can stay long enough for me t'get down there. And by the way, is Lee in his office?"

"No, he ain't come in yet. Hold on while I ask Mr. Parker."

"Tell 'im I'll wait as long as he woants me to."

Eustis got there about thirty minutes later. "Lee hasn't come in yet, so let's talk in his office."

"Now, Jason, I woant t'help you if I can. But before we start, I woant to assure you that whatever information you can furnish me will be strictly between me'n you. Since we don't have much time, let me ask you a few questions. Is that alright?"

"Eustis, that's why I'm hyere. Ask me anythang you woant to."

"Fine. Now, Jason, tell me first of all, where were you when Lee got there?"

"Me'n Miss Eula was on the back porch. I'd brung 'er some potatoes an' we was talkin' when we seen Lee comin' roun' the house."

"And did ju ask Lee why he was there?"

"No, Miss Eula did."

"And what did he say?"

"He said ju told 'im to come git Bo Arthur'n take him back to jail."

"That's right. Now tell me everything you saw an' heard after that."

Jason gave as accurate an account as he could, considering that he had previously cautioned himself against expressing personal opinions about any of it, yet, at the same time, he reminded himself that he would need some flexibility, he must not sift too finely or he might unintentionally leave out some significant something that could possibly make a difference, no matter how small. He knew Eustis wanted as much pertinent information as he could get and nothing else.

"Now, Jason, if you don't mind, I'd like to ask you a few more specific questions. I need to know as much I can possibly get in order to make a fair judgment of what happened out there a while ago. For instance, did Miss Eula ask Lee why he'd come out there in the first place?"

"Yeah, he tried t'tell Eula why, but I could tell he was bavin' trouble doin' it."

"What d'you mean by that?"

"Well, I guess he was a little embarrassed'n dittn't know how to describe it."

"I see. And where was Bo Arthur at the time?"

"Miss Eula said he was still sleepin'. She said she'd go wake 'im up, but Bo Arthur must'a hyeard 'em talkin' an' got up t'see what was goin' on."

"Then what did he do?"

"Now, Eustis, I can only tell ya what Miss Eula told me."

"Yes, that's fine. What did she say?"

"Well, she said as soon as Bo Arthur knew what was goin' on, he hit the ceilin', you might say, then run up to Miss Eula's bedroom'n got her shotgun. He dittn't know the shotgun wuddn't loaded'n she dittn't woant him t'know it. She said that way he couldn't kill nobody.

"Well, the next thang I knowed, Bo Arthur, he was out chonder gittin' ready t'shoot Lee without knowin' they wuddn't no shells in the gun. I could see'im. He sidled up to the corner of the house, the north side, that is, an' dittn't lose no time puttin' th'aim on Lee. Lee was standin' over on the other side of the steps. When Bo Arthur pulled the trigger and nuttin' happened, he jumped back out'a sight, an' when he stuck his head back around the corner and aimed the shotgun ag'in at Lee, Lee shot 'im as soon as he seen 'im. They wasn't a half a second b'tween when he seen Bo Arthur and when he shot 'im. Bo Arthur dropped to the groun' right then'n Lee put his pistol away'n left, just like he didn't care if Bo Arthur was dead or not. He got rid of'im, awright. It seemed t'me like that's all he woanted. Of course that's just my opinion an' maybe I ought not be sayin' it. Anyway, Miss Eula was kneelin' over Bo Arthur on the groun' when Lee passed by on his way out. She told me later what he said."

"And what was that, Jason?"

"He said, 'I done what I was ordered t'do.'"

"Of course that was not what he was ordered to do. That's a matter I will discuss with him as soon as he shows up. In the meantime, Jason, I woant chu to know how much I appreciate what chu've told me. I know, also, how to what extent this tragedy has hurt your family as well as Miss Eula's. I will keep all of you in my prayers. But there's one other matter I woant to talk about with you. That's Bo Arthur's funeral. I know Miss Eula won't be able to take care of that, and I don't think you should have t'do it. I wish you would tell her when you get back that I'm goin' t'take care of that. I think I can find several men who'll do it for a small fee. Assure her, now, that that's my project, and not t'worry about it. And tell her, also, Jason, that I plan to go back to see her as soon as I can. And Jason, I appreciate your concern for justice, no matter at what level. I wish more people felt the same way. Keep in touch, an' let me know how things go."

Eustis wanted to talk with Lee and wondered why he hadn't come yet. Tracy called him. He said he would be there in just a few minutes. That was enough time for Eustis to put his thoughts together. He was eager to hear Lee's version of what happened this morning.

Lee was obviously surprised. Eustis could see that he was. "How long you been waitin'?" Lee asked.

"Not very long. Since I was already here, I thought I'd hang around long enough to see how things went this mornin'. D'ju have any trouble getting' Bo Arthur t'come with you?"

Lee was slow to answer. "Well, Eustis, it didn't turn out the way I woanted it to."

"What d'you mean by that?"

"Bo Arthur resisted. He tried t'kill me."

"Now how in the world could he do such a thing, Lee? What brought that on?"

"Well, when Miss Eula told 'im I was waitin' for 'im, he come out the front door with a shotgun, an' he didn't lose no time pointin' it at me."

"And what did ju do?"

"Well, I done what anybody in his right mind would'a done. I aimed my pistol at him."

"And then what? Did he shoot at chu?"

"Well, he tried to, but I guess he just dittn't know how to use that shotgun. It dittn't go offn he pulled back, I reck'n he must'a done sumpn to it, then stuck his head out and aimed at me ag'in. I figgered I better stop him, so I did. I dittn't have no other choice."

"What d'you mean, you didn't have no other choice? Didn't chu see the shotgun wuddn't loaded? Bo Arthur didn't know it wuddn't. Why, then, would you shoot him without first wondrin' why the gun didn't go off?"

"Well, Eustis, I didn't have no way a knowin' that."

"Lee, don't give me such a stupid answer. Haven't you been around guns and pistols long enough to be able to sense such things?"

"I don't know how I could'a knowed. He was determined t'kill me, Eustsis."

"And you were determined t'kill him, weren't chu?"

"No, Eustis! Of course not. I would'na shot him if I'd'a knowed that. Honest t'God, Eustis, I dittn't have no choice."

Eustis stood up, walked over to the door, waited, then turned around. "Lee sit down! I woant chu t'listen carefully t'what I'm goan tell you. First of all, you've lied t'me. You knew from the moment I told ju t'go get Bo Arthur'n bring him back to the jail that chu would be able once more to get even with him for the way he's done you. Whatever he's done t'you, it cannot be said that any of it justified killin' him. There was somebody who saw everything you did. He was watching from his own yard. He could see, the moment Bo Arthur came out of the house with the shotgu, that he didn't know the first thing about how to use it.

Now, if Jason could see that, why couldn't chu? . . . Don't answer, I'm not through.

"Lee, almost for as long as you've known Bo Arthur, you've hated him for some reason or other. You've tried countless times to prove that he's done something bad enough, either to be put in jail, or even worse. And, furthermore, Bo Arthur has known that and hated you as much or even more than you hated him. No doubt, both of you had justifiable reasons for hating each other. Now it wasn't bad enough that you paid a hundred dollars to have Daisy work him over to see if what you'd already made up your mind about was good enough to prove somehow, how, I don't know, that he killed Frank Haley Bankston.

"That was about as stupid as stupid can get. But, a few hours later, you would do something even more stupid. You let two of your cronies convince you that Tyler Canfield had raped and killed Dulcie Dykes, so you go over there with them, hoping to get chureself another case, one that might prove beneficial to your ailing reputation. You actually tried to arrest Tyler while he and Mr. Wallace were rescuing Dulcie. Now, how do you explain such stupidity? You even argued with Mr. Wallace that Tyler was the one who'd raped Dulcie.

"Now, Lee, you've topped all of that foolishness off by killing Bo Arthur Bilbo. Your orders were to get him and bring him back to the jail. At some later point he would have been tried, and his punishment would have been determined legally by a jury of twelve people. Now you, Lee, have made yourself judge and jury. You, Lee, couldn't wait for that to happen. You only knew that you finally had the one opportunity you'd been waiting for. You could kill Bo Arthur and then say you did it in self-defense.

"As for now, Lee, this very moment, you are suspended from your duties as sheriff. Shortly hereafter, this suspension will be validated by the proper county officials. In the meantime, I'm asking Tracy to assume the duties as sheriff of Ellisville. That's all."

"You mean you aint goan let me defend myself?"

"Why should I, Lee? Did ju let Bo Arthur defend himself?"

* * *

Bo Arthur Bilbo was buried on Monday afternoon, at three o'clock. Eula, Jason, Myrtis, Lorice, and Dodger were the only ones in attendance.

Eustis Eubanks had done what he said he would do. He sent six deputies to Eula's place to prepare for the burial.

Dodger had watched the deputies for as long as they worked. When Eula walked back to the grave that evening, Dodger was still there.

Next day, when Eula came inside after visiting Bo Arthur's grave, she saw a man driving a car into her yard. A lady got out and told him to wait, she would need only a few minutes. She took the steps slowly and carefully, holding firmly onto the banister with her free hand. Eula watched her as she came up the steps. She had no idea who it was. She could use a little company, but maybe this wasn't the kind of company she wanted at a time like this.

The knock was barely audible. Then came another one or two. Eula opened the door just enough to see a beautiful lady she couldn't remember ever having seen before.

"Hello, Miss Eula," the lady said. "I don't think you know me. I'm Gayle Bankston. May I come in?"

"*Gayle Bankston?* Why, I never! Well, of course you may come in. I cain't hardly believe it's you, though. Come on in, Gayle'n have a seat. Hyere, you sit in this hyear chair. It's just 'bout the most comfortablest one in the house."

"Thank you, Miss Eula. Yes, it is comfortable."

"Now, Gayle, you just put whatever that is you're totin' on that little ol' table over yonder."

"Well, now isn't that cute! It looks like it's hand-made."

"That's 'cause it is. Brandon, he made that for me a long time ago. Now, what can I do for ya?"

"Well, Miss Eula, you may not believe this, but I just woant t'sit here with you for a while. Oh, but wait, though, I brought chu a little gift. Here, Miss Eula, open it."

It was a beautiful, full-size afghan, jade green and wrapped around with crisp tissue paper, in an elegant green gift box. "Well, as I live'n breathe, Gayle, I don't reck'n I've ever seed anythang this beautiful in all my born days. Now, you aint goan sit there'n tell me you made this yoreself, are you?"

Gayle reached over, they hugged and cried. "Yes, Miss Eula, I did, durin' some of my long and lonely hours. I hope you like it and can use it."

"Why, Gayle, I don't hardly know how t'thank you. I'm afraid you've caught me at a time when hit doan't take much t'make me cry."

"That's perfectly alright, Miss Eula. I know what a sad time this is for you. In fact, I was a little hesitant about comin' today."

"But I ain't the onliest one. You've had more'n yore share, too. Oh, by the way, Gayle, would ju like a cup a coffee? I can heat it up real fast."

"I was hopin' you'd have some."

Eula watched Gayle as she took the first sip of coffee. She had been putting the pieces together since Gayle came. So far, she hadn't been able to figure out why she'd come for a visit.

It was as though each could hear what the other was thinking.

"Miss Eula, I know you must be wonderin' why I decided to come see you today."

"You must'a been readin' my mind, Gayle. It ain't hard t'do since they aint much of it left."

'"Oh, Miss Eula, don't say things like that. If I have as much of mine left when I'm your age, I'll be satisfied. But I should get to the point, because I have someone waiting and I don't woant to stay too long. So," she said as she took another sip of coffee, "I came here because I suddenly realized that you and I are related in a strange way. No, not by birth, but by a common denominator, you might say."

"An' what d'you mean by that, Gayle?"

She started to take another sip of coffee but looked around at Eula. "Miss Eula, neither you nor I have ever been mother or grandmother to Bo Arthur, have we?"

"Sadly enough, Gayle, we ain't."

"Nevertheless, both of our lives, yours'n mine, have been drastically affected. I know you must've been terribly shocked to learn that Brandon wasn't Bo Arthur's father, weren't chu?"

"I shore t'God was!"

"And I was shocked, also, that Bo Arthur was the son I never had. I decided to come see you, most of all, to talk with you about how you and I are related. Not by blood or ancestry, but by Fate. That's somethin' you and I had nothin't'do with. What I'm tryin' t'say is that you and I should take advantage of and enjoy that rare bond, meaning Bo Arthur. In other words, will you be my friend? I woant to be yours. I woant to be able to come see you whenever I woant to, and I woant chu t'feel free to contact me whenever you feel the need or even the desire to see me."

Eula, in the meantime, was thinking about how intelligent Gayle was and how beautiful, inside and out. Her mind went suddenly out there, where he was. She could feel the ache of loneliness and a strong urge to be with him.

"Miss Eula, I must go now. But before I go, there are two things I hope you'll do for me."

"An' what's that, Gayle?"

"First of all, will you tell me you understand why I woanted t'come see you today?"

"Yes, of course, Gayle."

"And last of all, will you take me to where Bo Arthur is buried?"

"Of course, Gayle. I've just been havin' the strongest urge t'go back out chonder myself."

As long as Dodger lived, there would be no need for a marker. He was lying stretched out on top of Bo Arthur's grave."

ON THE PREVIOUS Saturday morning, a little after nine o'clock, Annie Lois was cooking breakfast for Wanda Faye. Her mind was on everything except what she was doing. She used to say on occasion that she'd done so much cooking in her lifetime that she could do it in her sleep if she had to. Sadly enough, she'd have no chance to prove it anytime soon. She had lain in bed for a few hours only because she thought it might make Wanda Faye feel a little better.

Wanda Faye, too, was having trouble trying to figure things out. She was too new to the world to understand what had happened to Dulcie, yet she was old enough to realize that life without her was going to be sad and lonely. It would be a while, though, before she would see and feel to what extent her own brief and bewildered world had been changed.

Annie Lois heard someone knocking at the front door. Who could it be? No matter, it was *someone*. Hays Younger had just heard about what had happened, and he knew that Annie Lois was shocked, inconsolable, and in dire need of someone to talk with. She had been so consoling and otherwise helpful when Hanna died. She had shared his grief and now he wanted and felt compelled to share with her what he knew was going to be a long and painful few months.

"Annie Lois," he said as soon as she opened the door, "I'm not going to say 'good-mornin'. As a matter of fact, I don't know what t'say. I just heard about what happened. May I come in?"

"Oh, Hays, thank you for comin' over." Without giving it a thought, she threw her arms in his direction and he put his arms around her. That's all it took. The already threatened moat wall tore asunder, her tears drenched his shirt. How unexpected! How unlike either of them! It was an emotional moment of such intensity that her tautly leashed inhibitions were unable to prevent it. "Oh, Hays, I'm at my wits' end. I haven't any idea whatsoever about what I need to do."

"That's why I came over, Annie Lois. I know what chure goin' through. What were you doin' b'fore I got here?" he asked as he closed the door.

"I was cookin' breakfast for Wanda Faye. It's so hard to do!"

"I know. Go on and finish it. I'll sit in the kitchen an' watch."

"Are you hungry?"

"No, I've eaten."

When Wanda Faye finished eating, Annie Lois put the dishes in the sink and washed her hands. "Can you stay a while, Hays?"

"Yes, that's why I came. I'd like to help you do what I can to make it a little easier for you."

"You don't know how much I appreciate that."

They talked for over an hour. He thought Dulcie's funeral should be special. He would take care of bringing her home from the clinic, and he would also take care of the burial. He assured her that he would gladly help her with the finances if she needed or wanted him to. She thanked him; she would be able to do what had to be done. Together, they decided the wake should begin Monday evening. *She'd always hated the word "wake." Why was it called a wake? Was it a designated time before a burial, no matter how long, to make sure that the one who died stayed dead?*

The funeral was set for two o'clock, Tuesday afternoon. After Hays left, she felt somewhat better. There was, however, another difficult task to take care of. She must call Penny Welborn as soon as possible.

Penny's immediate response was, "That cain't be true! She was here just yesterday! *What am I goan do, Annie Lois?*"

Voncille called shortly thereafter to express her sorrow, then called Father Seranno.

So far, it seemed that Annie Lois had not considered the difference Monday would make. Sophronie would be with her. The more she thought about it, the better she felt. At some juncture in her thinking, she realized for the first time that Tyler was the one who found Dulcie; he was the one who walked back to Shep Wallace's house to tell him about it. She remembered, too, when Dulcie was sick, and he said he would stay with her while she called Dr. Cranford. There were the other times, too, when she had been made aware of how much she needed Sophronie. Come to think of it, what had anybody of Sophronie's color ever done to hurt her? Had her own mother ever treated her and Dulcie as decently and lovingly as Sophronie had?

As she went from one recall to another, she realized she'd have to clear her mind of whatever had distracted her. This was no time to take an alternate route especially one she'd never taken before.

After delivering the sermon on Sunday morning, Brother Stanwell said he had two announcements to make. First of all, he would be away next week. "I'll be attending a conference of southern Baptist ministers in Biloxi." The other, he cautioned, was a sad one. "We've lost one of our own, Little Dulcie Dykes passed away yesterday morning." Some of the church members who had been mentally away during the sermon, now squirmed alive. It would seem that Dulcie, in a week's time, had become a model of Godliness that others should emulate. He asked the congregation to pray for her, then added something that had suddenly come to him last night: Dulcie was, after all, one of the *children* cited by Jesus as having all the virtues He represented and wanted others to acquire as soon as possible.

Sophronie almost fell, coming up the back steps on Monday morning. She was carrying a lot of grief and was in a hurry to share it with Annie Lois. She had also brought a pillow case full of things she would need while she was away. Annie Lois was waiting for her in the kitchen.

She dropped what she was carrying as soon as she saw Annie Lois, then hobbled over to where she was and threw her arms around her. "Oh, Miss Annie Lois," she said, "what we goan do wifout 'er? Go on, Honey, cry yo' eyes out. Dat's what I been doin' evuh since Tyler tol' me."

It was another instance of deep-seated inhibitions having to yield to strong, pent-up emotions. Clinging with both her arms around Sophronie's neck was a comfort her mother had never provided. Such was a sign of weakness, she had been told.

Yet, Annie Lois, herself, had felt the same way about letting Tyler be in the house while Dulcie was sick, yet she had needed him, and he provided a bit of comfort by watching over her.

"Sophronie," she said as she pulled away, "you are a God-sent and wonderful friend. I've just realized how valuable you've always been for as long as I've known you, and how beautiful you are. I love you. Thank you so much for coming prepared to stay a while, to see me through this sad, sad time of my life. Dulcie would be so happy to know you were here."

That afternoon, around two o'clock, someone knocked on the front door. It was Father Seranno. Annie Lois was surprised. When he told her who he was, she was also suspicious. He was a Catholic.

"Mrs. Harper, I know you're surprised to see me. I'm a friend of Dulcie's. Did she ever mention me?"

"No, never. I don't understand. Did you know she had died?"

"I heard yesterday. May I come in?"

"If you're a friend of Dulcie's, of course you may come in."

He told her how it had started, his interest and curiosity about

why she was so sad and lonely. Yes, at first she was scared about being in a Catholic church, but he had assured her that God was everywhere. When she said God never answered her prayers, he suggested she speak softly enough that only He could hear. She did.

"Mrs. Harper, I wanted more than anything in the world to help her. I looked forward to Friday afternoons. She told me she did, too."

As time passed, Annie Lois's respect for him increased. Her feeling of inadequacy also increased. What she couldn't recognize, he could. He had made Dulcie happier than she had ever been before, yet she never let Annie Lois know. Knowing it now only added to her pain.

"Mrs. Harper, when will the funeral be?"

"Tomorrow afternoon, at two o'clock."

"Is there going to be a church service before the burial?"

"No, there won't be. I'd rather have a graveside service of some kind. I'm not sure yet what would be most appropriate and comforting."

"Will your pastor prepare a eulogy for Dulcie?"

"No. As a matter of fact, he'll be out of town. There's a meeting of Baptist Ministers in Biloxi."

"Then, may I ask another question?"

"Yes, of course."

"Would you let me say a few words on Dulcie's behalf? I would love to be able to do that. Would you permit me to do that?"

"Well, of course! How strange and wonderful! It seems that God has planned it that way."

"I can't tell you how happy that makes me."

Annie Lois was surprised to see how many people came for the wake. Several of them had to be introduced. Where had they come from? And *why?* She was pleased with the way Dr. Cranford had prepared Dulcie. Even the spitcurls had been made and seemed to stay put. There were two large stands of flowers from Hays Younger and Marcus and Elsie Tatum. Others had brought some of whatever had bloomed in their yards or gardens.

Now it was Tuesday, the dark day she had dreaded so much. Hays Younger had kept his word. He had even called Father

Seranno and, during their telephone visit, told him where the burial would be. Father Seranno said he would be bringing a friend, and planned to stop by the house before the funeral. Elsie Tatum and Nell Wallace said they would bring food to the house after the funeral. It was an old southern custom, like salve on an open wound.

Annie Lois had not slept last night. *She's here, she's home again, but she won't be staying. And what will I do? I don't know how I'm going to hold up. I'm so scared I woan't be able to. Oh, dear God! Help me!*

Marcus and Elsie Tatum came around twelve-thirty. "Hello, Sophronie," Marcus said, taking off his hat. "We've come a little early intentionally, in case there's something we can do to help."

"Yessir, dat be mighty fine, an' Miss Annie Lois, she goan be glad. She say she be ready in a jiffy."

Sophronie apparently hadn't noticed that Elsie was holding something in a paper bag. "An' by de way, doan't Miss Dulcie look mighty pretty?"

"Yes, she surely does," Elsie said.

"Well, now, y'all jes have a seat. I goan see how Miss Annie Lois and little Wanda Faye be doin'."

She couldn't leave yet. Somebody else was knocking on the front door.

It was Father Seranno and Voncille Martin. They introduced themselves, then sat and visited.

"Voncille," Marcus said, "how are you related to Dulcie?"

"Oh, I'm *not* related to 'er. She'n Melissa used t'come t'my house every Friday afternoon and we'd visit. That's how I met Father Seranno. Every time Dulcie'd come back from vis'tin' him, she seemed so happy and always said he made her feel good." She suddenly felt foolish. She was embarrassed. "Oh, ya'll, I'm so sorry for talkin' too much. I apoligize."

"You needn't apologize," Father Seranno said. "I can attest to the fact that you helped Dulcie, too. She often said you did."

Sophronie was visibly distressed, yet she never stopped long enough to be distracted out of control. Annie Lois, unaware that by now her limited effort to avoid an emotional breakdown was depleted, was unable, on two occasions, to do so. "Go on, Miss Annie Lois, dey ain't nuttin' t'be gained by you pretendin' you's not human lak evuhbody else is."

Wanda Faye seemed unaware that anybody else was in the room. She tiptoed over to the casket and stood for a while, apparently puzzled, then slowly reached over and touched Dulcie's face and folded hands, not knowing or understanding what everybody else already knew and understood. *"Dulcie, why don't chu move? Has the cat got chure tongue?"*

Marcus and Father Seranno stood when Annie Lois came into the living room. She thanked Father Seranno and Voncille for coming. She seemed momentarily to have forgotten why Father Seranno was there. After Elsie hugged her, Marcus put his arms around her. "Everything's goan be alright, Annie Lois. God will make all things right."

That's what I'd like to believe, but I don't.

"Annie Lois," Elsie said, "I have a little surprise for you."

"At a time like now?"

"I don't know a better time. Here." She handed her the paper bag.

"Oh my God!" she cried, sobbing out of control. "Where did ju find it, Elsie?"

"I *didn't* find it, Annie Lois. Little Beebee Burnside found it on her way to school. She said she'd seen Dulcie carrying it. It was in a ditch over behind the court house. She took it to Marcus yesterday."

Annie Lois collapsed into a rocker, holding the wicker purse to her chest and squeezing it. When she had done with crying, she opened it, put her hand inside and brought out first one item after another, each one like a knife to her heart. Then, at the bottom, there was something else. A crumpled piece of paper. She started to pull it out, then, realizing what it was, she slipped it back inside and pushed it to the bottom, then laid the purse beside Dulcie in the casket. She closed her eyes and fought the impulse to let go. She remembered what Sophronie had said earlier. But Sophronie was not always right. This was not the time to lose control. *I must get a'hold of myself, if only for Wanda Faye's sake.*

She did not know, or, if she did, she had not yet reconciled herself to knowing that Wanda Faye, even now, was learning more than she wanted her to know.

Hays had instructed the driver of the hearse to be at Annie Lois's house at two o'clock. That meant that Annie Lois, Wanda Faye, and Sophronie would soon need to say their good-byes. Marcus, Elsie, Father Seranno, and Voncille Martin waited outside.

Sophronie put her arm around Annie Lois' shoulder while she waited her turn, knowing she wouldn't be able much longer to keep all the hurt inside. Then she bent over Dulcie and kissed her, then said "You ain't goan suffer no mo', my Baby Dulcie. You's in God's hands now. Nobody goan make fun a you no mo' an' ain't nobody goan' hurt chu nevuh no mo'. Oh God! Bless dis sweet angel. *Oh God'n Hebben, bless Miss Annie Lois and little Wanda Faye. Please, God!*"

It was a bright and sunny day, with a small, dense cluster of clouds that never seemed to change shape or intensity. The grave was under a huge oak tree. There was a plain, rusted, and all but illegible metal marker indicating that Dora Dykes lay below, feet facing south. It was run over with weeds and even a deprived blackberry bush. That was because Annie Lois had always been paranoid about cemeteries. She would still swear to having seen, at the age of thirteen, parts of a decomposed human body covered over with nothing but a thin layer of red clay. She could never be convinced that it was a dream.

She knew she should say something. But what? How could she? But she *must!* As soon as she saw all the friends gathered around the grave, a daring thought came to mind. At some other time, she would more than likely have buried it where all the other unwanted thoughts were, but not today. Today everything had changed. Nothing would ever be the same. Why not say what she felt?

"First of all, to each and every one of you, I woant to let chu know how grateful I am that you've come to help me bear what I'm having a hard time bearing. Every one of you know how your emotions take over and cause you to feel and say things you might not have said otherwise. After I've said a few words, Marcus Tatum and Father Seranno will speak on Dulcie's behalf. I promise I woant talk too long.

"As many of you already know, Dulcie was color-blind to the extent that she was often happiest when she was with her black friends. I don't think I need go any farther into that. You can understand, therefore, how touched I am that so many of her friends have come to see her for the last time." She almost choked on the words. "Now, you will surely understand why I say this to each of my black friends. Don't be afraid to come over here and stand with her white friends. She loved you and you loved and treated her well. It's only right and fair that all of you get as close together as you can. For me, this is a time to forget everything except how much you've meant to Dulcie and how you've loved her, and how you made her life happier than it would have been otherwise. So, please come forward. Please, all of you, for Dulcie's sake, in loving memory of her."

If Marcus Tatum had not said the same prayer hundreds of times before, he would have been at a loss to know what to say after hearing what Annie Lois said. But he made the transition quickly, as he had many times before. He simply had to substitute "Dulcie's friends and loved ones" for "faculty and students." Moreover, he had been told many times that he never knew when to stop talking. He brought that with him today.

When he finished, he introduced Father Seranno.

"First of all," Father Seranno said, "I think I should let you know I'm not going to keep you standing here all afternoon. I *will*, though, tell you I'm here because I've lost one of my dearest Friends."

He told them how he met Dulcie, about their Friday afternoon visits, her reluctance to tell him why she was unhappy, and how, after their first few minutes together, he had discerned what she was afraid to tell him.

"The first time I saw Dulcie, she was sitting in one of the pews in the sanctuary of Sacred Heart Catholic Church. That's my church. She had slipped in and was curious and, as she said, surprised to see how pretty the Catholic church was. She seemed obsessed by the statues here and there in the sanctuary, so much so that she told me she'd always heard that Catholics worshipped statues. I told her that was not true, that each statue represented

MEN AS TREES WALKING | 361

someone who had done good things in his or her lifetime, that a statue is like a photograph, only a representation of someone or something, that everybody is a statue or photograph in a way. I could see she was confused, and I can certainly understand why, and so can you.

"I told her that when you look at a statue or a photograph, you see only what the person *looks* like. I attempted to tell her that those people who had made fun of her or had insulted her in other ways, had no way of knowing what she was *really* like inside and, furthermore, that nobody, I mean *nobody*, can ever know anybody else *completely*. Each person is like a book; the cover alone will tell you practically *nothing* about what's inside.

"Finally, I hope and pray that each of you who knew and loved her will never forget her. Whether it's in your sad heart or with your crafty hands, make you a statue of Dulcie. And *please!* Keep your statue where you can see it and feel it every day. May God bless us all."